BOMBAY RAINS, BOMBAY GIRLS

A doctor by profession, Anirban was born and brought up in Ranchi, and has, at various points in his life, called Mumbai, New York City, Atlanta and Rochester, home. He was assistant professor of medicine at the University of Rochester, NY, till he packed his bags and returned to India in 2007. Other than writing he is passionate about music. He now lives with his wife and two children in Kolkata.

BOMBAY RAINS, BOMBAY GIRLS

Anirban Bose

HarperCollins *Publishers* India
a joint venture with

New Delhi

First published in India in 2008 by
HarperCollins *Publishers* India
a joint venture with
The India Today Group
© Anirban Bose 2008

ISBN: 978-81-7223-683-0

Anirban Bose asserts the moral right to be identified
as the author of this book.

HarperCollins *Publishers*
A-53, Sector 57, NOIDA, Uttar Pradesh - 201301, India
77-85 Fulham Palace Road, London W6 8JB, United Kingdom
Hazelton Lanes, 55 Avenue Road, Suite 2900, Toronto, Ontario M5R 3L2
and 1995 Markham Road, Scarborough, Ontario M1B 5M8, Canada
25 Ryde Road, Pymble, Sydney, NSW 2073, Australia
31 View Road, Glenfield, Auckland 10, New Zealand
10 East 53rd Street, New York NY 10022, USA

Typeset in 10.5/14 Charter
Jojy Philip New Delhi - 15

Printed and bound at
Thomson Press (India) Ltd.

For my children, Nina and Nikhil:

may you find love like I did

ONE

Adi's Prologue

On learning that I was going to study medicine in Bombay, someone said to me, 'You've got to see two things in Bombay: the Bombay rains and the Bombay girls.'

At that time it seemed kind of inconsequential; one of the hundreds of 'drugs are bad', 'don't smoke', 'you must call every week' pieces of advice that people litter on an impressionable eighteen-year-old about to live alone 2,500 kilometres away from home. Amidst the chaotic litany of arrangements that such a long, unexpected move generates, my recollection of its author got mired in the ambiguity of the advice itself. However, this semi-pubescent line stuck in my brain simply because of its inherent quirkiness.

On a hot, sticky afternoon in July, Baba and I boarded a train from Ranchi station, waving our goodbyes to a crowd of family and friends there to see us off. Two years of intense studying had come down to this: my roll number had appeared in the newspaper as one of the successful ones in the All-India Medical Entrance Exams – a fact I verified repeatedly to assuage my doubts and my family's disbelief. A week later, a rather nondescript letter in the dimensions of a glorified receipt arrived in a plain brown envelope. It read:

Candidate Number: 0069385

Candidate Name: Adityaman Bhatt

Rank: 166

Medical College: Grant Medical College and Sir JJ Hospital, Bombay

Course: MBBS

Date of Joining: July 15th, 1990

I accepted its dullness readily, reconciling it to reflect the ordinariness of my achievement. In fact, to my parents, given my terribly mediocre academic record in school and college, my success as one of the 900 lucky ones out of the 120,000 who had taken the exam was as much of a surprise as my choice of college. And thus, Grant Medical College, being so far away from Ranchi, had become the source of some consternation at home. Although I feigned innocence, I had deliberately put it as one of my choices without consulting anybody. Not that the choice itself was bad. On the contrary, it was an old and reputable college. But I felt too embarrassed to confess to the truth. For, when I had filled in the eligibility forms, 'success' had been just a wishful thought, a cynical chuckle, and I had listed the best colleges in the most distant places with an ill-defined angst – a sort of revengeful rebuttal of my mediocrity. I suppose there was an inescapable humour, however puerile, in the incongruity between my lofty choices and my paltry expectations of success.

Bombay, however, was the icing on my cake of accidental achievement. In my otherwise mundane small-town existence, I had often let my imagination ruminate about getting away to someplace where the highlight of the year wouldn't be the arrival of the circus. So, while I was joyous at this unexpected turn of events, Baba and Ma didn't share my unbridled enthusiasm. Several discussions and deliberations followed with friends and family alike, the final consensus being that although Bombay was a 'fast' town for simple, innocent boys with 'pristine hearts' like myself, the opportunity to study at such a

good institution should not be passed up. I
knew that in their hearts, Baba and Ma realized
my success in the Medical Entrance exams was
a flash in the pan, akin to having won a lottery
ticket, and so the debates were essentially
exercises in semantics. I sat through the discussions with silent indulgence at their
delusional, self-serving arguments, secure in the
knowledge that nobody in their right mind
passes up a chance to study medicine in India,
especially not when success was essentially a
fluke. It would be a close second to throwing
away a winning lottery ticket because you didn't
like the numbers.

After two days of exhausting travel, as our train
slowly rolled into Victoria Terminus, the first
thing that struck me was the size of everything.
The platform seemed to continue forever, before
the train lurched to a sudden stop with an array
of loud clangs and forceful hisses, as though
begrudging the absence of tracks ahead. People
spilled onto the platform of the cavernous
station, emerging briskly from the train like
angry termites from wood. They straightened
their crumpled clothes, paused for a moment

to orient themselves, and then hastily joined the hordes swarming towards the exit with an asynchronous orderliness. Thin porters in blood-red uniforms balanced a pyramid of suitcases on their heads, their sweat-lacquered faces frozen with concentration as they advanced towards the main gates with curious bobbing strides. The passengers followed them closely, finding it difficult to keep up with the porters' pace despite carrying nothing but themselves. An official looking gentleman, braving the heat in his authoritative black coat, stood collecting tickets while his experienced eyes scanned the crowd for potential freeloaders. Departing passengers, waiting for their train to arrive, fashioned makeshift beds out of their luggage, whiling time in a game of cards or with music on the radio. Everybody else, including the stray dogs that gallivanted around uninhibited, understood their plight, carefully sidestepping their sprawled-out arrangements despite the limited space and the traffic jam they produced.

Outside, Victoria Terminus stood like a spectacular citadel of beauty, shining amidst her bedraggled surroundings like a lotus in the middle of a mud pond. Her yellowish brown granite walls, intricately decorated with domed clock towers, stone animal filigrees, soaring phallic spires, stained-glass windows and cathedral-like pointy arches, glowed mystically under strategically placed lights. Atop an enormous central tower was the figure of a lady with a torch in one hand, whose facial features clearly pointed to the building's colonial heritage. Large silver coloured letters with the insignia of the Indian Railways announced current occupancy by the Central Railway offices. Although more recent non-architectural additions like the rear ends of air conditioners and makeshift wooden partitions clashed with the historic pomposity stamped all over the building, the overall effect was still stunning.

In contrast to her stately, dignified silence, a boisterous sea of humanity hummed outside her perimeter, buzzing with manic energy. People moved with a keen sense of purpose as though no one had a minute to spare. Music blared from the shops, taxis and ubiquitous loudspeakers. Giant billboards and gaudy cinema posters cried for attention. Roadside vendors, selling every-thing from roasted peanuts to jazzy electronics, sat with their colourful wares, intoning their products in strange accents and harmonious phrases, each trying to outdo the other through sheer decibel power. Their eyes keenly searched for gullible newcomers in the crowd who could be lulled into inspecting their wares. Bulky double-decker buses, bursting with passengers, farted great plumes of thick black smoke as they chugged along languidly. Smaller, more intrepid mini-buses jostled for space with a hundred other cars on the narrow roads, the sides of which were steadily compromised by both vendors and pedestrians. Mopeds and scooters skirted in and out of the traffic, finding room where none existed, while a hapless traffic cop tried to maintain some semblance of order in this chaos.

I was mesmerized by the carnival-like atmosphere and a sense of impending adventure of exploring this city on my own began titillating my senses. Unable to contain it effectively, I chortled with glee. Baba looked at me questioningly. I sobered up immediately and shook my head to indicate it was nothing.

With a rigidly straight jaw line and a thick moustache that sat gravely above his lip, Baba looked every bit the disciplinarian that he was. Unimaginative dark-rimmed rectangular spectacles complemented the effect. Everybody who knew the two of us agreed that other than the glasses, his broken nose and his receding hairline, I was a spitting image of Baba's youth – an observation that gave me considerable pride. A recent growth spurt had seen me shoot past his head rather rapidly – a phenomenon that had made Baba proud. But there was nothing other than irritation on his face at this moment as he looked away, the exhaustion of the long journey making his battle with the heat and noise less successful than mine. Dark circles of perspiration had turned the cloth around his armpits into a darker shade of the blue that imbued the rest of his shirt. His forehead had creased into glittering lines of sweat as he scoured the area for an empty taxi. Soon he spotted one and flailed his arms wildly to hail it down.

The driver swept in next to us, screeching to a halt amidst a dust cloud inches away from our feet.

'How much to go to Grant Medical College?' asked Baba.

'Where?' asked the taxiwala somewhat cagily, his beady eyes squinting at us.

'Grant Medical College,' repeated Baba. 'My son has got admission there to become a doctor.' His voice was a mixture of pride at his son's achievement and irritation that the taxiwala did not recognize it right away and treat him with the respect and envy such news arouses in small towns like Ranchi.

'Never heard of it,' said the taxiwala, waving his thin arm dismissively.

'What? Never heard of it?' exclaimed Baba. 'It is 150 years old, the top college in Bombay… How can you drive a taxi here knowing so little?'

The taxiwala scowled. 'What is the whole address?'

'Here it says…' scolded Baba, waving my letter of admission in the taxiwala's face, 'Grant Medical College and Sir JJ hospital…'

'Arre! So say JJ Hospital then! You should have said that first,' retorted the taxiwala. 'It's about ten kilometres from here!'

A brief, awkward silence followed.

'So how much do you charge?' asked Baba, his voice full of hesitation at the inauspicious beginning.

The taxiwala gave him a strange look. 'By the meter,' he said.

'What? By the metre?' started Baba. 'We have to go so many kilometres and you are going to charge per metre? Bombay is so expensive, I tell you! This is extortion…in broad daylight! I will write to the newspapers…'

'Arre, sahib, this meter shows the charge here!' mocked the taxiwala, cutting Baba off and pointing to the square piece of machinery jutting from the front door panel on the left. 'Haven't you ever taken a taxi before? Which village have you come from?'

Baba was suddenly at a loss for words. Suitably embarrassed, he shot one quick glance at the meter before looking away from the pointed gaze of the taxiwala.

'Okay, okay, let's go. No point debating these things…we are getting late,' he said, followed by a host of mumbles under his breath that I couldn't catch.

The taxiwala tossed our luggage into the trunk. He returned to his seat and slammed the door after him. He scanned our faces in the rearview mirror – his own bursting with righteous indignation – and then set off.

The taxi weaved its way through the crowded roads. A cool breeze rushed in through the rolled down windows, bringing sudden relief from the sultry heat of the July sun. The air was laced with the mouth-watering aroma of melted butter and fried onions, sizzling in the cast iron pans of the roadside pav-bhaji stalls. I put my head against the window, staring at the stratospheric buildings that flew past. The crush of people on the crowded sidewalks had transformed into a faceless, featureless blur. A thrill ran down my spine, filling me with a giddying sense of achievement. Having never accomplished anything worth crowing about in my life, just getting to Bombay seemed enough to justify this elation.

Baba, meanwhile, was keeping an eagle eye on the meter. Finally, the taxiwala, in the high chair of the victor, decided to break the silence.

'So where are you from?' he asked.

Baba, unsure if this was the beginning of an innocent conversation or the onset of more 'small town' ridicule, replied somewhat hesitantly, 'Ranchi, in Bihar.'

'Arre, sahib, I am from Hazaribagh,' said the taxiwala, his face lighting up with a smile.

The taxiwala's delight at having found someone from a place separated from his hometown by fifty kilometres of dusty, single-lane roads wasn't something Baba empathized with right away.

'Then how can you treat someone from your place with such disrespect?' he complained.

I looked at him with incredulity. 'Stop trying to pick a fight, Baba!' I whispered.

Baba nodded. 'So…how long have you been in Bombay?' he asked light-heartedly, before the taxiwala could say anything else.

'This is my eighth year, sahib,' replied the taxiwala with a cheer that completely belied any memory of the recent acrimony. 'But my family is still in Hazaribagh... You know, my parents, my wife and three kids...two boys and one girl. I send them money from here. Work is tough to get in Hazaribagh.'

'So how often do you go back home?'

'Maybe once or twice a year, sahib.'

Within a few minutes of discovering common ground and trading sentimental memories, both of them acquired the engrossment reserved for long lost brothers re-discovering each other's past. They launched into a discussion of life in Bombay and Bihar, fondly reminiscing about small-town innocence and its corruption in big cities. I could sense Baba's apprehension about leaving me alone. The temptations that exist in a city this size and the opportunity to study at such a good institution were at loggerheads in his mind.

The air was heavy with small-town nostalgia when the taxi came to a screeching halt in the midst of traffic, sending us lurching forward in our seats. As we recovered our bearings while trying to discern the cause of such sudden deceleration, I felt the front of our taxi bump into the rear end of the car ahead of ours. The other car's owner turned around and glared at us. He shifted gears to park his car, and then began to emerge from it.

'Nothing happened... It just touched...no

problem...don't worry,' said the taxiwala, reassuring us as well as himself. His eyes meanwhile were nervously tracking the other car's owner, now striding menacingly towards us. The man was a giant, and snorted angrily as he opened the passenger door and got in next to the taxiwala.

'Bhai...nothing happened... Just a small mark on the bumper...No damage!' pleaded the taxiwala, reflexively backing into his corner.

Before he could say more, the man clasped the taxiwala's head with one hand and started raining blows with the other.

'Saale, bhaiya...harami! Don't know how to drive...bring your filthy ass to Bombay, fucking son of a bitch!'

The taxiwala shielded his head between his arms and tried to duck under the steering wheel. The man kept throwing blows with such single-minded focus that he paid no attention to our presence less than a foot away. Baba and I stared at him as though we had lost our tongues.

Then Baba said, 'Arre, leave him; it's only a small scratch, if at all.'

The man stopped and turned to look at us. 'Get out,' he said.

Baba started to protest. 'But, mister...'

Still holding the taxiwala's collar with one

hand, the man reached into his back pocket and flicked open a vicious looking knife. Holding it menacingly, he snarled, 'Get out!'

I clutched Baba's hand tightly and whispered, 'Don't say a word...just get out.'

We scrambled for the doors. Although terrified, a morbid curiosity overcame me. I kept stealing glances at the continued punishment of the hapless taxiwala, even as we spilled into the middle of stalled traffic. Meanwhile, the traffic lights changed to green and the rest of the vehicles on the road started to honk. The incessant beeps probably saved the taxiwala's life. The other man got out of the taxi, folded his knife, strode up to his car with supreme nonchalance, and drove off. Baba and I scampered onto the sidewalk, from where we managed to catch a glimpse of our taxi racing away with most of our possessions.

Standing on the sidewalk as though rooted to the spot, neither of us could think of saying or doing anything for the next few minutes. Around us, life continued uninterrupted, completely oblivious to the drama that had unfolded just a few feet away.

Finally, Baba spoke. 'Do you have all the necessary papers and certificates to complete your admission?'

'They're with me, in my handbag,' I mumbled, suddenly having lost the strength in my voice.

Baba let out a long sigh. 'Let's at least get that done,' he said.

Thankfully, the college was only a few minutes' walk from where we were. Wary of getting into a taxi again, we trudged along on foot. I followed Baba closely, somatizing the shame of my cowardice by wringing my hands and clenching my jaws. Baba had at least tried to defend the poor man, while I had meekly plotted our exit. Had Baba noticed? How could I have been so afraid? God!

We could now see the gates of the JJ Hospital campus. A dilapidated, rust-stained sign that read 'Grant Medical College and Sir JJ Group of Hospitals' arched from one post to another. Beyond the gates was a driveway that curved in front of the main hospital building. We followed it to the hospital's main entrance, Baba maintaining his stoic silence, while I burned with shame a few steps behind.

As we reached the turn in front of the building, to our surprise, there was the taxiwala, waving to us enthusiastically. Baba and I walked towards him in astonishment. His face showed a few bruises from the assault, but other than that, his spirits seemed fine.

'Your luggage was still here and I thought you might not get a chance to get your son admitted if you didn't get your documents...you know...' he explained.

Baba's eyes were brimming with tears. 'I can't thank you enough...' he began, stretching his arms out to hug the man.

'Arre, no problem, sahib,' said the taxiwala, reassuring Baba with an emphatic pat on his back. 'We are like brothers, you know...from the same place. Your son is like my son...'

'Listen,' said Baba, 'if you want to file a report with the police about that chap, I will be a witness.'

The taxiwala gave him a look of bemused surprise that quickly changed into a defeated smirk. 'Arre, no no, sahib, these things happen in this place,' he said, dismissively. 'As long as you are not seriously hurt, you just learn to ignore. If something happened to me, all the taxiwalas would have called a strike tomorrow. But this is not like Ranchi or Hazaribagh, where somebody hitting you hurts your pride and you have to do something about it. In a big city like this, nobody knows or cares...and you just learn to continue like nothing has happened. You even tried to help. Thank you for that...but here, you have to be like Gandhiji's monkeys and learn to see no evil, hear no evil and speak no evil. That is the best way.'

The taxiwala's casual, brush-it-off-your-shoulder attitude to what seemed a major event to us left us unsure of how to respond. We looked at each other uncertainly; more shaken by the incident than the man who had actually taken the beating. I was already burdened by my earlier inaction and the irony of this situation left me even more confused.

We collected our stuff and Baba gave him ten rupees extra (to buy sweets for his kids in Hazaribagh, Baba explained). Then we proceeded to the administrative office to complete the formalities of my admission.

❧

That evening we found a hotel after an exhaustive search. Our budget was rather meagre for the amenities we sought in a city like Bombay. It was a simple room with white plastered walls, minimal furnishing and a small attached bathroom, the fixtures on which left a lot to be desired. But more than the room's shortcomings, it was the sweltering heat of the evening that really bothered us. The squeaky overhead fan tirelessly waged a losing battle against the suffocating humidity in the room. I opened the windows to let in some fresh air. Not that it made any difference – the outside was filled with the damp of the impending monsoon. The hotel manager had said that the monsoon might break over Bombay that very night. 'That will cool everything down, sir,' he had promised in a raspy voice. We squirmed in the sticky sultriness, trying to find faith in the hotel manager's ability to forecast the weather.

Baba sat alone on the bed, the newspaper open in front of him but his eyes focused far beyond the pages. His spectacles had made their stealthy journey down his nose to where I found them uncomfortable, adjusting my imaginary ones a couple of times.

'Baba, your glasses...they'll fall off.'

'What? Oh...yeah...hmm...'

Baba readjusted his glasses, then promptly went back into the state of contemplative void.

'You know Baba,' I began, testing the silence with caution. 'The taxiwala was really honest. I didn't think such guys existed here...I mean...he could easily have disappeared with everything.'

'Hmm? Oh, yes, that's true,' replied Baba, his mind clearly preoccupied with something else.

His inattention irked me. 'Why don't you say what's on your mind, Baba?'

'What…no nothing, really.'

'Are you upset with me because I…I didn't do anything in the taxi other than run out?'

Baba looked confused. He put the newspaper down, smiled amiably at me from behind his glasses and said, 'Were you scared in the taxi when that chap flashed his knife?'

'A little,' I blurted, well aware that my actions had spoken louder than my words.

'Yes, yes…me too,' he said. 'I was very scared.'

Baba's admission surprised me. After all, he had been the brave one.

'Then why are you so quiet, Baba? What is bothering you so much? My safety? You know I won't mix with the wrong crowd… I can take care of myself.'

'Oh, yes, I am sure you can.'

I didn't respond, unsure if his remark was laced with sarcasm.

Baba sighed deeply. 'I am troubled by the taxiwala's reaction. How could he be so calm and casual after such a thing?'

I was baffled. The taxiwala's reaction…that was bothering him?

'You heard what he said, Baba. In big cities you have to take such things in your stride.'

'See… I cannot get over that, Adi. After all, what is life devoid of dignity? I can understand being scared and unable to do anything, but to not feel hurt or angry? How can you get to be like that? Does the anonymity of living in a big city come at the price of one's pride? Or is it merely a convenient excuse to carry on living?'

'Well, he has to feed his children and family and sometimes that calls for a compromise, Baba.'

Baba smiled, then removed his glasses and began wiping them with his shirt. He held them against the light for a brief second before placing them back on his face.

'You know Adi,' he said, 'I don't worry about you getting into drinking, or drugs, or smoking… If eighteen years of our upbringing cannot come to use now, it never will. But I worry about what new lessons you will learn here that will shape the rest of your life… Because life is all about learning, and living off what's learned. I mean, look at my life – not a success by anybody's standards. I haven't had my name in the newspapers, nor do I own a big house. But I'm not ashamed of that, Adi, because it is more important to succeed in one's own eyes than to live up to someone else's expectations. You know, I have lived my life following certain principles because of which I have often got into trouble at work. Despite all my qualifications, my experience, I've remained a deputy manager at the engineering plant for the last eighteen years. I've been tempted time and again...and believe me, it's been hard to resist. But I have never compromised, never. So, after working for thirty years, I still drive a scooter, have one suit, and travel second class, but – you know what, Adi – every day I walk with pride, I feel comfortable in my skin, and I sleep at night with a clear conscience. That is who I am...my being, my soul. I cannot compromise on that.'

'That's easier said than done, Baba. You've never had to live 2,500 kilometres away from your family to feed them.'

Outside, a loud clap of thunder startled us momentarily.

Baba walked over and put his hands on my shoulders. 'Where does so much doubt come from?' he asked, his face searching mine, as though looking for the source of such scepticism. 'I am glad that you have such a practical approach to life, but sometimes it is good to look at life in the simplest of terms. You know Adi, I hope you will still feel bad when hurt, outraged when wronged, pained when sad, happy when right...I hope you will continue to believe in goodness, and right, and justice, and truth, however much your faith is questioned by circumstance. Idealism, however impractical, gives a meaning to our existence. At your age you must be able to wonder at the beauty around you, as well as question wrong without doubting its injustice. Doubt comes at my age after going through life...' He chuckled. 'But you're already ahead.'

'You see,' he continued, 'compromises are also a part of life, but they make you cross a line that starts to disappear the first time you cross it, until one day it disappears altogether. Then wrong becomes right and lies seem like the truth; everything becomes just a matter of inter-pretation because truth loses its best quality – its simplicity. That's when you should look in the mirror and see if you recognize yourself as the person you wanted to become. That is the day you'll know if you will sleep well or keep awake the rest of your nights, talking to your conscience...'

Outside, a thunderclap announced the arrival of the monsoon rains. A sudden cool breeze rushed in and took my breath away.

Oh, these Bombay rains...

TWO

Untraditional as it was, Adi's introduction to Harsha, Rajeev and Toshi was not even an event any one of them cared to remember afterwards. It occurred in the shielded isolation of a dormitory, at the end of a long and narrow passage on the third floor of the men's hostel – a place infamous for ragging.

Ragging marks the unofficial beginning of many a distinguished career in medicine. Rivaling an ancient Roman sport in its viciousness, the stories from this cold, brutal tradition get repeated like an old maid's tales amongst the incoming group of 'freshies'. They curse the custom with helpless rage, only to turn into its major proponents the following year, when an infusion of fresh faces unfailingly entices them into this orgiastic revelry. And so the hideous heritage thrives, carried on by the victim-turned-aggressors baying for their share of fresh blood.

Despite being an inescapable part of the initiation into the fraternity of hostelers, the existence of ragging is vehemently denied by college authorities. In fact, a cursory glance at the hostel premises during the day would easily reinforce the deceptive image of a placid building full of fraternal bonhomie. But, come evening, and in a Jeckyllian transformation under the stealth of deepening darkness, ragging resurrects its ugly head, tormenting freshies in the seclusion of the nocturnal hostel.

That night, they were the chosen ones.

Nervousness gnawing at his insides, Adi quietly surveyed his room, feeling his heart sink at the sight of the dismal decor. The huge room was sparsely furnished with a few wooden chairs and a worn out metal table that somehow managed to stay upright on three rickety legs. The four of them sat on the only other piece of furniture – a hard, creaky, cast-iron bed strategically placed in the centre of the room. On the ceiling above their heads, an array of dusty light bulbs spat out an anaemic glow that only served to accentuate the ominous milieu. Dark windowpanes effectively shielded any light from outside. A lonely wall clock above the door reminded Adi that it was almost midnight.

With the automatic sympathy of kindred in misfortune, Adi looked at the others more closely. Two of them stood out: Toshi, because of his Mongoloid features looked unlike anyone else in the room, and Rajeev, who was very handsome, and possessed the air of self-confidence such knowledge brings.

Scared and anxious, they sat there quietly as their tormentors – snickering, sneering and expectant – poured into the room and surrounded them. Then a loud cheer erupted as a stocky, bearded guy walked into the room.

'Aha...Pherwani...'

'Pheru...Pheru...'

The crowd's enthusiasm made Adi's heart sink even further.

Salim Pherwani (a.k.a. Pheru), stuck in second MBBS for the last four years, had developed a special talent – ragging. He lived a semi-hermetic existence, his own classmates having long since become doctors. Once a year he appeared out of nowhere to render his rowdy welcome to the newcomers and then returned to the shadows of hushed whispers and cagey glances. His exploits were legendary, and for good reason. Tales of how he had ragged a politician's snobby son so mercilessly that the poor guy had left medical college and taken up fashion designing were discussed with hallowed reverence amongst the hostelers. Rumour had it that this was the reason Pheru had spent the last four years trying to clear the Pharmacology exams in second MBBS. Nobody dared to confirm or contradict this fact for fear of incurring his wrath. The tale added a touch of martyr-like legitimacy to Pheru's operation, and as he chalked up more victims and gorier stories, it bolstered his reputation as 'ragger extraordinaire'.

Pheru's physique and attitude served his image well. A few inches short of six feet, his thick neck and huge chest lent him a bullish stockiness. The muscles on his arms rippled under the white sleeveless undershirt. A ragged stubble peppered the hard, sardonic face. He sized up his victims with sharp piercing eyes while a sly smile played on his lips.

An eerie silence descended on the gathering. Everyone followed Pheru's moves as he surveyed the four of them with the look of a champion gladiator about to pick his kill.

'Freshie!' He motioned towards Rajeev. 'Introduce yourself!'

Rajeev jerked upright. Tall, lean and broad shouldered beyond what could be accounted

for by his eighteen years of life, Rajeev wore a
fashionably outspoken red T-shirt over tight blue
Wrangler jeans. His eyes narrowed, searching
for a friendly face in the crowd. Then, smiling
disarmingly to reveal a perfect set of white teeth,
he said confidently. 'My name is Rajeev...
Rajeev Varoach, sir.'

'Hmm... Varoach, huh? Nice name,' said
Pheru, nodding his head approvingly. Rajeev
smiled, pleased to have begun the interaction
on a positive note. Pheru seemed lost in thought
for a few seconds. Then he said, 'So...how is
your brother... Cock?' Everyone burst out
laughing. Rajeev looked confused. Pheru
clarified: 'You know, your brother, Cock, as in
Cock-roach, Va-roach.'

'F...Fine,' blurted Rajeev.

'Do you like Cock? Do you play with Cock
often? Did you play with Cock when you were
a kid?' continued Pheru. More laughter
emanated at the double entendre.

'No, sir,' Rajiv muttered, his voice suddenly
weak.

'What! You don't like your brother?'
demanded Pheru. 'How can you not like your
brother? If you don't like Cock, what do you
like, huh?' Rajeev didn't reply. 'Come on,
man...what do you like?' asked Pheru again.

Rajeev stood looking around nervously, fidgeting with his hands that suddenly seemed to be out of sync with the rest of his body. His forehead glistened with beads of perspiration. His self-assured demeanour had melted into the darkness of the night. He thought for a few moments, his eyes fixed on a spot on the floor. 'Physics,' he said finally. 'I like Physics.'

Pheru smiled wryly, recognizing Rajeev's attempt to choose a topic that would give Pheru little opportunity to dish out more humiliation.

'Physics, eh? So you are really good at Physics, are you?'

'Yes, sir. Very much so...I topped Physics in Delhi,' said Rajeev, his voice trying to match the confidence of his assertion.

'Well, let's do an experiment to re-evaluate Newton's first law,' said Pheru. 'Let's assume that the floor of this room is absolutely frictionless. Zero friction, okay?' Rajeev nodded. 'Now, suppose you begin to masturbate on this frictionless floor...you know, play with your brother, Cock,' continued Pheru. Rajeev's ears turned a curious shade of red. 'What happens then?'

Rajeev looked confused.

'Arre...' Pheru explained, very matter-of-factly, 'you ejaculate. Don't you?'

Rajeev nodded. 'So,' continued Pheru, 'as you ejaculate, the drops move forward, and by the law of conservation of momentum, you move a few millimetres backward. Don't you?'

'Yes, yes…sir,' replied Rajeev lamely.

'Now, Newton's first law says that any object tends to be in a state of motion or rest unless acted upon by an *external* force, right? But here the drops are moving forward and you are moving backward without any external force at all, right? All the forces are *internal*, aren't they? So this neat experiment of yours proves that Newton's first law is just bullshit. Doesn't it?'

Amidst raucous laughter, Rajeev fidgeted nervously. The fine beads of perspiration had coalesced into big drops of sweat that now started to track down the bridge of his aquiline nose. His tall, lean figure acquired a self-conscious stoop as he tried to muster some bravado on his clean-cut good-looking face. He dabbed his forehead with his sleeves, fighting his diaphoresis with limited success.

Pheru smiled and said, 'So this is your task for tonight. Sit at that desk and start writing an article on your experiment and we will send it to the Nobel Prize Committee to review and publish, stating how you, Mr Va-Roach, and your brother, Mr Cock-Roach, have disproved

Newton's first law just by playing with each other.'

The crowd howled with delight. They cheered Pheru, waiting for him to deliver more humiliation. The opportunity came in the form of Harsha, who, studying the proceedings with his mouth agape, had the temerity to let loose a short laugh.

Pheru turned on him with the speed of a cheetah. 'Shut your mouth, freshie! Who the hell are you?' he barked.

Harsha pursed his lips, gulping like a guppy. He stood up gingerly, unsure of responding lest that be construed a direct defiance of Pheru's instructions. Then he blurted a hurried introduction. 'Harsha... Harshvardhan Bhanot, sir...from Rohtak.'

Even with the generous contribution of a few inches from his scruffy old shoes, Harsha was the shortest in the group, barely reaching five and a half feet. His round pudgy face, speckled with wispy strands of wayward hair, hadn't outgrown its pre-pubertal quality. Hopelessly unfashionable steel-rimmed spectacles disappeared amidst the wavy whorls of black, oil-drenched hair peeking from behind his ears. An unpretentious plain white shirt hung loosely over a fledgling paunch as he stood nervously still, an uncertain slouch maiming his stance.

In a sharp contrast to Rajeev, Harsha's rough, heavily accented English spoke loudly of an underprivileged upbringing.

'What was so funny, eh?' bellowed Pheru. 'You stupid Jat! This is a serious scientific study and you find it funny! What...you've never masturbated? How many girls have you screwed?'

'Sir...no, sir,' mumbled Harsha.

'No what? You don't masturbate or you've never fucked a girl?'

'Never...with a girl, sir,' replied Harsha, his face expressionless with fear.

'Really?' said Pheru, suddenly softening his voice. Putting his arm around Harsha, he said, 'That is terrible. It is a requirement for this hostel that you lose your virginity. Look around you...do you see any virgins? Huh?'

With a nervous grin Harsha acknowledged that he couldn't spot any.

Pheru smiled. 'See? So tonight, we will help you lose your virginity. Right here, right now.'

A loud cheer rang out in the crowd. Harsha smiled uncertainly.

Pheru continued, 'So who do you think is the girl of your dreams... You know, the one you think about when you fantasize?'

'Princess Diana, sir,' said Harsha with a spontaneity that immediately ratified the sincerity of his reply. A loud cheer of approval echoed around the room. Pheru looked pleased. 'Excellent choice,' he said, smiling at Harsha. Harsha's smile broadened in reciprocity.

'Now imagine,' continued Pheru, his voice full of sensuality and passion, 'you are alone with her on a beautiful island, and all she has left to wear is a black, lacy negligee. She is hot and horny for you. Her beautiful buttery breasts heave with every breath, and she spreads her silky thighs and tells you, "Harsha, oh Harsha, I want you. I want you so bad." So what will you do next, Harsha?'

Harsha looked around uncertainly and said, 'Sir, I will…I will…ask her if she has AIDS.'

This time even Adi burst out laughing along with the crowd. Harsha's face quivered nervously at the reaction he had generated. Pheru stared at him, his mouth agape.

'Man, you are cursed! You will remain a virgin! You are hopeless!' he roared. 'What the hell is wrong with you? Ask Princess Diana if she has AIDS? It is a bloody fantasy, you idiot! She is not…I mean….' His voice trailed off in exasperation.

When the crowd had settled down, Pheru turned towards Adi and Toshi. 'Freshies!' he barked, 'on your feet and introductions!'

Toshi and Adi snapped to attention. 'I'm Toshitenga Lotha,' said Toshi. 'I'm from Nagaland.'

'Hmm,' said Pheru. 'What part of China is that, Ching-chong?'

Toshi kept a straight face and said, 'Sir, Nagaland is in the north-east, along the Burmese border...'

'Yeah... I know where Nagaland is, you Chicken Chowmein,' said Pheru. He turned towards Adi. 'And you?'

'My name is Adityaman Bhatt, sir,' Adi replied. 'I'm from Ranchi, Bihar.'

'A Bhaiya. What does your name mean, Bhaiya?'

Before Adi could reply, Pheru held up his hand and said, 'Let me figure this out. Hmm...let's see...A-dit-ya-man...hmm...sounds like "I-did-a man".'

Some light laughter arose from the crowd.

'And "Bhatt" sounds like "butt",' continued Pheru, looking very pleased with his efforts. 'So you are the first example of someone being born out of doing a man's butt...and your parents named you "I-did-a-man's-butt" to commemorate the great event.'

Adi could only smile stupidly at this brutal desecration of his name. He stole a glance at the clock on the wall. Two hours had passed and there was no reprieve in sight.

'Wouldn't you like to help your friend Harsha here? The poor guy is a virgin and needs to be taught the art of love. Wouldn't you love to help him out?' said Pheru. 'You guys are not virgins, are you?'

'No way!' scoffed Toshi. Pheru looked at Adi questioningly.

The discovery of Harsha's virginity, Pheru's corruption of his name to caricature his manliness, Toshi's virile scoff, all conspired at that moment to convince Adi that the knowledge of his virginity could only be a vulnerability. He let out a manly guffaw.

'Yeah, me neither!'

'Perfect!' said Pheru. 'Toshi and you can demonstrate to our dear friend Harsha how it's done. By the end of the lesson, Harsha should be a master.'

It was Adi's turn in the swelter pit. Sweat dripped from his forehead with such profusion that it alarmed him, and his heart began to race at the speed of a runaway train. His mouth turned dry as he and Toshi stared awkwardly at each other.

'Come on freshies!' growled Pheru.

Toshi walked towards Adi. Then, much to Adi's embarrassment, he began acting coy, performing his role with inadvertent diligence. Amid loud cheering, he started to go through the motions of deflowering Adi.

Adi's inexperience showed almost immediately.

'Come on, Bhaiya,' called out Pheru. 'Show us, man. What does your girlfriend do when you touch her?'

Toshi's sensuous seduction left Adi paralysed. He stood cowering in the middle of the room, his gaze fixed on his shoes.

After a few minutes, Pheru called out to him, 'So you are a virgin too, aren't you?'

Unable to look up, Adi nodded quietly.

Pheru let out a loud groan. 'What the hell is this world coming to?' he said. 'Damn it... except Ching-chong here, you guys are all virgins? This is unbelievable! We have to do something about it. You guys need BP!'

Although Adi had no idea what BP meant, at that moment, he was willing to try anything else.

BP stood for 'Blue Picture' or pornographic movies. The crowd murmured its approval and almost immediately, as if by magic, a TV and VCR appeared in one corner of the room. Within a few minutes, somebody had inserted a tape into the VCR, and an orgy began unfolding on the television screen.

Adi stood wondering what part of this was ragging when Pheru pointed to the screen and said, 'Okay, Rajeev, you are this guy; Bhaiya, you are this other guy; Harsha, you are this blonde girl; and Ching-chong, you are this girl.' Then he turned down the sound and said, 'All right! You have to make up the dialogues.'

For a few minutes the four of them stared blankly at one another.

'Start, freshies!' barked Pheru.

Toshi was the first to begin, grunting with gusto. Painfully awkward at first, the other three joined in, providing the soundtrack to the wanton sex on the TV screen. They dug into new depths of their raunchy onomatopoeic repertoire, grunting, groaning, moaning, squealing and screaming through the night. It was easier as a group, each losing his inhibition in the lewdness of the other, burying his humiliation in their common misery. Luckily for them, the movie commanded a lot of the audience's attention, and slowly the crowd dissipated to the privacy of their rooms, offering explanations of fatigue and early lectures the next day. By the time the sadomasochistic ritual was over, the wall clock had chimed thrice and then some.

❧

Finally, only the four of them remained. Having been publicly humiliated and most of their intimate details exposed, the need for introductory niceties was easily skipped.

'I hate that guy...man, I'm going to kill him if I get a chance!' seethed Rajeev.

'Can't we tell the warden?' asked Adi, wiping the last drops of sweat from his face. 'They say there is no ragging here...that was brutal...they should take some action against these guys!'

'I think the warden already knows. He just behaves as though he has everything under control,' said Rajeev. 'Assholes...I hope they break their legs!'

'If I was a local, na,' said Harsha, 'I would get friends and teach this Pheru-beru a lesson. Saale, naani yaad dila deta.'

'What does that mean?' asked Toshi.

'You don't know Hindi?' asked Harsha.

'No, not very well,' said Toshi.

'What?' said Harsha. 'How do you not know your rashtrabhasha? You know – national language?'

'Well, it's a little different in Nagaland,' replied Toshi.

It was Adi's turn to be surprised. 'That's still

India,' he said, then quickly added, 'are you from Imphal?'

'No, I am from Mokukchung,' said Toshi. 'Imphal is in Manipur. The capital of Nagaland is Kohima.'

'Arre,' said Harsha, 'but everybody is teaching Hindi in India…and also Hindi movies…and songs… If you can't understand, then you can't speak in Hindi?'

Toshi looked at him with exasperation and said, 'You guys aren't talking much in Hindi either.'

The discussion halted abruptly with Toshi's simple, yet potent, rebuttal. The clock on the wall chimed to indicate it was 4 a.m. It suddenly reminded them of their overwhelming mental and physical exhaustion and effectively disqualified that moment as the time to discuss India's geopolitical make-up. They dragged their weary bodies to the dishevelled cots and collapsed on them, too tired to care about the books and clothes that lay strewn everywhere.

Adi lay silently in the darkness, feeling the rush of blood into his legs sapping up the tension in his muscles. He tossed and turned on the creaky cast-iron bed, the surfeit of adrenaline from the evening's experience making it difficult for him to fall asleep.

As he stared blankly at the bare ceiling, he heard Rajeev say, 'Ask Princess Diana if she has AIDS? What the hell...!'

Suddenly, they were all laughing. Exhausted, Adi fell back and was almost immediately overcome by sleep.

THREE

If he had had any inkling about the incident that would give him his first shot at fame – or, more appropriately, infamy – Adi would have chosen to sit somewhere else in class that day. Either way, it was the beginning of a series of events that propelled him to a prominence he had seldom imagined in his hitherto humdrum existence.

The little drama occurred in the Anatomy lecture hall of Grant Medical College.

Established by the British in 1845 to introduce western medicine in India, Grant Medical College is one of the oldest institutions in the country. Its campus, spread over a few square miles in the heart of Bombay, reflects a lot of its history – from the distinguished buildings that are the Anatomy and Physiology schools, to the fort-like hospital with its empty gun turrets and crumbling wooden staircases. Dates etched on the stone facade commemorate important incidents in the life of the 150-year-old institution. Years of expansion have led to the grounds being remodelled, landscaped, structured and restructured again and again, in ways that reflect a lack of coherent planning.

Yet, it was this lack of a discernible plan that fascinated Adi. There were dark buildings with sombre padlocks; strange coffin-like nooks; unpredictable turns with sudden dead-ends; dizzying spiral staircases that led nowhere, and dark passageways that mysteriously opened onto vast naked terraces – all of which lent the campus a maze like mystique. Adi loved exploring these architectural idiosyncrasies, his imagination flirting with a bygone era, conjuring stories about these halls steeped in history. And nowhere was this perception of historic grandeur as heightened as in Anatomy Hall.

The lecture hall was built like an amphitheatre, thirty rows of seats rising thirty feet in the air to complete a semicircle around an ornate central podium. Portraits of past luminaries smiled benevolently down at the students from the walls on either side. Bright metal plaques below the decorative wooden frames extolled the accomplishments of each one. Breaking the parade of pictures and covering most of the wall behind the podium was an antiquated six-panel blackboard. In an ambiguous attempt at scientific art, an assortment of dissected body parts sat in a display case near the door, instantaneously inspiring awe among the newcomers.

One particular dissected out face, tracing the innervation of the facial nerve into the muscles responsible for human expression, enthralled Adi. The filleted face sat motionless in a jar, staring at him from within the formalin, an expression of perennial surprise in its dehiscent eyes. Whenever the wall-mounted speakers boomed out the lecturer's voice, Adi thought he perceived a distinct grimace crease those facial muscles. The outrage with which the dead face responded to such auditory impertinence would send a queasy tingle down Adi's spine. He'd scrunch up his face and savour its flexibility before returning to admire the hideous beauty of the grimace again.

That day, Adi sat in the lecture hall, busily trying to get the pages of his notebook in order, when he noticed the guy sitting in front of him turn back to look up every few seconds. Finally, out of curiosity, Adi followed his gaze. When he saw nothing of interest, he turned back.

'Did you see it?' asked the guy, sitting in front.

'See what?' asked Adi.

'You can actually look up Sheetal's skirt, man,' he said with a naughty smile. 'She has nice legs.'

'I…I didn't see anything,' said Adi defensively.

'Come down here. It's a view of heaven. Check out those legs, man.'

Adi hesitated for a few seconds before quickly gathering his stuff and climbing down, just as Dr Gomke, the head of department of Anatomy, was getting ready to begin her lecture.

'Hi,' said Adi. 'I'm Adityaman Bhatt. Adi.'

Shiny black pupils sized up Adi as they shook hands warmly.

'Hi, Adi. I'm Sam, Samuel Ashok Biji.'

Adi's first and overwhelming impression of Sam was the engaging congeniality of his broad smile. A few inches shorter than Adi and a few stones heavier than him, Sam's tight black jeans, bulged between the stitches to contain the excesses of gluttony. A head full of curly black hair, generously speckled with bits of dandruff, inevitably invited a look of disgust from the beholder. Not that it registered on Sam. His dark brown impish face glowed perennially with a sprightly smile, unseating any other emotion that tried to manifest itself.

'Check out the view, man,' he said, pointing behind.

Adi turned to look up. He jerked back almost immediately, half expecting Sheetal to catch him red-handed.

'Did you see?' Sam asked, excitedly. Adi nodded.

Sam closed his eyes and purred. 'Man... Sheetal is something. Imagine licking those milky thighs. Mmm...'

'Quiet!' hissed Adi. 'Gomke will throw us out of class. She is strict *and* crazy!'

Sam gave Adi a cavalier shrug. 'Relax, man. Don't freak out...this is the best place to sit for the view. Check out Rupa; if she moves a little bit I'll tell you the colour of her panties.'

He laughed. The humour escaped Adi's worried mind that was now re-evaluating the merits of his decision to sit next to Sam. Sensing his discomfort, Sam cast Adi a sympathetic glance.

'Don't worry, Adi. I'll let you know if anything else shows up. You keep up with Dr Gomke.'

Adi focused on the podium where Dr Gomke looked all set to begin her lecture.

She was a specimen of old-fashioned propriety. Tall and buxom, with a gratuitous accumulation of fat in all the wrong places over six decades of life, she could be best described as un-aesthetically plump. Her hair, pulled tightly into a huge bun, stretched the skin on her face like a taut elastic sheet, making the veins on her forehead look like rivers that emerged from the depths of her eyeballs only to be squished at the hairline. A huge red bindi centered those veins, looking from a distance like the perfect bull's-eye for target practice. A curved pinched nose, scant eyebrows artificially darkened by the liberal use of eyeliner and narrow lips on a pale white wrinkled face conveyed a distinct aura of unapproachability. She wore a red sari and the matching bangles on her wrists clinked noisily every time she raised her hand to write on the board.

She began her lecture in a funny nasal voice, absolutely devoid of inflections. 'Today, we will start the series of lectures on the lower limbs – thigh, leg and foot.'

'We have a head start,' whispered Sam, and Adi chuckled softly.

Everybody dived for their notebooks. The collective enthusiasm was contagious; Adi opened his books and prepared to take notes.

He was trying to keep up with the lecture when Sam whispered excitedly, 'Adi, Sheetal just crossed her legs. Check out her thighs.'

'Sam, you'll get us into trouble!'

'Don't miss this, man. Don't!'

Mostly in an effort to get him off his back, Adi turned around to look in the direction of Sheetal, sitting three rows higher. Oblivious of their lascivious stares, Sheetal had crossed her legs, catching the fabric between them. The slits now exposed her firm, smooth thighs all the way up to her underwear. Lost in the world of scholarly pursuit, she was eagerly taking down whatever Dr Gomke said, unaware that three rows away, her anatomy was the subject of another, rather non-academic, discussion.

This time Adi did not make a hasty retreat. Sam joined him. 'Man...what a view. If only I was a fly that could sit beneath her legs and admire what's between them.'

'She would squash you, Sam!'

'But at least I'd die happy, man.'

Following their line of sight, a couple of other guys joined in surreptitiously, enjoying the spectacle that was Sheetal.

Suddenly, as if awakened from this outrage by some sixth sense, Sheetal looked in their direction.

The speed with which some of them looked away could have given them whiplash. Sam lowered his head and began laughing. Adi scribbled furiously in his notebook, suddenly feeling his ears go red when he realized that their antics had attracted Dr Gomke's attention.

She stopped in the middle of her lecture. Her eyes narrowed; the artificial eyebrows furrowed quizzically as she stared sternly in their direction for a few minutes.

'You!' she barked, pointing in their general direction. 'Get up!'

Adi's heart began palpitating so loudly he was afraid she would hear him. He looked up, trying to muster the most innocent look his fear would allow. Sam didn't budge.

Dr Gomke tried again. 'You! Yes, you, there!' she shouted, pointing at Sam. Her pale face was suddenly suffused with colour.

Sam sat unperturbed. He turned to look behind him casually, as though Dr Gomke's pointed glance couldn't possibly be implicating him.

Dr Gomke, firmly entrenched in the Anatomy division for twenty-eight years, was not blessed with patience. Unmarried and unattached, her life revolved around teaching Anatomy and running the department – a commitment that automatically authorized a gargantuan demand for respect.

Striding up the steps rapidly, she approached their row. With her face approximating the colour of her sari and the veins on her forehead looking ready to burst, she bellowed, 'You...yes, you in the blue shirt. Stand up, now!'

'Who...me?' asked Sam, his eyes wide with incredulity.

'Yes, you! What is going on? What are you doing?'

'Nothing, ma'am...just...studying,' replied Sam calmly.

'Studying? Studying what?' she hollered, showering the air with a thin mist of saliva.

'Thighs...I mean, legs...I mean, the lower limbs,' replied Sam.

By now, Adi's appreciation of anything comical had vanished. His mouth felt dry and the perspiration on his palms made it difficult for him to hold on to his pen.

Dr Gomke was not amused. 'So where is the disturbance coming from? Or am I imagining things?' she yelled, spewing anger liberally with her salivary fireworks.

Sam stared ahead with the same look of incorruptible righteousness.

Dr Gomke pointed at the guy sitting next to Sam. 'You, there...yes, you, Sardarji...stand up. What is your name?'

Adi felt relieved that Dr Gomke had chosen to pursue her inquisition on Sam's wrong side. However, his heart sank upon seeing the studious looking Sikh guy stand up slowly, bewilderment and fear written all over his face. He looked around uncertainly, and then said softly, 'Jagdeep Singh, ma'am.'

'Where was all the noise coming from?' demanded Dr Gomke.

Jagdeep looked unsure for a few seconds. He glanced at Adi, as though expecting him to own up to his culpability. Adi caught his stare but looked away, his guilt finding refuge in his fear. When Adi didn't respond, Jagdeep looked down at the floor and said, 'I...I don't know, ma'am.'

Dr Gomke was not amused. 'So, none of you know what happened, even though it was loud enough to disrupt my lecture?'

Nobody said anything. In the pin-drop silence of the huge hall, Adi could almost hear himself perspire.

Dr Gomke stared at them for a few minutes, her eyes narrowed, her jaws clenched. Then she declared, 'Fine...since you were paying attention, you should know what I have taught so far. If you can answer my question, I will let you stay here. Otherwise neither of you will come to my lectures...for the rest of the year!'

The class broke into a shocked murmur at the severity of the punishment. Two careers in medicine were about to be nipped in the bud.

'Silence!' yelled Dr Gomke, and two hundred voices went mute.

Jagdeep looked horrified. He opened his mouth to speak, but stopped. Sam took a deep breath and clenched his jaws tightly.

'So, do you know what happened?' asked Dr Gomke, testing their resolve one last time. No one spoke.

'I see…Okay…Are you ready to answer this question?'

Sam nodded. He straightened up, as though preparing for the guilty verdict and the subsequent martyrdom of being falsely accused.

'In the thigh, what is the relation of the femoral artery to the femoral vein?' asked Dr Gomke.

An eerie silence descended on the class as two hundred pairs of eyes focused their attention on Sam.

The question was not a random pick. In fact, it was specially chosen to *prove* Sam's guilt. For, not only did Sam not know the answer, he didn't even know that Dr Gomke had not yet *taught* that part. Dr Gomke was killing two birds with one stone – making sure that Sam got booted out of her class while confirming her suspicion that he was the source of the disturbance.

By some heavenly coincidence, Adi had glanced at a diagram of the femoral vessels in his anatomy book just before class had begun. The book had fallen open on that page and, for some unknown reason, he had spent a few seconds studying the diagram of the two blood vessels lying next to each other. His mind raced to recall the details, and within seconds he knew that the answer was 'lateral'.

Sam was lost. His expression inspired a faint smirk of satisfaction on Dr Gomke's face. The redness on her face receded rapidly. As she turned to go down the steps, contemplating her next move, Adi quickly scribbled 'lateral' on a piece of paper and pushed it towards Sam. He read it; then crumpling the paper into a miniscule ball, swallowed it.

Just as Dr Gomke turned to look at him, eyebrows raised, ready for the kill, Sam said in a loud clear voice, 'Lateral, ma'am.'

In the uneasy silence that followed, two hundred pairs of eyes turned to focus on Dr Gomke, nervously awaiting her reaction. She went red in the face again. Her fingers bit into the chalk in her hand, turning them pale and sickly. Her lips hardened and her breathing became uneven as she scanned the faces for potential suspects who could have helped Sam. Finally, after a few anxiety-ridden moments, she growled, 'Sit down!'

Sam sat down with a satisfied smile and shot Adi an appreciative glance. Adi could hear the entire class of two hundred let go of the breath they had been holding for the last fifteen minutes.

⚘

When the class got over, a crowd gathered around Sam, eager to hear his version of the story. Sam enjoyed being the centre of attention as he repeated the story over and over, regaling the audience with a liberal sprinkling of his own masala. His audacity landed him the cape of the champion-of-the-wrongly-accused-and-threatened-junta, with Adi as his genius sidekick.

Smiling to himself, Adi headed outside. He stopped at the display case and studied the expression of the dissected face again. The bewildered eyes stared back at him; the confrontation seemed to have transformed the grimace into a wince. Adi felt an inexplicable sadness and curled his own mouth a few times, as if to coax the dead muscles to contract by imitation. Studying the face for any signs of compliance, he started to back towards the door, bumped into somebody and fell.

'Keep your eyes where you are supposed to…that includes in the class too!'

Adi looked up to see a girl staring at him with annoyance. She stood a foot away, one slender arm holding a notepad with a few loose sheets of paper, while the other one dangled an oversized leather bag. She wore a sleeveless light-green top that disappeared around her narrow waist into a tight-fitting black skirt. The skirt ended just above her knees, revealing smooth and shapely legs protruding elegantly beyond the hemline. She ran her fingers through her wavy hair, coaxing them back into place. Even though Adi had a worm's eye view, her glamorous good looks were very striking.

'Oh! Sorry!' he exclaimed, quickly scrambling to his feet.

'Are you going to say that to Sheetal too?' she asked, smiling mischievously as she bent down to help him pick up the books that lay scattered on the floor.

'Say what to Sheetal?' Adi asked.

'Oh, come on!' she smiled naughtily. 'I know what you and Sam were doing. I was sitting just behind.'

'Oh, I see…well…um…what…no, we were not doing anything,' stammered Adi, struggling to regain what was left of his composure.

She looked at his face closely, smiling at his efforts to keep the guilt from showing.

'You look so guilty,' she laughed. 'By the way, I'm Renuka.'

'Oh, yeah. Hi, I'm Adi...Adityaman Bhatt,' he replied.

'So where are you from...Adityaman Bhatt?'

'I'm from Ranchi, in Bihar. How about you? Where are you from, Renuka...? What is your last name?'

'I'm from Bombay. And why do you want to know my last name?'

'Just...I guess...for general knowledge...in case they ask me on Quiz Time.'

She laughed. 'You're funny...and cute, too.'

'Th...thanks,' mumbled Adi.

Renuka looked at him intently, probing his reaction to her compliment. Adi didn't disappoint. She could see the blood rushing to his face. The bemused smile never left her lips.

Being from a small town and having studied in a boys' school, this was the longest conversation Adi had ever had with a girl not related to him. He decided to get away quickly before he made a fool of himself.

'I guess we are late for the next class,' he said. 'We'd better be going.'

'What? Aren't you going to say something?'

Adi stared at her blankly.

'You know, one good turn deserves another,' she said. 'I said you were cute and so...'

Adi tapped his forehead lightly and said with a sheepish smile, 'Oh, yeah...you too.'

'You too, what?'

'You know...the same...'

'No, I don't know, Adityaman Bhatt. Perhaps you could be a little more specific?'

She raised her eyebrows expectantly. The smile continued to play at the corner of her lips.

Adi's mind went blank. He tried desperately to say something smart. However, it seemed unimaginative and lazy to repeat 'cute' and yet, no other description seemed apt. He struggled with his vocabulary, trying hard to be complimentary without being overtly flirtatious.

'Yes, yes...you look...*nice*...too...very much...' he mumbled, kicking himself for his verbal constipation. He had heard of writer's block, but what was this, flirter's block?

She started to laugh. 'I didn't mean to corner you, Adityaman Bhatt. Why is it so hard for you to say I look good?'

'I...I don't know.'

'So you do think I look good but cannot say it, is that right?'

'Well, no...I mean...I guess I don't know you

well enough,' he said, weakly. 'I don't even know your last name.'

'So you do think I am good-looking, but cannot say it because you don't know my last name? Is *that* right?' Adi nodded. 'But if you do get to know me better, you *will* tell me that I'm good-looking. Sounds fair?' she said. He nodded again. 'Well then, I will have to let you know me better, won't I?' she said, grinning coquettishly. 'Anyway, I think it's time for the next lecture now. And by the way, my last name is Seth. Renuka Seth.'

She turned around and began to walk away.

Adi stared at her shapely figure disappearing through the graceful archway. He smiled to himself, an inexplicable happiness buoying his spirits. He began to head for the next lecture hall. Suddenly, his eyes fell on the display case once more.

The face in the formalin…it was smiling…*yes, it was smiling*.

FOUR

Far from all forms of familial restriction, Adi's days in medicine began to pass rather quickly. Armed with a new found emancipation from accountability, he, along with Toshi, Rajeev, Harsha and Sam, began to explore the glitzy allure of downtown Bombay, magically drawn to its charms like moths to a flame. Every evening, as soon as classes were over, they would clamber aboard the bright red BEST buses, choosing the double-deckers for the bird's eye view they provided. Their ride along the crowded roads, with the wind in their hair and the sun on their faces, readily justified the two rupees the conductor charged for the trip. Their pace would peter to a crawl at Kalbadevi, the chaotic marketplace, where the earth appeared blanketed with a quilt of bobbing human heads. The bus would inch ahead in fits and starts, honking angrily at anyone who dared to dart across its path. The harried honking rarely dissuaded anyone, be it the sweat-stained, sunburned handcart pullers anxious not to break the momentum of their efforts, or the impassive neighbourhood cows ambling over to check out a green leafy tidbit in the middle of the road.

The rides usually ended at Flora Fountain. They would alight amidst the hundreds of makeshift stalls, sprouting on the sidewalks like mushrooms after a summer rain. They would loiter around rudderless, captivated by the histrionic chants of the thela-wallas or the electronic crackle of newfangled gizmos. They would ogle at college girls in miniskirts hunting for bargains on Fashion Street; sip nimbu-pani while watching cricket matches at Cross Maidan; gulp down tangy pani-puris outside Churchgate station; or admire the Mercs racing down Marine Drive, over a warm packet of seng. Occasionally they'd stumble onto the sets of a movie, where watching the celebrities up close and personal would inevitably generate an excitement-filled phone call home that evening. When tired of all the activity, they would rest on the rocks overlooking the sea at Nariman Point, admire its vertiginous skyline and smell the moisture-laden winds blowing inland.

In the midst of discovering the city's nuances, they talked, joked, argued and chatted, slowly getting to know one another during these never-ending sessions of idle banter. Adi enjoyed these times immensely, hanging on to the smallest details of their conversation, as his image of the others began to get coloured by their opinions. He learned of Toshi's love of music, Harsha's love for his mother, Sam's love of jokes and Rajeev's love of himself.

This routine kept repeating itself with amazing monotony, even though Adi's life was anything but monotonous.

'What is the use of all this studying?' pondered Rajeev solemnly one day when they were sitting in the driveway of the hostel, lazily sipping tea. The bittersweet warmth of the brew was particularly effective in stimulating thoughtful discussion. They had just returned from Marine Drive where the sight of a bunch of voluptuous models entering a discotheque in tight skirts and halter-tops had struck a particularly resonant chord with Rajeev. 'Saala, we'll slog for the next twelve years and still earn less than what a model earns in one year,' he concluded.

'Yeah, poor Rajeev,' smiled Sam. 'Any more "slogging" and he may actually have to buy *Gray's Anatomy*.'

'That's not the point, Sam!' replied Rajeev. 'I mean, we worked our butts off to get into medical college and we're supposed to be the bright ones, right? Yet some idiot with a half-brain will smile with some soap in one hand, then carry off a paycheck in bloody crores along with a bunch of babes willing to spread their legs for him every night.'

'Idiot with a half-brain…hmm,' reflected Sam. 'Rajeev, you have a great future in modelling.'

Amidst the laughter Rajeev shook his head in frustration. 'You're useless, Sam! Everything is a joke for you. You'll realize later.'

'So why are you joining medicine? Do modelling, na?' asked Harsha.

Rajeev shot him an appreciative look. 'It's not that easy, man. I had a few offers but I'd be in the background in those ads for sanitary napkins and…'

'Hey guys…how do you define women's periods?' interrupted Sam. After a brief pause, he said, 'It's a bloody waste of fucking time.'

Everyone laughed. Smiling to himself, Adi swirled the tea around a few times, preparing for a final swig of the sludge at the bottom of the cup, when his eyes fell on the noticeboard next to the hostel's main entrance. He was surprised to see an official looking notice stuck to the tattered green cloth. The only message the mutilated board had ever conveyed in the past was its state of neglect, a plight emblematic of the generally run down state of affairs in the hostel. Consequently, hostelers usually just walked past the board without giving it a second glance.

Adi walked over to read the notice. 'Have you guys read this?' he called out to the others. 'It says that the rules of room distribution in the hostel may be changed, to be based on marks in the exams!'

'It's probably a joke,' suggested Sam.

'A joke?' said Adi. 'It's signed by the warden!'

Suddenly rattled out of their sense of complacency, they quickly walked over to read the notice.

'How can that be?' asked Rajeev. 'If they decide based on marks and not by the distance from Bombay, then the locals might get rooms before us.'

'This is crazy,' said Toshi. 'Mokokchung is 3000 kilometres from here. I'm screwed if I don't get a room... We can't live in dorms forever. We should do something about it.'

'What can *we* do?' fretted Harsha.

'We have to do *something*!' said Sam. 'Maybe we can talk to the warden!'

'It's not a rule yet,' said Adi. 'The notice says that this is one of the proposed changes that will be voted on by the hostel committee, after the next election for the Hostel Secretary. But I think we should talk to the warden right now.'

'Talk? What will talking do?' asked Rajeev. 'This is more serious, man. This calls for action!'

Suddenly one of the windows above their heads opened and someone said, 'Freshies! Up to my room! Now!'

Their discussion abruptly halted, they looked up to see Pheru scowling down at them from the window of his second-floor room. They looked at each other uncertainly, reluctant to obey Pheru, yet undecided about the ramifications of ignoring an order from a senior of his reputation. After a few seconds of silent wrangling, they acquiesced to their fears and trooped up to his room, trying to find consolation in the fact that, in the normal scheme of things, freshers were subjected to Pheru's torture only once. They filed into the big room slowly, lining up against the wall like prisoners about to be executed.

'Close the door,' instructed Pheru. Harsha, closest to the door, complied.

Although it was a double room, Pheru remained its sole occupant, no one else in the hostel willing to brave the bogeyman's company. His prolonged occupancy had turned that section of the hostel into the eerie tower of the abominable beast in the castle, only to be crossed under duress, swiftly and silently.

Adi, however, was pleasantly surprised as he studied the room. Instead of instruments of torture, books of all shapes and sizes lined shelves on two sides. A neatly organized table stood next to a tidy bed, the walls around it decorated with a few posters of Eric Clapton. The sun streamed in from the generous windows, lighting up the room with its orange brilliance.

Silence reigned for the next few minutes. Then Pheru addressed Sam. 'You've become famous. I heard about the incident with Dr Gomke.'

They sighed in unison, suddenly able to breathe easier now that their apprehension about renewed persecution appeared unfounded.

'You know, you should stand for Class Representative,' said Pheru. 'Everyone knows you in your class now, and it will be really easy for you.'

Sam's eyes sifted uncomfortably. 'Why?' he asked finally.

Pheru shrugged and said, 'Don't you want to be CR? If you are CR, you can be anything after that…you can stand for College Representative, or General Secretary or Hostel Secretary…'

Sam chuckled nervously, hoping he was right in identifying some cryptic humour in Pheru's advice. When Pheru didn't reciprocate, Sam shifted hesitantly, afraid to antagonize him, yet unable to generate enough enthusiasm for the idea.

'Really? You think I can be one?' he asked.

'Of course,' said Pheru enthusiastically. 'You'd be perfect. Lots of guys, even from other classes, admire your guts in standing up to Gomke. It does take guts to stand up to her, man. Besides, you're smart, you're quick, and you have a great smile. You'll easily become CR. If you get to become CR, you'll be known throughout campus and then you can stand for Hostel Secretary…'

The attraction of the proposal began to show on Sam's broadening smile. 'What do I have to do?' he asked.

'Well, stand for Class Representative first and campaign hard. You'll definitely win in your class. That way you will be well known throughout campus and then you can stand for Hostel Secretary.'

The recurrent mention of Hostel Secretary caught Adi's attention. 'Why Hostel Secretary?' he asked.

Pheru smiled quickly and said, 'You can be anything. I just said that because of the new rules in the hostel. Did you guys see the notice?'

That was when it dawned on everyone that something in the new rules bothered Pheru, and *that* was the primary motivation for calling them up to his room. They nodded silently.

'It's all that bastard's doing. Bloody son of a bitch!' said Pheru, suddenly angry. 'All of us are in trouble with this new rule. I heard you guys talking about fighting it out. I have a plan, but I'll need your help. Are you in?'

Without waiting for their response, Pheru motioned for them to surround him and said in a sinister voice, 'The warden is the dean's chamcha. All this is a charade…education my ass, he is doing this because the dean asked him to.'

Pheru studied their faces, somehow expecting this tidbit of information to induct them as co-conspirators into his mysterious plan. Although no one said anything, the real reason for Pheru's agitation was apparent to all of them. Clearly, his days of unhindered intimidation were numbered by his academic calendar.

Adi felt a sudden rush of power at the naked helplessness of his former tormentor. He felt like laughing at Pheru's pathetic efforts. Surely, Sam would never agree.

'What can we do?' asked Sam.

Taken aback by Sam's offer, Adi looked at the others out of the corner of his eyes. The same question adorned each face – what was Sam doing?

'Sam', said Pheru enthusiastically. 'First you have to become the Class Representative. The election of the CR of the new class is a big event on campus. Everyone tries to find out who is the most prominent person in the new class. First CR, then that will be the launching pad for Hostel Secretary. Once you are the Hostel Secretary, you can change the rules...you have time...the new rules will come into effect only after the elections next year. But the time to prepare is now.'

Then – much to the consternation of the others – Pheru and Sam began plotting political strategy.

❧

Sam returned to the dormitory later that night, having stayed back for a few hours after the others had left for a session of personal and political brainstorming with Pheru.

Rajeev confronted him as soon as he entered. 'What is wrong with you, Sam?'

'Why...what happened?'

'Why did you decide to help out Pheru?'

Sam fell silent. The others looked on expectantly, awaiting the explanation that would explain his betrayal. Instead, Sam said, 'Pheru is not what he seems. He is actually not a bad guy...'

Rajeev cut in. 'Not a bad guy? Pheru? Saala, are you fucking nuts? Is that why he fails every year? Is that why he almost made us cry? Is that why he is so afraid of the dean?'

'You don't know much about him, Rajeev.'

'Why don't you tell us what we don't know? So that we can like him like you do,' mocked Rajeev.

'Pheru has a long history here,' began Sam. 'I know that the authorities, especially the dean, have been after him for some time...'

'That is bullshit, man. Maybe the authorities have a good reason. Maybe he *needs* to be afraid of the dean!'

Sam didn't reply.

'Don't you see it, Sam? He is using you. He knows that other than freshies like us, nobody is under his control. You were not there that night when he ragged us...he is a bloody bastard. Now he wants to be friends with us to use us. This is the *best* chance we have to get rid of him, man.

This is the revenge we've been waiting for. If they changed the rules to get rid of him, maybe it's because he *needs* to be got rid of!'

'Rajeev, this rule could hurt us just as much. Remember we were talking about doing something just a few hours ago? The dean hates Pheru…'

'That's what Pheru says, Sam. Why would you believe him? He has shown you all these starry dreams and now you cannot think for yourself. Saala, he is fucking using you, man!'

Sam grimaced but didn't reply.

'Why don't you say that you want to be CR? This stuff about Pheru is just an excuse,' accused Rajeev.

'Maybe I do! So what?'

Toshi intervened. 'Stop it, Rajeev. If Sam says we should help Pheru out, maybe we should. After all, if the new rules do apply, even we could be in trouble. And Sam being CR or even Hostel Secretary will only help us.'

Toshi's mediation brought about an uneasy calm. He quickly brought out a pen and paper to expand on the political strategy Pheru had initiated. Within a few minutes, they were engrossed in trying to devise a catchy but believable message.

The elections were scheduled for the day after

the class picnic. Sam's only opponent was a local lad, Manish Torwadkar, whose campaign had no theme other than the fact that he was from Bombay.

They agreed unanimously on the central message of their own campaign – Sam's confrontation with Dr Gomke, showcased as a fitting testament to his courageous leadership. But the method of getting the message across to everybody took more decisive planning. It didn't help that Rajeev's participation was begrudging, slowing down their decisions. After a lot of debate and discussion they agreed that the class picnic, which was a week away, would be crunch time.

At a hundred rupees per person, Adi had decided to forego the pleasures of the picnic. He could think of ten better uses for the money.

'Rajeev, you have to bring in the girls to vote for Sam. Adi and Harsha can go after the guys,' suggested Toshi.

'Maybe I can talk to the other guys in the hostel,' suggested Adi, hesitant to mention that he was planning to skip the picnic due to monetary concerns.

Toshi nodded unconvincingly. 'Oh…okay. Anyway, let's get the list of people who are going to the picnic from one of the organizers. The picnic is the best time to promote Sam. It'll be fresh in their minds when they vote the next day. Anyone know any of the organizers?'

'I think Renuka Seth is one of them,' said Sam.

Adi's ears perked up at the mention of Renuka's name.

'Yeah, she is one of the organizers,' said Rajeev. 'By the way, Adi, she asked me if you were planning to go to the picnic.'

A sudden elation arose from somewhere deep within Adi's heart, filling him with a sense of optimism for reasons he couldn't quite fathom.

Renuka had asked about him...about *him*? Well, she had smiled and spoken to him a few times. And a few days ago she had walked down twelve rows to sit next to him. Last Tuesday, she had waved at him...not a simple goodbye, but an affectionate twirl of the fingers along with a wave that was a special...

'Hey Adi. Are you going to the picnic? And why are you smiling?'

Adi hurriedly focused his eyes to find the others staring at him. Then smiling cheerfully, he said, 'Of course I'm going to the picnic. Why wouldn't I?'

The chosen picnic destination was a small fishing village with gorgeous white beaches hemmed by stretches of shady coconut groves. In addition, it boasted of an uninhabited island fort that was approachable by foot when the tide was out. On that picture perfect August day, clear blue skies and miles of azure water simmered before Adi's eyes.

Despite the promise of fun and frolic that lay ahead, they were focused on using the day to campaign for Sam. Or at least that was what Adi ascribed Rajeev's activities to.

Rajeev was having a great day. The graffiti on his bright red T-shirt, 'Nobody's Perfect…I come close', was not an accidental pick; rather, it described his state of mind fairly accurately. Hidden in his back pocket, he carried a small mirror that helped him adjust his hairstyle every so often. He sat under the coconut trees with a couple of girls, holding their hands open while his index finger ran over the lines on their palms, apparently en route to their future. In a perfectly symbiotic alliance, the girls stood close by, expressing surprise or cheer or outright glee at his visions of their fate with implicit faith in his credentials as a palmist. Adi hoped one of those predictions involved voting for Sam.

Wherever Rajeev went, Harsha couldn't be far behind. Rajeev's charismatic good looks and popularity with the girls had serendipitously transformed him into Harsha's fashion, attitude and style guru. Harsha even helped himself liberally to Rajeev's language skills, spotting his otherwise broken English with a 'cool, man' here and a 'holy cow' there with little thought to the propriety of his diction or grammar. Adi could easily see the synergy of their relationship: Harsha hoped some of Rajeev's glitter would rub off on him while Rajeev's pleasure in having a perennial admirer of his wit and grace was evident in the confident smile he carried around.

Adi stood debating whether to remind Harsha of their duty to campaign for Sam when he heard Renuka's voice behind him. 'Hi Adi, do you want to go to the fort?'

Adi turned around to see her standing behind him, sipping on a straw stuck into a decapitated coconut. She wore a simple white sleeveless dress with bright yellow flowers that hugged the curves of her body. A slender arm held a large straw hat in place, keeping the sun out of her pretty face.

'Hi,' he said, smiling. 'I was looking for you.'

She smiled back. 'Why?'

'To...to...talk to you.'

'Hmm...Talk about what?'

Adi shrugged. 'Just stuff. You know...'

She smiled. 'No, I don't know. Anyway, do you want to walk up to the fort with me and tell me what you wanted to talk about?'

'Sure,' said Adi, enthusiastically.

They walked along the beach, making small talk as they headed towards the old, uninhabited fort. The soft, wet sand tickled their feet and caressed their soles. The gentle splashes of the inch-deep water played with their ankles, sputtering with effort as the tide rode out into the sea. A few shells floated lazily on the surf while tiny crabs scurried around among the pebbles.

The fort stood atop a giant rock formation that looked distinctly out of place amidst the flat shiny sand surrounding it. The fort was small and in an advanced state of ruin. Banyan trees clung to the cracks on the walls, sending snake like root trails scurrying towards the ground. Huge, moss covered rocks in various shades of green bore the names of previous visitors and the brunt of their need to commemorate such visits. Tall, unkempt grass covered the uneven land inside. Although a few rooms remained intact, the cracked walls and termite ravaged wooden beams didn't invite a closer inspection of the interiors. Small square windows along the hallways provided an unrestricted view of the sea stretching all the way to the horizon. Even in its advanced state of disrepair, those empty turrets and crumbling halls gave the fort a distinctly regal flavour.

'Wouldn't it be great to be a queen?' said Renuka.

'Really? Hmm...I'm not so sure,' replied Adi, trying to think pragmatically. 'Imagine having to live all your life with the fear of being killed or dethroned.'

Looking out through the windows she said, 'One day, I'll be rich and buy an island.'

'Why should we live on an island...' said Adi. Renuka turned and looked at him, a saucy smile playing on her lips.

Flustered, Adi tried to change the subject quickly. 'I hope you are voting for Sam tomorrow,' he said.

'No.'

'What... Why not?' said Adi, shocked. Then, remembering their slogan, he said, 'Sam is the best...Gomke's put him through the test. Vote tomorrow night for the one who'll fight for your rights.'

'Nobody asked me to vote for him.'

'*I'm* asking you,' said Adi.

'Then I can't refuse, can I?' she said, smiling sweetly.

❧

By the evening, Adi had crossed off almost everyone on his list of potential voters. The sun had shed much of its warmth and a light breeze was blowing in from the sea. Adi clambered into one of the buses and found a window seat. He looked outside expectantly, hoping to spot Renuka and find the courage to invite her to sit next to him.

He heard someone say, 'Can we sit here?'

Half-expecting Renuka, he turned around to see an attractive girl with a very pretty smile looking at him.

For a moment, he stared at her as though he hadn't heard her question. Then, gathering his wits, he said in a mock-serious tone, 'Let me see. What are your ticket numbers?'

She laughed at his silly attempt at humour. Her laughter rang with a sweet, innocent quality that complimented her looks. Her face was slender, with high cheekbones and soft unblemished skin that seemed completely unaffected by the exertions of the day. Beautiful, bright eyes glowed with vivaciousness, heightened by the twin dimples that appeared on her cheeks when she smiled. A lovely light-blue dress hugged her lissome body and seemed to lighten the damp of the evening. But what caught Adi's eye was a subtle vulnerability in her beauty that made him instinctively like her.

'Hi, I'm Isha. Ishita Banerji,' she said, occupying the seat next to Adi. Then pointing to her friend, she said, 'And this is Payal Chawla.'

'Hi... I'm Adi.'

'Yeah, we know who you are,' said Isha. 'Ever since that day in class when you and Sam almost got into trouble with Dr Gomke, you guys have been famous.'

'Infamous, you mean.'

Again, that beautiful laughter.

'And very, very lucky,' added Payal.

'That's true,' smiled Adi. 'So are you both from Bombay?'

'Yeah. We've been friends from school through to college, and now medical college.'

'Wow! That's great,' he said. 'Listen, before I forget, I hope you are voting for Sam tomorrow. Sam is the best...Gomke...'

'...Put him through the test. Vote tomorrow night for the one who'll stand up for your rights,' said Payal, completing his sentence. Adi smiled.

The bus showed no signs of moving. Although it was humid inside, Adi didn't complain. He enjoyed talking to the girls and each time Isha laughed, Adi felt like laughing as well. Her laughter was as contagious as it was beautiful.

Suddenly, Adi spotted Rajeev and Harsha standing about twenty feet away from the bus in animated discussion with a bunch of boys. Adi couldn't hear them, and the possibility that they had gotten into trouble while canvassing for Sam worried him. He excused himself from Isha and Payal's company, and headed outside.

The situation turned out to be different. The bus driver claimed that his bus permit didn't allow more than ninety-six people. There being a hundred occupants, he was refusing to go back.

'The driver counted the numbers now. Claims there were less in the morning,' explained Rajeev.

'Can't we reason with him?' asked Adi.

'The bastard just wants some extra money.'

Adi shrugged. 'Then why don't a few of us go back on our own?' he said. 'The train station is pretty close and once we reach Virar, we can take the locals trains.'

Rajeev turned to look at him. 'That is a great idea. Why don't you suggest it?' he said.

Adi broke into the discussion and enthusiastically offered the solution. A few 'why-didn't–I-think-of-that' smacks on the forehead followed, after which everybody dispersed towards the bus, eager to find a seat to get back. Adi, stuck with being the idea's proponent, assumed that Rajeev would join him, which meant Harsha would agree readily. He turned around to look for one more volunteer, only to find that Rajeev had disappeared.

A few insipid announcements and some gentle cajoling later, three other volunteers joined Adi. The four of them set out on foot for the nearest train station. As the bus drove past, Adi spotted Rajeev sitting near one of the windows in the rear of the bus, talking animatedly to the girls around him.

The train station was a twenty-minute walk from the beach. The sun had set, and in its absence, a refreshingly calm breeze blew in from the sea. Tall palm trees swayed gently in the wind as they made their way through the open farmlands along the narrow, dusty foot-trails.

Adi, walking with one of the guys, realized that this would be the ideal time to sell him Sam's candidacy.

'Hey, Yogesh,' he said. 'I hope you are voting for Sam in tomorrow's election.'

'Hmmm...I'll see.'

'See what? You know Sam is the best, Gomke's put him through the test. Vote tomorrow night for the one who'll fight for your rights!' said Adi enthusiastically.

Yogesh didn't respond. Undeterred, Adi pestered him some more. Unable to convince Adi of his sincerity or shake him off with his indifference, Yogesh said, 'He won't win the election, you know that.'

Adi was taken aback. 'Why won't he win? Sam is the best choice...'

'But he is not from here!'

'What do you mean?'

'He is not...Maharashtrian.'

'Sure he is. He is from Pune...very much in Maharashtra.'

'Yeah, but not *really* Maharashtrian.'

'What? How can he not be Maharashtrian, having been born and raised in Maharashtra?'

Yogesh averted his gaze. Then, softly, with some guilt in his voice, he said, 'He is not *pure* Maharashtrian, you know... I mean...he...he is not Hindu.'

FIVE

In contrast to his breezy social evolution, Adi's academic transition from high school to medical college was nothing less than tumultuous. Anatomy, Physiology and Bio-chemistry – the three subjects to be taught over the sixteen months of first MBBS – were whole new worlds to him. It didn't help that laborious words with roots in Greek or Latin described esoteric terms that neither made sense nor sat easy on his tongue. Learning turned into a process of confining facts to memory with limited understanding of the actual content. To further complicate matters, a plethora of notes on every subject circulated clandestinely; hushed whispers and cryptic nods conveyed their caliber and an incipient advantage to the recipient, thereby automatically inducing him or her to guard the secrecy of their existence with passionate zeal. Lost in this competitive world of undergraduate medicine was the fact that there were so many versions of the same message floating around, they spent more time chasing them than reading them.

This undercurrent of fanatical competition was effectively camouflaged in the animated bustle of the huge dissection hall where the entire class gathered to dissect cadavers and learn about the intricacies of human anatomy. Eight batches of twenty-six students huddled around a corpse, trying to figure out what in the world they had sliced their way through. Adi's batch was a motley crew of late arrivals. He chose to limit his fraternization to Rajeev, Toshi, Sam and Harsha, never finding the courage to approach the other person in his batch who held his interest – Renuka.

'So, Adi, have you done something yet?' asked Sam one day as they hung out on the periphery of the gathering around the cadaver while the others dissected with an enthusiasm that completely eluded the two of them.

'Done something about what?'

'Renuka, man. Have you taken her out...like a date?'

'No...I've never done it.'

Sam gave him a disapproving look. 'You've never dated anyone?' he asked.

'No. I guess it's not too common in a small place like Ranchi.'

Sam looked shocked. 'Man, what is this...the eighteenth century? Did you at least talk to the girls in your class?'

'I went to an all-boys' school.'

'Aaargh,' said Sam, hanging his head in mock despair. 'Adi, you'll need a lot of help. Someone else in your place would have had a few kids with Renuka by now.' He laughed at his joke while Adi could only smile indulgently.

'I don't know what to do,' said Adi. 'I mean, she hasn't ever said anything.'

'What do you expect her to do, man? You've got to make some moves too.'

'I suppose...but you know, I'm not even sure she likes me or has feelings...'

Sam gave him a perplexed look. 'Going out with her doesn't mean you have to marry her tomorrow, Adi. If you like her, you have to try to get to know her better and let her get to know *you* better. How is she going to like you if all you do is give her sly looks in class?'

Adi nodded, mulling over Sam's advice, wondering if he had the gumption to act on it.

Maybe he would ask her out. Ask her to a meal, or a movie...or both. But what if she refused, or worse, stopped talking to him?

Suddenly Sam whispered, 'Grab Cunningham, Adi! Gomke!'

They dived for their Anatomy dissection guidebooks. In the aftermath of that incident between Sam and Dr Gomke, she kept an eagle eye on them.

Dr Gomke waddled to the middle of D-hall. 'Class,' she declared loudly. 'I have an announce-ment. Since the class is now complete, we will reassign roll numbers according to last names and form new batches.'

Loud groans ensued. Nobody, it seemed, wanted this rearrangement. Adi empathized: except for Sam and Harsha, they would all be in different batches. That meant no Rajeev, Toshi or...Renuka. He joined in the loud chatter, voicing his indistinguishable protest.

'Silence!' demanded Gomke, and silence materialized immediately. 'The new roll numbers and batches have been put up on the notice board downstairs. You can look at it after dissection is over.'

She shot one parting glare at Sam before slowly ambling out.

The class broke into loud chatter as soon as she was out of earshot. The displeasure at the turn of events was almost unanimous.

'I thought she was going to eat me alive,' said Sam. 'I hope the witch goes to hell and has to dance nude for the devil. Imagine her dancing on the table with her tits jiggling like dried oranges. I think the devil might just quit hell.'

Adi laughed. He began to arrange his bag, preparing to follow the rest of the class to the notice board downstairs.

'So, you think this is funny?' said Renuka, who had quietly slid up next to him.

Adi sobered up immediately. 'What...no, no,' he said. 'Sam cracked a joke about Gomke. So that's why...'

'But does this bother you or no?' Clearly it bothered her.

'Of course,' he said.

'Why does it bother you?'

'Why...? I don't know. It was nice in this batch.'

'That's it? Nice in this batch?'

Adi fumbled, looking for something smart to say. 'No... I guess we will have to make new friends...'

'So you'll make new friends too?'

Adi couldn't understand why it was so hard

for him to say the things he wanted to say. He wanted to tell her that the prospect of separation bothered him, and that he too had protested this move, and that he would miss her. But in her presence, his tongue always twisted into a dyslexic lump.

Renuka stood waiting for him to regain his eloquence. Then, with an exasperated sigh, she said, 'Well, see you later,' and began walking away.

'No, no Renuka...wait,' said Adi, running behind her. 'Would you like to have coffee with me?'

Whereas Adi's sudden bravado surprised her, it shocked him, leaving him immediately with a terrible knot in his stomach. It grew knottier the few moments she spent contemplating her answer.

Then, the edges of her lips curled into a smile, and she said, 'Okay... how about 4:30? Where do you want to go?

'The Central Canteen?'

'CC? Oh, well...okay.'

'Great!' smiled Adi, now that it was easier to breathe. 'I'll see you there.'

She smiled and walked away.

Everyone else had crowded around the notice board, trying to locate their names on the new list. Adi ignored the list and ran out. He found Sam and Rajeev walking towards the hostel.

'Sam... Sam,' he called from behind. 'I did it. I did it, man!'

They stopped and stared at Adi.

'I asked her out, man... and she agreed!'

'That's great.' Sam grinned and filled Rajeev in.

Rajeev broke into a smile. 'All right, Adi! Where are you going? Movie? Dinner? There is a great movie for couples in Sterling...'

'No, no. It's just for some coffee in the canteen,' said Adi.

Sam and Rajeev looked shocked. Then, almost simultaneously, they started laughing. Sam put his arm around Adi's shoulders. 'Man, Adi... you need a lot of coaching. You are terrible.'

'Why? What did I do?' asked Adi.

'What did you do? You are going to take her out for the first time, and decided on the campus canteen to have coffee for Rs1.50? This is how you plan to impress her? Take her somewhere nice, man; you know...a nice restaurant on Marine Drive. Have dinner if possible; if not, then coffee is fine. Take a walk along Chowpatty. Not the bloody rat-infested, noisy, dirty canteen, with its steel cups and twisted spoons, man!'

'Oh... okay. But I told her I'd meet her there at 4:30.'

'Well, you still have half an hour. Why don't you go and freshen up in the hostel and then meet her in the central canteen? Then you can suggest real casually that CC looks kind of dirty and that you know a good place on Marine Drive.'

'Oh...okay,' said Adi, nodding appreciatively.

They showered him with advice while heading back to the hostel.

'Use only taxis, no buses.... and open the door for her.'

'Brush your teeth now.... Use my aftershave.'

'Carry a handkerchief...the way you are sweating, carry two.'

'Don't forget to laugh at all her jokes.'

By the time Adi reached the hostel, only twenty minutes remained. He showered, quickly brushed his teeth and changed into a new set of clothes. Sam emerged with some aftershave and Rajeev lent him his clean pair of jeans. Toshi offered him his new Nike shoes. Someone filled his wallet with a few hundred-rupee notes. Dressed to kill, Adi looked in the mirror while Sam, Rajeev and Toshi stood back and admired their handiwork.

Adi was about to leave when Pheru walked into their room.

A sudden silence descended on the gathering.

Adi stared at Pheru, wondering what he wanted *this* time. Why wouldn't he just leave them alone?

Before Pheru could say anything, Toshi said, 'You'd better leave, Adi. You don't want to be late.'

Adi felt an immediate need to get away from Pheru. He was about to step out when Pheru said, 'Don't forget, she is a vegetarian.'

Surprised, Adi said, 'What? How do you know?'

He winked and said, 'The place to go is Pandits. A little expensive, but the best for vegetarians. Short walk from Churchgate'

Adi smiled. Another round of advice followed.

'Good luck champ and don't burp!'

'Go easy on her boobs, man,' said Sam, and everyone laughed.

Adi ran towards the canteen. He was at the front entrance just as the wall clock inside the canteen proclaimed it was 4:30 p.m. Out of breath, he looked around the crowded canteen. She wasn't inside. Somewhat surprised, he scanned the faces again, unsure of what to make of her absence. He felt silly hanging around aimlessly at the door of the busy canteen, and decided to wait inside. He found an empty seat next to a window and occupied it. A twinge of nervous excitement ran through his body as he scoured the faces of those walking towards the canteen. Was that her in the red salwar kameez...no, Renuka wore her hair down and she was far prettier.

Adi smiled to himself, reassured that he had made it on time. His thoughts drifted to Pheru, and how he seemed to know everything. His resources were amazing. But something about Pheru's presence was also ominous. He carried bad luck like a stray dog carries fleas – fleas that could bite hard if you came too close...like they bit Sam...

Adi chuckled nervously to himself. How could Pheru influence his plans with Renuka? After all, she had said she would meet him. It certainly wasn't his imagination.

Five minutes rolled into ten. The waiter made two trips to see if Adi wanted to order anything. He decided against it, hoping to leave as soon as she arrived. Shetty, the canteen owner, kept shooting nasty glances at Adi, irritated that he was tying up a seat without generating any business. Adi looked away, pretending to be deeply engrossed in a torn sheet of newspaper. Every now and then he stole glances at the door.

Fifteen minutes passed and then twenty. Adi's palms started to feel moist. He wiped them on his jeans, reminding himself of the necessity to keep his palms dry should fate present the opportunity to hold her hand.

Thirty minutes later, when Renuka had not yet put in an appearance, a hint of doubt crept in. He had heard her say yes…hadn't he?

He debated what to do next. Waiting forever obviously wasn't an option. She was from Bombay, and would no doubt return home in the evening. Should he find his way back to the hostel? Perhaps he should leave word with someone?

After forty-five minutes had passed, Adi decided to order half a cup of tea. That would be easier to abandon when she showed up. The increasingly nasty expression on Shetty's face made his decision easier.

The half-cup was over pretty soon, closely followed by two more half-cups. Adi sipped the dark brown concoction, gingerly glancing at the wall clock every so often, his mind tensely revisiting the events of the afternoon.

She had said yes…she had *smiled* and said she'd be there. He was there on time…wasn't he…of course he was…his watch was working fine.

If only that blasted Pheru had not walked in.

Ever since the day Pheru had advised Sam to

stand for CR, nothing other than bad luck had come their way. Sam had suffered a humiliating defeat and, as it turned out, for no reason. The hostel's warden had decided that he liked the idea of room distribution according to marks so much that he would implement it at the next distribution with or without the hostel secretary's blessing. That evening Pheru had dropped into their dorm, uninvited, to cheer Sam up. However, instead of raising his spirits, he had managed to spread misery yet again. Rajeev had kicked the door shut angrily after Pheru's departure, only to fracture Toshi's thumb in the process. Then there was the toaster Pheru had 'gifted' Harsha that had blown out some fuses and left them sweltering in the dark dormitory for three days. The worst part was that Pheru hadn't learned his lesson. He would walk into their room as though such frequent intrusion was a natural extension of his acquaintance with them. They would quieten down immediately and hope that Pheru would take the hint and leave them alone. Instead, his visits only grew more and more frequent.

Damn Pheru…it was his fault…all his fault.

Adi leaned against the wall and stared at the clock, feeling his expectations wither with every tick of the clock's hands. Outside, the shadows of the trees grew longer, stretching to twice their actual height. Everything started to acquire a bright orange glow as the sun hung low in the horizon. A cool breeze began blowing through the open windows. Adi stared ahead blankly, thoughts buzzing through his head without being able to drop anchor. In the background, people seemed like ants, scurrying about their business with scant regard to his gnawing insecurity.

So many people. So many voices. So much noise.

More half-cups of tea followed: the warmth of the brew provided a vague comfort to the ache in his heart. He stopped looking up the road, focusing his attention instead on the few that walked in through the door. His palms had stopped sweating and the small tea stain on his shirt didn't bother him anymore. He stretched out his legs, only to realize that Toshi's new Nikes hurt from being too tight around his feet.

The clock marched on to half-past five, then six.

No matter how many times Adi visited the scene from the afternoon, the images played out with adamant consistency – she had *smiled* and said she would come. There had to be a reason

...a mal-alignment of the stars perhaps. An astounding reason of infinite significance had to have delayed her...or, did it have something to do with Pheru?

It had to! Everything had been fine until he showed up. Pheru was a walking disaster... bringing misery to whomever he touched. Rajeev was right – he needed to be got rid of! God knows how many other lives he had ruined!

Finally, at half-past six, Adi decided to leave. He headed towards Shetty to pay for the six half-cups of tea that had kept him company. As he laid the crisp twenty-rupee bill on the counter, Shetty asked in his thick south Indian accent, 'What...you sat for over two hours and only had tea? How will my business run like this...you should eat something, no?'

'Sorry,' blurted Adi. 'I was actually waiting for someone. A girl... Renuka.'

Shetty's face changed expressions like a chameleon changing colour. He slapped his forehead, bit his bright red tongue, and exclaimed, 'Arre...so it was you? A girl came at 4.15 or so and said someone was to meet her here and to tell him that she was going home because she got a ride in somebody's car, and that she would not be able to meet today... But she said you would be wearing a blue shirt and black pants, not a red T-shirt and jeans pant... Oh, Rama...sorry...sorry, but how do I know? I have to serve so many people and if the fitting is not right, what can I do? Now, she said blue shirt and black pant...Oh Rama, Rama...okay, okay... You...you only pay for two cups, okay? Don't feel bad. Okay? Don't feel bad.'

❦

Adi headed towards the hostel lost in a maze of haphazard thought. 'Don't feel bad' Shetty had said to him. What did that mean? Was he feeling bad for himself or was he sad to have missed her? Should he feel bad about her betrayal or get mad at Pheru? Or was he just glad for Shetty's explanation?

Bad...sad...had...mad...glad...

It had started out about going for coffee, when had it transformed into a date? Was it so important to get a ride home? Could she not have waited a few more minutes for him? And why had Pheru come into the room? Who had asked him to come in? How dare he walk into their room just because they were freshies who couldn't say no?

Mad...sad...bad...glad...had?

Stumbling through the long corridor, Adi made his way towards the dorm. As he passed Pheru's room, he noticed that the door was slightly ajar. He paused outside, for the first time in no hurry to rush past. The bastard was probably asleep after having ruined his day.

Adi's heart began to race and his breath acquired a turbulent warmth. His hands folded into tight fists. His temples began to throb, and blood rushed past his ears, drowning out all warnings of Pheru's rung in the hostel's pecking order.

He pushed open the door roughly and walked in.

Pheru's back was towards him, his head buried in his arms as though seeking shelter from the sky that was about to fall down. Wedged between the fingers of his right hand was a card that he hastily flicked away upon hearing the door open. He turned around swiftly, smiled at Adi, and quickly drawing up his shirt, started wiping his face. His motioned Adi to take a seat.

'So? How was it, man? Did you have fun?' asked Pheru from behind the impromptu veil, his muffled voice soggy with the heaviness that tears impart.

'Yeah...yeah,' Adi replied evasively, shocked to see Pheru in this state. He stepped back, suddenly unsure about his presence in the room. His fists unfolded spontaneously and the heavy thudding in his chest subsided to a gentle rhythm.

Pheru...crying? Was he crying? Did he cry? *Could* he cry?

'What...what's wrong?' asked Adi. 'Were you...crying?'

'Ahh...no man,' chuckled Pheru, looking away, trying hard to hide his embarrassment. 'I... I just got a card from Abbu...my father. That's all. Nothing to it.'

'Is he all right? Were you missing him or something?'

'Missing him?' smirked Pheru. 'No, Adi. I'm not missing him. Abbu sends me a card for everything. I tell him that I'm happy, he sends me a card. I tell him I'm sad and he sends me a card. I tell him that I might get thrown out of the hostel in another year and might have to stop studying medicine...and he sends me a card. His secretaries probably fill it out and sign it. Fucking shit!'

He fell silent, staring angrily at the card lying on his desk.

'So, what is wrong with a card?' asked Adi.

'What is wrong with a card? What is wrong with a card? What does a card mean? Who am

I, his colleague's wife? I want him to say what he feels, man. I want him to be my fucking *dad*!'

Pheru's outburst surprised Adi.

Pheru caught Adi's look. 'My dad is different, Adi,' he said, his voice edgy with exasperation. 'My mother died when I was very young and I've grown up with Abbu alone. But growing up with him was like growing up with a picture on a wall. You wouldn't understand, Adi…we have a lot of problems…'

'But he cares for you, man. That's why he sends you the cards, right?'

'That's what everyone thinks. His cards aren't sent to wish me well!'

Adi stared at Pheru incredulously, trying to decipher the contorted logic of his statement.

Pheru sighed and fell silent. 'It's funny when I think about it,' he said. 'Everyone else gets into medicine to become a doctor, but I got into medicine to irritate him. Abbu wanted me to stay in the family business. I am the only man left to carry on the Pherwani name and Pherwani Constructions. But I wanted to get as far away as possible from him and from what he wanted me to be. So I studied like a madman to get into medical college. It pissed him off. But now that I'm going to be thrown out of college, he sends me a card. Don't you see? This card is his victory.

This card means I've lost! He knows that I'll
end up doing what he wants me to do!'

'But why don't you want to join the family
business?' Adi asked.

'Because that's what *he* wants me to do!'

'What is wrong with that?'

'No… I'm not going to give him what he
wants. He was never there for me when I needed
him and just because he's old now he expects
me to forget everything…Saala, no way…no
fucking way! I have to become a doctor. I just
have to…even if it takes me a hundred fucking
years!'

'I… I don't understand Pheru. What is wrong
with your dad expecting you to join his
business? What is this fascination with
becoming a doctor?'

'It's not a fascination, Adi. It's a fucking
necessity!'

Adi stared at Pheru, a silent question adorning
his puzzled face. Pheru caught that look and
shook his head in frustration. He leaned back
against the wall, letting his eyes drift aimlessly
over the ceiling. Then, after a few minutes, he
said, 'My life is too bloody complicated, Adi.
My mother committed suicide when I was about
five…no one knows why. She had five kids…the
fifth, me, probably tipped her over. One day she

walked to the ledge of the naked terrace and just kept walking. One year later, to the exact day, my eldest brother Khalid and my sister Samina disappeared in a Hindu-Muslim riot. Khalid was eighteen years old and all set to join Abbu in his business. He was the son Abbu always wanted. Khalid was the best in anything he did, studies, sports, drama…and Abbu would go to all his sporting events and elocution contests in school. So when Samina and he didn't come home and they found his headless body in a field near his school, Abbu went crazy. He started going to vague dargahs and crazy babas, preparing for another fucking calamity the next year! I used to feel very scared seeing all kinds of weird people come into the house at all times of the day and night and perform these bizarre rituals. His business started to suffer…we almost got thrown out of our house.

'Abbu recovered somewhat in the next few years, but remained cold, barely throwing me a glance. And I was only a kid… I couldn't understand why. I tried so hard to please him, you know, just to get him to fucking look at me. But he'd either scold me and turn me away or just walk out of the room silently. Then, from when I was about seven or eight years old, I began to have these terrible nightmares. I'd see

Ammi walking on air and Khalid and Samina calling out to me. I'd try to follow them only to realize that there was nothing under my feet. I'd wake up shivering and bathed in sweat, with such headaches that I felt my head would explode. I'd stay awake the rest of the night …afraid to go back to sleep…afraid of the dream coming back. But I couldn't tell Abbu… I was so scared of him! So I would sit alone in my bed the rest of the night and cry till I could cry no more. It went on till one night when I couldn't bear it anymore, I ran to Abbu. Just outside his door, I could hear him arguing loudly with someone. They were talking about me and that's when I heard Abbu say that I was the family's curse! One of these fucking babas had told him that…that everything bad had happened to him after my birth – Ammi's death, Samina's disappearance, Khalid's murder, his business problems. I stood there feeling like I was still dreaming…only it wasn't a dream any more. But you know the funny part, Adi, I had stopped crying and my headache had vanished. And from that day, the nightmares were gone!'

He paused. Then, his voice trembling with hurt and anger, he said, 'So, from then on, I've carried the curse of my birth, Adi. The curse that sits on my shoulders like it was stitched on to me. I ruin everyone's life, Adi, everyone's... I fuck up their happy little existence, I cloud their bright sunny futures, I ruin their precious dreams. I am the ghost that haunts everyone... Just like my image in the hostel...grotesque, fearful and terrifying... They all wonder, what will Pheru do to me next? Everyone is scared of me, Adi, including my own father...! They don't know that I'm as afraid of the fucking curse because it rules *my* fucking life!'

Mad...sad...bad...glad...had?

'Maybe your dad is trying for a reconciliation, Pheru.' he said.

'No, he isn't!' scoffed Pheru.

'Maybe this is your opportunity to get back what you missed out on!'

'Didn't you hear all that I just said?' said Pheru, irritated.

'You're living in the past, man.'

'It's not my past, Adi. I'm still living that fucking isolation!' he shouted. 'Nothing's changed...it's the same in the hostel! I see the others stare at me from a distance...I see the unwelcome faces when I walk into a room. I can hear their footsteps run past my door... I know they pray for me to get thrown out of college! It's the same fucking loneliness. While I walk around hoping to find someone...anyone, to talk to, everyone finds ways to keep me away. Everyone is afraid of what I'll do to them. Nobody wants to be around me: all they want me to do is fucking rag, rag, and rag. It fits my terrifying image… Pheru the monster! But that's not me, Adi, that's not me. I dislike ragging but there is nothing I can do, man. That is what they want me to do. That is the *only* reason they will talk to me or respect me. If I don't rag, I'm nobody…if I do rag I'm somebody…but not the person I want to be…' His voice trailed off, chasing his agonized confusion.

Adi gulped and stared at Pheru silently.

Pheru dabbed his eyes with his shirt and said, 'So you see, Adi, becoming a doctor is not a dream for me, it's a necessity. I have this thing in my head that I'll remain cursed till I become a doctor. I just know it. I just know that I'll cure myself *only* if I become a doctor. I *have* to pass my exams or I'll never be rid of this curse. That is why I desperately cling to medicine while the dean tries to kick me out! Otherwise the curse of my birth will take hold of my life again.'

'Pheru, that's just ridiculous.'

'No, no, it's true…don't you see it? The fucking baba or whoever was right… Khalid, Samina, Ammi, Abbu all felt it before. I've been stuck in second MB for the last four years in the same fucking subject. There have been so many other incidents. Sam lost the election as soon as I tried to get him to contest. And now that you've talked to me, I'm sure something will go wrong with you...if it hasn't happened already. Was everything okay today?'

Adi smiled, but didn't respond.

'What? Did something happen? It did...didn't it?' said Pheru.

'She...she didn't show up,' replied Adi.

Pheru face fell. 'I can't believe it!' he said, clutching his head as though unable to deal with the terrible accuracy of his own prediction. 'Don't you see what I'm saying? I do this to everybody. I'm sure none of this would have happened if I had not shown up to meet you.'

'Pheru, I'm not superstitious,' lied Adi.

'No Adi, it's true. This bloody thing never leaves me! That is why I must become a doctor, Adi. I *have* to become a doctor, not to give medicines to people, but to cure myself of this scourge!'

Adi stared at Pheru wrestling with his demons. He couldn't believe this was the same guy who had nearly made them cry; whose name evoked images of torture and terrible humiliation, whose influence had ruined his...

Mad...sad...bad...glad...had?

'Pheru,' said Adi. 'This is just nonsense. Has anyone told you...you are an absolute psycho. Sam lost because Manish and his gang played dirty. I don't know why you are stuck in second MB, but your influence on the events of today have as much significance as the...as the... influence of an Asian grasshopper's fart on the...pattern of rainfall in the Kalahari Desert!'

Pheru stopped agonizing and stared at Adi as though someone had yanked the power supply to his misery. Then he began to laugh. He sat on the bed and laughed till tears started streaming down his face. Adi joined in, deriving more mirth from Pheru's laughter than the absurdity of his metaphor.

Finally, when he had calmed down, Pheru sat reflective and silent for a few minutes. Then, turning to Adi he said, 'It's scary to be so scary, Adi. I... I'm so afraid of myself.'

Adi smiled and hugged him. Mad...sad... bad...glad... had?

Glad. Yes...definitely glad.

SIX

It rained heavily that night. A freak October shower – a leftover from the monsoon that had flooded the roads and caused the drains to overflow two months ago. The deluge prophesized a similar aftermath, but threatened to wreak even more havoc on an unprepared populace this time. But, while everyone hoped the uninvited drencher would die out soon, Adi prayed for it to go on forever and drown out any possibility of ever meeting Renuka again.

He dreaded meeting her. He prayed for the rains to miraculously wipe out the memories of that evening. If only to assuage his own insecurity, he fantasized about a heart-wrenching, earth-shattering, superbly persuasive explanation for her choosing a car-ride home over meeting him. The thought of being unable to camouflage his sense of betrayal in her presence in the event of a less than satisfactory explanation, terrified him. He prayed that he wouldn't run into her, but as so often happens, she was the first person he bumped into upon entering the Physiology Hall the very next day.

'Hi,' she said excitedly. 'Did you check your new batch?'

'Not yet,' Adi replied.

'It's on the board...right there,' she said, pointing towards the far wall. 'Why don't you look at it? I'll wait for you here.'

Confused that she had made no mention of the previous day's fiasco, Adi headed towards the board and began going through the names half-heartedly. He located himself on the board as number nineteen. Predictably, Sam and Harsha were his batchmates. Then another name on the list caught his attention.

Ishita Banerji was number fifteen.

Reading her name close to his brought a smile to Adi's face. He hadn't foreseen this pleasant surprise. The memory of her gentle beauty, her vivacious laughter and the few minutes they had shared on the bus during the picnic, suddenly buoyed his spirits.

Smiling to himself, Adi withdrew from the board. Suddenly he wasn't feeling all that bad any more.

He could see Renuka's silhouette at the door, talking to someone. As he headed towards them, he saw them laugh in unison, and then the other person walked away. Renuka was still laughing when Adi reached her. She turned towards him.

'What is your new number?' she asked.

'Nineteen. Yours?'

'One five five,' she replied.

Adi smiled. He was feeling rather good, and the events of the previous afternoon had stopped bothering him. He looked forward to being in the new batch.

'Neil is in second MB,' she said.

'What? Oh…who's that?' said Adi.

'Neil Kapoor. You know… I was just talking to him. He gave me a ride home yesterday. Didn't Shetty tell you?'

'Oh, I see… Shetty did tell me, but only about two and a half hours later,' laughed Adi.

'Why? What happened?' she asked.

Adi did a quick recap of the events, leaving out his feelings and abridging his story to the canteen.

She smiled apologetically. 'I'm sorry. I'm so, so sorry.'

'That's fine. It's all right; not your fault, really.'

'Look, I'll make it up to you. How about I

treat you to a movie and lunch today? We can skip dissection, that way I'll have enough time to make it back home.'

Adi was a bit taken aback by the sudden turn of events.

She sensed his hesitation and said, 'I promise, I won't take a ride with anybody else.'

Adi laughed. 'Which movie do you want to go to?'

'Does that really matter?' she said, smiling.

❧

The theatre was fairly crowded for a matinee show. Even though she had promised to treat him, Adi insisted on paying for the tickets which, at Rs 50 apiece, meant he'd have to miss a few breakfasts in order to manage his monthly budget. Of course, at that moment, managing his monthly budget was the farthest thing from his mind.

They settled into their seats while the advertisements and trailers played onscreen. The seats were small and close together, and for the first time, Adi felt very aware of her physical proximity. In the flickering light of the huge screen, he stole surreptitious glances at her.

Her pretty profile looked like one of those exotic faces embossed on the sides of a coin. Her neck was long and slender. The outline of her breasts underneath the tight-fitting top moved gently with her breath. Smooth, shapely legs stretched out seductively beyond the skirt's hemline. One foot lazily dangled a shoe at its end. Her wavy black hair spilled gently over her shoulders, and the faint whiff of her perfume reminded Adi of jasmine flowers.

In the sumptuous anonymity of the dark surroundings, Adi felt his mouth turn dry and a familiar tingle in his loins made his heart thump noisily in his chest.

'A penny for your thoughts,' she said.

Her words startled him. 'What? No, nothing …I was just…you know, daydreaming.'

She smiled and said, 'Adi, I've got to ask you something.'

'Sure.'

'Why did you wait close to three hours for me?'

'I didn't know you wouldn't show up.'

'But three hours?'

Adi thought for a few seconds and said, 'Well… I didn't want to have an inauspicious start to my dating life.'

She looked at him and said, 'You've never

gone out on a date before? And, by the way, I'm not exactly sure yesterday was a date.'

'That's true,' he agreed sheepishly, kicking himself for his gaffe.

'What's true? You've never been out on a date before?'

Adi nodded.

'So no girlfriends at home getting jealous?'

'Well,' said Adi. 'I've been the secret admirer of this girl in my neighbourhood and I think she knows it too, but both of us are too timid to make any moves.'

She smiled. 'So you don't write to her every day telling her how much you miss her?'

'I've thought about it. But you know the joke about the soldier who goes off to war, promising to write to his lover every day and then comes back to find that she's married the postman? So I decided against it.'

She began to laugh. A few people glared at them. Adi mimed apologies.

'I'm glad you waited for me, though,' she said.

Adi gulped, unsure of her meaning. The sentence was pregnant with possibilities.

She slid down her seat and rested her head next to his shoulder. Adi fought to control the dryness in his mouth.

'How about you?' he asked. 'No guys waiting in line?'

'Why do you want to know?'

'Well, just so that I don't suddenly get beaten up by a bunch of guys after being seen alone with you.'

She laughed again. More angry stares followed from the crowd.

'I think we stand a good chance of being beaten up by this crowd,' she said. 'Are you watching the movie?'

'No, not really.'

'Then let's get out of here.'

❧

They walked into a small restaurant right next to the cinema hall. Over coffee, they talked about their childhood, comparing and contrasting their upbringing 2500 kilometres apart. The difference was not just in the distance. Her privileged background contrasted sharply with the iron spoon Adi had been born with. He was surprised she had chosen to enter medicine, ignoring the relative luxury of an established family business.

'Is that the trend nowadays…nobody wants to join their family business?' asked Adi.

She smiled. 'I didn't want to follow anyone else blindly... Why did you choose medicine, Adi?'

'Me? Hmm...honestly, I don't know. Everybody was taking the medical entrance exams, I did too. Nobody expected me to get through ...least of all me. But I guess I got lucky...so here I am.'

She smiled. 'Are you always this self-deprecating?'

'I'm just being honest, Renuka. Nobody had any confidence in my abilities – least of all me. You should have seen how surprised my parents were when I told them it was *my* roll number in the newspaper...'

She laughed again. 'You should be a little more confident about yourself, Adi.'

Adi shrugged. 'I suppose...but all this is rather new to me. I have to remind myself everyday that someday I'll become a doctor. I'm from a middle-class family; if I had a rich business family like yours, I'd probably stay in it.'

'Yeah, I suppose,' she said. 'It's different in old, traditional business families like ours. If I weren't doing medicine, I'd end up with a few kids, perennially hosting parties for my husband's clients.'

Adi smiled. 'It's funny how the grass is always

greener on the other side. I guess you are not very traditional.'

'Are you?'

Adi hesitated for a second. 'No... I'm not.'

'Would your family mind that you are out with me?'

Her question quickened Adi's pulse. 'No, not really. My parents are fairly non-traditional. How about yours?'

She sighed. 'They wouldn't be too happy. They are very traditional and I'm the only daughter in the family. I think they even expect me to marry this guy from a family they know ...sort of bringing together two business houses, you know...'

She looked away.

Adi stirred his coffee slowly, unsure of how to react. He didn't even know his status: friend...boyfriend...shoulder to cry on?

'So, you don't like him?' he asked finally.

'It's not really a matter of liking or disliking; I think I should have a say in my life. I should get to decide who I choose to be with.'

'Absolutely! But shouldn't you try talking to this guy or your parents, and tell them this?'

'My parents would never understand.'

'You might be surprised, Renuka. I think parents put up a fight initially but nearly always agree with what their children want,' said Adi, feeling rather proud of his excellent advice.

'No, no, you don't understand, Adi. There are three generations involved in this decision. There would be hell to pay in the house.'

'Then maybe you should listen to your parents. Lots of arranged marriages work, you know.'

Adi regretted his remarks almost as soon as it left his mouth.

Surprised, she shot back, 'Whose side are *you* on?' Then, consulting her watch, she mumbled, 'It's time for me to head home.'

She picked up her bag and started to walk away.

Adi abandoned his coffee and ran after her. 'Renuka...hold on!'

The restaurant manger noticed him rushing out without paying and sent a waiter hurrying after them.

'Eh...pay for your coffee!' the waiter shouted at Adi.

Adi tried to ignore the waiter as he tried to keep up with Renuka. 'Renuka... Renuka. Hold on... I didn't realize what it meant to you. I was just trying to say something smart... wise...funny...'

'Smart? Wise? Funny?' she repeated, her voice dripping with condescension.

Adi rolled his eyes skyward and sighed. 'What can I say?' he said, trying to keep up with her. 'I didn't mean to make you feel bad. Look, I'm an idiot in these matters. I think I need to buy a book on How To Talk To Girls And Impress Them or, better still, write a book on How To Talk To Girls And Un-Impress Them...'

She held her head down and kept walking ahead resolutely.

'Why don't you pay me and then run after her,' said the waiter.

'We are coming back to finish our coffee!' retorted Adi.

'She's not coming back,' said the waiter, 'you can wait forever for her.'

Adi looked at the waiter and smiled at him appreciatively. Then, with Renuka a few paces ahead but still within earshot, he said loudly, 'I waited for three hours for you yesterday because I enjoy being with you, and would really like to get to know you.'

She stopped dead in her tracks. Then, as the waiter's face crinkled with surprise, she turned around, looked at Adi, and smiled.

SEVEN

His transition into the new batch turned out to be much easier than Adi had anticipated. Finding his bearings wasn't hard and suddenly, the 'small-town' feeling didn't weigh so heavy on his shoulders. Instead, a newfound prominence deified him, stemming from the common speculation that Renuka and he were a couple. Thanks to the incident with Sam and Dr Gomke, Adi had even managed to acquire the reputation of being brilliant, an image that he struggled to keep with a lot of late-night reading. He often worried about the moment the true mediocrity of his mettle would be exposed. But initial impressions stick fast – and so he learned to enjoy it, sparing no opportunity to actively fuel the adulatory fires.

Despite the academic environs, most of the discussion in dissection hall centered on the upcoming events in the class. As a result, the next big event – 'Rose Day/Traditional Day' – an incongruous amalgam of two distinctly puerile celebrations, dominated the buzz. On this day, the entire class dressed in traditional clothing and gifted roses to one another, messages being conveyed in the colour of the roses. Red signified love, orange meant friendship (bordering on love) while white stood for the plain platonic kind. Although no one had ever figured out the roots of this celebration, it provided great service to the silent, lovelorn sufferers who, emboldened by the anonymity as well as the pressure of the occasion, would be spurred on to declare their feelings.

Amidst all this riveting talk, the process of dissection went on uninterrupted, often inspiring feelings of being closest to real surgeons as they slashed their way through dead human tissue.

'What in the world is this?' asked Sheetal in the polished English she had acquired from her frequent travels abroad (or so she explained). At the end of her forceps dangled a small black organ, which she had dug out from the abdomen of the cadaver they had lovingly christened Chachu.

'Uterus,' suggested Sam.

'Sam... Chachu is a male, *ya*,' said Sheetal.

Everyone started laughing and Sam joined in the laughter.

Amidst this merriment, Adi's eyes fell on Isha. God, her laughter was beautiful! Her pretty face had curled up with delight while two dimples on either cheek accentuated the glee. Her mouth opened to reveal beautiful white teeth, and then followed the vivacious sound – clear, warm and effervescent with happiness. He'd start feeling happy just watching her laugh.

'Isha, you have a beautiful laugh,' said Sheetal.

'Really? Thanks,' smiled Isha, somewhat embarrassed but clearly enjoying the compliment.

'Yeah, I think so too,' said Adi.

Almost instantaneously everyone turned around to stare at Adi as though he had said something uncomplimentary.

'What?' asked Adi, taken aback.

'Adi, you are not supposed to admire somebody else's smile!' accused Sheetal, 'You are almost a married man.'

'I'm not.... Come on,' protested Adi.

'Come on, spare him,' said Sam. 'He is allowed a little variety. You know, variety is the spice of life…for Rose day he is ordering six red roses.'

'What? No. You know that's bullshit, Sam.'

'Six red roses, Adi…*ya*?' teased Sheetal. 'Somebody is getting six red roses…'

Adi recoiled feeling very uncomfortable with the situation. Not only did he find the attention unwarranted, he hadn't even planned on what to give Renuka. His intent had vacillated between red and orange (and in some moments of extreme insecurity – white), primarily because he wasn't sure where their relationship stood. Sometimes, even calling it a relationship seemed excessive. They did hang out together during the breaks between lectures, and sometimes ate together in the canteen, but, other than that, it had not progressed. Time was a major constraint; she returned home in the evenings whereas Adi lived in the hostel. The pressure of studies along with the numerous small exams squeezed out any chance of some intimate tête-à-tête. The batch redistribution had only made it worse. So, while he enjoyed being called a couple and the attention it generated, he was privately besieged with doubts about the accuracy of such an epithet. Unable to pin down her affections or his feelings with accuracy, Adi often burned in the insecurity of this confusion.

He decided he needed to clarify this with Renuka away from the prying eyes of the class. Making a mental note of meeting her by the end of the day, he returned to the conversation around the dissection table. Luckily for him, the discussions about him and his extracurricular activities had died down.

'That must be the head of the pancreas... Sam, you idiot, you have cut off the body and tail.'

'How would I know that the pancreas has a 'body' and 'tail'?'

'Let's call Dr Gomke...'

'What? Are you crazy? Let's look it up in the book.'

As Adi reached for his book, his eyes fell on Harsha, holding his copy of *Cunningham's Manual of Human Anatomy* upside down. He stood a few feet away from Isha, motionless, as if rooted to the spot. He stared at her intently, completely oblivious to his surroundings, mirroring her actions involuntarily. If she smiled, he beamed. If she spoke, his lips pursed. If she posed a question, his eyebrows furrowed. And when she laughed, he laughed with unbridled happiness.

Adi smiled: one red rose for Isha for sure.

❧

Adi spotted her walking down Mohammad Ali road.

'Renuka,' he called after her.

She turned around. 'Oh…hi, Adi… I didn't recognize your voice,' she said. 'What are you doing here?'

'I wanted to talk to you.'

'Oh, okay, but I'm on my way home.'

'I'll come with you. We can talk on the bus or in the train…'

'Can't we talk tomorrow, Adi? We could skip dissection and go for lunch or something.'

'No, no, I can't skip any more classes, Renuka. I've lost a lot on attendance already.'

'Okay, so what is it you want to talk about? Anyway, I hear I'm getting six roses from someone.'

'No, no,' clarified Adi. 'I hadn't planned anything of the sort.'

'And that is supposed to make me feel better?' she asked, smiling.

'No, no. How do I explain this? It is really a misunder-standing. Sam started this whole thing about the roses. I had actually not planned it like that at all.'

'Thanks,' she said, 'but I wish you hadn't clarified *that* misunderstanding.'

Adi was at a loss for words. Annoyed with himself for having shot his mouth off again, he said, 'I could actually send you the roses if you want.'

'You should do whatever you feel like, Adi, not what I want.'

'Look, Renuka, I'm not sure about us...or what we mean to each other...and that leaves me a little confused.'

'About what?'

'I... I don't know what rose to send you...I don't know what is appropriate for *us*.'

'Why should anything be appropriate for *us*, Adi? All that matters is how *you* feel, not what you *should* feel or think *I* feel. You've got to decide based on your feelings. Why is that so confusing?'

'I just wanted to be sure...about...about...'

She smiled. 'I guess you want to know what I'm going to send you, right?'

Before she could answer, a car pulled up next to them and someone said loudly, 'Hey...there you are!'

The door opened and out stepped Neil Kapoor. Neil was a year senior to them. His height and build matched Adi's closely, but his poise and attire clearly spoke of a privileged upbringing. Swinging his car keys with confidence, he approached them, looking like he had just stepped out of the pages of an advertisement for fine Italian clothing.

'Hi,' he said, addressing Renuka. 'I was waiting near the chowk.'

'I was on my way,' she replied. 'Oh, by the way, this is Adi...Adityaman.'

'Hi,' said Adi, smiling and shaking hands.

'Neil lives in Juhu. He is giving me a ride home,' said Renuka.

'Oh, okay,' said Adi, forcing a smile on his face.

A few seconds of awkward silence followed. The three of them shifted uncomfortably.

'Should we get going, then?' Neil asked Renuka. He followed his rhetorical question by holding the passenger door open for her.

Adi hoped she would answer the question she had posed just prior to Neil's arrival. Instead, she hopped into the passenger seat, rolled down the car's window and said, 'Bye, Adi.'

Adi lifted his hand to wave goodbye. The car pulled away, their silhouettes against the rear windscreen melting rapidly with the distance. Then, even before he could take a step, they were out of sight.

The incoherent babble, peppered with loud laughter from Toshi's room, was a persistent distraction. Adi tried to concentrate on the factors affecting cardiac output as he prepared for the upcoming Physiology examination. There were definitions to mug and graphs to commit to memory. There were headings and subheadings, sections and sub-sections as Guyton's *Physiology* described, in the span of twenty pages, why and how the heart beats. It explained in great detail why it speeds up and slows down, and how it works tirelessly to keep one alive. Yet, as the open book stared back at Adi, the details flew past his preoccupied brain, the words on the page barely registering their message.

His mind grappled with a hundred thoughts. He wondered why the others weren't worried about the exam. He worried about the remaining course-work. He wondered what colour rose Renuka would give him. He chided himself for doubting her. He wondered who else, if anybody, would give him a rose. He hoped Isha would give him a rose...just a white one...like he would give her and the others in the batch.

The open book suddenly came into focus

again. Adi cursed his lack of concentration and decided to take a break. He walked to Toshi's room and peered inside.

Sam and Rajeev stood next to the window. Harsha sat on the bed next to Toshi, who was idly strumming an old guitar. Pheru sat on the table, next to Jagdeep, his arm flung over Jagdeep's shoulder.

'Hi, guys, what is this? Group study for Physio?' asked Adi.

'Screw Physio, man,' said Sam. 'We are talking about more important things here.'

Loud shouts of 'yeah, screw Physio,' filled the room. The beer bottles lying spent on the window-sill readily explained their cockiness.

'So, Adi, are you really sending six roses?' asked Rajeev.

'No... I may send one.'

'Red?'

'Maybe...I'm not sure...orange or red.'

Toshi stopped strumming. 'What do you mean?' he asked.

'I'm not sure what to give her. I certainly don't want to give her the wrong impression.'

'Saala, this Adi is always confused,' said Harsha, 'and he is causing confusion for everybody.'

'Look who's talking,' said Sam, throwing

Harsha an accusing glance. 'You stare at Isha like your eyes are pasted on her.'

Everyone looked at Harsha.

'She is really good, man,' said Harsha, smiling shyly.

Adi smiled to himself. Harsha's trouble with English inevitably handicapped the verbal expression of his true emotions. His face, curled up with coquettish happiness, was easier to read.

'You seriously like her?' asked Rajeev. 'Not like just…time-pass?'

'Yes… I really like her,' grinned Harsha.

'She is a really nice girl,' blurted Jagdeep. 'She was in my batch before the redistribution. She made me feel very comfortable when I first came to Bombay and didn't have any friends.'

A smile surfaced on everyone's lips. The allusion of romance in Jagdeep's admiration left a distinctly adversarial silence hanging in the air.

'So, Jagdeep, are you going to send her a rose?' asked Rajeev innocently.

'I don't know,' said Jagdeep.

'I will send a rose,' declared Harsha immediately, as though the first one to say it reserved the privilege.

'All right!' cheered Rajeev. 'Red or orange?'

Adi noticed the lack of a white option.

'Orange...maybe,' said Harsha somewhat hesitantly.

'What? Why?' asked Rajeev. 'This is the time, man. Just tell her how you feel. Be a man!'

'I'm... I'm...' stuttered Harsha.

'Harsha, just do it man. Just show her how you feel, otherwise guys like Jagdeep may give her the red rose while you'll be left scratching your head and holding your balls!'

Harsha looked around the room, gathering strength from the expectant stares. His smile broadened. He rolled up his sleeves, pumped his fists in the air and declared, 'I will send her six red roses!'

EIGHT

The success of Rose Day depended on the enthusiasm of the class representative, and enthusiasm was undoubtedly one of the many deficiencies in Manish Torwadkar's character. The attribute he did possess in abundance was shrewdness, in keeping with which he limited his efforts to arranging the cancellation of classes scheduled for that afternoon, deferring all other arrangements to his self-appointed deputy, a short, plump, effeminate guy named Praful Sangvi. Praful, happy to have this extra assignment for some inexplicable reason, began to give the function some character. What he lacked in height, he made up for with an almost inexhaustible supply of energy. His boundless enthusiasm and machine-like efficiency were admirable, although those were the limits of his praiseworthy qualities. He carried a roster of lists on a clipboard, periodically brushing his hair back from his eyes to consult it, prior to making notes or checking off things with a theatrical seriousness. The lisp in his speech didn't dampen his air of authoritarian importance as he assigned roles to any unsuspecting victim who mistakenly lent him a willing ear. Watching Praful flit around, giving instructions and taking notes, one could be forgiven for mistaking the medical college for the high school drama club.

Adi was in Toshi's room discussing options for dinner, when Praful showed up unexpectedly. Ignoring Adi, he addressed Toshi. 'So, Toshi, what are you doing for Traditional Day?'

'Being traditional?' offered Toshi. Adi laughed.

'No, no, seriously…are you going to dress up as a Naga?' asked Praful, dutifully consulting his clipboard.

'Most people in Nagaland wear jeans and t-shirts, man.'

'I meant the kind of dress they show in the Republic Day parades, with the headgear and spears…the really lovely costumes,' said Praful. 'You must wear it, Toshi! You just have to!'

'But I don't have one here,' protested Toshi.

'I'll try to look for it in the emporia, or the state fairs,' pleaded Praful.

'Forget it, man,' said Toshi. 'I'm not doing it… I can't go to class wearing that stuff and anyway, nobody wears that stuff, even in Nagaland.'

'What? Why? No…please,' implored Praful.

'Praful, can you imagine people going to schools, colleges or churches in such an outfit?' explained Toshi. 'How would you like to be served by a bare-chested teller in a loincloth, wearing a helmet made of bamboo and carrying a spear, every time you walked into a bank?'

Adi began to laugh.

Praful raised his eyebrows skeptically. 'Oh,' he said. 'So you have banks in Nagaland?'

Both Adi and Toshi stopped laughing. For a minute, Toshi stared at Praful, unable to decide if he was serious. Then his eyes furrowed with displeasure and he glared at Praful.

'I'm sorry!' exclaimed Praful. He rolled his eyes back with dramatic intensity and folding his hands apologetically, beseeched Toshi, 'I didn't mean that… I meant to ask something else… I'm really, really sorry. Please forgive me.'

Surprised at his rather garrulous apology, Toshi said, 'It's okay, man. Forget it. I'm not offended.'

Praful clasped Toshi's hands and begged dramatically, 'You must forgive me, Toshi!'

'Sure, don't worry about it…it's fine,' said Toshi, trying to break away.

'Are you honestly not feeling bad any more? You are…aren't you?'

'I'm fine, Praful!'

'No…no…I've hurt you. I know Nagaland is a great place! I'm so insensitive!'

'Hey, Praful, relax, man. I said I'm feeling fine! What do you want me to do?'

'Okay, okay,' said Praful. His eyes suddenly lit up. 'How about I design the Naga dress for you and I will know you've forgiven me if you agree to wear it… Please, Toshi, please!'

Toshi was taken aback. He tried to think through this 'heads-I-win-tails-you-lose' situation. Praful clasped his hands tighter and went down on his knees. The silent pressure worked brilliantly and, mostly in an effort to get Praful off his back, Toshi nodded 'yes'.

'Oh, thank you…thank you,' gushed Praful, as he hugged Toshi. Then, eagerly scribbling on his clipboard, he beat a hasty retreat before Toshi had a chance to change his mind.

Adi began to laugh as soon as Praful had left the room.

'Why do I have a feeling I just got taken for a ride?' said Toshi, shaking his head in disbelief. 'That guy is something… I'm sure he's gay.'

'Hey, maybe he'll send you a rose…a red one,' joked Adi. Both of them laughed.

'Great,' said Toshi. 'That way I'll at least get one rose.'

'Why? Won't any of the girls in your batch send you a rose?'

'Send me a rose?' asked Toshi.

'Yeah, you…how about Naina? She's cute.'

'No, man, nobody wants to send this Chinese guy a rose…'

'Come on,' said Adi, 'that's not true.'

Toshi stopped laughing and studied Adi's face for any sign of levity. 'Are you serious?' he asked.

'Absolutely! I'm sure that somebody will send you a rose.'

'I don't think you understand, Adi.'

'What is to understand? You're part of the class and…'

'But I'm not from here, man.'

'I'm not from Bombay either, Toshi!'

'But you are Indian, man!'

Surprised, Adi stared at him. 'You are Indian, too!'

'Am I? Really?'

Adi stared at him in disbelief.

Toshi looked away, avoiding the look on Adi's face. He fell silent for a few minutes and then said softly, 'Do you know how different my being

Indian and your being Indian is, Adi? Do you think people on the road looking at me think, "oh, there goes another Indian"?'

'But that is their stupidity, their ignorance, Toshi! Everybody knows that Nagaland is in India and that Nagas are Indians.'

'It is not that simple, Adi!'

'Why is it not simple? If you're born in India you're Indian.'

'Look at me, Adi. Look at me. I *look* different. I stand out! I look more Chinese than Indian, man. People call me Nepali or Gurkha or Chang or Zhang... None of you know where Nagaland is. Praful asks me if there are banks in Nagaland. You guys are shocked that I don't speak Hindi well. Everybody looks at me and identifies my differences and then expects me to believe I'm Indian, ignoring all the differences that *they've* pointed out?'

'But that doesn't make you less Indian, Toshi!'

'How can *you* say that? How do *you* know what *I* feel and what makes *me* feel accepted or what doesn't? Do you know in Nagaland people call themselves Nagas and the others who have come from outside are called "Indians"?'

Adi was stunned into silence. Then, he sighed and asked, 'Do *you* feel Indian, Toshi?'

Toshi didn't reply. He turned his back towards Adi and stared out of the window.

Adi stood up. 'I can't believe it, Toshi. After eighteen years of growing up in a country, how can you say you don't belong? That is just being ungrateful!'

'Fuck you, man!' retorted Toshi. 'What is your problem? Why do you care? I've known you for what…seven months now? And I've lived eighteen years in a small state, out of the radar of most Indians. We are not in the consciousness or the thoughts of most people, and you expect me to just forget that? How does it happen? How can I suddenly feel all this love for everybody walking down the street when everyone on the street reminds me of how different I am?'

His eyes were flashing with pain and anger. His hands clenched the chair tightly, draining the blood from his bony knuckles. For those few seconds Adi couldn't recognize him.

'Toshi!' he blurted. 'I'm shocked. I…I don't know what to say. I'm so confused, man. I feel like I don't know you. I mean, I'm your friend and think of you as one of my best friends…and suddenly I find… I don't know you at all. I think of you as being no different from Sam, or Pheru or Rajeev…but maybe I should. You probably hate being here. Hate having to stay and eat with us…hate…'

Toshi's face softened. 'No, Adi… I don't hate anybody… and I think of you as a good friend too. But I can't explain it, Adi…or maybe you wouldn't understand. It's a constant *feeling*… something that *I* feel. It's not something that is obvious. I just *sense* it, man… There are hundreds of small incidents everyday that remind me I'm different. It's nothing that anyone does deliberately and many…many are my own shortcomings. I cannot talk in Hindi. I don't like Hindi movies; I cannot sing Hindi songs; I don't play cricket; I don't understand some of the jokes the people in my batch crack in Marathi… And when the teachers look at me, they think, "Ah…here is the guy who didn't deserve to come here, but came because of the reserved seats that the Government of India provides for tribals from Nagaland". You see, you don't have to do anything. It's everywhere, man, and that's why I *sense it*… I'm different…like an outsider in my own country!'

He paused. 'Haven't you heard of the insurgency in the North-East? Almost every state in the North-East has problems with violent rebel groups who attack the Indian Army outposts there.'

Adi nodded. 'I've heard of the ULFA, the Nagaland National something...'

'Yeah, the NNC,' Toshi continued. 'There are smaller groups too that come around trying to recruit people and get money. A lot of people support them, because of this feeling of being different. You have no idea how strong this feeling is, Adi. It runs very, very deep. They cannot identify with the rest of the country, and these guys feed into this feeling of being different.'

'But, do you feel this difference amongst us, Toshi? Do we make you feel different?'

Toshi sighed. 'No, man...but that is what is so confusing about it. I don't understand these feelings any more. Sometimes, I realize, maybe I *want* to feel different. All through my life in a small village in a small state, I've heard nothing but how different we are. I was so scared about coming all the way to Bombay...afraid of how I'd fit in. I was going to India, you know...a new country.

'The night before I took the flight to Bombay, my mom saw the fear in my heart. She talked to me for hours. She said that people are the same everywhere; that differences are not in how others see us, rather in how *we think* others see us. She said I'd meet three kinds of people:

those who I will know and understand, those who I'll know and never understand, and those who I'll know and think I understand but never will. Like Praful, who I know, but I'll never understand. Then there are the guys who I'm friendly with, but they cannot resist cracking a joke in Hindi or Marathi so that I can't follow …the ones I know and think I understand, but really don't. But you guys…you, Sam, Rajeev, Harsha, and now even Pheru…are the ones I know and understand. I laugh, joke, fight with you guys like old friends. And that is what adds to the confusion… I find all the differences disappear when I'm chugging beer at Mogambos with you guys; yet, they come roaring back when Praful asks his idiotic questions.'

Adi smiled. 'Your mom's advice is superb, Toshi.'

Toshi smiled back. 'Yeah…it is. She is very proud of me, man. When she realized I had done well in the state exams and was going to study medicine, she cried for a whole day. Then she gave me this.'

He reached for a thick, maroon, hardbound book lying on his desk. 'It's a diary,' he explained. 'She wants me to record the events of every single day that I am away from home. It is for her to read when I get back.'

He opened the cover and pointed to a couple of lines scripted in English on the inside flap. 'That is in the language we speak. It says, *"Toshi, today there is a rainbow in my heart; the sun shines because you are going to become a doctor, and it is raining because you leave me to become one."'*

His eyes were moist.

'That's very beautiful,' said Adi. He walked over and hugged Toshi.

'So are you going to write about today's stuff too?' Adi asked.

Toshi smiled and nodded.

'Well, you'd better put in there how this tall, handsome friend of yours created all this trouble,' said Adi.

Toshi smiled. 'That description is reserved for Rajeev.'

Adi laughed and said, 'Well then, don't forget to mention the not-so-tall, not-so-handsome guy who wondered if there were banks in Nagaland.'

They laughed again.

'Anyway, I'd better get going,' said Adi. 'Biochem tutorials tomorrow.'

Toshi nodded. Adi turned to leave. Then, as he reached the door, he turned to look at Toshi and imitating Praful's lisp, asked, 'So Toshi, are there any banks in Nagaland?'

Toshi laughed. 'Sure,' he replied. 'The Indians run them.'

NINE

Of the three subjects taught during the sixteen month First MBBS course, Biochemistry received a distinctly step-sisterly treatment – an outrage that echoed in the somewhat confused architecture of the department. The entire division occupied a nondescript corner of the Physiology school and managed to eke out a semi-respectable existence by straddling the first floor of Anatomy Hall. Its unobtrusive seclusion could only be navigated through narrow, dimly lit stone passageways that contributed heavily to the building's gloomy appearance. Wooden partitions divided the generous floor space into small cubicles, stopping at a height of about ten feet, as though lacking the effort or the intelligence required to make it all the way to the top. Ceiling fans dropped down from long poles, hanging from huge iron beams that crossed the roof and provided an ideal nesting ground for a flock of pigeons. These pigeons made their way in and out of the building through the vents above the doors, masters of their own free will. Occasionally, they proved to be an easy distraction, cooing loudly and flapping their wings nervously when disturbed by some event of avian significance. Other than the isolated mishaps of their droppings ruining clothes or botching up experiments, they shared the space rather amiably – the pitter-patter of tiny claws on the iron beams failing to intrude on the academic pursuits below.

Despite the unkempt surroundings and penurious spaces, the rooms served their purpose adequately for a class of two hundred. In fact, space was at such a premium that Adi's Physiology tutorials often encroached onto these cubicles. Their tutorial demonstrator for Physiology was Dr D'Souza, a young man with a kindly face and an equally benign bearing. Fresh out of training, his enthusiasm to teach was infectious, making his lecture one of the few that the students looked forward to. His discourse, however, was marked by a persnickety uneasiness on his part, the roots of which were fairly evident – his unruly body hair.

The thatch like growth covered his skin like a thick mat, pouring out of any area that didn't have the benefit of some cover. As a consequence, he wore long-sleeved shirts and turtlenecks, even in the middle of summer. It was strongly suspected, but never proven, that he shaved his beard at least thrice a day. Yet, despite his best efforts, hair seemed to peek out from everywhere. Every few minutes, Dr D'Souza would stiffen up and tug at his sleeves or tweak his collar with skittishness. Then, reassured that he had managed to keep his hirsute unsightliness at bay, he would afford himself a smile.

Although initially an annoying distraction, the students rapidly learned to adapt, overlooking his fretfulness out of respect and admiration for the man. After some weighty discussion they attributed his inordinate fussiness to being the only one to have beheld himself in the nude.

They filed into the tutorial room, where Sam and Adi sat at the back under the fans, while the more studious ones rushed for the ringside seats. Dr D'Souza began by writing some properties of nerve conduction on the blackboard. It was then that Adi noticed a plain steel tray lying on the desk with an inverted glass jar on top. Inside the jar sat a frog, deathly still except for its shallow, rapid breathing.

Dr D'Souza said, 'Okay, now I will demonstrate the experiment, and then you have to do it yourself.'

Adi's ears pricked up. Did that involve killing the frog?

As though having read his thoughts, Dr D'Souza said, 'You have to sacrifice the frog by inserting this needle into its spinal cord and brainstem from the cervical vertebral joint. Then, dissect out its femoral nerve and its innervation into the quadriceps. Then I will...'

Adi was aghast. A significant part of his childhood had been spent feeding stray dogs and nursing wounded cats, something that his parents blamed, not unfairly, for his lacklustre academic performance in school. Despite their admonishment he had continued his enterprise behind their backs, earning him little other than a steady following in the homeless animal population of his neighbourhood.

'Sacrifice? Who is sacrificing? The poor frog?' he whispered angrily to Sam. 'This is so bloody unfair!'

Unfortunately, in the small room, the whisper echoed all the way up to the front where, despite the furry canopy above his ears, it managed to strike Dr D'Souza's eardrums.

Dr D'Souza stopped mid-sentence. His eyes,

brimming with rage, froze on Adi. 'I heard that! How dare you! How dare you say that!'

Adi stood up slowly, surprised that his opinion had offended Dr D'Souza.

'How dare you! Who do you think you are?' said Dr D'Souza again.

Adi shrugged. 'I just think it is cruel to kill the frog, Dr D'Souza. This experiment has been done hundreds of times and I can't understand why we have to torture the poor frog. Calling it a sacrifice is an even bigger joke...sir!'

Everybody froze, staring at Adi with disbelief. In the overbearingly paternalistic education system, Adi had violated the sacred hierarchy of the teacher-student relationship – a hierarchy usually etched in stone. The onlookers waited with bated breath for the hammer to come down. Only the frog continued to breathe rapidly in the small jar.

Dr D'Souza looked surprised. 'What did you say?'

'I said, it's unfair to kill...'

'No! To your friend over there. What did you say to him?'

'The same thing,' replied Adi. 'It's unfair to kill these frogs for this experiment. We say sacrifice, but it is the poor animal being sacrificed without any say in the matter. And in such a terrible way. It is so cruel and unfair.'

For a few seconds, Dr D'Souza looked confused. Then suddenly, his face changed like magic, his anger replaced by an embarrassed smile.

'Oh, I see... I thought you said something else...not about the frog,' he said, breaking into a sheepish grin.

That was when it dawned on Adi what had happened. Instead of 'bloody unfair' Dr D'Souza had heard 'body hair', a word that caused him to reflexively bristle with rage.

Suddenly, Isha stood up and said, 'I think we shouldn't kill the frogs. Please sir, it's just so cruel. Like Adi said, this experiment has been well described hundreds of times.'

Dr D'Souza smiled, twitching and tugging at his sleeves. The tension in the room had evaporated along with his anger. A chorus of 'yes, sir' and 'let them go, sir' arose from the batch: some out of genuine concern for the welfare of the frog, others at the prospect of a shorter afternoon tutorial.

Their interest in discussing the frog's fate rather than his hairy predicament left Dr D'Souza decidedly relieved and deeply empathic.

'I have no problem with that,' he whispered. 'I don't like killing these frogs myself. But you have to derive the action-potential curves and then seal them in wax paper and paste them in your physiology journals. How are you going to manage that?'

The class fell silent for a few minutes. Then Sam said, 'There are lots of old physiology journals from the previous years lying in my room in the hostel. We could just take out those graphs and paste them in our journals.'

Adi smiled at Sam's audacious use of this opportunity to legitimize his pre-planned racket. A cheer rang out amongst the rank and file. Cries of 'let's do that, sir', 'please, sir' rent the air.

Dr D'Souza had little choice. 'Okay,' he murmured, rapidly revisiting his reassuring routine one last time. 'But don't tell the other batches. Otherwise, all of us will be in trouble. I guess the tutorial for today is over. And please, prepare the topic of membrane potentials well.'

Jubilant, everyone started filing out of the room. Some even patted Adi's back appreciatively.

Adi took another look at the frog, smiled and started making his way downstairs. Halfway down, he realized he had left his journal in the room. He turned and made his way back.

As he approached the room, he heard voices coming from within. He recognized them as Isha's and Payal's. He stopped, straining his ears to catch the discussion.

'Yeah... I think six red roses are too much.'

Then he heard Isha say, 'No, not a matter of too much; it's just that my mother has worked really hard and sacrificed a lot to put me into medical college and I shouldn't get distracted. I'm here to study and I don't want to disappoint her.'

'Yeah, that's true... So what would you do Isha, if somebody gave *you* six red roses?'

Adi's heart beat loudly while Isha contemplated her answer.

'I... I don't think I'd like it. Anyway, I'm sure no one will.'

Adi was stunned at the relevance of the information he was suddenly privy to. He would have to tell Harsha before his amorous flight suffered a crash landing. He slipped away from the door, turned and walked back towards the room, just as the two of them were coming out.

'Oh hi, Adi,' said Payal. 'What are you doing here?'

'I...I forgot my journal,' replied Adi casually.

'Adi, what you did today for the frog was really nice; nice and thoughtful,' said Isha.

Adi smiled. 'Well, thanks for helping,' he said.

'You're welcome,' she said, 'but I think the poor frog is even more thankful. You saved its life. Hey, maybe if you kiss it, it will turn into a princess.'

They laughed.

Adi's eyes lingered on Isha for a few extra moments. She looked even prettier up close. And that laughter was pure magic.

He stared after her as she waved goodbye and disappeared through the doors. Inside the glass jar, the frog sat in the same position, statuesque in its terrified stillness but breathing more evenly. Adi carried the tray outside and placed it on the lawn in front of the building. He lifted the glass jar that had held the frog captive. Then, with Isha's heartwarming laughter still ringing in his ears, he watched the frog leap away and disappear amidst the fresh green grass.

❧

Adi sat with the cards that went with the roses, trying to come up with funny or imaginative quotes for their recipient. After struggling for a few hours he decided to write a special one for Renuka and a generic *Have a great Rose Day. It's good to have you as my friend* for everyone else.

Well, almost everyone else. He wanted to write something special for Isha too.

He racked his brains to come up with something original for Renuka first. Some of the guys tried to help.

'How about "your roses are the smelliest"?' suggested Sam.

'Man, that sounds horrible,' said Adi.

'Yeah,' agreed Rajeev, laughing. 'Sounds like you're describing a fart.'

'What is it exactly that you want to say?' asked Toshi.

'I wish I knew,' said Adi. 'I think I'll know it when I see it.'

Pheru, sitting alone in the corner of the room, said, *'I feel wonderful because I've seen the love light in your eyes; and the wonder of it all is that you just don't realize how much I love you.'* He paused, surveying the faces frozen in admiration, then explained, 'Eric Clapton, "Wonderful Tonight".'

'Wow!' said Adi, 'that's perfect. Let me write that down.'

Harsha immediately turned and addressed Pheru: 'Pheru, tell me something also, na. I have to send roses too.'

'Are you sending six red roses?' asked Pheru.

'To Isha,' he said, smiling happily.

'You need to fill out six cards?' said Pheru. 'That's going to take a lot of thinking, man.'

Adi studied Harsha's blissfully happy face with some guilt on his own. Time and again he had toyed with the idea of telling Harsha what he had overheard Isha tell Payal. He had deliberated and dithered, a couple of times coming close to informing Harsha of the potential setback of his six red roses. But something always held him back – something he could not quite pin down. He knew Harsha would be terribly hurt by Isha's reaction. He realized that as a friend, he had an obligation to alert Harsha. He felt irresponsible and guilty whenever he imagined Harsha's disappointment.

But he just didn't do it.

He couldn't explain his procrastination, either. He wasn't jealous of Harsha. There was nothing to be jealous of.

Although Harsha had replaced his square steel-rimmed glasses with natty rimless ones, and fluffed his hair with the diligent application of conditioner under Rajeev's guidance, he had so little to champion his cause, Adi knew he didn't stand a chance. Harsha's simplicity, bordering on naïveté, made most people treat him with the sympathy reserved for a village simpleton. And so, Adi was never quite sure what held him back. The more he thought about it, the more he believed that with or without his help Harsha would fail.

Something in him *wanted* Harsha to fail.

TEN

As a natural extension of his organizational prowess, Praful was chosen to preside over the Rose Day ceremony. He spent the first few minutes taming the microphone's wails before bringing out the packet of envelopes that contained the cards. Much to the crowd's voyeuristic delight, Praful decided to randomly read out some of the more interesting messages that accompanied the roses.

He had a flair for the dramatic. His artistic gesticulations and expressive voice put a lot of feeling into those quotes.

'Sheetal has three white roses. *The road to a friend's house is never long.*'

'...One white and one red for Savita... *Sometimes the heart sees what is invisible to the eye...*'

Everyone clapped and cheered, the red roses

generating the maximum curiosity. Their announcement would immediately set the crowd abuzz with speculation about the likely author.

Then came Adi's turn.

As Praful announced his name, Adi sensed the heightened anticipation of the class. Everyone knew he would get a red rose from Renuka and were hoping that Praful would read a deliciously scandalous card to go with it. Adi began walking down the steps towards the podium, where Praful was going through his list and checking his envelopes. Adi saw him turn towards Manish, who had thus far been handing out the roses, and whisper something. Manish looked surprised and immediately started checking his own list. Praful covered his microphone as they traded hushed discussions and denials. Adi, meanwhile, reached the podium and stood looking around nervously.

Praful reached for the envelope and, avoiding Adi's eyes, said, 'Adi gets two white roses.'

The immediate reaction of the class was a few seconds of stunned silence. Then, quickly recovering their senses, some of them began to clap. Interspersed with the polite applause was the distinct sound of muffled snickering.

Adi could feel his heart beating faster and

the effort to maintain the grin on his face began hurting his cheeks. He quickly grabbed the envelope with the roses and started walking back to his seat, now twelve rows too high. His legs felt leaden. Confused, embarrassed and nervous, he accosted a hundred stares of sympathy, empathy or morbid fascination by fixing his eyes on his feet during the unbearably long ten-second journey up to his seat. Only when he neared the familiar figure of Sam did Adi look up and slid in next to him with the swiftness of an alley cat.

Adi opened the envelope to look at the cards. Sheetal had sent him one white rose...as had Renuka. He stared at it in disbelief. How could Renuka send him a white rose? He turned to look at Renuka. She sat rigidly straight, staring ahead unfazed.

Sam peered over Adi's shoulder. 'What happened...she didn't send you a rose?' he asked.

'A white one,' Adi replied. 'I don't understand it, man.'

Praful announced Renuka's name and Adi felt his heart sink. As she stood up and made her way towards the podium, Adi prayed fervently that Praful would not read aloud the card that he had sent.

Sam sensed Adi's anxiety. 'Don't feel too bad,'

he said, trying to cheer Adi up. 'Look at what somebody sent me – a thorn!'

Then, just as Praful announced, 'Renuka gets two red roses' over the speakers, Sam passed Adi the card that accompanied the thorn. It read '*I hope this pricks your hairy, stinky, black butt every day.*'

Adi chuckled.

Praful continued. 'And here is a quote from one of the cards...*My feelings for you are like this special rose, It blooms, it blossoms and slowly grows, Its scent drowns any painful past, Its hue conveys my love at last, And like the feeling that lingers, of the special touch, With this, I promise, I love you very much.*'

Sam whispered to Adi, 'I wonder who this person is who knows what my ass looks like?'

Adi began to laugh. Those who had turned to see how Adi would react to Renuka's roses, were taken aback to see him laughing. Seeing those perplexed faces, Adi laughed even more. Although he had been laughing at Sam's wisecracks, the whole mix-up now appeared ridiculously funny. The more he thought about it, the more he laughed, garnering even more startled attention. Soon the applause dried out and the entire class was staring at him in confused silence. This made Adi laugh even harder, till he was hysterical with laughter. Finally, he grabbed his stuff and ran out of Anatomy Hall.

❧

By the evening, Adi's embarrassment returned. He sat alone in his room, reliving the snickering laughs, the pitying looks, the confused stares and the astonished gawks over and over till he couldn't stand it any more. He decided to head out towards the beach, hoping that the time spent alone would clear some of his confusion. On his door he left a note about his whereabouts and reminded Sam and Toshi to wait for him for dinner.

It was nearing sundown when he arrived at Chowpatty. On the tiny expanse of sand bordering the water, hawkers and tourists jostled for space and jousted for business. Adi watched as the hawkers got into the tourists' wallets by enticing their kids, jangling their wares tantalizingly close for the tots to admire while the parents tried to drag the screaming children away. Inevitably, after a futile battle with a bawling brat, the parents would end up buying a balloon, or a toy gun, or a ride on a horse. They grudgingly parted with their money, often giving the hawkers a piece of their mind. The hawkers ignored the tongue-lashings with such a flat face that Adi could almost visualize the words bouncing harmlessly off some invisible emotional shield.

Adi sighed, deciding he needed to learn from them. He needed to be able to react similarly to the events of the last few hours. He needed to throw out those questions that kept popping into his head and concentrate on studying. He needed to ignore the anger of a white rose from Renuka, the disappointment of none from Isha, the guilt of not telling Harsha, along with the embarrassment of his behaviour in class. On top of that, every time he thought about Sam's thorn, he laughed.

'Can I sit next to you?'

Adi turned around to see Renuka standing behind him. Surprised and unsure how to react, he nodded.

'How did you find me?' he asked.

'I went looking for you. Then someone said there was a note on your door.'

A few more seconds of silence followed.

'Are you feeling bad?' she asked.

'I don't know what I'm feeling.'

'I liked your card and rose. They were very nice. Thank you.'

Adi remained silent.

'You know, your profile looks much better,' she said. 'You have a very nice nose.'

'Look, Renuka,' said Adi, with irritation. 'You are wasting your time. I'm really not in the mood for chitchat. And I think you can understand why.'

'No, I don't understand why,' she said. 'Why don't you tell me?'

Exasperated, Adi turned to look at her. 'What about...about the white rose?' he demanded.

'What about it?'

'I thought I'd get a red one from you!'

'Adi...calm down. That was *your* expectation. Not my obligation. Do you remember what I said when you asked me about the roses the other day?'

He stared at her, speechless.

She continued, 'Look Adi, I'm sorry that I couldn't fulfill your expectations. I'm happy that you sent me the red rose, but I'm not sure I'm ready to reciprocate yet. I need some time to think things through...and decide.'

'Decide on what? I thought you had decided already!'

'What makes you think that?'

'You said that you would be disappointed if I didn't send you the red roses. You said you liked being with me…you…you…' he trailed off, losing his voice in a cloud of anger.

'That's true. But I don't think I ever said I thought of you romantically. I enjoyed spending time with you and I still do, but what does that mean to you, Adi? And what does it mean to me?'

Adi suddenly remembered that someone else had given her a red rose.

'Wait a minute,' he said. 'Who sent you the other rose?'

She hesitated for a minute before saying, 'Neil did.'

So many things suddenly seemed to make sense now to Adi. Oh how could he have been so stupid!

'Let me try and explain it, Adi,' she said. 'I met Neil some time back and he is a nice guy too…just like you are, Adi. I like him like I like you. And that's why I'm so confused… I don't know what to think. Let's say we are committed to each other, and after some time you, or I, meet someone else who we think we are more compatible with, what happens then? How do we know who is *the one*? Can you understand my confusion, Adi…can you?'

She paused to see if Adi would reply. He didn't.

'You are a really nice guy, Adi, and I do like you…a lot. I enjoy spending time with you. I enjoy talking to you. I think about you often. But all of that applies to Neil too. And on top of that, Neil is…you know…'

'He is what?' Adi asked.

'He is…kind of…well-settled…you know.'

'You mean he is rich and I'm not,' smirked Adi.

'It's not that!'

'Then what is it?' he asked, enjoying her discomfort.

'It's about…it's about…'

'Money?'

'No, Adi! Please don't cheapen my feelings. I don't know how to explain it better… Look, every girl looks for security in the future and it's on everybody's mind, even if people choose to trivialize it…'

Adi began to laugh.

She looked at him with surprise. 'What's funny? Why are you laughing? And why were you laughing like that in class today?'

Adi was about explain, but stopped. Suddenly, his thoughts began to organize themselves like the pieces of a complicated jigsaw puzzle falling into place. The maze of confusion in his head melted like a dissolving fog, leaving him marvelling at the simple task ahead. He felt glad the events of the day had played out the way they had. And he was especially glad he hadn't warned Harsha.

For the first time that day, he felt really good.

Turning to look at her concerned face, he smiled and said, 'I've got to go back to the hostel. The others will be waiting for me for dinner.'

ELEVEN

Fifteen months had flown by, lost as much in the tests and tutorials as the picnics and rose-days, when Bombay University's First MBBS exams loomed on the horizon. Thanks to its solemn reputation, this inaugural assessment by the University in the four and a half year's curriculum, was especially nerve-racking. Conducted with a psychopathic rigour bordering on institutionalized torture, the hallmark of the exam was the agonizingly protracted timetable. Three papers in Anatomy, two in Physiology and, in typical step-sisterly fashion, a solitary paper in Biochemistry waited to challenge them over a ten-day period. The practical exams and viva-voce would follow in the three subjects after a week's lull, extending the torture by another fortnight. This four-week period promised them hell, and they could think of little else as they began burning the midnight oil religiously. The nagging uncertainty of covering the sixteen-month curriculum in the few weeks that remained, turned time into a precious commodity.

The excitement of Rose Day had settled by now. Everyone in the class accepted that Renuka and Adi had 'broken up'. Although Adi did think about Renuka now and then, his new-found sense of pride and the burden of the exams ensured that these moments were few and far in between.

Predictably, Isha began avoiding Harsha as though he carried an infection. Harsha even tried explaining himself to her, only to make things worse. His predicament earned him limited sympathy. He looked to Rajeev to guide him through, but Rajeev showed no interest in continuing his tutelage. He was lost in a world of his own, obsessing more about his looks and clothes than either Harsha's plight or the coursework that remained incomplete. He gazed into a mirror on his table as he studied, looking into it every so often to adjust his hair or prod the pimple on his cheek with his tongue while his adroit fingers squished out its unwelcome existence. His flashy smile and macho good looks had won him some modelling assignments. Many suspected that might have been the true reason for his choice of a medical college in Bombay: his academic performance had done little to buttress the crumbling image of him as the best student from Delhi. He, however, had a ready excuse for his under-performance. The problem was the silly subjective nature of the exams in Bombay.

Although clearly a rationalization, there was some merit to Rajeev's complaints. The essay-type questions demanded detailed, descriptive answers and, as a consequence, the outcome was directly proportional to the weight of the answer sheets rather than their content. Thus, irrespective of one's knowledge base or quotient, writing incessantly to fill up pages was a commonly employed strategy to obtain marks. It was a technique that Toshi had turned into a science by using his illegible but beautiful penmanship to great effect. A sound knowledge of the subject was the least important part of getting marks, often becoming a handicap for many. For example, to a question on 'eugenics' worth five marks, Toshi wrote a full page of nonsense. He had no idea what eugenics meant, but he filled up the sheet with descriptions like 'it is a part of genics' and 'it is a very important field of study'. He made up sub-headings, underlined them in colour and even drew a small graph, all of which nobody could interpret. Harsha, on the other hand, had read a small description of the term – exactly three lines that explained that it was the application of genetic principles to better the human race – and reproduced that verbatim. It didn't surprise anyone when Toshi got four out of five, while Harsha only managed one.

Toshi would clearly sail through.

Sam, however, was another story. He found the going tough, especially when it came to Anatomy, for Dr Gomke made sure that his life was no bed of roses. But he stood up to her torture without regret or remorse. Sam just didn't care – he treated the upcoming exams with as much seriousness as the dandruff in his hair. So while he accumulated more white specks on his head and Adi shuddered with what should have been Sam's worry, Sam's inscrutable optimism offered him an imaginary immunity, making him oblivious to the dangers of repeating another six months with Dr Gomke.

Two days before the exam, Rajeev walked into Adi's room. 'Hey Adi, do you have the class notes for Glycogen Metabolism?' he asked, looking harried.

'I do,' Adi replied, not looking up from his

books. 'I'm using them now. I have to finish them in the next thirty minutes.'

'I think somebody swiped mine from the library yesterday...fuck, this place is infested with thieves. Everybody wants to steal the brilliant notes that I've managed to gather from the seniors. They don't want me to do well.'

Adi kept his eyes steadfastly on his books, hoping Rajeev would take the hint and leave him alone. For a while Rajeev pottered about aimlessly. Then, after a pause, he said, 'Adi, I met Renuka today in the library...she was asking about you.'

'About me?' asked Adi, intrigued.

'She asked what you are up to and whether you go to the library to study, or study in your room...that kind of stuff.'

Adi nodded without saying anything.

'Do you want to talk to her?' asked Rajeev. 'I can send a message to the library if you want to....'

'I'm not interested,' Adi muttered firmly, returning to his books.

'What? Why? Is it completely over between the two of you?'

'Rajeev, I need to study now, man. You know it's over between the two of us, and anyway, I'm not going to let her get over it so easily!'

'What do you mean? Not let her get over what easily?'

'Rajeev, please let me study. I'm behind as it is. I'll fail, man!'

Instead of leaving, Rajeev pulled up a chair and sat next to Adi's desk, grinning expectantly.

'Oh come on, Adi! You can't leave me hanging with tidbits of information. I'll just keep thinking about what you meant, if you don't tell me about it.'

Adi clenched his jaws with impatience. He knew that Rajeev's rather predictably egocentric interpretation of priorities meant the only way to end this discussion was to oblige. He narrated the events of the evening of Rose Day briefly. He glossed over the details in an effort to get it over with quickly, and left Neil completely out of the description. When he had finished, Rajeev looked fascinated.

'So what are you planning to do?' he asked.

Adi thought for a few moments. Describing the events had opened some old wounds. He said slowly, 'I want her to feel what I felt. I want her to feel the pain of rejection and the humiliation *I* felt!'

'Why? She does have a point, you know.'

Surprised, Adi asked, 'What do you mean?'

'I mean, sometimes it is difficult for girls to

decide at the first instance. I mean, let's say she had gone steady with you and then *I* had started to show interest…then she'd have had to make a choice, right?'

'Rajeev, just leave me alone!' snapped Adi.

'Hey relax, Adi…it's not personally against you, man,' said Rajeev, smiling. 'It's just a general statement, that's all. It's not like I'm interested in her or anything.'

Adi didn't respond. Rajeev smiled and said, 'I wish you had told me before…I could have given you some good advice about how to charm girls. I'm very good at it…you can get girls like that with my advice,' he said, clicking his fingers to indicate the purported ease.

'Like the advice you gave Harsha?' said Adi.

Rajeev's face soured. 'What advice?'

'You know what advice. Six red roses…rings a bell? The advice you've conveniently forgotten now…because of which Isha avoids Harsha like he has the plague?'

'I was only trying to help, damn it! Harsha must have screwed up! It was not *my* fault!'

'Yeah, Harsha screwed up alright…he listened to you! If only I had told him about Isha, this wouldn't have happened.'

Rajeev stared at Adi. 'What do you mean?' he asked.

'Nothing!' hissed Adi, angry with himself for having shot his mouth off yet again.

'What should you have told Harsha?'

'It doesn't matter now, Rajeev. Forget it!'

Rajeev's voice softened. 'Look, you should tell me…maybe I can help Harsha…or work something out for him.'

'It doesn't matter now, Rajeev.'

'Not to you, but maybe to Harsha it does!'

Adi felt the old guilt return. He buried his head between his arms and tried to think it through. The anxiety of time being wasted added its weight to the guilt already burdening him. After a few uneasy moments he looked at Rajeev and said, 'Promise me you won't tell anyone.'

Rajeev sat down and put his arm around Adi's shoulder. He sighed deeply and said, 'Look Adi, I too feel guilty about what happened to Harsha…maybe I can help him…If nothing else, it'll at least make him understand why she avoids him…I promise it'll remain a secret with me, and it might even make *you* feel better.'

Adi studied Rajeev's face for signs of insincerity. A persistent voice in his head warned him not to disclose anything. Rajeev couldn't be trusted, it said. His promise was shallower than his skin-deep looks.

'Rajeev, you have to understand I feel guilty

about this too. So please, promise me you won't tell anyone else about this.'

'I promise.'

Adi sighed. 'I knew what was going to happen,' he said, hanging his head low while recounting what he had overheard Isha and Payal discuss. Rajeev listened with bated breath.

'Why didn't you tell Harsha?' he asked after Adi had finished recounting his story.

'I don't know, man. I didn't think he'd actually do it…I don't know.'

Adi looked up at Rajeev and noticed he was smiling. It unsettled Adi, and he wished he had retained the secret.

Rajeev said, 'Don't worry, man. Harsha had no chance anyway. He is just too unpolished… there is no way he can ever impress anybody.'

'Is that what you're going to tell him?' Adi asked, sarcastically.

Rajeev's lips curled into a smile. 'You've changed a lot, Adi. A lot!' He closed the door behind him and left without answering Adi's question.

Nobody slept the night before the first paper. Adi realized, after having studied for hours at a stretch, that he'd been reading the same line for the last ten minutes without being able to comprehend what it said. Panic-stricken, he forced himself to take a fifteen-minute break and walked into Sam's room. Sam was stuck on the fifth revision of his favourite book in medicine – *Medical Mnemonics*. Despite Adi's repeated entreaties in the past to abandon mugging-up mnemonics in favour of their meatier derivatives, Sam stuck to his guns, convinced that salvation lay in the thin book and the entertainment it provided. This time Adi didn't repeat his warning.

Sam woke him up after fifteen minutes of heaven.

The sleepless night rolled into a harried dawn, and a few hours later, Adi and Sam headed for the exam centre together. The scene outside terrified Adi even more than the one in the hostel. About five hundred students from all the medical colleges in Bombay stood discussing the likely questions with ardent fervour. In this state of mass hysteria, Adi tried to cram himself with more facts for almost immediate regurgitation. His anxiety rose a few more notches.

A bell sounded, signalling the start of the exam. Then the question papers arrived.

Staring at his paper for the next few minutes,

Adi suddenly realized that he actually knew the answers to some of the questions. His breathing suddenly felt natural again and his anxiety receded even further when he realized that *most* of the questions looked familiar. He sighed with a sense of reprieve and plunged into the task of writing.

Adi wrote and wrote till his fingers cramped, his arms hurt and the tetany in his hand left the pen's imprint on his fingers. Three-and-a-half hours, two pens, one pencil and forty answer sheets later, Adi walked out with the confidence that he had done fine. One down, five to go.

TWELVE

Then came the practical exams.

Although conducted on familiar territory, the circulating horror stories about the viva-voce gave the students a lot of heartburn. These sessions of intense one-on-one questioning, lasting five to ten minutes in an isolated austere room, were more akin to a police interrogation than an academic exercise. The internal and external examiners essayed out the roles of good-cop and bad-cop with élan. Out of courtesy to a guest, the internal examiner would let his colleague do most of the questioning, who would then proceed to revel in the suffering of the students, sparing no opportunity to show how little they knew.

One particular external examiner in Bio-chemistry, Dr Singhal, struck terror in their hearts with his notoriety. He was reputedly brilliant, but a symptom of his genius was an eccentric nastiness, attributed to a keen sense of underachievement because the doctor in his name alluded to a Ph.D. in Biochemistry, not the pedigree of a medical degree. This manifested as a sadistic trait that caused several students to leave his room crying, thus ensuring him the adulation reserved for a serial killer.

In the days that followed, a lot of amusing stories about the practical exams did the rounds of the hostel. Sure enough, Dr Singhal had made a few girls cry. Sam, picking up a dissected out tongue, had identified it as the heart. When both the examiners had burst out laughing, Sam had joined in the merriment. If Sam passed, Adi thought wryly, it would be purely a consequence of his entertainment value.

Finally, all that remained was the Biochemistry practical exam. Adi looked forward to it with a huge sense of relief, planning his well-deserved vacation to relax and recuperate at home while the exam results were tabulated. With most of the exams behind him, he even began to enjoy a vague confidence that he had done fairly well – a feeling that left him wondering if he'd be among the ones with a 'D'.

'D', which stood for Distinction, meant a score of more than 75%. Recipients of '3Ds' (i.e.

Distinctions in Anatomy, Physiology and Biochemistry) became instant celebrities in the class, while 2 Ds also offered significant recognition. Their titular use around campus, viz., there goes Meena Sinha 3Ds – led to instantaneous respect for both the achiever and the achievement.

Adi's performance so far had left him cautiously optimistic about being one of the blessed ones. All that stood between him and final glory was this Biochemistry practical. He took comfort in the fact that his schedule had left him an entire day to revise for the exam; enough time to feel confident about his tryst with Dr Singhal.

On the morning before the exam, just as Adi opened his Biochemistry books and prepared to sit down with them, a worried looking Sam rushed into his room.

'Adi, something is wrong with Toshi!'

Adi followed Sam into Toshi's room. They found him on his bed, curled up like a foetus, breathing noisily through his mouth. His face looked pale, and dark blotchy patches encircled his sunken eyes.

Adi shook his shoulder. 'Toshi, wake up, man! Don't you have to study today? Wake up!'

Toshi raised his right eyebrow and peered at

them. He tried to say something but his dry, cracked lips made no sound. He motioned weakly for some water.

Sam and Adi stared at each other in disbelief. Adi checked Toshi's practical exam schedule. Toshi had finished everything except the Anatomy practical exams. They were scheduled for the next day; the same day Adi had his Biochemistry practicals.

'We've got to take him to the hospital!' said Adi. Sam nodded and ran out to make arrangements.

Toshi fell back on his bed after having a drink. He closed his eyes again, breathing noisily through his mouth. Dry spittle immediately began to crust on his parched lips. His heart thumped rapidly underneath the thin shirt, creating swiftly moving ripples on the fabric. Adi felt his forehead; it was hot.

Sam returned after having arranged for a car. Adi slung Toshi over his shoulder and carried him down. Toshi flopped on to the back seat like a rag doll. They drove to the hospital just a few hundred yards away. Sam carried him inside while Adi went to arrange for the necessary paperwork to admit him to the hospital.

That was his first experience with hospital bureaucracy.

The clerk in charge of admitting patients needed an outpatient slip. The clerk issuing the outpatient slip was in the other building, and when Adi reached his desk, he had just stepped out for some tea. The junior clerk assured Adi he would be back in five minutes. And for the next forty-five minutes, he kept repeating his assurances that his compatriot would make a blessed re-appearance within the next five minutes. Adi stood patiently, deducting every minute he spent away from his Biochemistry revision by biting his nails down to their beds.

It was 10 a.m. His exam began at 7 a.m. the next day... twenty-one hours away.

The saga didn't end when the outpatient clerk re-appeared. He insisted that he needed a deposit slip of one rupee from the cashier.

'What for?' Adi screamed in frustration.

Taken aback, the clerk soured up and demanded an apology before he'd provide an explanation. Embittered but helpless, Adi apologized, following which the clerk informed him that he didn't make the rules, the Government of Maharashtra did. And the rules stated, rather explicitly, that Adi would have to obtain the deposit receipt. Adi felt like shooting him but realized that it wouldn't help matters. He ran in pursuit of the hallowed deposit receipt that gobbled up forty-five precious minutes. Then there was the information that needed to be filled out: Toshi's name, his father's name, his home address, the name of his local guardian, income, religion...information that was about as useful as the name of his cat and his favourite movie. There was much Adi didn't know, so he decided to oblige the bureaucratic appetite for nonsense by inventing Toshi's parentage and whereabouts right then and there. The clerk looked at him suspiciously a couple of times, but had no way of verifying the authenticity of the information.

By the time he completed the paperwork, it was close to noon... Nineteen hours to go.

After fifteen minutes of hunting around desperately, Adi discovered that Toshi had been admitted to one of the medical wards. A resident doctor with an intense, caustic face sat next to his bed, starting an intravenous drip. Sam and Adi waited for him to finish.

Finally, the resident doctor turned around and motioned for the papers, spiriting them out of Adi's hands. He scribbled on them and then he turned to address the two of them.

'Are you first-year students?' he asked. They nodded in unison.

The resident doctor nodded back sagely, as

though protecting Sam and Adi from their inability to comprehend what he was about to say was a key element of his job description.

'Your friend is very sick,' he said. 'I think he has either typhoid or malaria...we have...'

Adi cut him off. 'He is in the middle of his first MBBS exams, and has his practical Anatomy exam tomorrow.'

The resident looked at Adi with the expression a king might posses upon being rudely interrupted by the court jester. 'Do you even understand what malaria and typhoid are?' he barked. 'On top of that he is dehydrated, hypoglycemic and very fatigued. He may have been having chills throughout the night! Exams? No way!'

Adi had just about had his fill of un-pleasantness for the day. He looked at the wall clock. Quarter to two...less than sixteen hours remained.

Adi was a head taller than the resident. He took one step towards him, until their noses almost touched. He clenched his teeth and growled, 'Toshi has finished all his exams except the Anatomy practicals. We've been through hell to get to this point! He will take the exam tomorrow in whatever way, shape, or form. Either you help us, or we will arrange it ourselves!'

The resident doctor's self-righteousness vanished, replaced by a sudden understanding of their frustration. 'Yeah, yeah... I'll start the medicines, but he is going to be too weak...'

Adi ignored him and turned to Sam. 'I think we should talk to Dr Gomke to see if they can postpone the exam for Toshi by a few days.'

'You should talk to her, Adi,' said Sam. 'If I talk to her, she'll want to conduct his exam today! She hates me, man.'

Sam's remark had obvious merit. Adi ran out of the hospital and headed towards Anatomy Hall.

The steady stream of students exiting the building meant that Dr Gomke was still in her office. Relieved that he'd have a chance to talk to her, he rushed towards her room, only to be stopped by the scrawny peon sitting outside.

'Enh! Where do you think you are going?' he said, studying Adi suspiciously.

'I have to meet Dr Gomke! It's extremely urgent. Please!'

'Thamba! Thamba! Everyone has urgent matter to discuss with madam,' he admonished, motioning Adi to wait outside. Then, turning around, he disappeared into the room to check on her availability. He reappeared to inform Adi that 'madam' would be free in half an hour.

It was two thirty in the afternoon. Adi debated whether to use the half hour to get a Biochemistry book from the hostel. However, concerned that Dr Gomke might leave during his absence, he decided against it. Half an hour, he reasoned, only half an hour...

Adi should have known better. In keeping with the rest of that morning, the hands of the clock moved to 3:30 p.m. without any sign of Dr Gomke materializing. People popped in and out of the room at regular intervals, raising his hopes every time the door opened. But none of the emerging faces looked anything like the one he so desperately wanted to see. Adi waited, venting his frustration by wringing his hands and marching back and forth along the corridor with angry, impatient strides.

In sharp contrast to his fruitless, frustrated pacing, the peon yawned and stretched lazily, barely throwing Adi a glance. He scratched his beard, massaged his feet, cracked his knuckles, poked the crevices between his beetlejuice-stained teeth with a makeshift toothpick, and intermittently vented long bored sighs. Occasionally, he peered at the clock, awaiting the end of his shift.

Adi stared at him helplessly, jealous of the man's luxury of time, jealous that the same minutes and seconds flitting by left them on polar ends of an emotional scale.

Finally, at quarter to five Dr Gomke called for Adi. By the time he had finished explaining the situation, it was 5 p.m.... fourteen hours to go.

Dr Gomke's painted eyebrows frowned with concern. 'Has he been admitted to the hospital?' she asked.

'Yes, ma'am. Ward 6B.'

She reached into one of the drawers in her desk and pulled out a few thick manuals. Flipping through the pages she finally settled on one section and spent the next twenty minutes reading it with interest. The peon arrived with a hot cup of tea and placed it next to her on the desk. She ignored it and continued to underline a few passages from the manual and making brief notes for herself. Adi watched with helpless frustration as time evaporated in front of his eyes like steam from the teacup.

Finally, she said, 'Can you take me to his ward?'

It was more of a command than a request. Although Adi had initially planned to go to the hostel, he had no choice in the matter. It didn't help that Dr Gomke hobbled all the way to the ward whereas he would have preferred to jog.

Toshi was awake and sat propped up against

a few pillows on his bed. The hydration and defervescence had done him some good in the few hours Adi had been gone. In front of him lay *Chaurasia; Human Anatomy: Head and Neck.*

'How are you feeling, Dr Lotha?' asked Dr Gomke.

'Okay,' replied Toshi, his voice still weak. 'I feel very tired… But I don't want to lose a year. Please help me, Dr Gomke.'

Visibly moved by his plight, she ruffled his hair sympathetically and said, 'The problem is that the external examiner has left and I cannot make a decision about conducting one single student's exam later without consulting him. Those are the university rules. Even if I agree, the external may not…'

Adi felt his heart sink. Toshi's stared blankly at her, unable to react to the discouraging news.

'Look,' she continued. 'I will talk to the external and try and arrange something, but if he doesn't agree then he may still want to conduct the exam tomorrow. So, try to prepare as much as you can, hmm? I'll do whatever I can.'

She smiled at him hoping to inspire some confidence. Then she turned and ambled out of the ward.

It was 6 p.m. Adi sighed: thirteen hours to

catch up on a sixteen-month Biochemistry curriculum.

He turned towards Toshi. 'Who got you those books?' he asked.

'I asked Sam to get them.'

'Where is Sam?'

'I sent him back to study. He has his Biochem practs tomorrow…you do too, right?'

'Yeah, we're in the same batch,' replied Adi, pausing to think for a few minutes. 'How will you study? Gomke asked you to be prepared too.'

'I…I'll manage,' replied Toshi, his nervous eyes betraying his phony bravado. 'You go now, man. I think Gomke will get the exam postponed by a few days for me… I'll be fine. I know Anatomy pretty well.'

'You sure?'

'Yeah, man… I'm sure. Carry on, Adi. Thanks for all your help.'

Adi sighed with relief. Thirteen hours to revise Biochemistry was too little, but certainly better than no time at all.

Adi waited for a few minutes, feeling curiously uneasy. Suddenly, his anxiety to return to his books didn't seem so urgent anymore and even though he wanted to step out, a curious deficiency, as though he had left something incomplete, nagged him. Finally, he sighed, smiled benevolently at Toshi and made his way towards the door.

He had walked a few paces when, on an impulse, he turned around, pointed at his shoulder and asked, 'Toshi, what is the primary and secondary movement of this muscle?'

The question was simple, by design; one that Adi hoped would boost Toshi's confidence and, at the same time, reassure Adi. Toshi, unprepared for a question, looked confused at first. He stared at Adi and squinted in an attempt to focus.

Trying to give him a hint, Adi moved his shoulder, expecting him to spew out the simple answer any second.

When Toshi didn't reply, Adi's grin disappeared. He suddenly started to feel a hollow emptiness in his stomach. He tried again, making the questions simpler this time.

'Where is its origin? Where is its insertion?'

Toshi stared at him blankly, his face suddenly rendered expressionless with fear. Sweat began to shimmer on his forehead.

A few other simple questions later, Toshi's inability to recall a single answer left Adi close to panic. He cried out, 'At least tell me the name of this fucking muscle, Toshi!'

Rattled into a blackout, Toshi stared at him with the same vacuous look, unable to come up with the answer that could have been expected of a hardworking high-school biology student

Toshi shut his eyes and let his head flop back. Tears rolled down his face. He clenched his book tightly, the grip turning his knuckles white. His doom was imminent: even if the examiners were overflowing with sympathy, they wouldn't pass somebody who couldn't remember the word 'deltoid'.

Adi slumped into a chair next to the bed. He grimaced, unable to look at Toshi and yet unable to look away. He clutched his head and pulled at his hair, unsure of what hurt more: his scalp or the realization that not only was Toshi physically broken, he had broken his spirit.

Adi looked at the wall clock. It was 6.30 in the evening. Twelve and a half hours to go.

There was only one way out. Adi sighed, opened the Anatomy book and said, 'I'll teach you, Toshi.'

This time Toshi did not protest.

Fresh from his own Anatomy exams, Adi was well versed in the subject. They began their journey through the human body together: one figure, one page, one chapter at a time, familiarizing Toshi slowly with the origin of muscles, the distribution of arteries, the course of nerves, the location of organs and the movement of bones. Intermittently, he would flop back with defeat. Then, fighting fear, frustration and fatigue, he would begin again.

The nurses in the ward made them tea and cucumber sandwiches. The resident doctor paid them another visit, happy with Toshi's progress but still unconvinced about the usefulness of their effort. Nobody disturbed them, as Adi worked with Toshi through the stillness of the night.

The sky had begun to acquire a lighter shade in the east when they closed the last of the three books.

As Adi got up to leave, Toshi reached out and hugged him. 'Thanks, Adi. Thanks so much man,' he said, breaking into tears.

'Good luck, Toshi,' said Adi, fighting back his own.

Adi finally got to return to his room. The Biochemistry books lay on the table exactly as he had left them. He stared at them longingly, overcome by a sudden sadness – as though he had betrayed a good friend.

He decided to shower before heading off to the examination.

The cold water stung his skin like a whip, startling him, and waking him up from the trance-like state he was in. Suddenly, the enormity of his actions confronted him as he stared failure in the face. He hadn't revised at all: he would fail Biochemistry...fail! Far from his hope of getting a 'D', he would lose this year.

A sudden fear tore through him when he realized that this was the moment he had always dreaded. His mediocrity, his well-camouflaged secret, would be finally exposed. He had no way of hiding his unworthiness. He had cheated the system thus far, only for it to catch up with him at a time when he least expected it.

He clutched his head and stood motionless in the cold water, shivering, punishing himself for something he did not understand. He pinched himself, pulled at his hair, and squeezed his head in a vice like grip, hoping for something ...*anything*, to ease his pain. He cried silently, staring at the rising sun with hopelessness. A voice in his head wondered whether he should bother to show up for the exam: the outcome, after all, was predestined.

Adi dried himself and changed into a fresh set of clothes, performing the motions without thought or interest. He looked at himself while combing his hair, and studied his bloodshot eyes for a while. He took one long look at his room, feeling his tears return when his eyes fell on the books lying lonely and forsaken. Fifteen minutes to cover an eighteen-month curriculum – what were the odds? On his way out, he closed the door with a deliberate firmness, letting his hands linger on the latch for a few extra seconds. He wondered why the sun felt so warm as he trudged towards the Biochemistry building.

Adi spotted Sam outside the building. Sam's back was towards him, while his faithful book of Medical Mnemonics held his undivided attention. Adi heard him recite 'To-Taste-Ladies-Vaginas-My-Head-Pushes-A-SLIT: *Tyrosine, Tryptophan, Leucine, Valine...*'

Adi juggled the familiar words in his mind, the obscenity in the mnemonic failing to get his attention. Essential amino acids: that was what Sam was trying to remember.

'Oh! Hi Adi!' said Sam upon seeing him. 'I met Toshi in the morning. The resident let him go to the Anatomy hall in a wheelchair with an IV hanging from his arm.'

'So Gomke couldn't postpone the exam?'

'No, no, man. I think Toshi insisted on taking them today. He joked that he was better prepared than he ever would be. Also, he thinks that the examiners are going to be sympathetic to him, with his IV and all...' Then, in a more serious tone, Sam added, 'He told me what you did for him, Adi. He didn't want your efforts to be in vain. You really helped him, man.'

Adi nodded weakly and made his way to the room where his batch had gathered prior to being called in for the viva. He sat at the back, resigned to his fate, just waiting to get the ordeal over with. His head ached from having stayed awake the whole night, and his throat hurt from constantly fighting back tears.

His batch mates were discussing Dr Singhal's methods of torture.

'...He asked what vitamin is associated with the 3 "Ds"...'

'...Niacin–dermatitis, diarrhoea and dementia...'

Adi recoiled in agony. He hadn't revised a single vitamin.

'...there is also a fourth "D": Death.'

Death. *Adi liked the sound of that word*.

Death: the final solution to all problems. No exams to pass, no expectations to meet, no more desires and no more sadness – just the tranquillity of a conclusion. Soon it would all be over.

Adi's heart wept as he fought back the tears that threatened to break loose.

Then he heard his name announced. This was it, he thought. Lamb to the slaughter.

Adi walked inside slowly and took a seat across from the desk where Dr Singhal and Dr Bala (the internal examiner) were busy filling in some numbers while talking in hushed voices. They nodded their heads in final agreement and then turned their attention towards Adi.

Dr Singhal studied Adi through his thick spectacles. His smooth, bald head, framed by an unruly crop of long hair, shone brightly beneath the fluorescent lights. His round face sported a faint stubble which, along with the slightly crumpled shirt and a mismatched tweed jacket, completed the mad-scientist look. His knobby fingers twirled a pencil as he studied Adi.

'So, have you prepared well for this exam?' he asked.

Adi smiled nervously and gave a weak nod, wondering if Dr Singhal expected an honest reply.

'Really? Good. Then you should get 3 Ds!' said Dr Singhal.

Adi grimaced. This was clearly a harbinger of trouble.

When Adi didn't respond, Dr Singhal said,

'Well then, if you are going to get 3 Ds, why don't you tell me which vitamin is associated with the 3 Ds?'

Adi thought he hadn't heard him right. His mind raced to recall what he had heard outside just a few minutes earlier. His knees felt weak and his palms turned clammy.

'Niacin,' he blurted.

Dr Singhal nodded and asked, 'So what are the 3 Ds?'

Adi felt nervous with happiness. *Careful, do not panic...*

'Dermatitis, diarrhoea and...dementia!'

Dr Singhal looked at him with some interest. 'Good,' he said, surprised at Adi's pat reply.

Adi's spirits were starting to rise with cautious optimism. Maybe...just maybe, he had a chance...

'Do you know...there is a fourth D?' Dr Singhal asked, smiling.

'Death,' Adi replied calmly.

'Good!' said Dr Singhal. 'I see you know your vitamins. You must be one of the better ones. How about protein metabolism? Name the essential amino acids.'

Adi couldn't believe his luck. Silently thanking Sam and his book *Medical Mnemonics* Adi blurted, 'To-Taste-Ladies-Vaginas-My-Head-Pushes-A-SLIT.'

Before he had a chance to realize his faux pas, Dr Singhal broke into peals of laughter. Dr Bala joined in, enjoying Dr Singhal's uncharacteristic mirth. They laughed until Dr. Singhal's eyes began to water. Then, removing his spectacles and wiping his face with his handkerchief, Dr Singhal said, 'I have to write down this mnemonic, it is too funny. Tell me once again what you said.'

Adi repeated it somewhat hesitantly. Dr Singhal wrote it down on a piece of paper and read it to himself a few more times, each time finding something else to laugh about.

Then, turning to Dr Bala, he said, 'He has obviously prepared well and I have not laughed like this in a long, long time! You can go…your viva is over.' On his way out, as he was closing the door behind himself, Adi heard Dr Singhal tell Dr Bala, 'He was easily the best one today.'

THIRTEEN

Adi could never have dreamed of such a sweet end to the month-long vacation. The heady results of his exams – distinction in all three subjects and the second rank in class – immediately catapulted him to the prominence associated with such achievement. Sam and Toshi's description of his 'heroics' on the day of Toshi's illness and his silent suffering after the betrayal of Renuka's white rose consecrated his accomplishment leaving him a halo short of being beatified by the rest of the class. Slowly but surely, the outpouring of admiration and sympathy started adding up to a constant chatter in the background that Adi would make the natural choice for the next class representative.

He was on top of the world. The power and prestige of the class representative's position enticed him with unfailing seductiveness. In public, he dismissed the suggestion with an ambiguous nod, neither denying nor confirming his interest. He had six more months to make up his mind, a period that presented a number of other interesting possibilities.

Thirty-three students had not passed, and one of them was Sam. Adi was surprised to learn that it was not Anatomy but Biochemistry that had turned out to be his Achilles heel. Sam had fallen victim to Dr Singhal's verbal assault, and had made matters worse by laughing at the taunts Dr Singhal threw at him. Sam couldn't help laughing at any joke he heard, even if he was the intended target, and his humiliation the intended outcome. This had denied Dr Singhal the sadistic satisfaction of seeing the student sitting across the table squirm at his jibes, and the end result was that Sam was not in Adi's batch any more.

Toshi managed to squeeze through. He had a particularly nasty attack of malaria that relapsed and ended up leaving him hospitalized for five straight weeks. Upon his discharge, he felt so weak that he was mostly confined to his bed in the hostel during the vacation. He cancelled his trip home, making up some excuse about doing extra clinical work, which his gullible parents, ignorant of his illness and 3000 kms away, accepted with a heavy heart. While this was consistent with the pattern of not informing parents of anything unless it involved money, it left Toshi very depressed. Pheru moved into Toshi's room during his convalescence – a coincidental juxtaposition of individual conveniences. Toshi needed the company while Pheru, having been thrown out of his room for failing yet again, simply needed a space to stay. Pheru promised to move out once he passed Pharmacology – an event, judging by his efforts, didn't seem destined to occur any time in the near future. Toshi, on the other hand, began to enjoy Pheru's company so much that he looked forward to Pheru staying on indefinitely. What had begun as a six- or seven-week trial to tide them over their problems, unfolded into a symbiotic arrangement that wasn't constrained by time any more.

Rajeev's lukewarm performance distorted his image as the golden boy of the class. The heightened expectations from the combination of good looks and ostensible brilliance were surreal, and predicated his downfall with a fair degree of certainty. His dwindling glory left him even more reticent, leading him into a world of denial where he continued to believe in his inherent greatness and blame everything on some grand conspiracy in the campus. He restricted himself to his most loyal admirer, Harsha, and his circle of friends was limited to Toshi, Pheru, Sam and Adi.

Second MBBS is the best time in the life of a medical student. The four subjects – Pathology, Pharmacology, Microbiology and Forensic Medicine – are relatively easy, and since the foundation of medical knowledge is on firmer footing, the subject matter is easier to compre-hend. However, the piece-de-resistance of this momentous transition is the newly earned right to wear those hallowed white coats and carry stethoscopes around one's neck, which comes with starting to see patients. No second MBBS student could be caught anywhere near a clinical rotation without his stethoscope and long white coat. If the coats bore a few patches of blood, they added an arresting authenticity, the story of their acquisition becoming a natural conversation piece.

Adi's first clinical rotation was Obstetrics and Gynaecology (ob-gyn) in a peripheral hospital called Cama, right next to Victoria Terminus in the heart of downtown Bombay. Adi didn't care too much for the subject and reconciled to it reluctantly after some active encouragement from Pheru, who pointed out that if not the subject, the location at least was idyllic. Across from Cama was a huge open field, lined by numerous food joints; a few blocks down was St. Xaviers College, with the best-looking and most adventurous girls in Bombay, and within walking distance were all the major movie halls. If he played his cards right, Pheru suggested, Adi could be at the hospital in the morning, eye the Xavier girls in the afternoon over lunch, and with some debonair manoeuvring end up seeing a movie with one of them in the evening. More than luck, it would need an overdose of providential blessing for this scenario to materialize, but Adi's newfound confidence didn't have a problem with fantasies.

On the very first day, Adi managed to show up late. Negotiating the pedestrian traffic on the streets of Bombay during rush hour took its toll. By the time he reached the floor, rounds with the attending doctor were well underway.

Their attending, Dr Choksi, a tall, thin, serious-looking man, was dressed in a partially crumpled suit that had seen much better days. Wisps of long thin hair struck out defiantly from an awkward hairdo, and big glasses gave his eyes an owlish intensity. Huge ears, that seemed to bend under their own weight, framed his longish face and, combined with the way he stooped when he walked, seemed to convey a heightened susceptibility to gravity. Around him hovered a petite resident, dragging a cartload of charts. Behind her, in a procession of seniority and importance, followed two junior residents and the rest of Adi's batch, all twenty-four of them, in their spotless white coats and sporting brand new stethoscopes around their necks.

Adi tried to slip in unobtrusively. As he tiptoed across the ward to join the rest of the group, one of the patients called loudly out to him, 'Oh, doctor...can you come here?'

Everyone turned to look at Adi. He was about twenty feet from them, on tiptoes, trying to get the caught-in-the-headlights look off his face. Dr Choksi studied him through his thick glasses silently.

The patient called out again. 'Doctor... here...can you come here?'

Adi wanted to tell her that he wasn't a real doctor; the white coat he was wearing had been bought the previous night at the store across from their hostel. In the glare of everyone's gaze, he stood vacillating for a few seconds before smiling and waving at her sympathetically. Then he walked over to join the rest of the group.

'What did she want?' Dr Choksi asked him as soon as he reached them.

Adi shrugged uncertainly.

'What is wrong with her?' Dr Choksi asked again.

'I don't know, sir,' replied Adi. 'I... I just came in.'

'What do you think is wrong with her?'

Surprised at his persistent questioning, Adi ventured a guess. 'Maybe she is...pregnant.'

'Good diagnosis, doctor,' said Dr Choksi, sarcastically. 'This is the Obstetrics floor. *Everybody* here is pregnant.'

The others burst out laughing. Turning to the senior resident, Dr Choksi said, 'What is the case, Uma?'

Uma, the senior resident, replied, 'Sir, she is Mehzabeen, a 32-year-old G3, P2, admitted with a 28-week gestation for uncontrolled hypertension, pre-eclampsia.'

Dr Choksi turned towards Adi again. 'Did you find out what she wanted you for?'

Adi shook his head to indicate he hadn't.

'Don't you think it's important to know what

she wanted? Why don't you go and find out?'
ordered Dr Choksi.

Adi swallowed his embarrassment and
retraced his steps towards the woman. He felt
nervous dealing with a patient for the first time,
especially since he knew so little about the
subject. With the entire group looking at him,
Adi quietly walked up to her and asked her what
she wanted.

She pointed towards her foot, and Adi could
instantly see what the problem was.

A safety pin, used to keep her bedsheet in
place, had opened up. Every time she moved, its
sharp end etched long scratch marks on her leg,
punctuating it with droplets of blood. Sedated
and attached to the IV pole, she had tried to
remove her painful prickle, but had clearly found
such coordinated action impossible in the foggy
haze of her medicated brain.

A huge sense of relief washed over Adi when
he realized the simplicity of the solution. He
pulled out the safety pin and walked towards
the rest of the group holding the pin above his
head like a prizefighter's trophy. Dr Choksi
nodded and said to Adi, 'So, doctor...what is
your name?'

'Adityaman,' said Adi, confidently. 'Adityaman
Bhatt.'

'So, Dr Bhatt. What did you learn today?'

The fairly obvious conclusion that removing an open safety pin might prevent somebody from getting scratched by it was the first thing that sprang to Adi's mind, but he was quite certain that wasn't the answer Dr Choksi was looking for. He tried to think of the medical terms he had heard Dr Uma use, but he didn't really know what they meant.

Dr Choksi continued, 'I hope you learned that coming in late and trying to sneak into my rounds can get you into trouble.'

Everyone laughed.

'Besides that, what did you learn?'

Sheetal, eager to make a good impression, said, 'She has pre-eclampsia and we are giving her IV anti-hypertensive to prevent seizures and control her blood pressure.'

'Excellent,' said Dr Choksi, as Sheetal beamed happily. 'But that is not what I'm looking for. Why do you think she called out to you, Dr Bhatt?'

Adi didn't have a clue. He joined the others in staring at Dr Choksi silently.

'Because you wear a white coat, Dr Bhatt. She didn't know who it was that had walked past. But when she saw the white coat, her sedated brain reasoned that it meant *relief*. It meant an escape from her pain. She gave *your* coat the meaning *you* didn't, Dr Bhatt.'

Adi wrapped his coat a little tighter around himself, feeling a sudden respect for the modest garment.

Dr Choksi continued, 'It's a good lesson in the art of medicine: relief is the cornerstone of our profession. It is the oldest art, as old as life itself. Medicine arose from the art of providing relief, gradually transforming into a better, more exact science over hundreds of years. But the practice of being a doctor is using *both* the art and science of it. In olden times, it was mostly an art form, where you listened to the patient and prescribed medicines. With time, we have become better at the science . Our tools are more exact and give a wealth of information, and they have improved patient care tremendously. Unfortunately, as science has progressed, the art is slowly disappearing. Blood tests and CAT scans are replacing having a conversation with the patients. Under the guise of doing good, we are forgetting those we do good to. Like today, when Mehzabeen is sick and needs our care, she will get IV anti-hypertensives, she will go for an ultrasound, Dr Uma will prescribe medications to control her blood pressure, while somebody else will do a foetal stress test on her. The nurses will feed her and wash her, and I will examine her. But do you know what she'll tell her family when they come to visit her today? She will talk about you, Dr Bhatt...how you helped her by pulling out the safety pin that was hurting her. In spite of all the different interventions that we will perform on Mehzabeen, for today the only person who brought her real relief was Dr Bhatt. For today, her doctor was Dr Bhatt.'

Adi had never felt so proud of pulling out a safety pin before. He smiled self-consciously. As the batch slowly soaked in the wisdom of his message, Dr Choksi said, 'So, today, what I want you to learn is what wearing that white coat and carrying a stethoscope around your neck means. It means you provide *relief*. Soon you'll realize how little we can actually do to cure diseases in patients, but we can *always* bring relief by simply listening to them. I hope you will all remember this simple art of medicine: the art of listening.'

FOURTEEN

Every morning, at 6 a.m. sharp, the ob-gyn wards stirred to life. Junior residents were the first to walk in, gathering vital signs and examining patients for subsequent discussion with the senior resident and then formal rounds with Dr Choksi. The medical students' arrival was a less celebrated, often unnoticed affair, usually dependent on the student's personal interest in the subject. So, while Isha made it a point to walk in with the junior residents first thing in the morning, Adi barely managed to make it a few minutes prior to Dr Choksi's arrival.

Adi's passive participation was rooted in his dislike for obstetrics. It was not the usual image of the happy pregnant woman he had in mind. Most of them lay in bed, sleeping, or tossing and turning, pretending that the unnatural bulge in their middle was a natural part of their body. Those huge 'ripe' bellies with the upturned navels repelled Adi. After some tentative initial efforts, he learned to place his stethoscope over the spot marked with an 'X' by the trainee nurses (affectionately called missy babas) and convince himself that those vague rumblings in the distance were the tireless thumps of the foetal heart. As medical students, their inexperience in clinical medicine dictated an auxiliary role anyway, limited to hovering around the residents, inserting IVs or collecting blood, all the while trying to appear doctor-like in their demeanour. Adi often wondered if the patients noticed his lack of confidence or thought poorly of his abilities. Fortunately for him, the strata of patients seeking care in government hospitals like Cama ensured that he needn't have worried. Poor and illiterate, these women were easily impressed by the white coats and stethoscopes, not to mention the ability to discuss bombastic medical terms in English. Consequently, they accorded the medical students a level of respect distinctly out of proportion to their training.

Halfway into his ob-gyn rotation, Adi started coming into the wards very early, walking in with the junior residents at the crack of dawn. This dramatic shift in commitment had the desired effect of drawing Isha's attention. She, of course, ascribed his change of heart to a newfound enthusiasm for ob-gyn.

Adi knew Isha and Payal always ate lunch together. One day, he followed them to the canteen. He began to draw up a chair when they spotted him and beckoned him to join them.

'Hi Adi. Are you coming this evening?' asked Payal.

'Where?' he asked eagerly. 'Is everyone going somewhere?'

'No, no,' she replied. 'Dr Uma said that my patient is being induced this evening. We can watch her conduct the delivery.'

Adi's enthusiasm died.

'No way!' he said.

'Why?' asked Isha. 'We have to witness twenty-five deliveries this rotation.'

'I think I'll try and watch them while rounds take place, not spend extra time in the evenings,' replied Adi. 'That's why I've started coming in early.'

Isha nodded understandingly. 'What happened with Dr Choksi today?' she asked.

'Oh that,' said Adi. 'He asked me on rounds to tell him the foetal heart rate. I can't ever hear them. So I just put my steth close to the "X" that the missy babas made, and rattled out

"120". Dr Choksi was surprised and checked it himself. He couldn't hear anything at the site where I had placed my steth because, as it turns out, the woman had a breech. The missy babas make up the sounds and the numbers too. I felt like an idiot.'

Both of them laughed.

'Yeah, the venous hum of the uterine vessels in these patients is so loud that you have to press the steth really hard on their bellies to hear the foetal heartbeats,' agreed Isha.

'But don't you find that scary?' said Adi. 'Their bellies look like balloons and I feel they might burst if I press too hard!'

Isha started to laugh again. Adi couldn't help but stare at her face when she laughed. *She was so pretty*.

They chatted some more over lunch. As they got up to leave, Isha walked ahead to pay for her meal, leaving Payal and Adi a few feet behind.

Payal tuned to Adi and said, 'So, Adi, you are definitely not coming this evening, right?'

'Not a chance,' replied Adi. 'I have much better things to do in the evenings than watch a delivery.'

'Hmm...fine,' she said. Then, smiling mischievously, she whispered, 'I'm not going either.

Isha is going to be there alone. Nobody else from the batch.'

The look on Adi's face gave away the sudden change of plans in his head.

Payal grinned. 'I think Isha is meeting Dr Uma at around 6.30 in the delivery room.'

Then she walked ahead to join Isha.

❧

For Adi, it was a date any way he chose to look at it. The incidental distraction of parturition was an inconvenience that he schemed to turn into an advantage.

He went over the book on obstetrics and tried to memorize the stages and management of a delivery. A few hours into the confusing positions, lies and presentations of the foetus, he had managed to glean some very elementary concepts of childbirth. Concerned that the prefatory nature of his knowledge would be insufficient to impress Isha, he tried to think of a few jokes and some interesting anecdotes as he prepared to meet her.

Adi reached Cama hospital at 6.30 sharp. The delivery, he estimated, would last an hour or two. That would place them together right around dinnertime: a chronological convenience that would make his suggestion for dinner at 'Kamats' seem casual and spontaneous. He would naturally offer to share a taxi back to campus: another proposal as innocuous as the one preceding it. That way, he reasoned, any hint of his interest being overt, would be camouflaged in the spontaneity of the events.

The delivery room was situated at the end of the ward. A narrow, dimly lit passageway half-choked with rusty stretchers and crooked wheelchairs separated it from the rest of the floor. Adi had never been there before and would have been most happy if he could have avoided it altogether. Occasionally, while making ward rounds, he had heard the cries of women giving birth. Those screams, echoing along the dingy passageway, made the delivery room seem more like a torture chamber than a place where new life was ushered in.

Isha arrived while he was standing at the entrance to the passageway, staring in the direction of the delivery room and having second thoughts about his plan. She was surprised to see him.

'Hi, Adi!' she said. 'I thought you were not coming. How come you changed your mind?'

Adi smiled and said, 'I thought it would be a good opportunity to see a delivery being managed…what better way to learn more about Obs…'

'Great…you're really making an effort, Adi. I'm glad you are here. I think Dr Uma is already inside the delivery room. Shall we go?'

'Sure,' Adi replied, suddenly feeling very happy that she was 'glad he was here'.

He followed Isha into the shabby passageway. As they approached the delivery room, a terrible smell hit Adi's nose, sending a wave of queasiness through his body. The nauseating fetor of blood, urine, amniotic fluid and mucus seemed viciously pervasive and he held his fingers over his nose in a vain attempt at sieving out the smells. He tried to overcome his disgust by reminding himself of the impending payoffs.

Although much wider, the delivery room was only slightly better lit than the passageway. Its whitewashed walls were bare and, except for the green hospital curtains, the room lacked any hint of colour. Two stretchers separated by a flimsy white curtain served as the birthing tables. The sparse furnishings conveyed a sense of austere seriousness as if to remind one that childbirth was no joking matter. A couple of ceiling lights reflected off the glass panes on the cold steel cupboards which were full of neatly arranged obstetrical instruments,

awaiting their turn to pull out a baby. The
patient lay on one of the stretchers, struggling
in her semi-somnolent state with the
grogginess of pain-killing drugs and the agony
of contractions. Her belly straddled the space
between her splayed out legs, trying hard to
deliver its contents through the narrow
opening in between. Dr Uma and a nurse stood
beside her, helping her coordinate the
contractions. The sheet underneath her legs was
covered with a translucent, shiny fluid,
liberally spotted with jelly like blotches of
blood. Every few minutes she would clasp the
rails on the stretcher with desperate strength,
scrunch her face with superlative effort and let
out a bloodcurdling scream. Then, as the
contraction subsided, she would lie back,
thankful for a few moments of respite, even as
her eyes grew large with trepidation at the
thought of the impending one.

Adi felt sick to his stomach. But what dismayed
him more was the presence of five other students
from their batch, standing a few feet away from
the patient's legs, watching the birth. He stood
at the back next to Isha, behind the first row of
observers, feeling sorry for the poor woman and
sorrier still for himself. He couldn't imagine any
circumstance in which this ambience would be

conducive to his plans. Adi felt betrayed... Payal had promised there would be no one else!

Still struggling to breathe, he tightened his fingers around his nose as tactfully as possible.

'Chalo, Ameena, zor laga ke...' encouraged Dr Uma. Then, turning towards them, she said, 'Look closely...you can see the baby crowning.'

The audience leaned forward for a better look. Adi saw a mass of hair smudged with mucus appear near the gaping vagina. Adi wondered why God had made childbirth such a disgustingly agonizing ordeal. And why fate had afforded him an opportunity like *this* to try and make a suitable impression. As another wave of queasiness hit his insides, he reflexively tightened his fingers around his nose. He couldn't remember a time when he had felt quite so sick.

Dr Uma kept talking as Ameena's labour progressed slowly. The baby's head was almost out. The fetid odour grew stronger with the baby's burgeoning body, making Adi clasp his nostrils in a vise like grip. Then, as Ameena screamed like a woman possessed and along with the crinkled, slithery baby, a gush of slimy, blood-covered gunk started pouring out of her vagina, everything went black in front of Adi's eyes.

Adi opened his eyes to see six pairs peering down at him. Embarrassment washed him from head to toe. He tried to get up but his arms and legs refused to co-operate. He knew that the news of his fainting while watching a childbirth would travel fast and, from then on, he would fall into the category of 'misfits in medicine' who faint at the sight of blood or mucus. Since that was an automatic qualification for sissydom, getting to be vertical was, at that moment, synonymous with regaining his manliness.

He tried again, this time with more success.

Before he could say anything, Adi heard Isha telling the others, 'He tripped over my bag when he backed up... I shouldn't have put such a heavy bag on the floor.' Then, turning to Adi, she said, 'I'm sorry, Adi...I didn't realize you were going to step back... I put the bag there because it was too heavy. Your head must have hit the floor so hard...it knocked you out. Are you okay?'

Adi immediately saw the godsent opening to salvage his pride. Rubbing his head, he grinned sheepishly and said, 'Yeah, I'm okay... Just that my head hurts a little. Don't worry, it's not your fault. I was just trying to get a better look, that's all.'

Isha smiled apologetically. 'I'm so sorry... I

shouldn't have kept the bag there. You sure you're okay? You hit the floor pretty hard.'

Adi nodded, his face full of the machismo of a silent sufferer. Inside, he marvelled at his stroke of luck. Indeed, far from being an embarrassment, this was an explanation that evoked sympathy and satisfied everybody else. They redirected their attention towards the mother and her new baby. Adi sighed with relief, thanking God repeatedly for giving Isha the wrong impression.

❧

It was close to 9 p.m. when Adi finally grabbed the moment he had been waiting for. As it turned out, Isha and he were the only two returning to campus.

'Hey, Isha, do you want to eat something before we go back?' he asked.

She looked at him, somewhat surprised and hesitant.

Adi rubbed his head where he had fallen and said, 'The canteen will have closed by the time we reach campus.'

She smiled and let out a tentative 'okay'. They walked out of the hospital and within ten minutes stepped into a small, clean Udipi restaurant.

'Did you get a signature for the delivery?' she asked Adi as they sat down to eat.

'Signature? From whom?'

'You know, you have to enter every delivery you watch in the ob-gyn journal and get it signed by whoever is conducting the delivery... Dr Uma for today.'

Adi thought it best not to let on that his reasons for attending had been far from academic. Never mind getting a signature, he didn't even possess a journal.

'Yeah...I forgot to get it today... I think Dr Uma will sign it tomorrow. After all, she can't forget *my* presence today.'

She laughed. 'Does it still hurt?' she asked.

Adi felt like telling her that her laughter made it feel better, because it did, but he smiled and shook his head.

'Where was Payal?' he asked innocently. 'Ameena was her patient, right?'

'Yeah...although she had said she might have some stuff to do this evening. But I don't know why the others showed up.'

That caught Adi's attention. *So, she hadn't liked the five other students showing up for the delivery. Had she anticipated being alone with him tonight too? But she hadn't known he would be there...*

'Payal even asked Dr Uma for permission to be there for the delivery. Something important must have held her up.'

'Really? When?' asked Adi, unsure of why Payal had sought permission to witness her own patient's delivery.

'Remember after we had lunch with you? She spoke to Dr Uma about us attending the delivery and also said that you might show up too. Dr Uma said it was okay for the three of us to come, and that she would tell Ameena. But the others hadn't asked her.'

Adi suddenly felt very happy. *So, Isha had known that he was going to be there. She had perhaps anticipated being alone with him. No wonder she was irritated that the others had shown up!*

'Yeah,' he said, vehemently. 'They had no business being there!'

'It's just so demeaning, you know.'

Adi nodded as though he understood. *Demeaning? What was demeaning about it? What was she talking about?*

She said, 'I feel so sorry for Ameena.' Adi nodded again while trying hard to avoid the confusion from showing on his face. *What the hell was she talking about? Where did Ameena, fit into all this?*

Isha continued, 'It must be so painful during labour, and then these five show up to watch it as though it's a spectacle. Imagine, you are in labour, all naked, uncomfortable and in pain, with no control over anything, anxious to get it over with and concerned about the child being born at the same time...and then five people show up who you don't know, who have not bothered to ask you for permission, and simply stare at your most private parts, and then leave without a word after it is over... How demeaning is that!'

Adi had never felt shallower in his life. Here he was, immersed in his hormone-driven, egocentric interpretations of her words, while she was seething with indignation on behalf of the patient. Adi realized that he would have been one of those inconsiderate jerks had it not been for Payal seeking permission on his behalf. He silently thanked her from the bottom of his heart for more reasons than one.

Isha's eyes were moist.

'Well,' said Adi, 'you're right...but I guess it's tough for *me* to know what labour is like!'

She smiled. He felt happy to see her smile. He continued, 'But I think most of the others are new to clinical medicine and have not dealt with patients yet...'

'No, no, Adi. That's not true. You think these
five would dare to do such a thing in private
hospitals like Breach Candy or Bombay
Hospital? They know that if they want to see
anything there, they'll have to talk to the
attending doctor as well as the patient. They
know right from wrong, Adi. It's just that
Ameena is poor and has to be in a hospital
where she has no say in her own care. This has
nothing to do with clinical medicine and
everything to do with somebody being poor.
Because she is poor, Ameena is taken for
granted, her feelings don't matter...' Her voice,
filled with outrage, trailed off.

Adi stared at her, speechless with admiration.
The spirit beneath that sweet smile and the
beautiful face astonished him. Suddenly, she
looked so much more beautiful.

'You're absolutely right!' he said. 'I have an
idea. Why don't we take some sweets back to
Ameena in the ward and see how her baby is?'

She smiled, and Adi's heart lit up.

FIFTEEN

The ladies' hostel on the main campus of Grant Medical College was shielded like a fort. For some reason, the feeling that ladies were not 'safe' and needed protection from a pack of vicious, hormone-ravaged male medical students was built into the construction of the hostel and the psyche of its supervisors. A uniformed guard and two levels of barricade – a wooden door and a collapsible iron gate – defended the solitary entrance in front of the building. Other than the visitors' room, the ladies' hostel was strictly off limits to men. In keeping with this protective, paternalistic sentiment, rooms on the ground floor were devoid of living quarters. A six-foot tall steel wire fence surrounded the entire building, ensuring untouchability, even with a ten-foot pole. The area in front of the entrance was brightly lit, ostensibly to prevent any 'illicit, immoral activities' – a rather unnecessary waste of electricity since the guards kept a close eye on anybody who showed up. At midnight sharp, they locked the main gate with military zeal, after which, entering entailed the unpleasant task of rapping on the wooden door through the small openings on the collapsible gate – an act to which they didn't take too kindly. The night guard was especially terrifying. He was a crotchety character with a crabby face that complemented his disposition. His real name was a mystery, everyone called him Khadoos Baba, an epithet he took rather seriously. His beady eyes would narrow further, scanning the offenders suspiciously while he checked his watch a couple of times to indicate the unearthliness of the hour. With extreme reluctance, he would unlock the door, muttering angrily under his breath and occasionally slipping in some key words loud enough to make his displeasure obvious. The thought of having to get past Khadoos Baba was enough to dissuade a fair number of paramours, and ensured a rush for re-entry just before the dreaded midnight hour. Khadoos Baba was an ex-lab technician who had been fired for showing up drunk for work after his daughter had run away with a Muslim boy. He was an educated man, and in an effort to rehabilitate him, he had been given this opportunity to work as the nightshift guard at the ladies' hostel. Khadoos Baba saw in every unmarried couple, his daughter who would betray him and a Muslim boy who would instigate the betrayal: a vision that led him to do his job with a passion disproportionate to the responsibility it carried.

In stark contrast to the neurosis inside, the mood outside the hostel was very cosmo-politan. Groups of boys and girls hung out and chatted late into the night. Young couples sat close together, immersed in intimate discussion. From their balconies, single girls spied on the couples below, hoping to catch some of the snippets of conversation that would churn the gossip mills the next day. Cars and motorcycles stopped at periodic intervals to pick up or drop off the ladies. The more reserved ones, who didn't wish to be seen, went to the visitors' room to wait for their dates, only to realize that being discreet was not exactly the guard's priority. In the unsophisticated tradition of town criers, the guard would shout the girl's name repeatedly from the ground floor at the top of his voice until she showed up, alerting the rest of the hostel that she had a visitor at 6 p.m. on that day.

Adi was toying with the idea of asking Isha

out on a date – a real, formal date. He tried to be positive about his prospects – he was, after all, one of the most popular guys in class and the incident with Ameena had played out fairly well. Thanks to Isha's enthusiasm, Adi had attended quite a few deliveries, even managing to subliminally imbibe some obstetric principles while trying to impress her. But whenever Adi remembered her reaction to Harsha's advances, his enthusiasm would dampen. Finally, when no amount of scheming seemed to offer a foolproof solution, Adi decided to simply approach her and ask her if she would go out to dinner with him.

That evening, Adi put on his best clothes after a nice long bath with an especially expensive shampoo. He checked his hair a few times in the mirror, confirmed that his breath smelled good and that he had enough money to splurge. Then, ignoring the butterflies in his stomach, he headed towards the ladies' hostel.

It was still early in the evening when Adi approached the formidable entrance. Khadoos Baba wasn't destined to arrive for the next few hours. The timing seemed to be perfect: the crowd was thin and the faces unfamiliar. All the omens were right. He asked the guard to call Isha Banerji.

The guard stepped inside to announce her name.

That was when Adi spotted Sheetal in the TV room. She was busy watching some show and didn't look in his direction. However, as the guard yelled out, 'Isha Banerji...visitor', loudly and repeatedly, Adi could see Sheetal's interest suddenly get aroused. She looked in his direction just as he ducked out of sight.

Adi was certain that Isha would refuse to go out with him in Sheetal's presence, simply to avoid becoming the subject of class gossip. Out of the corner of his eyes, he spotted Sheetal approaching the entrance to satisfy her curiosity. Panic-stricken, he looked up to see Isha walking down the stairs. They converged simultaneously at the main door, both equally surprised to see Adi.

Isha smiled and said, 'Hi Adi. Did you call for me?'

'Hi, Adi. What are you doing here?' asked Sheetal.

Adi's desperate grin tried to hold off a reply while he searched for a simple white lie that would save the situation. But all he could come up with was, 'Nothing. I... I was just going to ask Isha out to dinner.'

Sheetal raised her eyebrows and looked at Isha.

A hint of surprise grazed Isha's face. 'Now?' she asked.

Adi nodded, bracing himself for a refusal. He hoped she would make it painless and at least offer him a way out...maybe she had already had dinner or she had to complete some assignment.

She said, 'Okay, give me ten minutes to change.'

It took him a few seconds to register what she had said. Then he smiled and said, 'Great. Thanks! I'll be right here.'

As Isha turned to leave, Sheetal smiled and said saucily, 'Have fun, you two.'

❦

By the time they finished dinner in a small restaurant near Churchgate, the night had darkened to the silence that afflicts downtown areas with empty office buildings and shuttered, padlocked shops. The last of the office workers hurried away towards the station, hoisting their bags and clutching their saris in the rush to get to their trains on time. The roadside vendors were busy packing their wares for the night, wearily bundling their meagre belongings into makeshift beds in one corner of their stall. A few scrawny dogs ran around intrepidly, picking up scraps of food and territorial fights in the comfortable absence of a crowd. Adi and Isha walked slowly towards the bus stand, their footsteps clattering loudly on the empty pavement.

Although they made small talk all through the evening, Adi sensed her uneasiness. He noticed her terse responses, her contrived smile; even her laughter felt synthetic to his ears. She avoided his eyes and intermittently stole quick glances at her watch while trying to avoid getting caught doing so.

Convinced that Isha's discomfort was rooted in the unpleasant thought of becoming the latest subject of gossip, Adi silently cursed Sheetal for messing up his evening. He tried to keep up the small talk, hoping that the constant chatter would distract her from such thoughts. In some corner of his heart he even felt afraid of inheriting Harsha's fate at the conclusion of the evening.

Finally, when it was obvious that neither of them was enjoying the evening, Adi stopped and asked, 'Are you tense about something?'

'Me? No...not really.'

'You look very ill at ease, Isha...and you don't lie very well.'

She smiled. 'It's nothing...it's just that I'm not sure about going out...and if Sheetal...'

'Yeah,' said Adi, cutting her off, 'I was trying to avoid Sheetal too. Believe me, I would never have called for you if I'd known she was there.'

'No, no...*I'm* not sure about *myself*, Adi. It's not about Sheetal...in fact, were it not for Sheetal, I probably wouldn't be here.'

Adi looked at her, confused. 'I...I'm not sure I understand. Are you feeling bad that Sheetal saw us?'

'No...why would I feel bad about that? In fact, if she hadn't been there today when you asked me, I wouldn't have said yes.'

Adi was flummoxed. 'What...what did Sheetal do to change your mind about coming out to dinner with me?'

'Sheetal didn't do anything. I just didn't want to hurt your feelings in front of her, that's all. I thought you would be embarrassed if I turned you down in front of her and so I agreed to come...but in all honesty, I don't know what I am doing here.'

Adi fell silent, feeling bitterly hurt, but feeling strangely guilty about feeling hurt. The paradox left him unable to react.

'Are you feeling bad?' she asked.

Adi shrugged. 'I...I don't know what I'm feeling,' he said honestly.

She sighed. 'Look Adi, you are a really nice guy and many girls would love to go out with you. But I... I'm not sure I'm ready for all this.'

'But you care about my feelings not being hurt in front of Sheetal?'

'Wouldn't you have felt bad if I had said no in front of Sheetal?'

'I... I would have felt very embarrassed...but why do you care what I feel?'

'Because it's very important to you, Adi. You like being popular and liked by the class.'

'Is that bad?'

'No, no,' she said, smiling disarmingly. 'There's nothing bad about it, but that is the reason I didn't want to embarrass you in front of Sheetal. For you, it is really important to have lots of friends and people who admire you.'

'But everybody likes that, right? Everybody likes to have lots of friends and to be popular.'

'I don't.'

'Really?'

She thought for a few seconds and said, 'It's different for you, Adi. You have grown so much in stature in the class, from the initial days in first MB to now. I remember you from when you were a quiet, simple chap, hanging around with Sam. You've changed so much…in a positive way. But I don't care about that… honestly, I don't. I mean… I have friends, you know, people I say hello to. But I'm good-friends only with Payal. It's not right or wrong, Adi…it's just a difference in personality…we are different people.'

'So is that why you're unhappy to be here with me?'

'No, not really. It's just that I'm confused…' She fell silent for a few minutes. 'See Adi,' she began, again. 'I'm from a middle-class family. My mother has spent all her energy, time, and money trying to give my sister and me a better life. She has paid for the best schools, classes and teachers, despite having a limited salary. She has really high expectations of me, and justifiably so. So, I feel that my time here in medical college should be spent almost exclusively on my studies. My results are a fruit of her labour, not mine. And I want her to be happy with it…not feel that her efforts went to waste.'

Adi smiled. 'I understand,' he said. 'I'm from a middle-class family too, with parents with high hopes.'

The natural beauty of her smile returned. 'Are you feeling bad that I said I wouldn't have come out with you?' she asked.

Adi wanted to say no, but her candour was contagious. He remained silent.

She said, 'If it makes you feel any better, I'm glad I came out today. I've enjoyed the time we spent together. I think you are a very nice guy, Adi, and that sometimes leaves me a little confused...'

She looked away without completing the sentence.

Adi seized on the small window of opportunity. 'Isha, I think you are a gem of a person, so I won't lie and say I'm not interested in seeing you more often... And I understand your hesitation. But all I would like to do is get to know you a little better and maybe you'll get to know who I am. That's it, no demands or expectations. And any time you feel this is affecting you too much or in a way you don't like, you can call it off. I promise I won't complain or demand anything.'

She didn't reply.

Adi continued, 'Look, Isha, if we do go out, I'll never talk about relationships, or expect anything. We'll go out as good friends and just enjoy each other's company. And any time you want to stop the arrangement or feel it is compromising anything, your studies, your comfort level, your happiness...your tennis game...you can stop. I won't protest. I promise.'

She smiled. 'You are hoping that after going out with you so many times, it will turn into a relationship, aren't you?'

Adi smiled. 'That is the general idea.'

She smiled back. 'That's honest.'

They walked along quietly, but for the first time, feeling comfortable in the silence. A young girl selling gajras ran towards them, hoping to make a fortuitous last minute sale before calling it a night. Adi obliged and Isha wove one of the strands into her hair. They reached the bus-stand and found seats in an empty bus. Adi bought two tickets to the campus.

'Can I have the tickets?' she asked.

'Sure. Do you collect them?'

She nodded, then neatly folded the two thin pieces of paper and put them in her pocket.

As the bus began to move, the rush of cool air from the open windows dispersed the sweet fragrance of the juhi flowers in her hair. It reminded Adi of the last time he had been this close to her, when the stench in the delivery room had knocked him out.

Adi chuckled softly, feeling a little contrite about letting her carry the guilt of that incident. 'Hey Isha,' he said. 'Do you remember that day in the delivery room when I fell?'

She nodded.

'Actually, I should be honest and tell you,' he said, 'I really didn't trip over your bag that day. I... I just fainted upon seeing the delivery.'

She smiled. 'I know,' she said.

Adi looked at her in surprise. 'What do you mean, you know?'

'I know because I was standing next to you, remember? We were behind all the others and I had my bag slung over my shoulder all the time.'

Adi was at a loss for words. 'So why...what ...I mean...why did you say that I tripped over your bag?'

'I thought you would be really embarrassed if people knew you had fainted while watching a delivery. It's like why I agreed to come with you today. I just happened to be there...so I said you had tripped over my bag.'

Stunned, Adi could only shake his head in disbelief.

She smiled. 'You probably don't realize it Adi, but you've changed so much from the initial days when you were a quiet shy guy, to today, when you have the confidence to walk up to the ladies' hostel and ask me out...and do it in front of Sheetal. Earlier, you always behaved as though you didn't belong...as if your presence in medical college was a mistake. But you've found confidence in yourself, cemented your position in class and it's very nice to see you transform ...so...so seamlessly. It's like watching a beautiful tree grow from a tender sapling and develop strong roots...you end up feeling protective, you know?'

Adi laughed. 'You feel protective about me?'

'Not you! Your persona, Adi. You like having lots of friends, and people looking up to you. It's great if you enjoy it, like you do, and I think, since you are friendly and caring about people, it's good if nothing happens to spoil that image.'

'But it's not simply an image, Isha. I do care about people.'

'That's true. I heard about you teaching Toshi before your Biochem exam. That was very selfless and courageous. That's why it is so nice to see someone genuine get respect in class. But I feel scared just thinking about how vulnerable it makes you.'

'I don't understand Isha...if you don't think of me as a good friend, why do you care what happens to my image?'

'As hard as you try Adi, you can't get me to admit I care about you.'

Adi laughed. 'Well, I'm going to believe that until you say something to the contrary.'

She smiled. 'Do you remember the frog you

saved in the Physiology tutorial? I don't know whether you kissed the frog or not Adi, but the frog was *really* a princess and she said so much about you. You know, it's strange how small incidents sometimes open such a big window into someone's personality.'

Adi smiled. 'I don't know what to say.'

'I should thank you for today's dinner.'

'No, no, please...today's dinner was for watching out for me when Sheetal was here. How about tomorrow evening? I could thank you for what happened in the delivery room.'

She smiled but didn't respond. They had reached the ladies' hostel entrance. The area outside was empty. Adi could see Khadoos Baba eyeing them with interest.

He asked again, 'Isha...Will you go out with me tomorrow evening to give me a chance to thank you for saving my pride in the delivery room?'

Isha was about to say something when he stopped her.

'Hold on,' he said, 'let me find Sheetal before you answer my question.'

She laughed and said, 'I guess you don't have to ask me in front of Sheetal again.'

SIXTEEN

The only virile facet of the Maharashtra Association of Resident Doctors was their acronym, MARD, the Hindi word for manliness. This organization of doctors in residency training spearheaded agitations every so often, protesting issues as diverse as the exorbitant price of meals in the canteen to the lack of toilets for the resident doctors on call. The residents were the bulwarks of the hospital, performing most of the actual work of patient care. From starting IVs to complicated surgeries, from examining patients to pushing gurneys, there was no hat that didn't fit those young, devoted heads. In addition, they carried the onus of teaching the students, for which they had to make time in the evenings, beyond their normal working hours. For their services, they received a stipend that was meagre by all standards; an outrage the administration sought to justify by reminding them that they were still students. They lived in miserable makeshift rooms in the hospital (named 'Resident Vista' by somebody's grandiose imagination) whose narrow, alley-like width inspired immediate claustrophobia on the so afflicted. The thin plywood walls separating one room from the next were rumoured to be porous to the sound of a cockroach's fart, and at the end of such pigeonholes were two bathrooms to be shared amiably by the inhabitants during the morning rush.

The residents worked tirelessly, ignoring these hardships with a fortitude that bequeathed on them a martyr like aura. However, a subtle undercurrent of exploitation periodically haunted the fraternity. It found a voice in the protests organized by MARD, though the issues were usually so trivial that the demonstrations took the form of black armbands worn for a week or posters put up outside the administration offices in the stealth of the night. Their ineffectual methods of protest were looked on by the hospital administration like the rebelliousness of a truant child who would eventually learn his lesson. The lack of financial backing and a reluctance to assume leadership for fear of authoritarian retribution during the exams were the principal reasons the organization lacked a coherent voice. In addition, the common sentiment that residency was simply a temporary state of torture to be endured for three years and then forgotten, led to half-hearted commitment on the part of most residents towards the protests organized by MARD.

Trouble began on a hot morning that June, when Dr Seema Mantri went to get her shot of penicillin from the outpatient department. Dr Mantri, a third-year resident in ophthalmology, had suffered from rheumatic fever as a child and needed prophylaxis with penicillin on a monthly basis. That day she had had her penicillin injection as on all other days, except that minutes after the injection, she started to feel nauseous and vomited. Although she was in the middle of a busy outpatient department, nobody paid her any attention. Within a few minutes she started to sweat profusely and collapsed on the floor. That got a resident doctor's attention. He immediately realized that she was having an anaphylactic reaction to penicillin. Pheru, who was posted at the outpatient department that month, happened to be with the resident, who told him what was going on. They rushed to the nearest nursing station, shouting for adrenaline. However, the

outpatient department had no adrenaline. They
would have to take her to 'Casualty', a hundred
yards away.

By then a crowd had gathered around her and
a mini-melee ensued. Somehow the resident
and Pheru managed to get her onto a stretcher
and started pushing her at breakneck speed
along the corridor towards Casualty. At that very
moment, the local municipal corporation leader,
known to everyone as the corporator, and a
couple of his good-for-nothing cronies were
coming around the corner of the same corridor.
Out on a cursory survey to show his concern for
the citizens of the area he considered his
personal fiefdom, the corporator was
completely unprepared for what crashed into
him. Furious at been rammed into, he
immediately started hitting out at Pheru and
the resident. The two tried to direct their
attention towards Dr Mantri who was gasping
on the stretcher, but to no avail. A crowd
gathered and pandemonium ensued. In the end,
by the time they got Dr Mantri to Casualty, she
was quite dead. It didn't help matters that in
Casualty, the supply of oxygen had stopped and
the nurse couldn't find the keys to unlock the
cupboard and retrieve an IV set.

To add insult to injury, the corporator and

his goons showed up at the dean's office to 'protest'. The Dean – a highly qualified but spineless political stooge – promised to take 'action' on the matter. Within an hour of having obsequiously wrung his hands in front of the corporator, he ordered the resident and Pheru to be suspended from duty.

This time the residents exploded in fury.

Dr Mantri's fiancé was a highly respected chief resident of surgery. Distraught with grief, he assumed the mantle of MARD's leadership rather naturally, finding unqualified support for his fury from his fellow residents. In a spontaneous outpouring of sympathy and anger, a rally was organized in the Anatomy Hall within hours of the incident. The news spread through the campus like wildfire and within minutes the huge hall was packed with medical students, residents, fellows, teachers and ward boys.

Everybody knew Dr. Sanjeev Chaddha not only as Dr Mantri's fiancé but also as a brilliant surgical resident. Tall and sturdy, with a dignified demeanour that inspired immediate respect, he stood silently in front of the massive gathering, waiting for people to quieten down. He cleared his throat, looked around at the hundreds of faces staring back at him, and began in a loud, firm voice.

'Thank you all for coming here,' he said. 'As you know, today Seema died. She died from an anaphylactic reaction to penicillin. Amit, our senior medical resident, and Salim Pherwani, a fourth-year medical student, tried to save her, but couldn't. So, we gather here trying to understand why a twenty-four-year-old, four months from completing her degree, now lies on a cold stretcher in the dirty morgue.'

Some of the girls began to cry.

He took a deep breath and said, 'So what killed her? Was it because there was no adrenaline in the OPD? Or was it because Casualty is so far away from the OPD that a patient will die ten times before they can reach it? Was it because there was no oxygen in Casualty? Or was it because Amit and Salim were stopped by a bunch of goondas who our dean does salaam to?'

He paused. Angry whispers and enraged nods filled the audience.

'No!' he said, raising his voice. 'We killed her!'

There were sharp exclamations all around.

'We killed her with our apathy! We killed her with our disinterest! We killed her with our uncaring attitude! If this was a patient, and not Seema, there would be no protest, no indigna-tion, no gathering! We wouldn't be sitting here, crying! We see this happen day in and day out, with so many of our patients. Medicines that don't work, IVs that give infections, surgical rooms without suture material, ob-gyn floors without painkillers, neonatal units without incubators... They are all around us. We see them every day and they don't even register in our brains! We walk over dirty floors, laugh when the nurse runs all over to find an IV, joke about the medicine having the wrong effect, harass the poor patient's family to get supplies, and count our days until we are out of this damned place. No wonder our patients do poorly and those who come to this hospital, come to die! So why should it be any different for Seema? Because she is one of "us", not one of "them"?'

In the room's pin-drop silence, the hurt in his voice was palpable.

'We are afraid to protest, afraid to bring it to the hospital's notice that they provide horrible service to their patients, that patients do well not because of us, but *in spite* of us! We fear that they will retaliate against us during the exams! We have made token protests against this with the administration, and they have, as usual, not responded. They reassure us, but don't act. They know our threats are empty. But this time...this time it has gone beyond our limits of tolerance! Not only did they not support Amit and Salim against the corporator, they suspended them! They suspended the two who tried to *save* Seema's life!'

The spark had been lit. Raising his hands in the air he unleashed the fury inside him.

'I am sick and tired of being pushed around! I am sick and tired of being a coward! I am sick and tired of being a voiceless slave! I am sick and tired of feeling worthless! I am sick and tired of the administration walking all over me! This is it! No more!'

Loud desk-thumping rent the air.

He waited for them to settle down. Then, picking up a sheet of paper from the desk, he said, 'This is a list of things that we want from our dean. We will put up copies everywhere... but what we want most is that Amit and Salim be reinstated immediately with a letter of apology from the dean, and we want a police case filed against the corporator who beat them.'

Another round of applause followed.

Dr. Chaddha raised his hand to silence the crowd. Then, in a steady voice he said, 'This is an ultimatum. If our conditions are not met within seven days, we will go on a strike...an indefinite strike!'

The applause continued. Amidst the loud

cheering, Dr. Chaddha spotted the look of concern on a few faces.

'I know some of you don't like the idea of a strike,' he said. 'You feel concerned about the patients who will be affected by it, but let me tell you this: they are *already* affected by it. They suffer the most from *our* apathy and carelessness. We do this to them! How could this terrible care get any worse if we went on strike? This strike is not against them but for *their* good. We are doctors, not magicians… We cannot do anything if there is no material for sutures or the IV fluid is dirty or the incubators leak! The responsibility of patient care lies not only with us, but with the administration, and this time the patients are in *their* hands. They can agree to our demands and prevent this strike from happening, but *laathon ke bhoot baaton se nahin maante!* Unless we threaten them, nothing will happen… Nothing will change, and Seema will have died for nothing! Nothing!'

The deafening sound of desks being thumped shook the walls of the huge room.

❦

The impending strike became the big news on campus. The dean did reinstate both Amit and

Pheru, and even gave them letters of appreciation for their effort in trying to save Dr Mantri. However, he refused to file a police case against the corporator, ostensibly because his had been an act of 'self-defense'. It was clear to everyone that the dean was under tremendous political pressure to ride out this storm on behalf of the corporator.

Pheru became an instant celebrity on campus. Suddenly he began to be recognized as the person who had tried to save Dr Mantri's life rather than the bully who enjoyed torturing freshies. His history of having languished for four years in Pharmacology got buried in the eulogistic descriptions of how he had tried to take a few swings at the corporator. One newspaper mentioned Pheru's name along with his photograph when describing the event. Pheru promptly cut out the write-up, got it framed and hung it on the wall of the room he now shared with Toshi. All this attention had a strange effect on Pheru. For the first time, he grew concerned that he had an exam to pass and a reputation to protect. He began to make regular trips to the library carrying his Pharmacology text under his arm. He started attending tutorials and participating in practicals that he had missed for the last four years. One night he woke Adi up to borrow notes on the subject. As Adi smiled and handed him the notes he realized that in the warmth of public adulation, Pheru had found the acceptance he had so hungered for.

Toshi saw the impending strike as a long awaited opportunity to go home. Since coming to Bombay two years ago, he hadn't been able to go home even once, and it left him extremely homesick. Dissuading a short jaunt was the distance between Bombay and Mokukchung that would consume five days by train and bus. Air travel could reduce this to one day, but the plane tickets were prohibitively expensive. It didn't make sense to go all that way, at such expense, without getting at least a few weeks at home – a scenario that was suddenly a distinct possibility if the strike materialized.

The dean tried all sorts of manoeuvres with the residents, but they wouldn't budge. The bone of contention was the police report against the municipal corporator, which the dean refused to file. As the situation reached an impasse, the strike loomed large on the horizon, seemingly as inevitable as the impending monsoon rains.

❧

Adi was sitting alone in his room when someone
knocked on his door. Adi opened it and was
surprised to see Neil standing outside with a
very apologetic look on his face.

'Hi Adi, I... I need to talk to you.'

'Sure,' Adi replied somewhat uncertainly.
'Come in.'

Neil walked in and sat on a chair next to the
window. He waited for a few minutes, looking
around, smiling hesitantly as though unsure of
what to say. Then, lowering his head, he said,
'It's Renuka... She won't see me any more.'

Adi sighed. 'What did she say? I mean, did
she say why?' he asked.

'No. She just called me up and said we
shouldn't see each other any more. I was going
to ask her to the Med Ball, but she called me
first. Now, she just won't talk to me.'

Adi wondered why Neil was telling him all
this.

Neil looked at him and said, 'I've thought of
slashing my wrists, man!'

The depth of his despondency suddenly
struck Adi. 'Hey, Neil! Nobody's worth dying for.
What do you want me to do, man? Come on,
man. It can't be that bad!'

Neil buried his head in his hands and began to sob. Adi studied him silently, finding it hard to believe that this was the same self-assured chap who had whisked her away in his car right in front of his eyes. He put a hand on his shoulder reassuringly and said, 'Calm down, man...you'll get over it. Your life is worth a lot more than just Renuka...You'll forget her.'

'Four years,' he sobbed. 'I've known her for four years...it's not easy to forget, man.'

Adi was surprised. Four years? Renuka had been at medical college for less than two...

'We met in high school, and have been going out for four years, but we were really serious in the last two years. I can't understand it, man...and the worst part is she won't even give me a reason... I wish she'd at least tell me why. Could you talk to her, Adi?'

Adi was taken aback. 'Me? What good would that do, Neil? I can't convince her of anything.'

'No, Adi, she thinks of you as a very good friend and thinks very highly of you. I'm sure she'll talk to you. All I want is a reason... I just want to know why.'

For the next few minutes Adi argued with him, trying to avoid a meeting with Renuka. Yet, somewhere within him was a nagging curiosity about Neil and Renuka's past: the history, Adi suspected, that would explain his own messy tryst with her.

Finally, unable to dissuade or dismiss Neil, Adi said, 'Fine, I'll try and talk to her, but don't expect any miracles, okay? And please Neil, don't do anything stupid.'

At that very moment, Toshi burst into the room. 'Did you hear?' he said, excitedly. 'The residents have decided to go on strike. Man, I'm going home.'

SEVENTEEN

It was the last day of the ultimatum.

Negotiations between the dean and the resident doctors had deteriorated rapidly after the dean had resorted to threatening the residents with jail time for dereliction of duty under the Maintenance of Essential Service Act. Until he discovered, much to his chagrin, that the very same rule which allowed them to pay a pittance for the resident's labour – they were students and not employees – excluded them from the provisions of the act. So he had the residents locked out of Resident Vista: 'If you don't work in the hospital, you don't need the rooms,' he had said, hoping that the prospect of becoming homeless in Bombay would break their back. Unprepared for the solidarity amongst the residents, he failed on both counts and only ended up strengthening their resolve even further.

Over at the ob-gyn wards, Dr Choksi looked very harassed. Dr Uma tried to give him a detailed plan of the patients' care before she along with the two other residents walked off the next day. They went over the fine points again and again, but Dr Choksi's worried eyes focused more on the unsettling future than on her detailed instructions. His clothes appeared even more crumpled and his awkward hairdo had acquired a new frizz. His coat pockets bulged with a sheaf of papers, which he kept pulling out, reading impatiently and shoving back in. He drifted around the ward purposelessly, finding the familiar area suddenly rather alien.

While on rounds that day, he turned to the students and asked, 'You are coming tomorrow, right?'

The students fell silent and looked at each other indecisively.

Dr Choksi was very surprised. 'Why... Why you are all not coming? '

As the natural choice for the next class representative, Adi felt it was his unwritten prerogative to be the spokesman. 'We are joining the strike, sir,' he said.

Dr Choksi's eyes widened with surprise. 'But this doesn't concern students...just the residents.'

'We have to show our solidarity with the residents, sir.'

'But...they really don't need your solidarity and I was hoping that if you are here, you would be of some help.'

'I'm sorry, sir. But the dean has treated the residents very poorly. Now he's thrown them out of their rooms... Where will they go with their books and luggage in Bombay with nowhere to stay? He still refuses to register a police case against the corporator, which shows where his sympathies lie. We all know, sir, that the residents do most of the hospital work. All of us are all going to become residents some day. So, we will show our support for the residents and join the strike. Maybe only then the dean will truly appreciate what the residents mean to this hospital.'

Dr Choksi looked away. He shook his head glumly, then shuffled across the floor to talk to the nurses – the additional blow of vanishing manpower adding a few more degrees to his lurching gait.

Adi started packing his books before heading back to campus, feeling rather proud of his extemporaneous little speech. A few appreciative pats on the back from the other students bolstered his confidence. He knew that this exchange would reach the rest of the class soon, making him even more eligible for the class representative's position. He looked at his name written on a piece of white tape stuck to his bag. Then, smiling to himself, he added the letters 'CR' behind it.

He looked around for Isha and spotted her talking to Dr Choksi. He waited till she had finished and walked back to join him. They began to walk out together.

Adi gloated secretly, expecting her to praise his brilliant speech any minute. When she didn't initiate any conversation, Adi said, 'I hope the residents are successful in their effort.'

'What? Oh, yeah,' she replied.

'The dean must apologize personally for what he did, and they have to arrest the corporator for his actions. Otherwise this could go on for a really long time.'

She nodded silently without looking at Adi.

Her silence surprised him. He decided to probe a little more. 'What were you talking to Dr Choksi about?'

'Hmm? No...nothing.'

'You know Isha, you don't lie very well.'

She smiled but remained silent.

'Poor man,' said Adi. 'He will have to deal with the entire ward by himself. I feel sorry for him but I'm glad we didn't agree to come to the ward tomorrow.'

She stopped walking. 'Adi, have you read a book called *To Kill a Mocking Bird*?' she asked.

Adi smiled. 'Sure. It is one of my favourite books. By Harper Lee, right?'

'Yeah. It's one of my favourite books, too...perhaps the best book I have ever read. Tell me, Adi, what did you like about it?'

'It's just such a great book. I especially loved how the lawyer...what was his name... Lazarus...'

'Atticus,' she corrected. 'Atticus Finch.'

'Yeah, Atticus... I specially like how his daughter, Scout, calls him by his first name— Atticus this, Atticus that... Someday, if I have a daughter, I hope she calls me by my first name, too.'

She began to laugh. 'Atticus is a lot easier than Adityaman,' she said.

Adi smiled. 'Imagine, when my daughter is ten months old and starts saying dada, I'll say, "No, no, forget dada... Call me Aaa...dit... ya...maan".'

She laughed again. It reassured Adi to see her laugh.

'Anyway,' she said. 'What I liked most in the book was Atticus's character. Even though he was white, he defied all the other whites in his small town to defend a poor black man because he thought he deserved a fair trial.'

'Sure,' agreed Adi. 'That description through the eyes of an eight-year-old child is riveting. It is a brilliant book. I've seen the movie, too… Anyway, why did you suddenly bring up the book?'

'Because of what I told Dr Choksi.' Then, turning around to look at Adi's confused face, she said, 'We are going back to the wards tomorrow to help out with whatever we can.'

He stared at her for a few minutes, shocked into silence. 'Who's "we"?' he blurted finally.

'Payal and I. Don't worry, you don't have to come or even know about it.'

'But what will you do? You guys are just second-year medical students!'

'I don't know,' she said calmly. 'Just hold a retractor while Dr Choksi operates, or set up an IV, or check somebody's blood pressure. There is a lot we have learned to do in the past few weeks.'

He stared at her with disbelief. 'But…what about the strike?'

'I don't support the strike. How can doctors endanger their patients' lives? I don't understand it. It's just not right.'

'But you know what happened, Isha! The dean and the residents...'

'Yes, I know,' she said, cutting him off. 'The dean is mean and the residents want blood and we want time off from the wards... Everybody has their own little agenda. But what about these patients? They didn't do anything wrong, yet they'll suffer the most. Their only fault is that they fell ill and are so poor that they cannot go to private hospitals. They are too poor to protest, and so poor that nobody really cares. Being poor is not a crime, and I am not going to be a part of this strike.'

'But Isha, we have to stand up for what is right!'

'Precisely, Adi. Stand up for what is right. Do you honestly believe you are right to join the strike?'

'What do you mean? I said we have to support the residents! They have been wronged!'

'And it's okay to let the patients suffer because of that?'

'No, it's not! But sometimes you have to make hard choices. That is the reason I support it.'

'Are you sure, Adi? Are you sure there is nothing else motivating you to ignore the plight of these patients?'

'What do you mean?'

'Ask yourself, Adi! You stood up for a frog when it needed help. Why is your decision so different this time?'

Adi fell silent for a few seconds. Something in her words struck a chord but he couldn't put a finger on it. He tried one last time. 'But what will the others think, Isha? I just talked about joining the strike! They will think that I am trying to get into Dr Choksi's good books. The whole class will feel let down!'

She smiled. 'Why do you care so much about what the class thinks or says, Adi? Why do you think it is so important to do what everybody else thinks is right? What do you feel about it? You don't have to join us, Adi. Payal and I are going... I guess that is the advantage of having only one friend. And that is why I was talking about Atticus...about doing something that you feel is right, even if everybody else is against it. Atticus was brave because he had strength of character, the courage of his convictions. Being brave does not mean taking a gun and killing five bad men...being brave is just having the courage to stand up for what is right and say it with conviction, ignoring whatever anybody else has to say.' She paused and added, 'Do that and your daughter may actually call you Atticus.'

Her words were still ringing in his ears when Adi joined his friends for dinner at a nearby restaurant later that evening.

Toshi was bursting with excitement about his trip home. 'Man, I leave in two weeks,' he said. 'Can't wait to see them... I haven't seen them in two years.'

'Why are you going after two weeks? Why not now?' asked Sam.

'I didn't have the money to get air tickets. My parents are sending me money and then I'll buy my tickets.'

'How long will you stay, Toshi?' asked Adi.

'A month at least... Maybe more, if the strike goes on longer. Pheru, you can have the room to yourself for a whole month. That should help you study for your Pharmac exams. And Harsha, you'll remember to be my proxy, right? Don't forget my roll number is 69...you know, like the position...'

Everyone laughed. Amidst the laughter Adi noticed Rajeev staring at him from the other end of the table, his eyes conspicuously devoid of any mirth.

'Man, I have my exams in less than four weeks,' said Pheru. 'This time I *must* pass...it is my seventh attempt. Pharmac can't be all that tough, man. And, I need my room back.'

'You can stay with me Pheru...for as long as you want,' said Toshi. 'But don't worry, I think you'll pass. It's different this time.'

'Why is it different this time?' asked Pheru.

'Maybe because this time you are studying?' said Toshi and everyone laughed.

The appetizing aroma of greasy Mughlai food filled the air. They pulled up their chairs and waited for the feast to be laid out on the table with hungry eyes and growling stomachs.

Toshi took a glass of water and proposed a toast: 'To the strike...may it last long.'

Everyone raised their glasses and cheered. Adi mumbled a few indistinct words.

'Speaking of the strike,' said Rajeev, softly. 'I've heard that some of the people from our class have decided to go to the wards despite the strike.'

Adi felt a funny sensation in his stomach. He looked at his food. The biryani seemed fine.

'Really? Who?' asked Sam, his face full of indignation.

Adi tried to nip it in the bud. 'What difference does it make if some second-year medical students decide to join the strike or not? We can't be counted on to give patient care...the strike will be effective with or without us.'

Pheru turned towards him. 'Are you going to the wards tomorrow, Adi?'

'No,' replied Adi, 'I'm not...but...'

'I heard somebody from your batch was going, Adi,' said Rajeev.

Adi grimaced, wishing he could sink his fist into Rajeev's mouth to stop the words from forming. 'What difference does it make?' he said with irritation. 'Let the ones who want to go, go!'

Pheru dropped his spoon and looked at Adi.

'What difference does it make? Are you joking, Adi?' he said, angrily. 'Do you have any idea what it was like to be punched and kicked by that corporator, that son of a bitch who probably cannot even spell his own name? The bastard held my collar and slapped and punched me...and even though I was furious, I begged him with my hands folded to try and get him to stop. I begged him, Adi... I begged him! And you think he hasn't done anything wrong? He killed her! He may not have strangled her, but he might as well have! If I'd had a gun, I would have fucking shot him that day. What difference does it make? Even now, I feel a hollow panic inside me when I re-live that moment. I could see her face turning dark and her body gasping for air like a fish out of water. So don't tell me that it doesn't matter that somebody is going to go against the rest of us, and go to the wards. This needs to be a total strike! Total!'

Adi quickly tried to think of some way to stop the situation from spiraling out of control. 'Calm down, Pheru,' he said. 'I'll find out who it is…'

Before Pheru had a chance to react, Rajeev said, 'I think it is Payal and her friend…what is her name…the one who Sheetal said you took to Kamats some time ago. Isha, right?'

Adi felt the blood drain from his face.

Pheru turned red. 'Those bloody bitches!' he started.

'Shut up!' shouted Adi. 'Just shut the hell up!'

Everyone stopped eating and stared at Adi.

Pheru stared at Adi in disbelief. 'Adi,' he growled. 'You…you fucking son of a bitch! You knew! You knew all along it was them!'

'You don't know them, Pheru! You have no right to talk about them like that! You can say anything about me but you don't know them, okay?'

Pheru's mouth opened and shut a few times without uttering a sound. 'You like Isha, don't you?' he sneered finally.

'That is besides the point, Pheru!' shouted Adi.

'Saala, Adi, you fucking bastard! And you've been leading us on all this while! "I'll find out who it is, Pheru!" You're protecting her...her? She's betraying our cause, she is betraying me! She is betraying all of us, and you want to help her? You forgot how she shut Harsha out...now you want to cover for her?'

Adi looked up to see Harsha staring at him with a vacant expression.

Adi didn't know how to react. He felt mortified and embarrassed, and yet angry and wronged. He felt that he owed them an apology and an explanation, just like they owed him one. He realized he had to do something quickly to manage the situation.

'Guys,' he said, trying hard to keep his voice calm, 'I'll try and talk to them to see that they do not go to the wards. I know I can convince them to join the strike. But don't disparage her like that...please... I can't tolerate that. You have no idea what she is like, so just fucking stop it!'

The table fell silent, the mood suddenly somber and hostile. They ate their food robotically, hurrying to minimize the time left in each other's company.

Only Rajeev hummed a tune while eating.

EIGHTEEN

For the next few days, Isha's work in the wards
and Adi's spirited defense of her position
dominated the discussion in their class. Even
though he hadn't gone to the wards, Adi was,
for all practical purposes, guilty by association.
He found himself haemorrhaging friends at a rate
directly proportional to the time Isha spent in
the hospital defying the strike. Helpless to stop
the defection, Adi fretted and fussed, bemoaning
the potential fallout, while Isha remained
completely unruffled by the feathers she had
ruffled. Now, the class representative's position
was not even in contention: Adi was left fighting
for a friendly face. Conversations with the same
guys with whom he had spent hours babbling
about the most irrelevant topics on earth turned
uncomfortable and stilted. And if Rajeev, Pheru
or Harsha were in the room, they would quietly

leave when he entered. The feeling that he had wronged Harsha and betrayed Pheru was on everybody's mind, even though it never formed on anyone's lips. Suddenly, the atmosphere in the hostel stifled him and Adi realized that unless he could convince Isha to join the strike, solitude would be his only steady companion.

He grappled desperately for a good plan, scribbling his options on a piece of paper and crossing them out because of their impotence in assuring a favourable outcome. Instead of useful ideas, these brainstorming sessions left him with monstrous headaches. Finding a persuasive argument proved as hopelessly arduous as his efforts to corner Isha and talk some sense into her. The watchman at the ladies' hostel always came back to inform him that there was nobody in her room, and Adi never managed to find a private moment to talk to her during the few lectures that were still on. He wanted to avoid following her to Cama – the act of asking her to join the strike within the hospital's premises seemed particularly unconscionable.

After a few days, desperation seized hold of Adi. He realized he had no choice but to confront her at work. Everything was at stake: his position, his popularity, his friendships, as well as any prospects of a future with her, rested in this do or die effort.

Unprepared and unsure, Adi could feel an emptiness gnawing at his insides as he entered the hospital. He spotted Payal sitting next to a patient a few feet from the entrance to the ward. Lurking behind the dark green curtains at the entrance, he whispered loudly, 'Hi, Payal…do you know where Isha is? I need to talk to her.'

Before Payal could reply, the sound of hurried footsteps distracted Adi as a young man rushed past him. Trailing him with an unsteady somewhat soporific gait was a young woman. Their clothes were cheap, and the dark blotches a few days of perspiration paints, accentuated the tawdriness. From his hand dangled a worn out cardboard suitcase that held on to its contents thanks to the tenacity of a single latch. She walked barefoot, the soles of her feet hard and callused, while the comparative luxury of his battered sandals flapped loudly on the cement floor. As he sat her down on the floor of the ward a few feet from the doorway, Adi realized that she was pregnant. She looked tired and was noticeably jaundiced. Her eyes had trouble focusing, and she held on to her husband's hand tightly, as though looking for a reassuring link to life and sanity.

The young man turned toward Adi, folded his hands and cried, 'Please, doctor sahib... please help us...please.'

Caught unawares, Adi tried to evade him, but the attention the young man drew towards Adi with his impassioned pleas, made him say, 'okay, calm down, calm down...tell me what is going on.'

Dr Choksi, having heard the commotion, came running out of the delivery room. He smiled upon seeing Adi. 'Dr Bhatt...thank you for coming. God knows we need help around here. Can you do the history and examination and tell me about it later? I'm needed in the delivery room.'

With that, he turned around and returned in the direction he had come from.

Adi felt trapped by Dr Choksi's expectations. He smiled nervously to allay the curious stares of the other patients and nurses, trying hard to prevent the discomfort from showing on his face. He decided to get the history for Dr Choksi and then leave as quickly as possible. He turned to examine the young girl.

The glow of impending motherhood, although heavily stained with bile, was discernible on her youthful face. Demure and groggy, she held on to her husband's hand, answering Adi's questions somewhat haltingly. Her husband prodded her through it, grateful for Adi's interest, peppering her story with small snippets of whatever he thought was relevant.

The couple had just arrived from a small village in Bihar. They had fled their village, escaping the wrath of the upper-caste Thakurs when, as Dalits, their crime of solemnizing their wedding in the upper caste temple and having a drink from the upper caste wells had spawned a murderous attack. His odd jobs as a labourer, laundry-worker and dishwasher had saved him just about enough money to buy two train tickets to Bombay. He had heard that Bombay was where all the jobs were and, in this amazing city, being from another caste was not a reason to kill one another.

His eighteen-year-old bride was six months pregnant and had developed a fever while on the train. He couldn't say how high, but she had felt very hot. She had complained that her stomach hurt while pointing to the area over the liver. The previous night she had thrown up whatever she had eaten, and the yellowish tinge on her skin had progressively deepened. Simultaneously, her urine had turned dark and so, as soon as their train stopped at the station, they had walked out to the nearest hospital they could find.

She allowed Adi to examine her hesitantly, clinging tenaciously to her husband's hand at the touch of another man. Although his knowledge of medicine was quite rudimentary, Adi was fairly certain that she had hepatitis. He donned a pair of gloves and sent off some blood tests while waiting for Dr Choksi to re-emerge from the delivery room.

An hour later, Dr Choksi walked in just as the results of her blood tests arrived. He presented her story to Dr Choksi who grew visibly upset. 'She should be getting her care from the medicine people, but now they will send anybody who is pregnant to the ob-gyn floors. This is terrible... terrible!'

Adi showed him the results of the blood tests. Her liver enzymes and bilirubin were high, confirming Adi's suspicion.

'She either has severe viral hepatitis or fatty liver of pregnancy... I hope nothing else,' said Dr Choksi. 'Either way, this does not look good. She is a little groggy too. I hope she is not going into fulminant hepatic failure. What is her PT– Prothrombin Time?'

'Normal,' said Adi, adding, 'the hepatitis serologies will take a few days to come back.'

Dr Choksi nodded to acknowledge the report, ordered a low-protein, fat-free diet and some general symptomatic relief measures. Then, smiling appreciatively, he put one hand on Adi's shoulder and said, 'Dr Bhatt, what you are doing shows that you are a doctor already. You don't need to pass any exams or get any degrees. You care, which is the most important quality a doctor can have. This caring is not learnt by reading big books...it comes from within. I thank you from the bottom of my heart and you should be very proud of yourself.'

Adi nodded diffidently and looked away.

Dr Choksi's smile faltered at Adi's hesitant response. For a moment, his eyes teetered on the brink of a question. But he held back. Instead, he smiled affably and patted Adi's shoulder before walking away, leaving Adi with a huge dose of guilt.

Adi arranged his bag slowly as he deliberated his next move. A strange doubt began to creep into his thoughts; a doubt that he felt scared to confront. He tried to reassure himself that he had gone above and beyond his duty – even Dr Choksi had said so. Yet, instead of a sense of accomplishment, he felt inordinately delinquent. He decided to leave the building immediately, hoping that his rapid exit would somehow douse his doubts.

As he stepped outside, the young girl's

husband came running out to meet him. His face had curled into an expectant smile. 'She will be okay, doctor sahib? She will, right?' he asked.

'She is very sick,' said Adi, finding it hard to convey an accurate prognosis without feeling a twinge of guilt.

'But you are taking care of her, doctor sahib. I trust you, sahib. The rest is the will of the one above...none of us can do anything about His will. But I trust you... I do.'

Adi sighed. 'Can't you take her somewhere else...like a private hospital?'

'Why doctor sahib? I trust you and the old doctor...I know you will do your best for my Neelmani.'

'It is not a matter of trusting us... In the government hospital, many doctors are on strike, so it's not good here.'

'But you are not on strike, sahib!'

'I'm not now...but I will be. I am not coming tomorrow.'

The young man's face fell. An uncertain smile stayed on his lips while his eyes flitted between incomprehension and bafflement.

'There was a fight between the doctors and the dean...the hospital's chief,' explained Adi. 'The doctors are doing this to improve the conditions in the hospital. They want to see that people like you get better care. They are doing all this all for you…for your good.'

The young man stood there with his mouth open, staring at Adi with vacant eyes.

'Do you understand what I'm saying?' asked Adi.

'But she will die! Neelmani will die, doctor sahib. If you don't come back, my Neelmani and our baby will die!'

'But if we don't do this, things will never get better!' replied Adi, trying hard to force conviction into his words. 'The resident doctors have to do this to protect more lives…to help more people like you and your Neelmani. Don't you see? Sometimes we have to make these tough choices. It is for everybody's good.'

The young man kept staring at Adi uncertainly, his apologetic face berating his inability to grasp the important principle at stake – a principle that was worth the lives of his wife and unborn child. Then, shaking his head ruefully, he said, 'You know, doctor sahib, when we were running away from the Thakur's men and hiding in the forest for five days without anything to eat or drink, my stomach would burn with hunger and I would wonder…why is our life worth so little? Neelmani would tell me we are achoots, we clean everyone's toilets and that is what we are worth. Then we learned that in this big city, nobody cares if you are achoots... Here everyone is the same...everyone's life is worth more than the toilet he cleans. But now, when my heart burns with the same question, I realize that we are not achoots any more doctor sahib, but we are poor. We are very poor – and I don't know which is worse.'

Then, clutching Adi's hand with both of his, he hung his head and began to cry.

❧

Adi returned to the hostel late that night without getting to meet Isha. He didn't turn on the lights upon entering his room. He opened the windows, tidied his bed, swept the floor and arranged his clothes, trying to lose the events of the afternoon in the small inconsequential things he usually did out of habit. His troubled mind kept wandering back to the young girl struggling for life and her husband pleading for her care. He wondered how to tell the other guys in the hostel that he had failed to convince Isha and Payal to join the strike.

His thoughts became noisier and an irritating

heaviness hung inside his chest, doggedly perseverant despite all his manoeuvers. He arranged his bag for the third time, hoping for some sort of a panacea in all this activity. Finally, frustrated with himself, he looked out of the window and stared into the vast calmness of the night.

A full moon smiled back at him benevolently. A light wind brought in the cool night air along with the beautiful scent of the jasmine flowers blooming outside. The leaves on the trees rustled playfully in the breeze. In the distance, the backwaters of the Arabian Sea shimmered like diamonds under the clear starry sky. Other than the occasional chirp of a cricket, silence hung heavy in the air.

Adi wondered how everything could look so deceptively peaceful, so starkly paradoxical to the malevolence in his heart.

His eyes wandered to the Textbook of Medicine sitting upright on the bookshelf. He gazed at the cover, feeling a strange calm materialize out of nowhere. He reached over and pulled out the book, the peaceful feeling now slowly gaining strength. As he opened the table of contents and thumbed through the list, the sensation coursed through his veins and buzzed down his spine. Suddenly, the questions in his head started to evaporate and the turmoil in his heart began to recede. He leafed through the pages with slow deliberation, savouring the steady percolation of serenity. By the time he opened the chapter on Acute Viral Hepatitis, the heaviness in his chest had completely disappeared.

Adi felt tears of relief well up in his eyes. He wiped his face with his hands and was about to begin reading the chapter on Acute Viral Hepatitis, when his eyes fell on the name taped on his bag. ADITYAMAN BHATT, CR it said. He smiled and pulled it off, then rolled it into a small ball and tossed it out of the window.

❧

The next morning when Adi showed up in the wards, he was shocked to find the young girl tied to the bed with cords fashioned from long reams of gauze. He could hardly recognize her as she twisted and turned, screaming obscenities at everyone during her intermittent moments of consciousness. Her jaundice looked markedly worse and she didn't make any sense as she thrashed around in bed like a woman possessed, tugging at the cords till they dug into her wrists. The shy, demure girl who had held onto her husband's hand in the presence of another man, was now oblivious to how her sari had ridden up her legs, exposing her thighs and buttocks. Her husband stood next to her, weeping at the sight of his sick wife whose condition was deteriorating so rapidly in front of his eyes.

Dr Choksi and Isha stood beside the bed. As Adi approached them, Dr Choksi turned to him and said, 'This is what I was afraid of: fulminant hepatic failure. She has Encephalopathy.'

Adi was horrified. He remembered having read the previous night about Hepatic Encephalopathy. It carried a terrible prognosis, especially among pregnant women, with abysmal survival rates even in the best centres in the world. This was Cama hospital, the ob-gyn floor, with a skeletal staff and no support services. It was a death sentence.

'I've put her on a zero-protein diet and started her on lactulose enemas,' said Dr Choksi. 'Her prothrombin time was normal yesterday, right?'

'Y...yes,' said Adi, his voice cracking up with emotion.

'Repeat it today. It should be very high and she'll need vitamin K injections. This time, get it done from Bombay hospital...I don't trust the lab here. Also... Dr Bhatt, her husband keeps asking me, but I cannot explain it to him. Maybe you can tell him that I'm not too hopeful for her… I don't think she is going to live. He says both of you are from the same state…is that right?'

Adi nodded. 'Yes, we are. I… I'll talk to him.'

Adi stared at the young husband helplessly, unsure how to begin explaining the inexplicability of her death. His heart felt heavy and a lump in his throat hurt every time he tried to talk. He had seen death many times before but had never known it could be so difficult to confront dying. Death at eighteen, an age that was supposed to be bursting with life's promise, a promise that was growing in her belly. A promise that was going to die.

He prepared to collect her blood. Isha helped steady her arm. As the dark red blood began to fill the syringe, he heard Isha whisper, 'Adi, I'm so proud of you.'

He looked up at her and smiled.

He carried the blood to Bombay Hospital. It wasn't far from Cama – a brisk walk of five minutes was all it took to get him there. Yet it may as well have been a world away. The grand atrium he stepped into was lined with dark wooden panels and recessed halogen lights, reminding him of a five-star hotel. Soft classical music wafted from the tiny speakers on the walls, as people in business suits and long white coats walked about, looking important. The air was cool from the central air conditioning, and some pretty ladies sat below a big sign that said 'Reception', staring into computer monitors and answering telephones with polished accents.

The ladies directed him to the clinical laboratories. He paid the forty rupees it would cost to run the Prothrombin Time and waited for the results.

In the cool comfort of the air-conditioned lab, Adi's mind wandered over to the meaning of life and the difference he had seen in its scope amongst the rich and the poor. He remembered pitying the beggar he had seen on the streets, the one whose torso, devoid of all appendage, would loll about aimlessly when trying to reach the comfort of a tree's shade. For the first time, Adi understood his miserable existence.

It was miserable, but it was *existence*. An existence enshrined by the innate and universal addiction to live. And it surprised him to think that this necessity to exist, so quintessential of life, was a privilege, not a right.

The cool air was such a refreshing change from the damp heat outside that Adi started to doze off. An hour later, the lady in the lab woke him and handed him the envelope containing the results of the test. Adi thanked her groggily and started making his way back to Cama. Halfway there, he realized he hadn't even checked the results. He opened the envelope to see that the PT was reported as twelve seconds. Normal.

Adi stopped dead in his tracks. It couldn't be…with fulminant hepatic failure the PT should have been markedly elevated. He was furious with himself. He had spent so much time on a test of dubious value, and was now carrying back a fallacious result. On top of that, he was forty rupees poorer.

When he reached Cama, Dr Choksi studied the result with astonishment. 'This was her blood, right?' he asked.

'Yes, sir,' replied Adi. 'I drew it and took it to Bombay Hospital personally.'

'If her PT is normal, then she is not in fulminant hepatic failure. It just cannot be. We are missing something… Let me call Dr Pershovan.'

Dr Choksi ambled to the end of the ward and dialled some numbers on the telephone. Then, with his eyes focused on a spot on the floor, he started talking rapidly to his old friend and internist, Dr Pershovan.

Adi was confused. What else could it be? Her liver enzymes were off the charts, she was severely jaundiced and now had encephalopathy…

'Did we check for malaria?' Dr Choksi asked upon returning, his eyes glowing with enthusiasm.

'No… I don't think we did, Dr Choksi.'

The glow in Dr Choksi's eyes got brighter. 'Dr Pershovan said she could have cerebral malaria. Because of the heavy parasitemia, the liver function can be abnormal. Let's get a peripheral smear for malarial parasite. We need it done right now. Send it to Bombay Hospital again.'

Adi found himself retracing his actions of the morning. His hands shook as he collected her blood…if indeed it was cerebral malaria, it was potentially curable! There was a chance…a chance for life.

This time he ran all the way to the lab at Bombay Hospital and waited outside the door anxiously for the results. Twenty-five minutes later, when the technician handed him the envelope, Adi opened it right away.

'Gametocytes and trophozoites of P. falciparum seen,' he read. Adi whooped with joy, kissed the sheet of paper in his hands and cried out, 'It's cerebral malaria, thank God… It's cerebral malaria!'

He suddenly realized that everyone there was staring at him with surprise. Adi smiled apologetically and then ran all the way back to Cama.

❧

That afternoon they started her on intravenous Quinine.

Adi stared nervously at the humble looking bottle hanging upside down on the IV pole. He watched as the clear liquid flowed along the thin plastic tube, ballooning into shiny drops in the air trap chamber. The drops hung precariously at the tip, vibrating with indecision before lurching into the collection below, only to be eagerly replaced by a sparkling new recruit. One after the other, like a well-trained battalion, they appeared with remarkable steadfastness, eager to wage battle as they flowed into her veins. She lay comatose, completely unresponsive except to painful stimuli. Her face was absurdly serene: other than her breathing and the occasional stirring of her baby in her swollen belly, the lack of distress belied the seriousness of her illness. If it hadn't been for the fact that she was hooked up to an IV, she could well have been sleeping peacefully at home.

Adi wondered if this was the quiet dignity of death.

Anxious, he looked for any sign of life. Anything: the twitch of a hand, the flutter of an eyelid, a groan of discomfort...anything to suggest the battle had not already been lost. Then, afraid that his expectations might somehow threaten the fickle temperament of her life, he switched to prayer instead. Hope, he realized, is a double-edged emotion. It provides as much anxiety as solace, as much doubt as faith, as much fear as courage.

He remembered reading about Quinine. Extracted from the bark of the cinchona tree, it is a highly effective but toxic medication. It kills the malarial parasite rapidly, but at the same time, it can lower blood glucose to levels that would starve the brain to death. It can stop the heart abruptly or send it into a tailspin, beating so fast that there isn't enough time for it to fill up with blood in between beats. Encumbered with this alarming knowledge, Adi decided to spend the night in the wards and keep a close eye on her. Her husband sat on the floor next to her bed, quietly running his hand through her hair.

Adi watched the nurses change shifts. One of the nurses got him some food, another offered him her chair. He watched some of the other patients watching him. Outside, the noisy bustle of the afternoon gave way to the disorderly hubbub of the evening. Adi stared at the life around him, waiting for the one that mattered most, to prevail.

Somewhere in between worrying about her and watching over her, Adi fell asleep.

The next thing he knew, someone was shaking his shoulder. He heard Dr Choksi's voice say, 'Dr Bhatt, wake up… It's 8 o'clock. Look at what you've done.'

Rubbing his eyes, Adi collected his thoughts, remembering the events of the previous day. As he focused to get a better look, he first saw Isha standing next to him, smiling. Then, he saw the reason why. On the bed lay the young girl, looking around with a dazed expression, as though woken up from a long, deep slumber.

She looked at Adi and gave him a shy smile.

It was a moment unlike anything Adi had experienced before. He raised his hands and started laughing even as tears raced down his face. His heart was bursting with happiness. He had never experienced so much joy in his life. He needed to share it with someone…someone close.

He turned around and hugged Isha.

NINETEEN

Although Adi had promised Neil that he would talk to Renuka, his heart was not in it. He could think of a host of reasons for his unwillingness, but most importantly, he had got closer to Isha and worried about jeopardizing their relationship. Isha and he were spending a lot more time together, both in and off the wards, and found themselves in the midst of an unplanned but enjoyable routine. Everyday, after wrapping up their work on the ob-gyn floors, they'd spend the evening together, strolling down Marine Drive, walking up to Mantralay or ducking into Gaylord's to watch the rain over a quick cup of tea. They sat on decrepit benches and chronicled the crowds, leafed through second-hand books on the pavements of Flora Fountain, admired on Fashion Street clothes they had no means of buying, sampled food that the vendors offered for free or walked barefoot on the wet grass of Cross Maidan, losing the weariness of a day's work in each other's company. Sometimes, engrossed in intense discussions for hours at a stretch, they would lose all track of time till the rapidly thinning crowd would remind them of the last bus to campus. Hurriedly racing towards the bus-stand they'd make it back to the ladies' hostel just in time for another round of suspicious glares from Khadoos Baba. Soon it became such a routine that Khaddos Baba gave up on them, yawning sleepily as he opened the door to let Isha in. Adi would stare at her figure disappearing into the labyrinth of corridors behind the collapsible gate before the wooden doors slammed shut on his face, suddenly reminding him of the long tread back to his room and the hundred things that still remained to be said.

Despite their growing proximity, a strange characteristic of their outings was the complete absence of any discussion about themselves. Adi's promise to keep their relationship platonic restrained him from letting it progress into anything physical, even though a nascent desire often nagged him mercilessly. It was especially acute in the hostel's inhospitable isolation, where Adi sat estranged, waiting to escape into the next day's arrival. So he'd tie his desire to denial and imagine how he would hold her hand while helping her up the stairs, or scheme to take her in his arms if she tripped. But there were no staircases on Marine Drive, and the only one to trip during one of their walks was Adi.

He sensed her physical presence every minute in her company, but didn't do anything for fear of losing what he had...the relationship he'd promised not to define. When frustrated with this arrangement, Adi would swear to abandon his pledge and demand a clarification the very next day – only to hastily abandon such thoughts the moment he laid eyes on her. He feared losing the contentment of having her next to him much more than his own aching insecurity. So he'd stash the thought at the back of his mind and continue to struggle with its meaning in the bitterness of his ostracized alienation. Somewhere, deep in his heart, he knew that the day they talked about Renuka would be the day they'd talk about themselves. Which led Adi to revisit the issue of meeting Renuka; not to keep his promise to Neil, but because he wanted to achieve some clarity on what he'd tell Isha. But his discussions with Isha remained self-effacing and platonic, and Adi felt too insecure to change their nature.

❦

The strike spilled over into its second week.

The night before Toshi was to leave for Nagaland, Adi walked over to his room to wish him goodbye. Toshi remained the only one to accord him any affection, and Adi's desperate need to hang on to this last vestige of friendship overpowered his reluctance to run the gauntlet of the others whose voices he could hear from outside Toshi's door. He hesitated for a few minutes in the hallway, waiting to muster up enough courage before finally stepping in.

Rajeev and Pheru were helping Toshi pack and immediately stiffened upon seeing Adi.

'Hi, Toshi,' said Adi. 'I just stopped by to say, have a good flight and enjoy yourself at home.'

'Hey, come in, man. Come in…come in,' said Toshi warmly, smiling from ear to ear.

'Toshi… I…'

'Come in, man…come in, Adi.'

Adi took one perfunctory step inside the room. He looked around, trying to search for a quick topic of conversation.

'Wow,' he said, 'you have too many suitcases, Toshi… Don't they allow only two per person?'

'Yeah…all these gifts I bought for my family won't fit into two suitcases,' he said. 'But I'll manage. I'll turn on my Toshi charm to convince them to let me carry more.'

'Make sure you go to the ladies at the check-in counter, not the men,' cautioned Adi in jest.

Toshi smiled. 'Unless it's Praful behind one of those—he may want to give me a personal ride,' he said, rocking his hips suggestively.

Adi laughed. Rajeev and Pheru remained silent.

'I should go,' said Adi. ' I have to get up early tomorrow…'

'To go to the wards!' said Pheru, cutting him off.

Adi stiffened. 'Yes…to the wards.'

Pheru snapped. 'Saala, Adi… I still can't believe you're doing this to us!'

Adi grimaced, trying hard to curb his irritation. He ignored Pheru and said, 'Bye, Toshi…have fun.'

Pheru shouted, 'Just remember, the next time…'

'What is your problem, Pheru? Huh?' said Adi, cutting him off angrily. 'What is it? Why do you care what happens to me? Isn't it enough that none of you talk to me any more? Isn't it enough that returning to the hostel makes me feel like it'll bite me? What do you want, huh?'

'You did that to yourself. Nobody asked you to…'

'I know that! I'm suffering for it...so why do you still have a problem? What the hell do you want me to do?'

Toshi intervened. 'Guys, stop it! Listen... tomorrow I need help to take this stuff to the airport. Adi, will you come to drop me off?'

Pheru did not stop. 'Don't ditch your friends... You're going to regret it!'

'When did you become an authority on friendship, Pheru?'

'You've betrayed the whole class, Adi! Think about that when this one dumps you too!'

Toshi interjected. 'Stop it, you two! I'm leaving tomorrow and this is not the way to say goodbye... Stop it. Both of you are being selfish! Adi...will you drop me off tomorrow?'

Adi and Pheru glared at each other. Then, as Adi turned to leave, he said to Toshi, 'Sure, I'll see you off at the airport.'

❧

Adi had trouble falling asleep that night. He lay in bed, staring at the empty ceiling, trying to rationalize his terrible loneliness. He wondered how so much bitterness had crept into what was so comfortable and familiar only a few weeks ago. He shuddered, imagining his impending isolation after Toshi's departure. It pained him to think that he was the common link in all this acrimony. Renuka, Pheru, Rajeev, Harsha…each and every one of his relationships had suffered the same fate.

And then it struck him. Isha…was Isha next?

His throat felt parched as he tossed and turned in bed, finding discomfort in every position he assumed. He covered his head with his blanket, curling up into a shivering bundle of insecurity. He stayed under the sheet as long as he could, giving up when he realized that he couldn't hide from himself. The simple truth was that he could neither define his relationship with Isha nor will it into anything meaningful.

It was in that panic-stricken moment that Adi decided he couldn't tolerate the ambiguity of their relationship any longer. He had to ask Isha to define it for him…he just had to!

But first, he'd have to talk to Renuka.

Homeward bound for the first time in two years, Toshi's joy knew no bounds. He smiled at everybody, shook hands with the guy who ironed his shirt, hugged the canteen manager after praising his food, all the while humming a tune under his breath.

The taxi arrived with uncharacteristic punctuality just as the breakfast crowd was gathering outside the canteen. Adi helped Toshi load his stuff into the taxi. Then, as he opened the door to get in, he noticed Rajeev and Pheru heading towards them.

Adi stiffened. He tried to back out but Toshi blocked his way, insisting on his company. After a few minutes of hushed wrangling Adi acquiesced to Toshi's insistence with great misgiving, expecting Toshi's clumsy effort at a last-minute reconciliation to backfire any minute.

The long ride to the airport began with tenuous tranquillity, the occupants maintaining a superficial civility in the confines of the car. Adi sat next to the driver, tensely awaiting the next round of unpleasant exchanges which, with Rajeev and Pheru together, would mean an unequal battle.

Rajeev fired the first salvo. 'Adi, don't you have to go to the wards today?'

'I have taken the today off...to drop Toshi to the airport,' replied Adi.

'Thanks, Adi,' said Toshi. 'Thanks for coming to drop me off. You are a good friend.'

Pheru scoffed. Adi smiled at Toshi,

appreciating his efforts to bridge the chasm with a plastic grin and forced joviality.

Then Toshi said, 'Do you remember, Pheru, how you made me try to screw Adi on the first night you ragged us?'

All of them smiled, welcoming the sudden diversion of that night's events two years ago. Despite the suffering of that moment, their memory of the event had mellowed so much with time that they were able to recall the torture with an absurd fondness.

'Ask Princess Diana if she has AIDS?' chuckled Pheru. 'How the hell did Harsha come up with that one? That is the funniest thing I've ever heard during ragging.'

All of them began to laugh.

'Hey, Rajeev, did you ever write to the Nobel Prize committee about your masturbation experiment disproving Newton's first law?' Toshi asked. 'That was a great one. Where did you come up with that one, Pheru?'

Pheru smiled. 'Like Rajeev, our physics guru from Delhi, I topped Physics in the Higher Secondary Exams of the state.'

Then, while the rest of them tried to digest the incongruity of his statement, Pheru launched into the correct interpretation of Newton's laws to explain his 'experiment'. As Adi listened to his elegant application of the concept of preservation of mass to explain the results, the paradox that had always bothered him came to the fore. He wondered why Pheru languished in second MBBS, unable to clear a relatively simple subject like Pharmacology.

'Pheru, why can't you clear Pharmac, man?' asked Toshi, mirroring Adi's thoughts.

Pheru sighed and said, 'It actually involves the dean... I was in second MB when I ragged a bunch of guys in the hostel. Not too bad, but one of them was this hotshot who was the dean's prospective son-in-law. He tried to get a statement from the others in the hostel about the incident, but nobody was willing to come forward. Since nothing materialized, he could not charge me or rusticate me. His son-in-law-to-be quit medicine to study fashion designing or something. So, the dean made sure that I failed the practical exams in Pharmac that year and he has been doing so every year. Initially, I tried very hard to study and pass, but I realized that he was going to keep doing it, so I just stopped studying. Now, I just show up at the exam and have fun. I say any nonsense that comes to my head and love to see the look of horror on the faces of the examiners. The last time they asked me what antibiotic I would use for bacterial meningitis, I said Vicks Vaporub.'

Everyone burst out laughing. 'So why do you continue?' asked Rajeev.

'What do you mean? Just quit medicine? I won't do that because that is exactly what the dean wants… There are too many things riding on my becoming a doctor. Someday the dean will drop dead and then I'll pass Pharmac and go on to third MBBS… Like a boxing match, what matters is who is left standing at the end; not how many punches are thrown. And since I am younger, I think I will outlast him.'

'Can't they terminate you because of repeated failure?' asked Toshi.

'No,' smiled Pheru. 'There is some great rule in the university: only three attempts allowed for first MBBS, but no limits on second and third. I guess they desperately need more doctors… even bad ones.'

Adi felt a twinge of sympathy for Pheru. His involvement in the strike was clearly personal at many levels. He wondered if this knowledge prior to the strike would have made him see things differently.

As though reading Adi's thoughts again, Toshi said, 'I wish all this had not happened. I wish we could be friends like we were before…you know, all of us together. What great times we've had, huh, guys?'

None of them said anything. They pretended to be lost in thought as the taxi drove into the airport. They helped Toshi unload his luggage and arrange it on a trolley. Then Toshi turned to say his goodbyes.

He hugged Pheru and Rajeev. 'Thanks a lot, guys,' he said. 'I'll see you all in a month…maybe more.' Then, smiling fondly, he added, 'Guys, I think we should all make up. I hope when I return, we can all go out like we used to, eat fish vindaloo at Tony's and ogle at the St.Xaviers girls… Huh? What do you say?'

Pheru and Rajeev nodded unconvincingly.

Toshi turned towards Adi and shook his hands. 'Adi, I'll never forget what you did for me during the exams,' he said. Then, pausing for a moment, he said, 'You…you make me feel Indian, Adi.'

Adi smiled and they hugged warmly.

Toshi walked away towards the terminal. He stopped at the entrance and turned back to wave at the three of them. Despite the distance, Adi could see the happiness on his face. Then, he turned around and disappeared into the crowded terminal.

TWENTY

That afternoon, the monsoon arrived in earnest, the first showers quenching the dry earth and quelling a nation's anxiety. At first, high clouds blocked out the sun, bringing immediate relief from the scorching heat of the long, arid summer. Then, underneath this altitudinous cover, dark clouds rolled in stealthily, rumbling and grumbling, suddenly transforming the brightness of the afternoon into an inky dusk. Sudden gales swept in from nowhere, and dust curled into hundreds of eddies, spinning in mid-air like frenzied tops. People ran helter-skelter in preparation for the oncoming deluge, trying to locate the nearest structure that would offer some shelter. A few rounds of lightning and thunder followed, after which it started to pour with a vengeance.

The pearl like droplets sizzled on the dry, parched land, the air suddenly redolent with the smell of wet earth. The rains pockmarked the dusty soil that hastily deliquesced into globs of mud. Like a hundred percussionists suddenly gone berserk, the rapid arrhythmic beats of a million droplets, ricocheting off cement sidewalks, tin roofs, dusty leaves and bare roads, filled the air. In the reflective silence of sudden inactivity, hundreds stood still, admiring the scene as though frozen in time, welcoming the first showers and their promise of plenty. Then, as abruptly as it had begun, the rain petered off and stopped, leaving behind small rivulets, hundreds of muddy puddles and a distant rainbow in the slowly brightening sky.

Adi watched the rains while waiting for Renuka at a small municipal park close to the hospital. The park was dotted with numerous gazebos that provided both protection from the rain and privacy from other people.

Renuka smiled happily upon seeing him. 'This is a surprise. I almost didn't believe it when Praful said you were waiting for me over here,' she said, striding eagerly towards him. 'How are you? Haven't heard from you for a long time.'

Adi held his smile briefly and said, 'I'm fine...but I know someone who is not.'

'Who? Are you talking about me? You have no idea how hard this has—'

'No. I'm talking about Neil.'

The smile on her face vanished and the laugh lines around her eyes melted into an icy stare.

'Neil came to my room some days back,' said Adi. 'He was very upset. Said you had broken up with him and wouldn't even tell him why.'

She remained quiet. Her face grew somber and she shifted her bag from one shoulder to the other for lack of anything better to do.

'Why don't you at least talk to him, Renuka? He deserves an answer!'

'Is that the reason you asked me to come here, Adi? To talk about why I should talk to Neil and give *him* a reason? Why don't *you* tell him the reason, Adi...you know why I stopped seeing him!'

'No, I don't! What are you talking about?'

'Oh, come on, Adi! You know it... Why do I have to spell it out for you?'

'Renuka, I don't know what you mean and I'm tired of drawing conclusions on your behalf. I'm tired of your interpretations of feelings and friendship. I thought Neil was special...you said that, remember?'

'Both of you have been my friends, Adi...and

I initially thought I was in love with Neil...but then you came along and you—'

'No, Renuka! Please, let's at least be honest with each other. I didn't happen to come along! You knew Neil two years before you knew me, and then you came and sought me out. Please don't insult my intelligence. I'm not the naïve, bumbling idiot I once was. At least, I hope you respect me enough to tell me the truth...the truth, as you, and only you know it!'

Renuka's eyes widened with surprise. She started to say something, only to find herself at a loss for words. She stuttered awkwardly, vacillating between denying her actions and defending them. Unable to do either, she opened and shut her mouth a few times. Soon, her malaise dissolved into a troubled silence, and Adi noticed the tears well up in her eyes even before she reached for her handkerchief.

'Will you be upset if I tell you?' she said finally.

'It doesn't matter, Renuka! But if we have to clear the air, we have to be honest with each other. I can't deal with half-truths any more.'

She dabbed her eyes and began in a voice that started to falter almost immediately. 'I met Neil in high school. He was a year senior and we worked on a play together – *The Merchant of Venice*. That was when I got to know him. He was Antonio and I was Portia, and we got close to each other. We spent a lot of time preparing for the play, for an inter-college competition. We were friends for a long time and… I thought he was such a nice guy.

'We started seeing more of each other when our play won a prize and we had to go for a national level competition. Neil was very sweet, very nice…so gentlemanly…and we started to like each other. I don't know how else to explain it, Adi…but I felt very strongly for him and started to get serious about him.'

She paused to dab her eyes some more. 'Do you remember Adi, I told you how my family wanted me to meet some other guy for an unofficial engagement… someone from another business family?'

Adi nodded.

She continued. 'But I loved Neil and I'd ask him repeatedly if he felt the same way. He would say he liked me but how could he be sure that what he felt was love? I was desperate, Adi. My parents were pressuring me so much and I wanted Neil to say that he loved me! I just wanted Neil to be serious about me… I was desperate, Adi. That was when I met you in Anat Hall for the first time… I'm sorry! I'm so sorry!'

Adi stiffened, trying to interpret the apology.

She sniffled. 'I just wanted to get to know you a little bit, Adi...somehow make Neil see...you know...' She started crying, unable to complete the sentence.

'So you wanted to make Neil jealous?' asked Adi. 'Is that why you tried to get close to me and pretended to have an interest?'

She kept crying. 'I'm sorry, Adi. I didn't mean to involve you to the extent that I did... I'm sorry, I'm so sorry!'

Adi stood still, staring at her as she buried her face in her handkerchief, weeping for having wronged him. Yet, his own lack of outrage surprised him. All he felt was a weight lifting off his shoulders.

Her eyeliner left dark smudges on her handkerchief as she searched for the next dry spot on the little piece of cloth. Then she wiped her eyes carefully and said, 'I'm sorry, Adi. I never meant to hurt you. Neil was right, I didn't know what love meant until I met you. I never anticipated falling in love with you, Adi. I stopped seeing Neil for you...for you, Adi!'

Adi didn't reply.

His silence unnerved her. 'What? What happened? Why are you silent, Adi?'

Adi shook his head. 'It's different now, Renuka,' he said.

'What's different?'

'Things change, Renuka.'

'What has changed? I remember you were so upset with me that evening after Rose Day.'

'I... I love someone else.'

She stopped sniffling and stared at him for a few seconds. 'You're not in love,' she said finally. 'You cannot be in love!'

Surprised, Adi scoffed at her. 'I don't think *you* should be telling anyone else about love, Renuka!'

'You're right, Adi,' she said, trying to smile through her tears. 'I shouldn't be telling anyone about being in love...but I know a thing or two about trying to get someone's love. It's Isha, isn't it? I know what you are trying to do, Adi...you are doing the same thing I did to Neil when I wanted his love...you tried to make me see that I did really love you...and you've succeeded Adi...you have. It has worked, Adi.'

'Renuka, that is nonsense!'

'Nonsense? No, no, Adi...don't you see? I did the exact same thing! And I'm not blaming you for it. You've succeeded...you've made your point!'

'I wasn't trying to make a point, Renuka. I'm really in love with...'

'How do you know that you are in love, Adi?

You told me that you loved me, and now you say you don't. How do you know you love her?'

'I never said I loved you!'

She held her distraught eyes on him for a few seconds before rummaging through her purse. She pulled out a card and read, 'I feel wonderful because I've seen the love light in your eyes; and the wonder of it all is that you just don't realize how much I love you!'

Adi stared at his handwriting on the card from Rose Day and recoiled with discomfort.

'What is this?' she demanded, her eyes digging into his face for an explanation. 'You wrote this, didn't you?'

'Yes! I sent it...but I didn't actually...mean...'

'You didn't actually what? You didn't mean it? Then why were you upset that evening? Why?'

'Maybe I meant it then...!'

'*Maybe* you meant it? *Maybe*...Adi? You said you loved me but you cannot even *remember* it now? And you're certain that you are in love *now*?'

Adi felt lost. He struggled to clarify, only to get even more embroiled in doubt. *This revenge was exactly what he had intended that evening after Rose Day!*

He fell silent. Renuka stared at him intently, his silence reinforcing her conviction.

'You don't know you are in love, Adi,' she said. 'I know what you are feeling now. You have feelings for someone because you want to fill the void I left in you. You are doing the same thing I did, when I wanted to feel loved, Adi.'

'No, Renuka! You are wrong! You have no idea!'

'Then tell me, Adi, what is it that you feel which is so different now? You said you loved me, but now you cannot even *remember* saying it? What is it that you call "love" when you think of her but didn't feel when you wrote this card for me? You said you were honest...so tell me, Adi what is it that you call love?'

❧

Renuka's questions haunted Adi as he prepared to meet Isha later that evening. Instead of clarifying matters, the acrimony of their meeting left him even more confused. It also left him desperate to avoid any discussion about his relationship with Isha: the very discussion he had so desperately sought in the isolation of his room just the previous evening.

Isha waved excitedly upon seeing him.

'Hi Adi. I got to conduct two deliveries by myself today. Dr Choksi said that I was a natural

...whatever that means,' she said, grinning uncontrollably.

'Great,' said Adi. 'This calls for a treat.'

'Yeah, let's go for a movie. There is a good movie in Sterling... "Ghost". If we run, we can make it before the evening show starts.'

Adi smiled, agreeing readily to her suggestion, hoping that the horror movie would be a welcome distraction that would thwart any discussion about their relationship.

He was wrong on both counts. The movie was a beautiful love story that made their hearts heavy with ardour as they stepped out of the hall into a night that was still young. Over dinner, she talked about the movie repeatedly, clearly moved by its romantic theme. Adi was deliberately evasive, hoping to avoid getting into a discussion about their relationship. He studied her face whenever her attention was elsewhere. She looked radiantly happy. Unable to participate in her happiness, Adi cursed his restless heart silently.

It was close to 10 p.m. when they walked out towards Marine Drive. The night sky hid the clouds well. The street vendors normally inhabiting the sidewalks had already deserted it. Dark and desolately beautiful, the drive curved along the shore before disappearing into the lights of Malabar Hills at the northern end. A few cars zoomed by, slowly melting into the distance. Adi and Isha splish-splashed along the wet stone paved sidewalks. Along the shoreline the waves crashed angrily against the ledge, their powerful surges brought on by the strong monsoon winds.

Then, without warning, it started to rain. The downpour drenched them before they could locate a shelter. They ran towards a lone taxi standing at the side of the road and knocked on the window. The driver let them in.

Adi followed Isha in and quickly closed the door behind him. The driver turned around to look at them. 'I am off duty,' he informed them in a perfect Bihari accent while sizing them up with the same suspicion he would accord a young couple on the verge of eloping.

'I know, I saw your metre,' Adi replied. 'We were just looking for a place to get away from the rain. Could you drive us to JJ hospital?'

'JJ hospital? Doctor?'

Adi nodded. He was rewarded with immediate respect.

The driver said, 'That area near Grant Road is filled with water. The taxi will get stuck. Anyway, not to worry...just sit in the taxi as long as you want. After the rain stops, I can take you to JJ.'

They thanked him profusely. The driver put some light music on the radio then stretched out on the front seat comfortably. Within a few minutes he started to doze off.

Outside, it continued to pour relentlessly. Huge waves crashed over the ledge, spilling gallons of seawater onto the street. Sheets of water ran down the glass panes, blurring their vision, disfiguring the traffic lights' red and green into a shimmering haze. The rains drummed a steady pitter-patter on the roof of the car, intermittently escalating into a crescendo of intense tapping when the wind bore down in gusts. The car shook when that happened, reminding them of the storm's fury.

As they sat in the taxi, calm, warm, with a lilting melody in the background, a strange sense of security began to envelop Adi. He could feel the knots in his muscles dissolve slowly and the tension in his head started to dissipate. For the first time that evening, he began to relax.

Both of them were soaked. Isha sat next to him, trying to shake the last drops of water from her hair. She had tilted her head sideways, letting her hair fall to one side while running her fingers through it. As she brought her hands down by her side, they touched his.

'Oh…sorry!' said Adi and retracted his hand.

'No, no,' she said, with a shy smile, 'I… I don't mind.'

He smiled nervously, put his hand on hers and gently rubbed the back of her fingers. She didn't protest. Slowly, he turned them over and held her hand tightly in his. He was surprised at how soft they felt. She moved closer to him. Adi eased his arm over her shoulders and intertwined her hands in his. He rubbed them gently, feeling the soft wetness of her long, smooth, graceful fingers. They smiled nervously at each other.

Nobody spoke. The radio crooned on, its beautiful melody filling the space between them. The rain continued unabated outside, lashing at the windowpanes with a ferocity that seemed to challenge them to step out. The waves whipped the rocky ledge. The winds howled, swaying the palm trees, swinging them back and forth as though they were made of rubber. Streetlights and traffic signs swayed in the wind, casting strange patterns on the road below.

Cocooned inside the taxi, Adi felt strangely content and very safe. In this small warm niche, his world was perfect, even if everything outside was crazy and chaotic. He sighed, feeling the warmth of Isha's body next to his.

In the faint glow of the radio dial, she looked breathtakingly lovely. The millions of droplets running down the windowpanes cast soft black and white shadows on her face, rippling on her skin like the gentle caress of a mysterious lover. Her wet face glowed like a beautiful wax doll. Her breasts moved gently with her breath, the stiff nipples straining against the wet fabric of the soggy T-shirt clinging to her chest. Her skin smelled salty-sweet, and he leaned forward to catch its comforting whiff. His heart began to race and he could feel goose pimples sprout on his arms. He felt blood rushing into his pelvis and a familiar tingle dried his mouth. He tightened his grip on her hands and blew softly on her neck.

She turned and looked at him nervously. Her breathing became heavier and her eyes began to droop. Her lips were lightly parted; her breath sweet and moist.

His heart beating wildly he leaned forward to kiss her.

He had got to within millimetres of her lips, when he heard someone shout, 'Stop this drama!'

They jerked away from each other as though struck by lightning.

The taxi driver was glaring at them from the front seat.

'Get out!' he bellowed. 'You call yourselves doctors! Get out of my taxi! Now!'

Trembling, they spilled out of the taxi, willing to brave the elements rather than their embarrassment. They plodded back to the bus-stand in silence, suddenly finding adequate protection from the storm by holding each other's hand.

'I can't believe what just happened,' she said once they were on the bus.

'I should have been watching out for him. I'm sorry,' apologized Adi. 'I just got so over-whelmed that.'

'No, no, don't be sorry about that, Adi... I'm just sorry we couldn't...'

Adi smiled at her and squeezed her hand. She gripped his hand tightly and went back to looking out of the window.

Adi bought the tickets from the bus conductor. Again, she insisted on taking them.

'What do you do with these?' asked Adi.

'I collect them,' she said, smiling mysteriously.

Soon they reached the campus. Hand in hand, they walked slowly towards the ladies' hostel, a light drizzle keeping them company. They sat on the ledge next to the hostel's entrance, unmindful of the soggy clothes that stuck to their bodies. Khadoos Baba shot them a disparaging glance from behind the collapsible gates, then went back to sleep. The clock on the wall above his head claimed it was close to midnight. The area in front was completely deserted. Adi held her hand, not willing to let go just yet.

She appeared to be lost in thought. Then, she said, 'Adi, I have to tell you something that I've never told anyone before.'

Adi nodded, waiting for her to begin.

'I… I have a problem trusting anyone… I'm extremely insecure about people,' she said.

'What do you mean?'

'I find it difficult to get to know people, or let them get to know me. I'm kind of…reserved …if you will. Remember what I said about having only one friend? It's actually my fault, not really my choice.'

'Why?'

She fell silent again. Then, after a few seconds, she sighed and said, 'My father left me about ten years ago.'

'Oh! I'm sorry…What happened? Did he die young?'

'No,' she said with a slow, deliberate effort. 'He left us…and went away.'

Adi could feel the hurt in her voice. He held her hand and rubbed it gently. Tears welled up in her eyes.

'Baba was everything to me when I was little, Adi. He was my world. He bought us books, toys, chocolates...took us to movies, spoilt us behind Ma's back. He was so full of life... constantly singing or playing with us or laughing. Every night before falling asleep, he would hug me, run his hand through my hair and tell me that I was his jaan. That's what he'd call me around the house...his jaan.'

She wiped the tears that had started rolling down her cheeks. Adi put an arm around her shoulder.

'When I was eight, Baba left to go to Germany for some sort of a six-month assignment. Initially, he would call every week from there and tell us how much he was missing us. He would still call me his jaan...jaan I miss you so much, jaan I am so disappointed that I have to stay longer for some more work. But when the six months were over, he didn't come back, and his calls became more and more infrequent. I remember Ma would cry after each call, and when I'd ask why, she'd wipe her face and say that she was missing Baba too and that Baba would show up some day and surprise us. From then on, every time the bell rang, I would expect him to be at the door with his suitcases full of stuff for us from Germany. Or suddenly find him sitting next to my bed after Ma had switched off the light, kiss my forehead and recount my favourite story. But…he never did and two years went by waiting for him to appear. Then his calls stopped completely. Ma never spoke about him and if I asked her anything about him, she'd just pretend she couldn't hear me. She grew so old in those two years, Adi. She had to work so hard to support us. Our life…our life changed so drastically in those years.'

'Then one day, when I was about eleven, I saw Ma packing away all of Baba's clothes. I was so angry with her… I began to fight her…she couldn't throw Baba out of the house! She tried to explain to me that he wasn't coming back…but I didn't believe her and I screamed at her and called her a liar. That's when she started crying and said that he had stayed on in Germany and started a new family there. He wasn't coming back…ever.'

She wiped away the tears that were now freely rolling down her cheeks. She turned to look at Adi and asked, 'Have you ever loved someone so much, Adi, that it hurts to love? Ever wanted something so much that it aches not to have it?

Ever wished for something so badly that your heart refuses to believe it doesn't exist any more? I have, Adi, and it has left a hole in my heart…a hole that fears the hurt that comes with love, long before love itself. I was scared to go out with you, Adi, because I'm scared of falling in love. I knew you had broken up with Renuka and that scared me, Adi. Not that you could have loved her once…but that you could have broken up with someone you loved; that you could feel nothing after feeling so much for someone…and I'm so terrified to love you, Adi!'

Adi stiffened in anticipation. Suddenly, the doubts Renuka had sown in his mind came rushing back.

'Isha,' he began, 'Renuka and I never had anything real. Honestly…for me it was just this feeling of importance, and for her…'

'Did you love her, Adi, or tell her you did?'

Adi was stunned by the sharpness of her question. It knocked his thoughts awry, leaving him unsure about what to say next. He didn't want to lie and he didn't want to tell her the truth.

'How does that matter, Isha… I don't…'

She stared at the disquiet on his face, lowered her head and began to cry.

Adi sighed, preparing to reassure her. He had

to tell her what she wanted to hear. He had to tell her he loved her. He took her hands in his and said, 'Isha, I like you. I really like you... I...'

Adi found himself unable to complete the sentence. He shook his head and tried again. 'Isha, I really like...'

What the hell! What was wrong with him?

He looked away, ran his hand through his hair in an attempt to clear his thoughts. 'Isha, I really like you... I really... I...'

Adi found himself unable to proceed. Shocked at his inability to complete the sentence, he stared at her, tongue-tied. She looked so beautiful, so fragile. He wanted to hold her hand, embrace her tightly and tell her he loved her and he would keep loving her forever.

But he couldn't. He just couldn't.

Suddenly Adi heard someone calling out his name. Surprised, he turned around to see Sam running towards them. As Sam got closer, Adi noticed that he was crying.

'Adi...he's dead!' screamed Sam. 'Toshi... Toshi is dead! His plane crashed. He's dead!'

TWENTY-ONE

Grief hung over the hostel like an invisible shroud. Everyone was awake, milling around on the ground floor in dismay and disbelief, waiting for any further news. The sight of anyone walking up the driveway brought some hope. Maybe Toshi had missed his flight in Calcutta...maybe there had been a mistake and it was some other flight to Dimapur that had crashed. But hope started to fade as time passed.

Toshi's flight had reached Calcutta on time and after the scheduled stopover of a few hours, had taken off for Dimapur. Then, on its descent into Dimapur, the pilot had lost control of the aircraft and had crashed into the mountainside. All ninety passengers, including the crew, were dead. Rescue efforts were soon called off because of the bad weather. A preliminary survey of the disaster site had shown that there were unlikely to be any survivors.

The news reached the hostel when officials from Indian Airlines came looking for Jagdeep, whose address Toshi had listed on the reservation form as the next of kin while buying his tickets. Unable to find him, they left a message with the canteen manager, who realized they were talking about the guy who had given him a hug that morning. He informed Sam who immediately called the airline office, hoping that there had been a miscommunication. Only when he replaced the telephone receiver, numb with disbelief, did it dawn on everyone that Toshi was actually dead.

Adi didn't bother to put on the lights on entering his room. The darkness surrounding him was resonant with the pain in his heart. The night air was cool and the beautiful scent of the jasmine flowers outside wafted in lazily.

A thousand images of Toshi flashed in his head like iridescent flashbulbs. Smiling, laughing, cracking a joke, strumming his guitar, studying late into the night. Lazing around on his bed talking to Adi; lying on it, weak with malaria. Adi remembered his fear the night before the exam and his joy at finally being able to go home. He could feel Toshi's hug from the

morning and his handshake still lingered on his
fingers. The last image of Toshi, waving from
the gates of the airport terminal before
disappearing into the crowd, haunted him.

Adi started to cry. He buried his face in his
hands and muffled his sobs, feeling the tears of
pain, loneliness, helplessness and insecurity
slide down his face. He cried for his friend, he
cried for himself, he cried wondering why
everything in his life was so topsy-turvy.

There was a knock on his door and someone
said softly from outside, 'Adi? Are you asleep?'

Quickly wiping away his tears, Adi opened
the door. It was Jagdeep.

'Hi, Adi,' he said. 'How are you feeling?'

'I'm okay,' Adi replied.

Jagdeep shook his head. 'I… I still can't
believe it, man.'

Adi tried hard to contain his tears. 'Think
about his parents, man. What must be going
through their minds? Losing a twenty-year-
old…and they haven't seen him in the last two
years.'

Jagdeep nodded. Then, after a pause, he said,
'I am planning to go to Nagaland to meet his
parents, Adi. Do you want to come with me?'

Adi looked at him, surprised. 'You're not
serious, are you?' he said. 'We can talk to them,

and write to them...but Nagaland is so far away, man.'

'Yeah... I know. But Toshi was a good friend and I want to go and meet his parents... I'll go alone if I have to, but I was wondering if someone would like to come with me.'

Jagdeep's determination surprised Adi. He had never known Jagdeep to be particularly close to Toshi. But the idea of going to visit Toshi's parents in Nagaland seemed not only foolish but foolhardy.

The one-way train journey would take four or five days, for they'd have to skirt the entire western and northern borders of Bangladesh to get to the 'other side'. Getting a reservation on the train would be the first challenge. With the onset of the monsoon, the Brahmaputra and its tributaries would inevitably flood the North-east, wipe out a few bridges and further complicate matters. Besides, Assam and Nagaland were racked by insurgency, with daily reports of rebels and the Indian Army killing each other. And even if he wanted to go, there was Isha. Their relationship stood at a crucial juncture, one that demanded his time and attention, both of which would be poorly served if he ran off on an ill-conceived, emotionally charged journey. Any which way he looked at it, the trip seemed like an invitation to disaster. He shook his head 'no.' Jagdeep accepted with a reluctant sigh and left.

Before shutting his door Adi looked in the direction of Toshi's room. In the dim light of the corridor he was shocked to see that the door was open!

Was Toshi alive? For a moment, happiness flooded his heart.

Maybe it was all a bad dream...and Toshi would be sitting in his room strumming his guitar!

He rushed to the room and looked inside. Pheru and Sam were rummaging through Toshi's stuff and looked up at Adi's excited face with surprise.

Adi groaned, rudely reminded that Pheru now shared Toshi's room. As he stood there broken-hearted, feeling his expectations crumble, his eyes fell on the maroon-coloured diary with Toshi's name printed on the cover.

It was the diary Toshi's mother had given him to chronicle his life in Bombay.

Adi stepped inside and picked it up. He began leafing through its contents. The memory of Toshi, sitting at his desk and filling out page after page late into the night, came flooding back to him. He held the diary in his hands and caressed it gently. Then, wiping his tears, he decided to give the diary to Toshi's mother personally, and tell her how proud he was of her.

❧

Adi mulled over how best to explain to Isha why it was so important for him to meet Toshi's family. He practised his lines again and again, recalling the time when Toshi had explained the diary's significance to Adi. He hoped Isha would understand that they would have to leave the discussion about their relationship for later, until after his return. When he got back...if he got back.

She came down promptly when the guard at the ladies' hostel called out her name. Her eyes were red and puffy. She sat opposite him, staring steadfastly at her feet, periodically dabbing her eyes with a yellow handkerchief. For the first time Adi felt self-conscious in her presence, unsure of what characterized their relationship – their physical proximity or their emotional distance.

'Isha,' he began softly, 'I am planning to visit Toshi's parents in Nagaland.'

She drew in a sharp breath. Tears welled up in her eyes as she looked at him uncertainly.

Then, trying hard to muster a brave smile, she said, 'I think you should go, Adi...he was, after all, a good friend.'

The tears she had restrained so far began flowing down her cheeks.

Adi looked at her in astonishment. With a single sentence, she had wiped away all his insecurity. 'And about last night...' he began.

'Shhh...' she whispered, laying her forefinger gently across her lips and smiling through her tears. 'Don't worry about that. We have all the time in the world to talk about us. When are you planning to leave?'

❦

Around noon, Adi knocked on Jagdeep's door. Jagdeep opened it and looked at Adi curiously.

'I'm coming with you to meet Toshi's parents,' said Adi.

Jagdeep smiled. Opening the door wider he ushered Adi in and said, 'Great. Now we have six people.'

Adi was surprised. 'Six? Who else is coming with us?'

'Rajeev, Harsha, Sam and Pheru. With you and me that makes six!' said Jagdeep, placing his clothes in a small, brown travel bag.

Adi's enthusiasm dampened upon hearing the list of names. He squirmed at the thought of having to spend almost a fortnight together with the others, confined to the small train cubicles and depending on each other for everything when he couldn't spend ten minutes with them alone in a room. He began to seriously reconsider his decision to undertake this trip. Trying to hide his discomfort, Adi asked, 'Doesn't Pheru have his Pharmac exam in ten days?'

'He does...and if he doesn't pass this time, he's done for,' said Jagdeep.

'What do you mean?'

'Well, he has nowhere to stay. Now that Toshi is dead, he'll have to give up the room. If Pheru flunks, his medical career is pretty much over since he won't have a place to stay in the hostel any more.'

'So why is he going?' scoffed Adi. 'Pheru should stay, especially since this time he has studied so hard...he is better prepared than ever. Instead of going to visit Toshi's parents he should try to pass his exam.'

Jagdeep stopped arranging his stuff and looked at Adi. 'I don't know, Adi. Pheru is a strange guy. He said something about this being his fault...his bad luck or something. I guess he does things that just *feel* right. You know...from the heart, not the head. Like you, Adi…staying overnight with Toshi to help him with his Anatomy practicals. It must have just *felt* like the correct thing to do, right?'

Adi nodded silently.

Jagdeep smiled and said, 'By the way Adi, can you arrange for the tickets?'

Adi busied himself in planning the trip. Even on a map, the journey looked long and complicated. The first, and probably the easiest leg, would be the train journey from Bombay to Calcutta on the Calcutta Express. The word 'express' was misleading. It was the slowest of the trains that plied the route, covering the distance in thirty-six hours. While that was the reason Adi managed to get reservations at such short notice, its scheduled and unscheduled stops along the way, slave to the whims of its driver, could easily add another six to twelve hours to the itinerary.

From Calcutta, a twenty-four-hour journey on the Kamrup Express to Guwahati would be the second leg of their expedition. A six-hour bus ride from Guwahati to Dimapur – the third section of the trip – would launch the final phase of their journey: a bus ride to Mokukchung. If all his calculations about the timings worked as planned, they would reach Mokukchung in four and a half days. Given the vagaries of Mother Nature and the whims of the Indian Railways, Adi realized that it would take nothing short of a miracle for them to complete their journey on time.

Their train was scheduled to leave for Calcutta at 9.30 that evening.

Adi hurried back to the hostel to pack. He sent word to Jagdeep about their travel plans and that he would meet them directly at the railway station. He put his belongings into one large backpack and carefully packed Toshi's diary amongst it.

Then he rushed over to meet Isha.

The guard called her name a couple of times, but she didn't appear. After waiting impatiently for half an hour, Adi left a note for her with the guard, informing her that he was heading for the railway station.

Adi met Sam, Harsha and Rajeev just outside the station. They exchanged cursory nods, maintaining a superficial civility before heading towards the train in silence. Adi located their seats in the middle of the bogie. He placed his bag on the bunk above and sat next to the window, gazing through the red-coloured window bars at the huge platform.

The station was abuzz with activity as people rushed about, looking for their compartments. They compared the numbers on the bogies to the small slips of paper in their hands, nodding with satisfaction when they matched. Rushing into the carriage they would quickly occupy their berths, spreading out anything handy to earmark the maximum space they could covet. Satisfied with their conquest, they would turn their attention to the day's newspaper or a film magazine, shifting impatiently every so often when the train didn't show any signs of moving.

Soon Pheru joined them, towing a huge suitcase.

'What is in that huge suitcase?' asked Rajeev. 'We are not going on a vacation, Pheru.'

'Still...' panted Pheru, 'I like to be prepared.'

'Where is Jagdeep? I thought he was with you, Pheru,' asked Sam.

'Jagdeep is going to fly to Dimapur,' said Pheru.

'What?' asked Rajeev. 'When did this happen? I didn't know he was that rich... Flights are so expensive.'

Pheru began to laugh. 'God knows what is wrong with that Sardarji,' he said. 'Indian Airlines announced that they will give one free round trip ticket to anyone related to the victim, to visit family. So, Jagdeep went to the Airlines office to tell them that Toshi was like a brother to our sardar. He claimed that that is why Toshi had listed him as the local next of kin.'

All of them burst out laughing imagining the look on the airline agent's face when Jagdeep, with the huge turban on his head, claimed that Toshi, a Naga Christian, was his brother.

'Pheru, don't you have your Pharmac exam in ten days?' asked Harsha.

Pheru nodded. 'They'll fail me anyway,' he said. 'Saala, this time I had actually studied, man. I'm sure I could pass if the bastard dean didn't interfere. But, you know, it would feel worse to fail this time…so I just won't show up. This time I won't give the dean the pleasure of seeing me fail at *his* hands…this time, I'll fail at *my* hands. And this failure is dedicated to the memory of our dear friend… Toshi.'

Outside, regular announcements of trains arriving and departing added to the din. Latecomers rushed for their bogies, their adroit manoeuvring across the platform with a pile of luggage in tow, defying all laws of physics. Passengers still idling on the platform began hugging members of their farewell entourage, warmly exchanging promissory nods to meet again soon. Animated porters, unconcerned that only a few minutes remained before the train set off, loaded huge sacks of cargo with practised ease.

As the giant moon-faced watch at the end of the platform turned to 9.29, the train jerked suddenly, as though rehearsing its intention to start moving. A green light shone from outside the guard's cabin. Adi craned his neck, straining to stretch his sight beyond what the bars would allow.

Suddenly, he spotted Isha at the edge of the platform, running towards them.

The train whistled and began to move. Adi got up and rushed out towards the platform, ignoring the look of surprise on the other guys' faces. He ran towards her, waving his hands frantically to catch her attention.

'Isha... I'm so happy you could come,' he said, when she caught up with him.

She smiled at him, trying hard to catch her breath.

'Sorry, I was late...bad traffic. Anyway, the train is leaving,' she said between breaths, 'you'd better get back on it.'

'I miss you already, Isha.'

She smiled. 'Here,' she said, and handed him a plastic bag.

'What is this?'

'It has some stuff inside,' she said. 'Some money, some magazines, some food and a bunch of postcards...write to me often. Run now, or you will miss the train.'

Adi grabbed the handrails next to the door and jumped onto the steps at the entrance to the compartment. She walked fast, trying to keep up with the train now slowly chugging out of the station.

Then she said, 'There is also a sealed envelope inside, Adi. Don't open it now...open it later, when you think you are ready; when you know what you feel.'

Adi was surprised. He looked inside the bag.

'The plain envelope?' he asked.

She broke into a jog to keep up with the train. 'Yes. Promise me you won't open it otherwise?'

Adi looked at her questioningly. The train had gathered speed and Isha had to run to keep up. Running and dodging the crowds simultaneously proved difficult. The distance between them began to grow.

'What is in it?' shouted Adi.

The train whistled loudly, drowning out her words. She tried to shout but this time the distance thwarted her voice. She slowed down and soon stopped running.

He watched as she stood at the edge of the platform, waving goodbye till she turned into a tiny black speck, indistinguishable from all the other specks that moved randomly in his field of vision.

TWENTY-TWO

By the time Adi woke up the next morning, the train was moving fast, cutting its way through small villages and farmland. He climbed down from his berth, yawning and stretching, trying to find his slippers to go to the bathroom. Rajeev was awake; he glanced at Adi and then looked away.

Adi stared at the scenery beyond his window. Hundreds of small paddy fields stretched for miles like a giant green patchwork quilt. Tender saplings stood in ankle-deep water, shivering in the wind. Men and women worked side by side, implanting the saplings into neat rows of green while their children splashed and jumped around in the pools of muddy water. Buffaloes roamed lazily in the fields nearby, periodically whipping their tails to chase off the crows conveniently taking free rides on their pliant backs.

It was cloudy and a pleasant breeze blew in from outside. Adi returned from the bathroom to find most of the others awake. The train was beginning to slow down for an approaching station. Sam stretched out his arms and yawned lazily.

'Sam,' said Rajeev, 'you better go and brush, man. There's a station coming up where we can have breakfast.'

Sam looked at him through sleep-filled eyes and said, 'I don't brush.'

'What do you mean, you don't brush?' asked Rajeev.

'I don't brush my teeth... Haven't done it for the last six years.'

The others stared at Sam, their faces crinkled with disgust. Sam saw the look and smiled. 'What? My teeth are as good as yours... Animals never need to brush; they do fine.'

'Sam, the last time I checked...I was human,' said Pheru.

They started laughing. Sam joined in the laughter. 'Go ahead,' he said. 'Make those corporations richer as they continue their mass fraud on millions of human beings, convincing them to use their misleading products... I won't brush and I won't let them perpetrate this fraud on my family!'

'Well, you'll never have that problem, Sam. No woman will let you come close enough to her to start a family!' said Pheru. Sam remained unmoved by the laughter.

As they entered Akola station, Adi checked his timetable to see if the train was on schedule. To his consternation, he realized that they should have been through Akola two hours ago. He cursed the slow-moving train and wondered if he should inform the others. After hesitating for a few minutes, he cleared his throat and said, 'We are behind…by two hours. Now we have only an hour's margin to catch the connecting train in Calcutta. If this train slows down any more, we'll miss the connection.'

'Maybe it will make up time,' said Sam. 'It seems to be travelling fast.'

'This train is always slow, Sam. If it was the Gitanjali, then maybe it could speed up, but not the Calcutta Express. In fact, sometimes they will let the next day's Gitanjali pass this one.'

No one else offered an opinion. Adi returned to staring out of the window, unsure if the others were deliberately ignoring him.

The train slowed into the platform and came to a halt. They waited for the initial rush of porters and passenger to subside before getting off to look for breakfast. Harsha volunteered to stay back and keep an eye on their luggage. Train stations were infamous as popular hunting grounds for petty thieves, and the price of a moment's inattention could be a suitcase.

Adi returned shortly, carrying a cup of tea for Harsha. He handed Harsha the earthen cup with a smile. Harsha, however, looked solemn and took the cup from him silently.

Adi sat opposite Harsha and looked out of the window at the crowds on the platform. People milled about patiently, waiting for the next train to arrive. Porters, in bright red uniforms, carried large sacks of freight all over the platform. Stray dogs hopped about effortlessly from one track to another, looking for scraps of food or the unexpected generosity of a stranger. Adi glanced at his watch, feeling his frustration rise when the train showed no signs of moving.

As he looked around idly, he noticed Harsha steal surreptitious glances at the top bunk.

Suddenly a couple of men came rushing down the passageway of their compartment. They looked very agitated as they scanned the faces of the passengers, looked under the bunks and knocked on the door of the bathroom at the end of the compartment. Intermittently, they called out a name.

Adi noticed Harsha looking up at the top bunk nervously.

One of the men reached their coupe and surveyed their faces rapidly. He stood up on tiptoe to look at the top bunk. His face lit up with excitement and he called out to the others. Three other men rushed to join him.

One of them began shouting angrily, addressing someone on the bunk, right above Adi's head. His face was flush with anger as he gestured animatedly, promising swift retribution unless the person came down willingly. His shouts drew an excited crowd, all eager to witness some act of instant public justice. Like everyone else, Adi wondered who was hiding and what, if anything, he had stolen. He craned his neck to get a better look.

His jaw dropped when he saw a young woman sitting up reluctantly.

She looked too well dressed to be a thief, and an arm full of red glass bangles along with the thick coat of orange vermilion on her forehead suggested she was a young bride. Her hair was dishevelled from being crammed into the tight space, and tears made black tramlines from the kajal around her eyes. A fine layer of dried blood caked the scratches on the back of her thin forearms.

She sat up whimpering at the sight of her tormentors.

The man who had found her was beside himself with fury. He lunged for her foot. She pulled her legs away and cowered in fear, sobbing uncontrollably. Cursing her loudly, he stood on the lower bunk, readying for another attempt to grab her.

Suddenly, Harsha stood up and blocked his path.

'Get out of our compartment!' snarled Harsha, pointing towards the exit.

The man was shocked to see Harsha, and, for one instant, backed away. Then, collecting his wits, he explained that she was his wife and she was trying to run away from home; he simply wanted to take her back.

'Saale! Harami!' shouted Harsha. 'You beat your wife, you beat your child. Get out now…nahin to aisa maaroonga!' Harsha broke into Hindi to explain what he would do if the man didn't leave her alone.

The man backed away, a look of disbelief on his face. The crowd fell silent, savouring the sudden escalation in the drama. Only the young woman's sobs grew louder in a constrained show of defiance.

One of the men looked much older. He

stepped forward and addressed Harsha. 'Beta,' he said, 'this is between a husband and wife – why do you care? Just let them go home with their child.'

'Why?' mocked Harsha. 'So that he can beat her up when he gets drunk?'

The old man backed off, muttering angrily under his breath.

The crowds were agog with curiosity. They piled over one another, blocking the aisles completely, trying to get a glimpse of the action.

The men looked at each other uncertainly. They traded irate stares and self-righteous nods before turning to glare at Harsha. 'Ehhh, bhadwa! Who do you think you are? Move or we'll skin you alive. You don't know who you're dealing with!'

Harsha stood his ground undaunted, silently seething with anger.

Rajeev looked around nervously. 'Harsha, you could get into trouble, man…just let her go with them!' he hissed.

'No! I won't!' Harsha snapped back.

Harsha's dissent shocked Rajeev. He turned to address the others. 'Guys, talk some sense into him! What is wrong with you, Harsha?'

The others looked at each other, unsure of what to say. Harsha meanwhile continued to stare at the men ferociously, unmindful of anything or anyone. His hands were curled into tight fists of rage and his round pudgy face was bursting with indignation. His meagre frame was trembling with anger, his eyes locked on the husband like a laser beam.

Harsha's courage amazed Adi.

Rajeev turned to Harsha again. 'Let her go, Harsha! It is for her own good, man!'

Harsha didn't even bother to acknowledge Rajeev.

Rajeev shouted angrily, 'What is your problem, Harsha? Who is she to you, huh? Why do *you* care?'

'Because nobody cared about my mother and me! Nobody!' Harsha shouted back, wiping away angry tears. 'I won't let anyone beat up this girl or her child, ever again! Saala... I'll cut off the hand that tries to touch her!'

A sudden hush followed his outburst: the source of Harsha's strength abundantly apparent.

Adi stood up. Putting his arm around Harsha's shoulder, he faced the men. Sam and Pheru followed suit. Seeing the others, Rajeev joined in.

The train hadn't moved an inch. The altercation brought the train conductor out of his cabin. Seeing him, the men started complaining that a group of young boys were refusing to let a husband see his wife and threatening to beat them up.

The conductor, a portly man with a thin moustache and a soft pudgy face, surveyed Rajeev, Pheru, Harsha, Adi and Sam suspiciously. Dressed in shorts, slippers and crumpled shirts, they were a sorry sight – one that did nothing to inspire any faith in the conductor's eyes. His eyes narrowed, and, placing his hands on his hips, he said, 'Tell me, why I shouldn't call the Railway Police and have you arrested?'

Before anyone could reply, Pheru whipped out his college ID card and flashed it in front of the conductor's nose. Then, in chaste, accented English he said, 'We are doctors from Grant Medical College, Bombay. We *would* like you to call the police. We want to report these men who have been threatening and abusing this young girl. You can ask her...she will testify. According to Indian Penal Code 324 section 2 clause 9, these men should be arrested for this crime...so please go ahead and call the police!'

Taking a cue from Pheru, the rest of them dug out their IDs and flashed it for the conductor's benefit, each wondering what was written under Indian Penal Code 324 section 2 clause 9.

The poor conductor was so impressed by Pheru's authority not only over medicine, morals and the Indian Penal Code, but also over the English language, that he immediately took off his cap and started addressing Pheru as 'Doctor sahab'. Pheru nodded with an authoritarian importance that completely belied the fact that none of them was qualified enough to prescribe aspirin, and 'Doctor sahab' had spent five years trying to pass the exam that taught him the properties of that drug.

The conductor verified with the girl that she didn't want to return with the men. Then he turned around and gave the men a severe tongue-lashing for stopping the train and causing a disturbance. He offered them the choice of getting off the train quietly or having a chat with the Railway Police.

The men got off silently, their eyes burning with anger. They stood on the platform, huddled in conspiratorial hatred, shooting loathsome glances towards the compartment. The crowds dispersed reluctantly, turning back every few minutes to confirm the conclusion of the drama. The conductor returned to his cabin, and after five minutes, the train began to move.

Adi checked his watch; they had lost another hour.

❧

The young woman's name was Aruna. At twenty, she had run away from home to get married to the charming young man who had promised her the world. Within a few weeks of marriage, she realized that he enjoyed beating her every night. She had borne this for a year, and they even had a child together. She had hoped this would make him less violent. Unfortunately, it was not to be. Instead, he beat her even more. His beatings had driven her to attempt suicide, but without much success, when the rat poison that the street peddler had sold her turned out to be fake. She had written to her father, but her husband had found the note before she could post it, and beaten her mercilessly that night. Finally, after waiting for a few months to regain her strength and having consulted the astrological charts to predict a successful escape, she had climbed through her bathroom window on the fourth floor, down the drainage pipes, while her fifteen-month-old boy slept peacefully in the sling she had strapped to her back. After successfully negotiating the most difficult part, her carefully planned escape had nearly been undone when her brother-in-law had heard the loud squeak from the old hinges on the house gate, and raised the alarm. She had run halfway across town to reach the station, just as the Calcutta express was pulling in. She had clambered aboard the train to try and reach Bhilai where her parents lived – a station fortuitously on their route.

Adi marvelled at the merits of the astrological chart: not only had the train's two- hour delay served her well, amongst the hundreds of passengers on the train, she had chosen to ask Harsha for help. Harsha, recognizing the look of terrified desperation on her face, had immediately conspired with her to evade her hunters.

She sat silently on one corner of the lower bunk, the object of prying eyes and hushed debate in the compartment. She was pretty and seemed fairly well educated. Her body was youthfully slender; her face long and graceful, with intense dark eyes and full lips. A smudged bindi adorned her forehead and a linear streak of orange vermilion disappeared among the roots of her long black hair. She wore a red and green sari, and the matching blouse hinted at an ample bosom. She sat encircling her knees with her arms, resting her head in its folds, occasionally burying her face in them to sob quietly.

A baby's wails suddenly disturbed the quiet in the coupe. She perked up and rapidly climbed up to the top bunk to tend to him. She stayed up there, nursing him for a while. Eventually, when no sound was forthcoming, Adi looked up to see that both mother and son were fast asleep.

❧

Pheru raised the obvious topic. 'What will she do in Bhilai?' he asked.

'Her parents are there, right?' said Harsha. 'They'll help her.'

'Yeah, man,' said Sam. 'I hope they go after the husband and take him to court. The son-of-a-bitch needs to be beaten up in the jails to set him straight. I think they should just cut off his balls.'

'Yeah, but socially she is really screwed,' said Rajeev.

'Softly!' admonished Harsha. 'She may hear you!'

'What do you mean she is socially screwed?' Sam asked Rajeev.

'You know...she'll have trouble getting back

into society. She's married and has a kid and has run away,' he explained.

'Rajeev, I can't believe you would say such a thing,' said Sam. 'For all your modernity and your latest fashions, your mind is still in the eighteenth century.'

'I'm just stating the facts, man,' replied Rajeev. 'It doesn't matter what I feel…the status of women in India is still second class. And married women…third class. A married woman with a child who has run away from home…no class. You think she'll find it easy to get back into society? She'll be lucky if her parents take her back. You cannot deny that her future is not going to be a rosy 'lived-happily-ever-after' even if you choose to believe in it. Don't lecture me…I don't care about it at all!'

'You may not care, Rajeev,' said Pheru, 'and it's because you don't that society is the way it is. But there are people like Harsha who see things differently and will give her the chance she needs and deserves.'

Harsha smiled.

'Yeah, Harsha obviously sees it differently,' joked Sam. 'She is cute!'

They laughed.

Rajeev chuckled. 'Aha! Now I understand why Harsha stood up for her. Hmm, very smart, Harsha.'

Harsha smiled but didn't say anything.

'I think her helplessness adds to her sex appeal,' said Rajeev.

'Rajeev, you bloody pervert!' whispered Sam. 'And you think I'm dirty because I don't brush my teeth?'

'Shh...!' hissed Harsha. 'She is coming down!'

They stared at her climbing down from the upper berth. For an instant, her sari caught the edge of a bunk on her way down, providing the onlookers with a flash of her firm thighs. They exchanged naughty looks before prying their eyes away and grinning slyly at each other.

She returned to her seat at the edge of the bunk, this time with her son in her lap.

The baby's back was turned towards them. She held the child close to her face and started playing with him. She mollycoddled him, gurgling childish gibberish while rubbing her face on his chest and tummy, and tickling him into throes of laughter. She played with him, laughing and smiling as though, for those few moments, she and her child existed without a shred of concern in a picture-perfect world. Then, smiling proudly, she turned her boy to face them.

The little boy had a silly senseless grin on his face. His eyes wandered in their sockets, as though unable to tether themselves to anything purposeful in their field of vision. Even at fifteen months, his neck was unable to support the weight of his head, and lolled to one side, sending clear white saliva dribbling out of the corner on to her sari. A few deformed teeth showed from behind the thin lips that showed no signs of forming any meaningful words.

Steadying him with her hands, she peeked out from behind his head, smiling at the five of them with immeasurable pride.

For a few seconds none of them could react. Then smiling briefly, they hurriedly looked away, their overwhelming shame feeling like a stinging slap on their faces.

❧

By the time they crossed Gondia, their train was already four hours behind schedule. Adi worried constantly about the possibility of missing the connecting Kamrup express and having to make the twenty-four-hour journey to Guwahati in the unreserved compartment of some other train.

It was past ten at night when their train slowed down to a halt for no apparent reason. When Adi looked out through the window, he could see little other than a set of parallel tracks separated by a small ditch, full of rocks and brush. His concern about these unscheduled stop-starts adding to the overall delay was lost on the others who sat huddled together, absorbed in a game of cards.

After a few minutes, Adi saw the headlights of a train light up the neighbouring tracks. The reason for their stop suddenly became clear to him. They were letting another train go ahead of theirs to use the same tracks. Adi grimaced with irritation. But his irritation turned to anger when he noticed on the sides of the compartments, printed in English and Hindi, the name of the overtaking train. It was the Gitanjali.

'I can't believe it!' he fumed. 'They are letting the Gitanjali go ahead of us! That train left Bombay this morning...and we have been travelling for almost twenty-four hours!'

The others didn't react, reserving their attention for the card game.

Suddenly, Adi noticed that the Gitanjali was slowing down too. Then it came to a complete stop on the parallel track.

Adi jumped at the chance. 'Guys!' he shouted, 'let's cross over to the Gitanjali! This may be our only chance to make the Kamrup Express from Calcutta!'

The others looked at him as though they had just woken up from sleep.

'Adi, there is no platform...we are in the middle of nowhere!' protested Sam. 'If we get off this train and don't make it to the Gitanjali, and then this train leaves, we'll be stranded in the middle of nowhere!'

'That's why we need to go now! No arguments, Sam! Let's go! Now!'

They began gathering their belongings, now lying scattered all over the coupe. Adi couldn't find his shirt while Sam looked desperately for his shoes. Pheru had the toughest time trying to repack his suitcase. Hurriedly they began heading towards the exit.

As he turned to leave, Adi's eyes fell on Aruna. She was staring at them from her berth, her eyes filled with anxiety.

Adi groaned. He had completely forgotten about her. He tried to explain the urgency in their situation. He explained that she would reach Bhilai in another three hours, and since the Gitanjali wouldn't stop in Bhilai, she should stay on this train with her child.

She nodded, unconvinced, and looked at Harsha.

Harsha waited for the others to leave the bogie. He walked over towards Aruna, took out a handful of money from his wallet and handed it over to her. Then he picked up Aruna's son, held him tightly and kissed him on the cheeks. Aruna began to cry.

Harsha handed her son back and said, 'You are so brave, Aruna. I...I wish my mother had been this brave. But both of us were so scared of him!'

Adi shouted from outside, 'Harsha! Chal yaar...let's go!'

Harsha picked up his bags to make the mad dash to the other train.

As they ran across the brush and rock-filled space in between the two trains in slippers and undershirts, the Gitanjali started to move. They searched desperately for a compartment with unlocked doors. Unable to find any, they clambered onto the guard's cabin. The guard was in the midst of a meal and came out protesting their unauthorized entry on a 'superfast' train. Despite his objections they clambered on quickly, fairly certain that the man wouldn't dare throw five young guys onto the tracks in the middle of nowhere.

As the Gitanjali started pulling away slowly, they could see Aruna staring at them from a window, tightly holding onto the iron grille that spanned the opening. They waved goodbye.

Adi's heart was heavy with the thought of her uncertain future, and yet something in him rejoiced at her liberation. And he refused to believe that those tears rolling down her cheeks were anything other than tears of joy at her newfound freedom.

The ticket collector let them into the main bogies after charging them a 'superfast fee'. Sam's sudden crying spell as he relayed the tragic story of Toshi's death evoked neither sympathy nor a discount. They managed to find two empty berths on the train and took turns to sleep.

When it was Adi's turn to be awake, he started writing his first letter to Isha.

≸⦿

Dear Isha,

I miss you.

Sometimes I cannot believe that we have begun this trip to meet Toshi's parents. Nagaland almost seems like another country, doesn't it? And then, travelling with this group that I can barely talk to! But it's been surprisingly calm...in fact it is turning out to be quite an adventure already.

Harsha helped save a young girl from her abusive husband. I was so impressed by his courage. He stood there and faced four men with nothing but the courage of his convictions...just like Atticus. I think his act not only won the girl's freedom, but his own redemption from his past. I had underestimated him, Isha. I thought of him as nothing more than Rajeev's unabashed fan. But I was wrong.

I don't know what will become of the girl or her mentally retarded child as she makes her way alone, but I would like to believe that her story has a happy ending. Sometimes, I wish I had a magic wand that I could wave and right all the things that are wrong in this world. But shouldn't God be doing that?

I am just rambling on...

Not much space in these postcards to write more, but there is so much more to write. So let me say what needs to be said urgently: I miss you very much.

Adi.

PS: I haven't opened the envelope yet, and the laddoos were delicious.

TWENTY-THREE

The Gitanjali, which makes a two-thousand-kilometre journey in twenty-eight hours, is a super-fast train only by the standards of the Indian Railways. Travelling across the widest part of the country, its reputation as a super-fast makes it a ready object of abuse at the hands of the proletariat. From the politician protesting the denial of a party ticket in the upcoming election, to the local college students protesting a tough examination, the Gitanjali is a sitting duck for the 'sit- down-on-the-tracks' form of protest called rail roko.

It was their ill-luck the next day, when a bunch of slogan-shouting, flag-carrying men, in white kurta-pajamas and open black sandals, decided to protest the vicissitudes of the local train timings by sitting in front of the Gitanjali's tracks, just outside Howrah. It was 5 o'clock in the afternoon and the train hadn't budged in the thirty minutes Adi had spent listening to the slogans emanating from the group in front. Their connecting train to Guwahati would depart in another half-hour. From their compartment, Adi could see the beginnings of the Howrah station platforms, the length of three or four soccer fields away.

Adi cursed his luck and rued the invention of brakes on the train: the Gitanjali could otherwise have resolved the nuisance of thoughtless public protest so effectively.

'Guys,' he said, 'let's pack our stuff and walk to the station. That is the only way we can make it to the Kamrup Express on time... It leaves at 5.30.'

The others looked at their watches uncertainly, as though delaying the decision would alter the train's inertia.

'Come on, guys!' urged Adi. 'We don't have much time!'

He picked up his bag and got off the train. One by one, the others followed suit.

They began walking along the rock-filled gutters next to the tracks. It had rained some hours ago and an angry, white sun beat down on them from a clear blue sky. The winds had died, leaving the muggy air around them in rigor mortis. Adi's handkerchief fought a losing battle against the sweat sprouting on his forehead. Pheru was having a hard time keeping his bulky suitcase above the stagnant water next to the tracks. But Sam, being stocky and overweight, suffered the most. He stopped every so often, rested his hands on his knees, and panted like he was breathing his last. Within a few minutes, all of them were soaked in sweat.

They were about a hundred yards from the platform when the Gitanjali's huge wheels started to moan and squeal, as though protesting being awakened from the restful nap. Surprised, Adi looked ahead. The train's path was now clear. In a fitting testament to the agitators' dedication to their cause, the demonstrators had dispersed spontaneously because it was past 5 p.m. — time to head home for dinner.

They clambered back onto the train, thanking their stars that they wouldn't have to make the rest of the journey on foot. Their clothes stuck to their bodies in a sticky salty mess. Adi looked at his watch again. It was 5:15 p.m. He sighed imagining what awaited them.

At five every afternoon, Howrah station turns into a madhouse, filled with local commuters eager to get home. Chaos reigns supreme for the next couple of hours, as the timings and platforms of local trains are displayed on giant boards or announced over jarring loudspeakers. People mill about in confusion, trying to decipher the message in those frazzled announcements. Long-distance travellers walk about with their cartloads of luggage, trying to sort through the jumble of train names and numbers. Beggars tag behind them interminably: the desire for good auspices before undertaking a long journey usually brings out the altruistic best in people. Piles of freight – from cotton bales to fresh fish – are pushed about the platform with scant regard for anyone in their path. Stray cows, goats and dogs wander about at will, their acclimatization to such chaos evident in their lackadaisical canter.

Adi knew that it would take nothing short of a miracle for them to make their way across several platforms in these milling crowds and reach the Kamrup Express on time. He turned to address the others. 'The Kamrup is part of the North East railway division and so the platform is farther off. Get ready, guys. We have to make a run for it, otherwise it will leave by the time we get there.'

The Gitanjali entered its platform at exactly half past five. They jumped off the still moving train, and began to run. The sight of the chaotic crowds disheartened Adi, and he prayed for a much-needed miracle. Their miracle came in the form of Sam who, inexplicably inspired after having recovered his breath, hoisted his bag above his head and began to run, shouting at the top of his voice, 'MOOOVE'. Seeing his bulky frame with the bag over his head barreling towards them, people quickly moved out of his path. Sam's personal hygiene had a significant contribution to the way the sea of humanity parted. The rest of them followed in his shadow, like ducklings trailing their mother. They made the distance in record time and found the Kamrup getting ready to leave. Grinning with relief, they clambered on board just as the train began to move.

The compartments were packed. Somehow they dragged their luggage to their coupe. To their surprise, all their seats were occupied. Adi pulled out his reservation slip and checked again. He confirmed the numbers...S-6, seats 41-46.

Adi turned to the men sitting in their seats. Tired, hungry and dirty, he easily skipped the part about being polite. 'Those seats are ours!' he said.

Some of them looked at Adi, then looked away as though he was selling a packet of peanuts rather than demanding his seat. Their collective cold shoulder annoyed Adi.

'I said these seats are ours!' he shouted.

'Hold it, young man,' said one of them. 'We are local passengers; we'll get off after a few stations.'

Adi couldn't believe their gall. But his irritation turned to anger when he spotted the familiar white kurta pajamas and open black sandals...these guys were behind the protest that had delayed the Gitanjali.

Adi felt blood rushing into his head and his temples start to throb. 'Get up right now!' he demanded angrily. 'Those seats are ours. We have the tickets!'

A murmur of infuriation arose amongst the locals. Drawing strength from their numbers, their anger seemed to acquire a justification of their own reckoning. They looked angrily at Adi.

'Who do you think you are?'

'You've bought tickets, not the whole railways!'

'Your father owns Indian railways?'

Some of them started to gesticulate at Adi angrily.

Adi realized he was challenging the lion in his den. They were far away from home, amongst a bunch of people who commuted this route daily, who could muster trouble at a moment's notice and outnumbered them ten to one.

But Adi couldn't care less...his anger clouded all judgment.

Pheru came from behind and said, 'Cool it, Adi...these guys are locals...'

'So what?' shouted Adi. 'What'll they do...kill me? Saala bastards... I'll die for my seat!'

Sam quickly positioned himself between Adi and the men. Pheru pulled Adi back towards Harsha and Rajeev who promptly restrained him. Adi tried to free himself from Rajeev's clasp.

Then he heard Sam address the local commuters in a gentle voice. 'Look, please excuse my friend. We have been travelling from Bombay for three days now. We are going all the way to Nagaland and we are very tired. All we would like is that you give us our seats, and then we can try and adjust to get most of you to sit with us.'

Sam's politeness only served to heighten their absurd outrage.

'Too bad and too late! Your friend should have spoken nicely, like you. We also travel this route every day and we have been working the whole day too. You'll just have to wait for us to get off!'

'Yeah! We travel this route every day.'

'Where will we sit?'

'And look at you...you will take the place of four people when you sit.'

'I can sit on your lap, if you let me...you look like you have a lot of cushion,' said someone and the snickers turned to outright laughter.

Adi peeked at Sam; he was laughing with them. Adi wondered for the hundredth time how Sam always managed to laugh about everything. How could he possibly see any humour in his belittlement?

Then Sam smiled sweetly at one of them and said, 'Is it okay if I stand in front of my seat?'

Unsure of what to say, the man nodded uncertainly.

'Thank you,' said Sam. Then, clambering over crossed legs and tightly packed bodies, Sam positioned himself right in front of the person he had addressed. He leaned over in front of the man, lifted his arms, rested his elbows on the bunk above his head, and flanked the man's face with his sweat-stained armpits. Then, with his face inches away from the man's nose, Sam started breathing through his mouth. Adi noticed his extra effort to exhale.

Adi didn't dare wonder what Sam's body and breath must have smelled like. Three days of accumulated perspiration and not having brushed his teeth for the last six years had a profound effect. If Adi had not seen it that day with his own eyes, he wouldn't have ever believed a human being's reaction to such olfactory torment. The man in front of Sam could neither breathe nor hold his breath: he was turning green if he did and blue if he didn't.

Sam continued to smile and breathe on him. Soon the man wheezed an apologetic 'you can sit here' to Sam, abandoned his seat and desperately lunged for some fresh air.

Sam had no intention of sitting down. He motioned for Adi to come and occupy the seat. Adi immediately did, after which Sam assumed the same position in front of the guy sitting next to him. Nobody lasted more than a few minutes of Sam's torture. The beauty of Sam's method was its indolent effectiveness – most people couldn't understand why these men were abandoning their seats so meekly. But they did, and with astonishing regularity. Sam even offered his lap to the person who had suggested it as a seating solution, only to be turned down rather hurriedly.

Within fifteen minutes, the entire row was empty, leaving the five of them with ample room to rest their weary behinds. Sam stretched out his legs and arms to relish the abundant space around him, the smile on his face ringing with the sweetness of his victory.

As the local passengers stared at them angrily, the train rushed on though the countryside, tearing through the darkness of the evening. Adi put his face next to the open window and took a deep breath. A beautiful earthly scent floated in. He recognized the smell. It smelled of victory.

He began writing another letter to Isha.

My dear Isha,

I miss you very much.

We are on our way to Guwahati from Calcutta. The journey to Calcutta itself almost didn't take place. We just managed to make it to the Kamrup on time thanks to Sam's inspired charge like a raging bull. On the Kamrup, I learned how not bathing or brushing your teeth can be a deadly secret weapon. (I'll explain when I get back, but believe me, it is remarkable). In fact, it makes me wonder: if Mahatma Gandhi had preached that seven hundred million Indians should not take a bath or clean themselves for days before his satyagrahas, maybe the British would have left this big, beautiful country in our hands a few years earlier.

And it is as beautiful as it is big.

For three days now we've been travelling, and still have another two to go before we reach Toshi's home. Sometimes I wonder if we'll be able to actually complete it, or may have to turn back halfway. Even when we meet his family, I wonder what we'll tell them. I wish we were carrying better news than that of his death. I wish we were going to attend his wedding, or his graduation. After all, what solace will we provide to his grieving family when we don't even know them, and require an introduction to their culture?

The trip so far has been without any major incident between the rest of the guys and me. In fact, today was a remarkable achievement of camaraderie. I remember Toshi trying to patch up our differences when we took the ride to the airport that morning, to see him off. I think that is the last image of him in our memory and so, right now, the goal of getting to Nagaland has sort of preceded any individual bitterness. But I still travel with the constant fear of having to defend myself...

Maybe Toshi's death will teach us to forgive and forget.

But again, I ramble on...

I miss you even more than before. I think about

you all the time and I can't wait to get back to see
you and talk to you.

    Adi

    PS: I still haven't opened the envelope. (I am so
confused!!!)

       ❧

By the time they reached Guwahati, all of them
had turned into ragged, tired, dirty versions of
the human beings that had begun the journey
in Bombay four days earlier. Travelling on slow-
moving, crowded trains, unable to shower or
shave, eating any junk they could lay their hands
on, and sleeping in fits and starts on hard
wooden berths, had brought them close to
exhaustion. The prospect of more travel
weighed heavily on their minds as they walked
out of the station in bone-weary silence. Even
by a conservative estimate, they still had
fourteen hours of travel left.

    'We'd better make our return reservations
back to Bombay from here,' said Adi, hating to
make the suggestion for fear of being stuck with
the responsibility of organizing it. An insipid
debate ensued, each trying hard to shirk the job.
Pheru took the easy way out by falling asleep on
his suitcase.

Finally, the responsibility of buying the tickets was Adi's, while Sam and Rajeev were to look for buses to Dimapur. Adi decided to buy tickets back to Bombay after a three-day stay with Toshi's family.

As he stood in line at the reservation counter, Adi's eyes fell on the newspaper the man standing in front of him was reading. Most of the headlines concerned the trouble in the North-East states. ULFA rebels had killed six Army jawans in an ambush, while a Hindi-speaking family of eight, including women and children, had been murdered in their home at night. Elsewhere, the Manipur Maoist Rebels had called for a two-day strike in that state, while the Border Security Force had shot down four 'terrorists' trying to enter India from Bangladesh. The violence was worse in the smaller towns and villages. Bigger cities still maintained some semblance of security and the local administration tried its best to keep trouble at bay. But out in the countryside, posts manned by Indian Army jawans were often the sole providers of security.

Thousands of miles from home, amongst inhospitable strangers, Adi had to remind himself that they were in their own country.

The bus-stand was right outside the train

station. Sam had an excited look on his face when he returned. 'Guys, you won't believe this,' he said. 'We found a bus that will take us to Mokukchung directly... We don't have to go to Dimapur at all.'

Everyone was happy at the prospect of having shaved off six hours of travel time. They followed Sam without a moment's pause.

The bus was a sweet sight for their sore eyes and weary bodies. It was luxurious, with spacious, cushioned seats that reclined to almost become beds. Soundproof glass kept the noise of the engines outside and individualized lighting and overhead fans provided personalized comfort. They found their seats and Adi immediately reclined his seat all the way. He checked the time. It was 9 p.m. He fell asleep long before the bus started to drive through the quiet night.

Adi awoke to the sounds of loud noises coming from the front of the bus. In the hazy awareness of his a semi-somnolent state, one of the voices sounded disturbingly familiar. He struggled to shake off his fatigue and get a better look.

Sam and Rajeev were arguing with the bus conductor. The two of them were gesturing angrily and were demanding that their money be returned.

'What is going on?' Adi asked Harsha sleepily, feeling the gummy tightness of his mouth hold back the words.

'Saala, this conductor is a bastard,' said Harsha. 'He lied to us about going to Mokukchung... This bus is going to Jorhat, and he says we can catch another bus from there.'

Although it was a major inconvenience, Adi was enjoying his sleep so much that he decided he wouldn't mind taking the extra ride to Jorhat. 'So what, man?' he said wearily. 'Let's go to Jorhat. Like he says, we can catch a bus from there to Mokukchung. Let's just go back to sleep.'

He lay back wearily, hoping the hollering would stop. However, the shouting match continued. 'Why did you lie? We want our money back!'

'Saala, are you deaf? I said you'll get a bus from Jorhat!'

'No, take us to Mokukchung or give us the money back!'

Adi curled up tighter to drown out the noise. He looked at his watch: it was four in the morning.

Suddenly there was a blood-curdling yell from the front. Startled, Adi looked up to see Rajeev and Sam in a mad dash towards the rear of the bus. The conductor stood brandishing a huge machete that glinted brightly even in the frugal light inside the bus. His face had deformed into a demonic scowl as he waved his weapon maliciously, foaming at the mouth and screaming frantically. 'I'll cut you into a thousand pieces! You don't know who I am…bastards… motherfuckers… Come out now!'

He charged towards them.

Adi's weariness bolted in a flash. The newspaper pictures of swollen rotting bodies with wide gashes caked with dried blood flashed through his mind. The terror in those photos suddenly came to life. He felt nauseous with fear and a hollow feeling of impending doom washed over him. His body froze. His legs felt like jelly and even though he tried, Adi couldn't move from the spot.

Suddenly, a man stood up from among the passengers and pointed a revolver straight at the oncoming conductor. His fingers tightened on the trigger as he shouted, 'Stop!'

The conductor saw the revolver's barrel facing him and stopped in his tracks. For the next few minutes he held his angry stare, as though testing the man's resolve to keep him in check. Sweat gleamed on his forehead and his eyes shone with manic intensity. No one moved.

Then, the conductor put his machete down slowly and walked away, disappearing into the driver's cabin. Only when he had closed the cabin door behind him did the other man lower his revolver and sit back on his seat.

Then, turning towards Adi, he said, 'You guys better get off with me at the next stop near Golaghat... He'll kill you if you stay on.'

Adi nodded dumbly.

The man smiled and said, 'I'm Major Nair. Major Arjun Nair.'

Adi had never realised it could be so difficult to muster up a smile. In fear, his facial muscles refused to comply. When he reached out to shake Major Nair's hand, Adi suddenly became aware that despite the heat of the night, he was shivering like a leaf in the wind.

TWENTY-FOUR

Major Arjun Nair was a dashing man. Tall, broad-shouldered, and with a booming voice to match, he looked like a natural born leader. His eyes were dark, probing, intense. A sharp jaw line and a prominent chin outlined his handsome face. A trim moustache spanned the breadth above his lip, stretching the distance on either side with exquisite symmetry. Not a single blade of hair had permission to grow anywhere else on his dark brown face. He walked with a confident air, returning his jawan's salutes with a snappy nod.

Adi, Harsha, Pheru, Rajeev and Sam got off the bus with Major Nair and followed him silently. His base stood next to an army checkpoint along the main road that ran towards the Nagaland border. It consisted of some large tents in a small clearing, surrounded by rolls of

mean-looking barbed wire. A couple of green
army trucks, with dark red numbers stenciled
inside bright white circles were parked neatly
on one side. Lookout posts on two sides hosted
uniformed jawans, scanning the area with
suspicious eyes while their machine guns stared
faithfully at the iron gates across the road. Tall
evergreen trees surrounded the base on three
sides and stretched as far as the eye could see.
Other than the occasional roar of a passing
vehicle, the only sounds were the anonymous
squawks of birds from deep within the forest.

The morning was sunny but pleasant. The
five of them were completely clueless about
their whereabouts. After the terrifying ordeal
in the bus, reaching their destination had ceased
to be such a pressing concern. They readily
soaked in the security of being surrounded by
barbed wire and machine guns.

Major Nair was pleasantly surprised when he
learnt of the reason behind their trip to Nagaland. 'We are at the border of Nagaland and
search all the buses that pass this check point,'
he informed them. 'If a bus is going directly to
Mokukchung, you can get on it; otherwise there
are lots of buses that go to Dimapur. You can
take one of those and then get a connection to
your friend's place.'

They nodded readily, relieved with the easy solution Major Nair had laid out.

Then Major Nair said, 'I suppose you have your permits.'

They looked at each other blankly.

'You know that you need to have permits to enter Nagaland, don't you?' said Major Nair.

'Permits?' exclaimed Adi. 'Why do we need permits to go to a place in our own country? We are Indians!'

'Other than Nagas, all others, Indians or foreigners, must carry permits issued by the government to enter Nagaland.'

'Does that mean we won't be able to get into Nagaland?' asked Pheru.

Major Nair shook his head. 'Sorry,' he said, 'you have to have permits to enter Nagaland... What do you think we check at this checkpoint? You can get one from Dimapur, but it'll take at least a day or two to get one made.'

They were stunned.

'That is insane!' Adi protested. 'Can't you just let us in...please? I mean, who will know?'

'I'm sorry, but I can't let you in. I think permits are a foolish idea too...but I have my orders. Besides, if you get caught inside Nagaland without permits, you'll be in bigger trouble.'

The five of them stared at each other in

disbelief, half expecting Major Nair to break into a smile any minute and tell them it was all a prank. But it was too cruel to be a joke: after having made this long, exhausting trip to the other end of the country, just when they were less than one hundred-and-fifty kilometres from their destination, their fate depended on a piece of paper.

'Major Nair, this means our entire trip is wasted...we leave for Bombay in three days. Please, please you must help us!' pleaded Rajeev.

'Well, you can try going to Dimapur, but it'll take some time...there is no way around that.'

'There is just no time. This is so idiotic, so bloody senseless!' said Sam. 'Who made these stupid rules?'

Major Nair shrugged understandingly. 'Unfortunately, some bureaucrats and politicians decide to do what they think is right for the country and everybody else suffers. I agree, it is ridiculous...but I cannot do anything about it. You and I have no power. Power resides not with the common man, but with a bunch of old fools sitting in Delhi and telling everyone else how to think. No wonder people everywhere are revolting!'

Major Nair's statement surprised Adi. 'I... I

don't understand,' he said. 'What do you mean people are revolting?'

'You know…all this insurgency and fighting,' said Major Nair.

'But those are terror groups…they kill innocents and want to break away from India!' said Adi, making his displeasure obvious.

Major Nair smiled and said, 'I think I've upset you. You probably think I'm being unpatriotic.'

Adi didn't reply.

Major Nair continued. 'Look, democracy doesn't work at gunpoint. I cannot point my rifle at a Naga and tell him to believe he is Indian. People have to want to be Indian. Like you said before, how can you be free if you need a permit to enter a part of your own country? India is too diverse, too big, to let a few elected representatives and mindless bureaucrats sitting in Delhi tell everybody else how to think.'

Just then a jawan entered the tent to inform Major Nair that they were going to search a bus on its way to Mokokchung.

Adi looked at the others, his frustration and helplessness echoing on everyone's face.

Major Nair sighed. 'Sorry… I know the feeling. So close and yet so far. But this is why we need a revolution to give the power back to the people. You are Indians and yet you have *your* freedom to move in *your own* county dictated by some mindless bureaucrat in Delhi. See, people *must* get to participate in their government locally, not get told by a bunch of ministers in Delhi that we need to carry permits or—'

'Or that everyone must speak in Hindi,' said Adi, suddenly remembering an old exchange.

'Exactly,' said Major Nair, as they started to walk out towards the bus. 'See, I am from Kerela, where people don't like Hindi being imposed on them. But they will sing 'Khaike pan Banaraswala' with Amitabh Bachchan in 'Don', cheer loudly when Sachin Tendulkar clobbers a bowler and salute the flag on Republic Day just like the rest of the country. A country cannot exist as lines drawn on a map unless it exists as a concept in people's minds. People will always find a way to draw more lines, erect more boundaries unless they can *feel* the belonging to a country. That feeling comes from the freedom to *differ*, from the freedom to be different. That is the…' He stopped in the middle of his speech, suddenly distracted by loud shouts that caught everyone's attention.

'Adi… Rajeev…Pheru!' yelled someone from the bus.

They stared in disbelief. It was Jagdeep!

❧

Jagdeep's success at convincing the Indian Airlines officials of his and Toshi's brotherhood defied rational explanation. But he had managed, and had reached Dimapur four days ago where, upon learning of the need for permits to enter Nagaland, he had spent two days trying to arrange papers for the six of them. He had kept a lookout for the others and stayed an extra day after the permits were ready, hoping to make the final leg of the journey with them. But when waiting in vain had begun to pinch his wallet, he had given up on finding company and set out on his own.

It was sheer fortuitous coincidence that the rest of them had been threatened by the bus conductor and had got off with Major Nair at his base, where the bus that carried Jagdeep and those all-important permits had been stopped for a routine search.

Major Nair inspected the papers, and confirmed that everything was in order. Thrilled that they had cleared the last hurdle on their way to Mokukchung, they cheerily clambered onto the bus.

They were struck by the sudden change in mood inside the bus. Fifty pairs of Naga eyes

stared at them coldly, completely lacking any
sign of welcome or warmth. Nobody moved to
offer a seat. The five of them walked in and
stood silently in the aisle, their happiness
suddenly tempered in the glare of those
unfriendly stares.

As Adi stood in the narrow passageway, his
eyes fell on a row in the rear that was occupied
by a solitary man sitting next to the window.
The rest of the seats looked empty. Adi walked
over, hoping to find a place to sit. However,
when he reached the seat, Adi was surprised to
discover a Naga woman stretched out on the
empty seat. She lay with her head on her
husband's lap, her hands propping up her huge
pregnant belly. She looked distinctly uneasy as
she shifted position every few minutes.

A gush of his previous not-so-memorable
trysts with obstetrics flooded Adi. He backed
away quickly, suddenly feeling very
uncomfortable.

Meanwhile, a jawan boarded the bus and
motioned for one of the Naga men to follow
him. They got off the bus together and
disappeared into one of the tents.

Ten minutes passed and then fifteen. The
driver, who had been expecting the inspection
to be a short affair, switched off the engine and

stepped outside. Taking a cue from him, some more passengers trickled out of the bus.

Adi looked outside. The road was deserted as far as his eyes could see. A few other vehicles passed by the checkpoint uneventfully, their tires searing the tar road as they disappeared into the distance. Other than the soft rustle of leaves and the chirp of crickets, the area was exceptionally quiet for the time of day.

An hour passed in wait. The sun began to bear down hard. Soon most of the passengers had abandoned the bus, escaping its suffocating heat for the cool comfort of the shady trees nearby.

Adi sat underneath a leafy tree, silently studying the movements within the tents for any sign of a resolution to the problem. Soon Pheru joined him. He sat quietly for a few minutes, tearing up a dry leaf into small bits and flicking them.

'What is the use of all this studying, huh Adi?' he said suddenly. 'I mean…all you need in life is a nice wife, a little land and a couple of buffaloes, right?'

Adi looked at him questioningly.

Pheru continued to mangle the dead leaves and said, 'Buffaloes can give you milk, and till your soil…and all you need is a wife to cook, clean and love, right Adi?'

'I suppose.'

'You think some nice girl like that will marry me?' he said, looking ahead.

Adi followed his line of vision and saw a pretty Naga girl, squatting by the side of the road, staring into the distance.

Adi smiled at him. 'You'd better propose to her and find out, Pheru. Since you won't show up for the Pharmac exam this time, you'll fail. If she says yes, start looking for a piece of land and the price of buffaloes.'

'No, no... I'm serious, Adi.'

'I think your brain has fried in the heat, man.'

'No, Adi... I mean it. I know I'll fail and I have nowhere to stay when we go back. So this is it...no more exams. I'm tired of this nonsense. I'll do something else. Farm...sell chickens... milk cows...Fuck it, man...no more medicine.'

Adi hadn't realized he was serious. 'Don't give up, Pheru. Look, even if you flunk this time you can stay with me. You've begun to study hard and I'm sure you'll pass eventually...like you said...you want to be the last one standing, remember?'

Pheru shook his head and sighed. 'No, Adi. I don't think medicine is for me... I took it up for all the wrong reasons and maybe that it is why I'm not destined to become a doctor. Abbu was right... I *am* cursed. I... I'll never beat it. Never. Maybe that's what I need to understand.'

'That is crazy, Pheru. Don't quit. You can stay with me and make more attempts, man. I think even Toshi would have liked to see you pass.'

'Yeah, but Toshi is dead, Adi...after he let me stay with him. Something will happen to you too if I move in with you... I should just stay out of everyone's lives!'

'Pheru, that is nonsense...and Toshi was really grateful for your company. Do you remember how sick he was during the time you spent with him?'

'Yeah, but he's not coming back...and it's better to be sick than dead, Adi,' said Pheru. 'So, I've been thinking about it for some time now. I can't spend my life just trying to prove a point, man. See...all my problems go away if I just quit medicine.'

Suddenly, Sam came running towards them. 'Did you hear what happened?' he said. 'During the search, they found that one of the passenger's bags had some bullets and this guy doesn't have his license to carry a gun. Major Nair won't let him go without verification, and the other Nagas won't leave without him. They are having a heated argument in the tent!'

The three of them walked over to the tent.

Inside, Major Nair sat behind a big wooden table on which lay a few unspent bullets and an open suitcase, its contents scattered all over. A couple of jawans stood behind him while he faced off with one of the Naga men.

'This is nothing but harassment!' shouted the Naga man.

Major Nair said quietly, 'You know that you have to carry your permit.'

'But I'm not carrying a gun! Why do I need to carry a gun permit if I'm not carrying a gun?'

'Look, you'd better sit down and wait. I have requested verification.'

The man stared at Major Nair in disgust, then stormed out of the tent. Outside, Adi could see him talking angrily to his fellow Nagas. Intermittently, they stared angrily towards the tent and Major Nair. A few of them re-entered the tent to talk to him.

'This is just harassment... There is a pregnant lady in the bus who needs to get to the hospital fast!'

'I know, but I can't do anything. My hands are tied!'

An angry silence ensued. Then someone from the crowd of Nagas said contemptuously, 'This is why Nagas get upset with the Indian government! You wonder why so many Nagas want a different country? We just don't want this harassment, that's all!'

Major Nair looked at him sternly. 'I'm warning you to stop your nonsense, otherwise I'll be forced to confine you.'

'So now you're threatening to arrest me?' challenged the man, raising his voice for everyone to hear. 'Go ahead…arrest me so that people will at least realize the problems that we face. Otherwise let us go!'

Major Nair stood up, trying to impose his size on the argument. 'I cannot let him go…the rest of you can take the bus and leave, but until I get verification of his gun permit, he cannot leave. Those are my orders… I am bound by the rules.'

The passenger stared angrily at Major Nair and then spat on the ground. He joined the group outside the tent, where everybody launched into an angry, animated discussion in a language Adi couldn't understand. The tone, however, conveyed their feelings adequately. Some of the men glared at the jawans around them. The armed jawans stood nervously still, holding on to their guns tightly, their fingers only inches away from the triggers.

Suddenly, loud incoherent shouting from the bus attracted everybody's attention. Within a few minutes, some of the Naga men came out of the bus, carrying the pregnant lady. Her face looked ashen and she was crying.

One of the men ran ahead towards Major Nair and said, 'She says that she cannot feel the baby moving. She feels the baby may have died!'

Major Nair immediately made way for the men to take her inside. They laid her on a cot in one corner of the tent. Her husband began to fan her with his shirt.

Major Nair looked lost. He turned towards the six of them and said, 'You guys are doctors, right?'

'Third year medical students!' came the rapid clarification.

'But you guys have seen patients, right? You know first aid and simple stuff, right?'

Pheru, Harsha and Sam shook their heads in unison before turning to look at Adi. Adi had been dreading this. Aside from him, none of the others had ever taken care of a pregnant woman, an inexperience that served well as an obvious disqualification from the responsibility of taking charge. Adi, on the other hand, had spent extra time in obstetrics, even defying the class to do so.

Adi cringed.

Jagdeep said, 'Adi, you've conducted deliveries, right? Let me go and get my stethoscope for you.'

With typical second-year-medical-student pride in the new tools of his trade, Jagdeep had remembered to pack his stethoscope. He ran to retrieve it from the bus.

Major Nair spoke to the lady's husband. Adi noticed the word spreading quickly among the gathering that they were 'doctors', and Adi was the ob-gyn specialist.

Adi froze. His heart began to race and his mouth turned dry when he remembered the trouble he had identifying foetal heart sounds even when a large 'X' identified the location on those protuberant bellies. He gulped, wishing he could confess that his interest in obstetrics hadn't exactly been academic. He silently cursed his hitherto cavalier approach to the intricacies of childbirth. Finally, unable to avoid the onus, and conscripted into service by the invisible spotlight of expectant stares, Adi felt obliged to involuntarily volunteer his 'expertise'.

All eyes were upon him as Adi slowly approached the pregnant woman. She lay on the makeshift cot, her eyes wide with anxiety. Sweat glistened on her face.

Adi stood beside her for a few seconds, unsure of what to do next. Then, very tentatively, he placed the stethoscope on her belly.

He smiled almost immediately, marvelling at

his acoustic windfall. Adi could clearly hear the sweetest, most beautiful sound in the universe: the sound of life. A tiny heart inside her belly went dub-a-dub-a-dub, pounding away at the pace of a fast-moving train.

Adi shouted excitedly, 'The baby is alive... I can hear its heart! I can hear its heart!'

A collective sigh of relief arose from the crowd that quickly condensed into a murmur of admiration. Major Nair beamed happily while the prospective parents broke into relieved smiles.

Bolstered by his initial success, Adi's confidence grew. He wondered why the baby wasn't moving if it was alive. He looked again at the spot where he had heard the foetal heart sounds. It *was* low in the pelvis... Could it be that the baby had stopped moving because it had engaged deep in the pelvis? But that would mean she could be in early labour!

That was the first time Adi noticed she was in pain. She was in labour! Adi's jaw dropped at the thought of impending birth. Sweat began to run down his forehead when he remembered how he had blacked out while witnessing his first delivery. The dryness in his mouth returned and his panic-stricken heart began to race even faster when he realized that the responsibility of holding the slippery, slimy, blood-covered infant as it came sliding out of the vagina was his. He didn't dare imagine what would happen to them if he dropped the baby.

Taking a couple of deep breaths to control his mounting panic, Adi tried to find faith in his abilities to guide a baby out of its womb. Sure, he had seen a bunch of babies being born, and thanks to Isha's enthusiasm he had even managed to supervise a few. But those had been with the comforting presence of Dr Choksi only a few feet away.

Trying to emulate what he had seen Dr Choksi do so many times, Adi asked for some privacy to examine her. Major Nair immediately cleared the tent. Adi was surprised to find that she was very advanced in labour. Her cervix felt soft and indistinguishable from the rest of the womb and he could even feel the frizzy hair on the baby's head. Her water must have broken while she was in the bus; she just hadn't realized it. She would deliver soon.

He turned to Pheru. 'Pheru, I think she is in labour...in fact, she is progressing really fast! I'll need your help!'

Pheru nodded uncertainly. 'Me? Yeah...okay, what should I do?'

'She is fully dilated and effaced. The

presentation is vertex and LOA and I'll try and manage her labour. But I... I have no idea about pediatrics or neonatal care. Can you take care of that...can you just hold the baby as it comes out?'

Pheru nodded uncertainly.

Outside, the hostilities had vanished. The jawans and the Nagas milled about, awaiting more news.

Adi turned around to give orders. Some of the jawans ran to boil water while Rajeev found some simple instruments in a first-aid kit. Some thread, a pair of moustache-trimming scissors and a couple of plastic meat-cutting gloves received a thorough boiling. A partition was fashioned out of a bedsheet hung across bamboo poles to provide privacy in the open tent.

Adi tried to think through the steps of childbirth. He asked her to bear down during her contractions. He felt her push the baby vigorously. A couple of Naga women stood around her, talking to her, helping her through it, while all eyes remained focused on Adi.

Adi barked instructions loudly while praying silently in his heart. The baby's head was crowning; the face would be out soon.

Her labour proceeded at good speed. In the next half-hour, Adi had managed to draw out most of the baby's head. As the chin turned and escaped the confines of the passage, he was completely unprepared for the sudden spurt of the rest of the squiggly body. He managed to hold on tightly to the slippery, rubbery mass of humanity, still attached to the umbilical cord.

Pheru rushed to wrap the baby in towels. They tied two knots in the cord and cut it. Pheru took the baby while Adi applied pressure on the mother's belly to expel the placenta.

The silence that followed her painful screams was deafening. As everybody stood rooted to the spot, Adi realized something was wrong.

The baby was not crying. It looked dark, limp and lifeless.

'Pheru?' Adi hissed, looking at him anxiously. 'Why isn't it crying?'

Pheru put his fingers into the baby's mouth to clear the passageway. Unable to find anything, he flipped the baby around in an effort to drain its mouth. The baby flip-flopped in his hand like a lifeless rag doll. Pheru started sweating profusely as he tried different manoeuvres to get the baby to breathe. Adi felt his heart sinking in the unbearable silence.

Then, more out of frustration than intent, Pheru spanked the newborn's bottom and shouted, 'Come on, damn it!'

The sharp slap echoed loudly in the room.

As if woken from a deep sleep, the baby suddenly cried out loudly, protesting its entry into an uncertain world, away from the comfortable confines of its mother's belly.

Everyone broke into a loud cheer as the indignant cries of a little girl filled the room. The louder she cried, the happier their faces got. People smiled and hugged the father. Within a few seconds the baby turned pink as they showered her with more looks of admiration. Then, when the crying had stopped in the tight and cozy confines of Pheru's arms, he handed the beautiful little girl to her mother.

Tears of joy and relief were streaming down Adi's face. He turned and hugged Pheru. As they embraced, Adi heard Pheru whisper quietly, 'Adi, I'm so bloody glad you didn't join the strike!'

TWENTY-FIVE

Her birth changed everything.
Tightly wrapped into a small bundle, she
gained instant eminence – the centrepiece of
interaction amongst her numerous admirers.
They fussed over her complacent pout, laughed
at her cantankerous cries, and gushed at her
content little face, finding kinship with one
another in the familiarity of these simple
emotions. The astounding beauty of her life
trivialized all that had seemed so important only
moments ago.

Pheru held the little girl for a while. She
curled up cozily in his arms as he stared at her
contented little face with a mixture of pride and
sadness on his own. She was like the beautiful
dream that deceives the slumbering mind, its
lucidity inspiring belief – only to leave behind
the bittersweet emptiness of its illusion when

awakened. For the first time in his six years of studying medicine, Pheru felt the need to become a doctor for the same reasons that usually makes someone want to become a doctor. Yet, this true calling came with the reminder of its inherent improbability. His failure was imminent: his exam was to take place in another five days when he would be 3000 kilometres away from any chance of success.

Major Nair agreed to let them board the bus without waiting for the gun license, happily flouting the laws he had insisted on upholding only a short while ago. This time when they re-boarded the bus, the animosity had vanished, replaced by welcome stares and admiring nods. The best seats in the bus awaited them along with enthusiastic offerings of whatever little food the Nagas carried.

As the bus started to drive off, the new father raised his newborn to the rear window for the jawans to say goodbye. They stood on their tiptoes and waved enthusiastically, leaning on each other's shoulders in order to get a better look as though bidding farewell to a distant but special relative. Their guns hung by their sides, the nozzles pointing harmlessly towards the ground.

Soon they began climbing the eastern range

of the Himalaya. It was late afternoon as they made their way along the sinuous roads that snaked through the mountains. The bus paced along the empty road, slowing down for the sharp turns or the shallow stream that cut across its path. The verdant hills on both sides were velvety lush. Sunlight glinted off the emerald green leaves that glowed brilliantly after the recent showers. The graceful slopes merged into one another, or flattened out into quaint valleys with clear, sparkling streams. Small villages with thatch-roof houses and smoking chimneys dotted the valleys. A few desultory clouds floated in the pale blue sky, meandering aimlessly after having dropped their wares. Far away on the eastern horizon, snow-covered peaks broke the monotony of the barren altitudes, looking like a disgruntled artist's brush strokes on the giant canvas of the sky.

They crossed the hills just as the sun flirted with the western horizon, glowing like a giant orange fireball and transforming the snowcapped mountaintops into reddish orange smudges of incandescent beauty. Soon, someone pointed out the village of Mokukchung to them. It cradled an entire hillside and looked like a bigger version of the villages they had passed on the way. As soon as the village came into view, the Nagas in the bus spontaneously broke into song.

The sun had set by the time they reached the bus-stop. Jagdeep had managed to contact Toshi's parents by telephone from Dimapur and they had assured him that someone would meet them at the bus-stand. A gentleman stepped forward when he saw them alight, and identified himself as Toshi's uncle. He embraced them warmly and loaded their bags onto a waiting jeep. Making their way across town on narrow, steep roads, they headed towards Toshi's house. As they got closer, Adi could see a small crowd waiting for them near the door. He scanned those expectant faces, feeling his heart grow heavy with sadness when he realized that they must have waited in a similar manner for Toshi's arrival.

Toshi's father and mother stepped forward. Although they had never met before, Adi hugged Toshi's father tightly. Toshi's father began to sob.

A series of introductions followed. Adi hugged Toshi's mother and gave her the diary that Toshi had so carefully maintained for her. She looked a little surprised at first and then, recognizing it, she held it close to her chest and kissed it. She turned to Toshi's sisters and brothers and said something excitedly. All of them gathered around her as she opened the diary and stared lovingly at his handwriting. Then, reading some of the entries to her other children, she smiled and cried, laughed and wept, grinned and sniffled in a strange medley of mixed emotions. The six of them looked on silently as Toshi's family savoured those moments of Toshi talking to them through his writing.

His brothers and sisters were full of questions: what was Bombay like? Did Toshi like it in Bombay? What did he eat, and where? Why hadn't he come earlier? Had he, or any of them seen any filmstars in Bombay? They talked late into the night, recounting stories, incident and anecdotes, reliving the two years of Toshi's life that his parents hadn't had a chance to know. Between them, they recounted every nitty gritty detail of Toshi's life in Bombay, to an audience whose hunger for Toshi's memories was insatiable.

Then Toshi's father recounted his experience of the fateful day. He had been waiting for Toshi at Dimapur airport that afternoon when he learned that the plane wouldn't be landing. Initially, there were rumours that it had been hijacked. After six hours of bureaucratic inertia they were informed that the pilot had lost control of the plane in the inclement weather and crashed into the mountains surrounding Dimapur.

The heavy rains had delayed his efforts to survey the wreckage site on his own. Keeping a father's hopes alive were his prayers, until he found, scattered on the hillside, the remains of what looked like the seat of a pair of corduroy trousers. He recognized it as the one he had given Toshi on his eighteenth birthday. Neatly preserved in the back pocket was a wallet that contained a photograph of his family.

That's when, sitting in the rain amidst the plane debris scattered over the hills, he had begun to cry.

He turned to address them. 'I thank you all for coming to meet us,' he said haltingly. 'I am just an old man grieving for his son. You know, I can still remember Toshi from the day he was born. He fit in my two hands...'

He smiled, staring at his empty hands held out in front of him, holding an imaginary baby.

'Twenty years,' he continued. 'Twenty years of memories, twenty years of hopes and expectations, all just suddenly seem to mean so little in actual time. Every moment is so little and yet, a lifetime in itself.'

His voice began to falter and his eyes grew moist. He stopped for a few minutes, biting his lips to hold back the tears. His wife put an arm around him and gently rubbed his back.

'I could go on living the rest of my life thinking of how many moments I have lost forever. But now, the worst part is that the last two years of not being able to see Toshi made it feel like his life was almost as unreal as his death. You know, his casket was empty because we couldn't find much of him...and so, sometimes, I wonder... was Toshi truly on that plane? Maybe he wasn't on the plane that day. Maybe he never took the flight. I mean, how could he if he never went to Bombay? Maybe I was mistaken that I had seen him grow up. Did I just imagine those eighteen years with my son? What did his voice sound like...I forget. What did his touch feel like... I cannot remember. What was Toshi's smile like... I cannot see. But everyone says he is dead... *He is dead*, they tell me, when I can't even remember him alive!'

Tears started rolling down his cheeks. Steadying himself between his wife and children, he continued, 'But you have given meaning to those two years like you give meaning to my memories. With your journey, you have filled up that hole in my heart from when Toshi wasn't here. It comforts me to think that these two years he had such good friends so far away from home...and that he felt loved and happy there. You give meaning to Toshi's life and you give me back two more years with my son. You make Toshi live in my memory again. You comfort my suffering. You ease my pain. You help me say goodbye. You…you help me bury Toshi.'

Then he and his wife started sobbing inconsolably.

❧

Even in the darkness of the night, Mokukchung was a beautiful place. The town lit up the mountainside, glowing with the specks of human habitation all the way from the stream at the bottom of the valley, to their destination for the night – the bungalow at the top. It was the government guesthouse where Toshi's parents had made arrangements for them to stay.

The guesthouse was a colonial legacy where supervisors from the British Viceroy's office maintained a nominal presence in the area. Since Independence, the local government had been using it to put up guests and entertain visiting dignitaries. However, because not many high-profile dignitaries visited these parts, its services were available to anybody who carried any clout in the village.

The bungalow occupied the most picturesque

spot in town. The top of the mountain had been flattened to accommodate this modest, single-storied, brick and limestone structure. A dusty, stone- and gravel-lined driveway arose from the solitary road on one side of the hill, and arched its way up to the portico in front of the building. The portico led into a roomy reception area, on both sides of which an array of rooms fanned out like the splayed out wings of a bird. The rooms opened out into a spacious chair-lined veranda that provided an ideal hangout to watch the beauty of the lights glowing on the dark mountainside merge with those in the pristine night sky. There was a kitchen in one of the wings and the central area was an open courtyard. An unkempt garden consisting of a few wild plants, a moth-eaten lawn and some large mossy boulders surrounded the bungalow on three sides. The perimeter was marked by the presence of a dozen half-rotten wooden posts, relics from a fence in the past. Beyond the posts, the gently sloping hill was streaked with foot trails that joined the road below.

As with most old colonial buildings, this one too shared the reputation of being haunted. The driver of their jeep was an old Naga man who managed to convey in his broken English that many people had reported seeing figures darting in and out of rooms at all times of the night. His furrowed forehead, widened eyes and retracted lips conveyed the horror better than his diction, but once Adi hit his comfortable bed after having slept on hard wooden planks the last five days, he was out like a light.

The ghosts would have to wait for another night to terrorize him.

❧

The next afternoon they visited Toshi's grave. It was on a piece of ancestral land, an easy trek up the gentle slope of a mountain. They walked along the narrow foot trails surrounded on all sides by miles of dense bamboo thickets. A light breeze blew through the trees, stirring the leaves soundlessly. A misty haziness floated around them, reminding Adi that they were in the midst of a cloud. The air felt pleasant on his skin, tickling it with its wet touch and leaving a million goose bumps in its wake.

On top of the mountain, in a small clearing, was a recent grave, the small patch devoid of the lush green grass that bordered its perimeter. A simple stone cross sat on one end, bearing an epitaph.

The sight of the grave suddenly filled Adi with

a strange sense of completion. It was as though their journey had finally ended, but with a conclusion he didn't desire. The neat pile of earth stood telling him that the twenty-year-old who had lived just a few rooms away, would not open his door the next time Adi knocked on it, nor dash into his, trying to figure out what the next set of tutorial questions would be. He would never again come around looking for toothpaste, nor would he share Adi's loneliness in the 2 a.m. discussion about friends and family.

Preparing to say his final goodbye, Adi closed his eyes, hung his head and took a deep breath. The crisp mountain air rushing into his lungs suddenly reminded him of Toshi singing 'Annie's Song'. Adi smiled to himself, then, feeling guilty about the impropriety of his smile, sobered up immediately. The image of Toshi with his eyes closed in melodious rapture while he enthusiastically strummed his guitar, returned, making it impossible for Adi to grieve. Adi wrestled with his thoughts, trying hard to muster the obligatory melancholy demanded by the moment. He tried to imagine Toshi's broken body lying deep inside the earth. He tried to imagine his pain when the plane hit the hills. Yet, standing amidst the serene and silent mountains, all Adi could remember was how Toshi's chipped front tooth made his grin look asymmetric; how he constantly bit the calluses on his fingertips; how his eyes twinkled as a prelude to his laughter.

Adi stood there silently, painfully aware that in his final moments with Toshi, he just couldn't say goodbye.

TWENTY-SIX

Although it was only 9 o'clock when they returned to the bungalow after dinner that night, the inky darkness of the east made it seem like midnight. Parked on the driveway was an official-looking car with miniature Indian flags fluttering above the headlights. An array of red sirens sat like ornaments on the car's roof. They looked at the government license plate, idly wondering about the identity of the dignitary who had decided to spend the night there. Discounting the cook and the ghosts they had yet to encounter, they had assumed they were the only other inhabitants of the bungalow.

The night sky was clear and a million stars dotted the heavens. A half-moon stayed up on the horizon, highlighting the crests of the mountains with a silvery tinge. A cool breeze whistled through the mountaintops. Surrounded by dense forest on three sides, the bungalow looked eerily beautiful in the moonlight. The only other source of illumination was a solitary bulb hanging precariously from the lamppost along the driveway, casting weak shadows that danced with every gust of wind. Millions of bugs flew frenziedly around it, crowding whatever little light the dim bulb could cast. The driveway disappeared abruptly into the darkness just beyond the reach of the lamppost's rays. A few streetlights illuminated the roads below, while most of the houses were dark in the quiet peace of slumber. Other than the occasional howls of some street dogs in the distance, the surroundings were encased in silence.

Pheru retired to bed early. The others sat on the rocks at the edge of the garden, silently enjoying the beauty of their surroundings.

'I haven't seen Toshi's girlfriend,' said Sam. 'He said he was going to see her pretty soon after he landed.'

'I think she was there yesterday,' said Rajeev, 'the one with the short hair and the brown dress standing next to his sister... I think that was her.'

'How do you know?' asked Harsha.

'Toshi had shown me a photo a while back,' replied Rajeev.

'Wow...she was pretty,' said Sam.

They smiled, remembering how Toshi had kept them entertained with descriptions of his escapades with his girlfriend. They'd sit around him, marvelling at his sexual prowess, as he'd describe positions, postures, passion and performance.

'Lucky guy,' said Rajeev. 'At least he didn't die a virgin.'

They laughed.

'This place is so full of good-looking chicks that even we could get lucky,' said Sam.

'Yeah, man,' said Rajeev. 'We should have stayed here a few more days. Then we'd definitely get lucky.'

A fog was moving in from the distance, and the few lights in the valley below them began to slowly disappear under its blanket.

Suddenly, the sound of footsteps caught their attention. The clinking of anklets accompanied each footfall and appeared to get stronger as if headed straight for them. Intrigued, they shared nervous glances and stiffened in anticipation, straining their ears to discern the source of the sound. Soon they could make out the hazy figure of a woman walking up the hill along the narrow foot-trails. They watched with a mixture of fear and fascination as her form took shape gradually, emerging from the fog like a phantom. The bungalow's spooky reputation crossed their minds and, for an instant, the thought that she was a ghost frightened them. But nothing about her seemed ghostly as she approached them and stopped a few feet away.

She was a young woman, barely out of her teens. A dark shawl covered her torso underneath which, a thin white gown outlined the silhouette of her slender hips and shapely legs. In the soft glow of the moonlight she stared at them, said something that they didn't understand and smiled at them expectantly.

She was the sexiest ghost they had ever seen.

Suddenly rendered speechless, they stared at her, afraid of making any move that might make this beautiful apparition disappear. Then, as they looked on, she took off her shawl and let it fall around her legs.

All of them gasped in unison.

Her breasts showed underneath the thin gown that was hanging from her shoulders by two flimsy straps. Her nipples cast faint shadows on the fabric above. Her skin looked taut and unblemished. It was obvious she wasn't wearing anything underneath.

Her move to get them to talk rendered them speechless. Something about what she said clearly involved sex, but nobody could figure out what. In this anonymous place, far away from home, just after their discussion about Toshi's sexual escapades, they stared at this sexy beauty propositioning them, living that moment straight out of an adolescent's handbook of sexual fantasies by doing absolutely nothing.

Suddenly, the cook came running out of the bungalow and said something to the girl. They exchanged a few rapid words as she quickly rearranged her shawl around her shoulders. The cook wrapped his arms around her and smiled apologetically at the five of them. Mumbling explanations that they didn't understand, he began to walk her towards the bungalow. She turned one last time to smile at the five of them before following the cook. They watched as he ushered her into a room and rendered a few comically apologetic bows to its invisible occupants, then carefully closed the door behind him and rushed off towards the kitchen.

None of them said a word. They stared at each other, feeling brutally let down by their expectations, trying hard to rein in their imagination.

Finally Rajeev blurted, 'Wow! Man...was I dreaming? Tell me I was...I wish we had taken her into our rooms before the cook came out.'

Sam shook his head with disbelief. 'God! She has the most beautiful boobs I've ever seen. She was so close... I can almost feel them, man!' he sighed, squeezing the air in front of him ardently. He grimaced when the sensation didn't satisfy, and said, 'I'll bet Toshi sent her for us from heaven.'

Everyone laughed.

Rajeev had a glint in his eyes. 'We could still get her, you know', he said.

The others stared at him uncertainly.

'She doesn't live here,' he said. 'She has to come out of the room some time...'

They looked at one another, letting the suggestion soak in.

Adi turned to Rajeev and said, 'Forget it, man... It's not right. We are here for Toshi's funeral.'

'Fuck you, Adi!' retorted Rajeev. 'You stay out of this!'

Rajeev's belligerence surprised Adi.

'What the hell?' he began.

Rajeev cut him off. 'Listen, you two-timing son of a bitch, stay out of this! Don't come and lecture us about right and wrong!'

'I was not...'

'Shut the fuck up, Adi! You are the biggest hypocrite I've seen. You talk about right and wrong and then turn around and screw everybody!'

Adi was dumbfounded. 'What do you mean?' he said. 'I've not screwed anyone.'

'Yeah?' said Rajeev. 'What about Harsha? Huh? You knew he liked Isha, didn't you? What about Renuka? Huh? You got her all excited and then dumped her for Isha... What about Pheru? You lied about joining the strike when he asked you to, just so that you could impress Isha. You have screwed so many people over Isha that I hope she is worth it. You wonder why you have no friends now... How could you, when all you have done is stab them in the back whenever it suited you! So don't come around here like some authority on morality: you are the last person who should be giving a sermon about stuff like that!'

Sam tried to intervene. 'Come on, Rajeev...that is not true...Stop it, man...'

Rajeev didn't stop. 'What is not true, huh? Do you know, Sam...he *knew* that Isha was going to dump Harsha if he gave her the roses for Rose Day...yet he never warned Harsha about it! He *knew* it...ask him...he told me himself!'

Harsha and Sam looked at Adi questioningly. Adi remained silent.

Rajeev continued, 'He walks around like he is some kind of a do-gooder, always trying to do what is right and trying to be popular. But behind their backs he screws everyone! Everyone thought of him as this great guy who would make this great CR in class, till finally the strike showed him for what he is! Look at him…even now he wants to fuck that girl, but is advising us on morality.'

Adi struggled with the barrage of accusations, his initial instinct preparing a fight back. But something in Rajeev's tirade struck him as unerringly true. He suddenly felt a weight lift off his shoulders. He looked around at the others and smiled.

'You know, Rajeev, for the first time I think you are absolutely right,' he said. He turned to address Harsha. 'Harsha, I don't know what to say other than I'm sorry, I'm really sorry to have hurt you. I can only hope that someday you will forgive me.'

Then, as the others stared in surprise, he turned towards the bungalow and headed back towards their common room. He looked at Pheru, sleeping peacefully in his bed, before slipping into his own. He thought of Isha and felt a burning desire to see her right then and there, before quickly being overcome by sleep.

❧

Adi woke up briefly in the middle of the night, disturbed by hushed voices and hurried footsteps.

'Close the door...close the door!'

'Just shut up, man, and go to sleep...'

He recognized Rajeev's voice. He looked at his watch before pulling the blanket over himself snugly, happy, that at two in the morning he had six hours of sleep left.

The next thing he knew, someone was shaking his shoulder vigorously and shouting, 'Get up...get up now!'

Adi awoke with a start to see Toshi's uncle staring at him. Adi smiled and stretched lazily, hoping to steal a few more minutes of the cozy bed's comfort.

'Come on...get up! Now!' shouted Toshi's uncle.

Surprised, Adi looked around to see Jagdeep, Pheru and Sam in various stages of getting dressed. He looked at his watch; it was five in the morning. Adi wondered about the reason for such haste, but the look on Toshi's uncle's face made him decide to save the questions for later. He began to get dressed hurriedly.

As Jagdeep started putting toothpaste on his

toothbrush, Toshi's uncle snatched it from him and yelled, 'No time now! Let's get out of here now! Right now!'

They stared at each other, unsure of the reason for this urgency. Except for the fact that Rajeev and Harsha were not in the room, nothing looked amiss.

Seeing their indecision, Toshi's uncle barked, 'Listen, do you want to go to jail?'

Dumbfounded, they shook their heads.

'Then get your stuff and put it in the jeep! We have to leave in five minutes. Now, let's go!'

That got them moving at top speed. As they loaded the jeep, Adi saw Rajeev and Harsha sitting quietly in the front, avoiding everyone's eyes.

'Remember,' instructed Toshi's uncle. 'Make sure you have everything! Leave nothing behind!'

He ran into the main reception area and re-emerged with a sheet of paper in his hands. Adi noticed him crumple it and shove it into his pocket.

The official-looking car they had seen the previous night was gone. They clambered hurriedly into the jeep as it started to roll out of the driveway of the bungalow. Adi turned to look back one last time, only to see the cook staring at them with hatred in his eyes.

The jeep flew along the mountainous paths. After a few minutes of driving, they passed a police car heading up the hill towards the guesthouse.

Adi found the suspense unbearable. Unable to control himself, he asked Toshi's uncle, 'What's...wrong? Why do you think we'll be arrested?'

Toshi's uncle turned around to take a quick look at Adi and said, 'For murder!'

TWENTY-SEVEN

Murder? How…when…who…what…where? A thousand questions popped up in Adi's head, like bubbles in boiling water. He sat in the rear seat of the jeep with Sam, Pheru and Jagdeep while Rajeev and Harsha sat next to Toshi's uncle, who was now driving like the wind. They exchanged anxious glances without saying a word as they raced down the mountains.

They hoped Toshi's uncle would expand his statement to an explanation. But he was a different person now – not the perfect gentleman who had escorted them around town. His face was full of fear as he drove like a maniac, running from something that they felt afraid to ask about. In the bizarre silence that followed, no one dared to ask what had happened, afraid of invoking what they didn't know and discovering their culpability in someone's death. Their hearts were dark with an illogical fear of the unknown, as they rode along silently, preferring the reassurance of an uneasy ignorance, and maintaining a wretched normalcy with their conspiratorial hush.

Only after they had crossed the border into Assam did they stop for a quick meal in one of the small food stalls next to the road. The original plan had been to spend the day in Mokukchung, but with this sudden turn of events, they had a whole day to kill before boarding the train from Guwahati early the next morning. Jagdeep had to catch his return flight from Dimapur. No one was sure of the plans for that day or their whereabouts, and no one dared to ask.

As they lounged in the small roadside stall, an article in a newspaper caught Adi's attention. He picked up a copy and began reading through it.

Govt. Hospital Strike Ends

(From the News Service) Bombay, Maharashtra: A spokesman for the Maharashtra Association of Resident Doctors (MARD) today declared an end to the three-week long strike that had crippled services in the J.J. Group of Hospitals. This followed an agreement between the doctors and the representatives from the State Health Ministry. The outcome was widely expected after the sudden reversal of the hospital administration's stance on the impact of the strike, following the death of Mr Adil Mohammed Sheikh, the local ward municipal corporation leader, who died after being shot at and taken to the hospital for emergency surgery. Incidentally, Mr Sheikh had been involved in the initial dispute with the resident doctors that had precipitated the strike. His death led to questions being raised in the State Assembly for over six hours, ending with the opposition staging a walkout. Opposition leaders have voiced serious concerns about the hardships facing the common man as a result of such a strike. In a further embarrassment for the ruling party, the health minister, Shri Bhaurao Damane, today conceded that the dean of J.J. hospital, Dr M.M Bhandarkar, had supplied him with false figures about the outcome of the strike that downplayed the mortality rates. He has issued a suspension order against Dr Bhandarkar and stripped him of his title. He has also conceded to the opposition demand for an all-party commission to look into the allegations of neglect and mismanagement in the services provided in public hospitals across the state.

Adi read the article again and again, each time deriving some more joy from same paragraph. In one of the most bizarre twists of destiny, the corporator whose arrogance had led to the strike, had now resolved it by his death. Adi marvelled at the divine justice of the bullet that had torn through the corporator's heart and finally given the strike meaning. In death, the municipal corporator had finally done his duty to serve his constituents.

Adi laughed. Oh...the irony was delicious!

The other big news was the dean's suspension. Pheru *was* the last man standing. But his exam was to take place in two days, and in two days they would be in Calcutta, 2500 kilometres from the exam centre.

Then Adi had a brainwave. He turned towards the rest of the group, waving the newspaper like a flag and shouting, 'Pheru, Pheru...the strike is over, man! And the dean has been suspended! You can actually take your Pharmac exam and pass it, man. You can go on to Third MB and to pediatrics...'

Pheru and the others read the article through while Adi brought Toshi's uncle up to speed on the developments in JJ hospital preceding their trip. Pheru's hands began to shake as he read the article over and over.

'Pheru, the only way you can make it to the exam is if you fly there using Jagdeep's ticket!' said Adi.

Pheru's eyes widened with anticipation and he turned to look at Jagdeep.

'Sure, man,' said Jagdeep, even before he was prompted with a question. 'If I can be Toshi's brother, so can you. I'll give you the ticket and you can check in as Jagdeep Singh.'

Pheru lifted Jagdeep in a bear hug. Then he began to laugh and shout, 'I've beaten him, man! I've fucking beaten him!'

The mood had changed dramatically from the sepulchral silence of the morning to one of boisterous hope. Everyone partook of Pheru's happiness as he pranced around, pumping his arms in the air repeatedly and grinning from ear to ear. Even Toshi's uncle seemed to relax a bit and decided to drive to Dimapur to let Pheru catch his flight. Only Rajeev and Harsha were a little restrained in their demonstration of joy.

They reached Dimapur in the afternoon. Pheru got off with his faithful suitcase. He was delighted to discover that there was an evening flight to Calcutta, from where he could take a late flight to Bombay that very night – two days ahead of his exam.

His check-in was smooth. He returned to say his goodbyes

'Use the two days to revise as much as you can, Pheru. This time you've studied…you'll definitely pass.'

'Good luck, Pheru!'

Adi mulled over the developments as he watched Pheru disappear into the crowd, finding justification, albeit poetic, in the interpretation of the brotherhood of a Sikh like Jagdeep, a Muslim like Pheru and a Christian like Toshi. He was sure the airline officials would see it differently: indeed, if they found out, they would call it fraud. But such a perfect adjudication to so many different problems made it impossible for him to believe they were doing something wrong. He smiled to himself...like beauty that exists in the eyes of the beholder, faith, after all, is in the interpretation of a believer.

❦

Toshi's uncle drove all through the night. They reached Guwahati early the next morning. The Kamrup Express was scheduled to pull into the station within the hour. Wearily, they started unloading their stuff.

As Adi was collecting his bag, he overheard Toshi's uncle telling Rajeev, 'Don't worry, it'll be all right...we'll take care of it...'

Adi was even more puzzled. Why was Toshi's uncle reassuring Rajeev? Take care of what? What was going on?

Then, as he turned, Adi noticed Toshi's uncle

reach into his pocket, pull out the crumpled ball of paper he had collected from the bungalow, and dump it into one of the wastebaskets on the platform. Adi waited for him to walk away before heading towards the wastebasket and shoving his hand into it. Adi's heart began to beat like a drum while his fingers felt around for the paper in the pile of trash. He managed to retrieve it and quickly shoved it into his pocket without stopping to scan its contents. Luckily, no one caught him in the act. Then he followed the rest of them onto the platform.

Soon their train arrived and they found their seats easily. The final goodbyes with Toshi's uncle were strained and artificial. A sense of relief rather than sadness marked the loss of each other's company. They promised to arrange the return of Toshi's belongings from the hostel and conveyed their sympathies, thanks and good wishes to Toshi's family. Adi felt awful: the terrible conclusion to their meeting felt like an emotional waste of the entire trip.

The train was to reach Calcutta the next morning. None of them had slept well the previous night. Within a few minutes of the train moving, they began to doze off. Adi climbed into the top bunk and lay down. In addition to relaxing, he needed the privacy to go through the paper he had picked out of the wastebasket.

He pulled it out carefully and pored over it. It consisted of three pages, now crumpled and crinkled with a million creases. The sheets were torn from the government guesthouse register that contained records of all those who had stayed there over the last few days. The top of each page read 'Nagaland State Govt. Guest House No. 6. Mokukchung, Nagaland'. The pages were numbered. Adi looked at the entries. At the bottom of page number 66 was written 'Lotha Guest'. The date of entry corresponded to the day they had arrived, and there had been no time or need to fill out the date of exit. The number of guests was listed as six. On the next page where the same columns continued, the solitary entry under 'name' had been scratched out. It listed the number of guests as two. However, clearly written in the adjoining column, in the same line as the name that had been scratched out roughly, was the license plate number of a car. Adi remembered it belonging to the official-looking car he had seen parked in the driveway that evening.

There were no other entries.

Adi was puzzled. It was obvious that Toshi's uncle hadn't wanted to leave any proof of their stay. But why had he also tried to erase the record of the other person who had come in the official-looking car?

Sam and Jagdeep had fallen asleep. Harsha and Rajeev sat next to each other, deep in conversation. Adi strained his ears to catch their words.

'But we didn't...'

'Just keep quiet, man...'

Harsha buried his face in his hands and looked like he was about to cry. Rajeev looked up to check on the others. Adi quickly shut his eyes, pretending to be fast asleep.

Rajeev put his arm on Harsha's shoulder and said softly, 'Look, we can talk about this later... Here these guys might wake up.'

Adi was stunned. He started thinking hard and fast.

Were Harsha and Rajeev involved in a murder? Who had they killed? Had they killed the other guest in the bungalow? Maybe, sometime that night they had had a fight over the young girl, and, being two against one, had killed him accidentally? Maybe that was why they had tried to scratch out the name of the person who had stayed in the bungalow that night. That had to be it! No wonder Toshi's uncle wanted them to disappear fast.

Adi's heart began to race as he wondered about the identity of the person they had killed. He had to be a dignitary…they are the only ones who travel in government cars with wailing siren lights on top. Adi remembered the police car shrieking its way up the hill towards the bungalow. He remembered the fear on Toshi's uncle's face as they raced away. And he remembered the hate on the cook's face as he watched them leave in a hurry.

Adi was suddenly seized with panic when he realized he was carrying an incriminating document. His pocket felt barbed as he tossed and turned, trying to get the morbid thoughts out of his head. His heart had travelled into his mouth and soon he was drenched in cold sweat. He loosened his collar, finding it hard to breathe without running his fingers around it again and again. He felt the urgent need to burn the pages, maybe even bury the ashes. He kept looking down the aisle, anticipating a posse of policemen charging down any moment, searching for them.

The train began to slow down as it approached New Cooch Behar station. Adi waited for it to come to a complete stop before climbing down from the top bunk warily. Despite his fears about showing his face in public, he couldn't stand the suspense of not knowing the victim's identity. A dignitary's death, he reasoned, would certainly be in the newspapers by then, twenty-four hours after the event had taken place. Adi decided to get a newspaper from the platform. Fighting his fear, Adi bought three English news dailies, half-expecting to see their photographs displayed prominently as runaway fugitives.

The Telegraph, The Statesman and *The Assam Tribune* didn't mention any sensational deaths in Nagaland. Adi combed through all the pages of the three dailies very carefully. Nothing caught his eye. He checked the dates again and again to confirm that they were the latest editions. There was no mention of anything that could be remotely tied to the events of that night. Although it didn't make sense that the death of a dignitary should go unreported, Adi found it easier to breathe again.

On an impulse, he picked up a copy of the *North-East Dainik*. This was a daily publication with a wide readership in the North-East, purely for the sensational stories it published. Elite society called its articles 'yellow journalism' while lapping up the gossip in the privacy of their bathrooms. However, a bold young man by the name of Arun Gogoi had recently bought the newspaper. Mr Gogoi, having inherited a publishing house from his ancestors, had decided to infuse some measure of respectability into the newspaper. Trained in journalism abroad, he worshipped freedom of speech. His newspaper had turned viciously anti-establishment and courageously adamant in its fight for freedom of expression.

On the pages of its afternoon edition was the story where Adi read with horror, the explanation of the night's events.

TWENTY-EIGHT

It was early morning when they reached Calcutta. They had twelve hours to kill before boarding their next train to Bombay. They walked into the station's waiting room, finding it surprisingly empty for a station this size. They sat in the room silently unsure of how to spend the hours that remained. They interacted minimally, finding it easy to maintain their distance by pretending to be involved in the sights and sounds around them. Rajeev and Harsha maintained a distinct segregation, with Rajeev keeping a constant vigil over the more emotionally distraught Harsha. Adi wished somebody would start a conversation about some mutually neutral topic.

Almost as if reading his mind, Sam said, 'Pheru should be in college by now, right? I hope he'll pass his exam this time.'

'Yeah,' replied Adi, 'he has a good chance if he just shows up...he was studying hard before Toshi died.'

'Yeah, and the examiners will be more sympathetic to him now that he's become a mini celebrity,' said Sam, smiling. Then, turning towards Adi, he said, 'You remember that day, Adi, before Toshi's Anatomy exam...we had taken him to the hospital and you taught Toshi through the night?'

Adi smiled. 'I was sure I was going to fail,' he said.

'Toshi asked me to pray to the Virgin Mary when I met him that morning,' said Sam. 'Not for him, but for you, Adi.'

Adi smiled. 'I suppose the prayer worked. Not only did I pass, I even got a D.'

They fell silent, reminiscing quietly. Then Sam said, 'I think that's why Toshi and I were close...as another Christian, he felt close to me. Toshi and I could sort of identify...'

'Because he was Christian?' asked Rajeev with annoyance, cutting Sam off. It was the first time he had spoken in a long while. His sudden participation after the prolonged silence startled everyone.

Sam shrugged uncertainly.

'What do you mean, Sam?' said Rajeev. 'We

couldn't identify with him because we aren't Christian...or you can't identify with me because I'm Hindu? What is it?'

Sam looked edgy. 'It's nothing man...nothing ...just forget it!'

'No,' said Rajeev. 'I won't forget it. I heard you. What do you mean he was close to you because he was Christian?'

'Look, Rajeev... I... I just thought so...it may not be true!'

'But if you say so, you must feel it!'

Sam's eyes narrowed with irritation. 'What is your problem, man?' he said. 'I said forget it... I take it back, okay?'

'Take it back? Take what back, Sam...that Toshi couldn't come close to us because I am a Hindu and Pheru is a Muslim...or that you are the only one who knew him because you are a Christian? What are you taking back?'

Sam didn't reply.

'What are you taking back, Sam?' repeated Rajeev with irritation. 'What can you take back...if you say something like that, you must mean it! Toshi and you were special friends because you were Christian...and Toshi was just pretending to be friends with us. Do you know how insulting that is to the rest of us?'

Sam remained silent.

'Don't make an issue out of a non-issue, Sam,' continued Rajeev, finding vindication in Sam's silence. 'You insult Toshi when you say something like that. Saala, you guys always do this…blame everything on being a minority in India. Don't indulge in minority-ism and blame every little problem you have on being a minority in India!'

Sam suddenly snorted with anger. 'Minority-ism? Is that what you call it, Rajeev?' he shouted. 'Hmm, let's see… Do you know why I lost the first election for the Class Representative's post? Huh? Do you…? I lost it because Manish and his gang spread the word about how I wasn't a true Maharashtrian. I was born and brought up in Pune. I learnt Marathi in school and can speak and write better Marathi than all of you. I burst crackers with the friends in my neighbourhood during Diwali, and they'd come over to our house to have cake at Easter. And yet, when the time comes to choose, I am not Maharashtrian?'

Adi had never seen Sam so upset. He had never known Sam could *be* so upset. He was shaking with indignation.

Sam continued, 'The worst part of it was that Manish's ploy worked. I couldn't believe that educated people, on their way to become doctors some day, would vote with such narrow minds and believe I'm not Maharashtrian because I'm not Hindu. And *I'm* narrow-minded? That day, I lost faith in people's judgment. And do you know who understood? Toshi. Do you know why? Because he could feel my hurt! Not the hurt of losing the election, but the hurt of being different...of not being accepted...of not being "one-of-us"!'

Sam's face was full of anguish. 'What do I have to do to be accepted, huh Rajeev? Why *should* I have to do anything to be accepted? What do *you* know about being different? You said it yourself: "you guys always do this"! *You guys...you guys,* Rajeev? How much do I have to demean myself, how much more fun do I have to make of my size, my stupidity, my teeth before you are willing to accept me as one of *you guys*? So, don't tell me it's not important that he and I were Christian, Rajeev. It was important because we were different from the rest of the crowd...and different in the same way. We could have been Buddhists or Nudists or Parsis, but our difference was our similarity – we both felt we didn't belong! Minority-ism, my ass!'

Rajeev was stunned. He tried to say something, but found himself unprepared for Sam's uncharacteristic outburst. 'Yeah...yeah...but

Toshi was my good friend, too, and Harsha's and Jagdeep's...'

'You shouldn't talk about being anybody's good friend, Rajeev!' said Sam, his voice dripping with condescension.

'What do you mean?' said Rajeev.

'You know what I mean. Your "friendship" almost got us into trouble. Your friendship is the reason we couldn't say goodbye properly to Toshi's parents and family. Your friendship is the reason God knows what Toshi's uncle thinks of us!'

Harsha looked visibly nervous. Rajeev tried to get a handle on the situation. 'Look, we didn't do anything!'

'What didn't you do?' asked Jagdeep.

No one spoke. In the uneasy silence, Jagdeep looked around nervously. 'What happened, guys?' he asked. 'I thought Toshi's uncle got us out of that place in a hurry because someone had died...but what did *we* have to do with it?'

'Nothing!' said Rajeev.

'What did Sam mean about Rajeev's friendship causing trouble? What happened? Are we in danger?' asked Jagdeep again, his fear mounting by the minute.

'Look, Jagdeep!' shouted Rajeev, 'nothing happened! Just forget it and shut up, okay?'

Sam looked at Rajeev coldly and said,

'Someone got killed, Jagdeep… And there was suspicion…that…' He couldn't bring himself to say the words.

Jagdeep's eyes widened. 'Suspicion of what?'

'Nothing!' shouted Rajeev.

Suddenly, Harsha started crying. 'We didn't do it, man…we didn't do anything!' he sobbed, burying his face in his hands.

'Shut up, Harsha!' screamed Rajeev.

'No!' cried Harsha. 'I won't shut up…you got me into this, you fucking bastard… You did this to me!'

Harsha's outburst shocked Rajeev. 'Harsha, cool down,' he said. 'Get a hold on yourself, man! We didn't do anything…what did I do?'

'You did this, Rajeev! You convinced me to go into that room…you made me, because you know that I want to be like you and I wouldn't say no to you… You used me! You couldn't do it alone, so you used me! You've always used me, Rajeev! You've always used me!'

Rajeev looked like an air-filled puppet that had just been stuck with a pin. He sat back quietly and turned to gaze at the clear blue sky just outside the window. After a few seconds, he said softly, 'She was still breathing when we saw her, man…'

Then, he began to cry as he related the events of that night.

TWENTY-NINE

After Adi had gone to bed that night, Sam, Rajeev, Harsha and Jagdeep sat staring into the depths of the valley in front of them, soaking in the silence of the hills. Their attention was sporadically diverted by the sounds emanating from the room they had seen the girl being escorted into. In the thin night air, the tinkle of glasses, the thump on a mattress, the creaking of wooden hinges and the light strains of laughter carried over like announcements and made their puerile imaginations conjure up images of lurid sexual acts. They smiled knowingly at each other and traded mischievous winks. Intermittently they stole longing glances at the room, wondering what fantasy of theirs was being played out in its confines. Afraid of making the wrong move, they sat about aimlessly.

Finally, when curiosity conquered their judgment, they decided to peek through one of the room's windows. As they were headed towards the room, the cook spotted them and hurried out to let them know that the room had a 'very-important-person' who should not be disturbed. When pressed for answers, the cook informed them that it was the Home Minister of Assam along with his friend. The importance of that information quickly doused the erotic fires and readily convinced them that the minister wouldn't want his extra-curricular activities spied upon.

They returned to their room where they sat around for some time and cursed their luck, before finally falling asleep around 1.30 in the morning.

A little while later, Rajeev awoke to the sound of a car starting up. His grogginess disappeared quickly when he guessed that the car melting into the distance must be the one carrying the Minister. Rajeev crept out of bed and tiptoed his way to the other room. He peeked in through the window, straining to see in the dim light of the moonbeams pouring in from the vents. His heart began to race when his eyes fell on the lovely figure of the girl sleeping peacefully in bed – this time wearing only her anklets. He marvelled at his luck, ecstatic that the major impediment to approaching her was well on his way to Assam. He stared at her for a few moments, trying to summon the courage to step inside. His excitement, however, was dampened by a nagging fear, one that convinced him to return to the room and wake up Harsha.

Harsha awoke from sleep quietly, and although unable to share Rajeev's excitement, he was eager not to displease him. The two of them slipped out and crept to the other room, where Rajeev introduced Harsha to the seductive sight.

They stared at her as she lay on her side, facing the opposite wall. Her back was towards them — the taut, flawless skin glistening in the velvety moonlight as it narrowed into an hourglass waist. Her buttocks were round and firm and disappeared where her legs curled away towards her chest. Lost in the tranquillity of sleep, she looked as comfortable with her nudity as someone posing for such a portrait.

As the two of them looked, their arousal, now set afire, blew away any doubts they'd had so far. A tentative knock on her door, to their surprise, actually caused it to open. In their excitement, it didn't strike them as odd that she should be sleeping in the nude with the door open. They stood near the door and tried calling out softly so as not to alarm her. When she didn't respond, they stared uncertainly at one another, unsure how to deal with the subtle inkling that something was amiss. After a few seconds of indecision, they tiptoed across the room to where she slept, straining in the dim light to tread a quiet path. Although reassured that they hadn't startled or scared her with their approach, the fact that she hadn't stirred even once during their stealthy trip across the room left them a little uneasy. But it was when they stood right next to her that they realized those marks across her chest were welts from a belt. Her right shoulder stuck out beyond its socket. Her eyes were swollen shut and her rapid shallow breaths formed bubbles of blood at her nostrils. The gag across her mouth was soaked with blood and a half-empty bottle lay dripping on the floor.

As they stared at her in horror, the enormity of their discovery left them panic-stricken. Unnerved and near hysteria, they ran out of the room, crashing into all the objects they had so carefully sidestepped earlier. The noise of their cumbrous exit shattered the silence of the night, awakening the cook, who rushed out of his room just in time to see their receding figures disappear into a room.

Rajeev and Harsha stood shivering in the

room, burdened with the guilt of knowledge.
The image of the dying girl haunted them, but
afraid of implicating themselves they could only
think of trying to hide from it. They shut the
doors and crawled under their blankets, only
to realize that it was the guilt of forsaking her,
over and above the horror of their discovery,
that was making them tremble so uncontrollably.

The cook discovered the battered body of the
dying girl. Having seen Rajeev and Harsha
disappear into the room in a hurry, he did what
he thought was best. He called Toshi's uncle.
Toshi's uncle arrived within the hour. Horrified
at what he saw, he had a quick discussion with
the two of them. Rajeev and Harsha recounted
their story, after which Toshi's uncle decided it
was imperative for them to leave as soon as
possible.

&℞

Pheru, Sam, Jagdeep and Adi had not known
about the exact nature of the events, although
Adi had read a fairly riveting description in the
pages of the *North-East Dainik*. Adi was
surprised at how accurate the report was. It
mentioned that the Home Minister's car had
been seen in the vicinity that night, while a

group of young boys were rumoured to have been staying at the same place. Being brutally anti-establishment, the newspaper had reported 'seeing' the official car, while the presence of the six boys was merely 'a rumour'.

An eerie silence descended as soon as Rajeev finished his story. His eyes were red, the pain of having to recount the events taking its toll. He looked around for understanding, hoping to have convinced the others of their innocence.

Jagdeep looked mortified. Sam looked away in disgust. He kept shaking his head and sighing. Adi remained silent, his bitterness towards Rajeev oddly unaffected by his story. He felt very sorry for Harsha, now sitting on the floor and weeping silently.

Sam was the first to speak, his voice trembling with anger. 'I thought you guys had witnessed something and that's why Toshi's uncle wanted us to get out so fast. I didn't know you guys had actually gone into her room to try and fuck her, man!'

Rajeev remained silent.

Sam continued, 'God knows what Toshi's parents think of us... My God, it is so shameful to even think about it! You guys... God knows what you did!'

'We didn't do anything!' cried Rajeev in despair.

'What do you mean, you didn't do anything?' Sam shouted back. 'You went to fuck that girl, and when she lay there dying…you…ran…'

'But we didn't do anything, Sam! I swear… we didn't!'

'Then why did you guys run away? Jesus, Toshi's uncle must be so ashamed of us being Toshi's friends…'

Adi looked at Rajeev and Harsha cowering with the shame. Their actions seemed particularly abhorrent, but staring at them, Adi had a sinking feeling of his own wrongdoing.

Harsha was crying silently. He squeezed his head, as though hurting from the terrible memory. 'Nobody believes us,' he whimpered. 'Nobody will believe us…'

Adi sighed and said, 'I believe you.'

A sudden silence followed. All of them stared at him, surprised.

'I believe you,' Adi reiterated. 'I heard you talking to each other at around two that morning. I think it was after you had returned from the other room. If Sam and Jagdeep had gone to sleep after 1.30, then you guys had less than ten-fifteen minutes to meet that girl and, you know…beat her or do anything. And besides, why would you?'

'But they were in her room, man!' said Sam,

glaring at Adi. 'They didn't go in to wish her goodnight!'

'Oh, come on, Sam. It's easy now, but do you remember what it was like that night when we saw her walking up the hill in those clothes? She was so beautiful, so sexy, and we guessed that she was there for sex. All of us looked at her with lust in our eyes. So, how would you have reacted if you had gone into that room and found her all beaten up like that?'

'But I didn't, Adi!' shouted Sam.

'And they did. But they didn't mean to harm her, Sam. They didn't beat her. Just like you wouldn't, Sam. Every time I imagine myself in their situation, I know I would have reacted like they did: scared, confused and ashamed...'

'I'm not ashamed! I didn't do anything wrong!' said Sam.

'Sure you did, Sam', said Adi. 'We all did. All of us share the guilt they carry. The guilt of an innocent girl's death being hushed up and not seeing justice because of our own fears. We may not have hit her with our hands, but our silence will hurt her as much. We are all involved in the cover-up, Sam, all of us. Do you think they will believe your story or that of the minister when the cook describes how he saw the two of them rush out of her room or how we left in a hurry? Do you think they'll believe us when all we did was run away? You and I are as afraid of telling everyone that we lusted for a girl who wound up dead after a few hours, as they were after seeing her dying that night. Would you go to the police and tell them everything that you know, Sam? Would you, Sam?'

Sam remained silent.

Adi sighed. 'You know, Sam, for the first time I realize why all of us kept silent for so long. We knew something bad had happened in that bungalow, but none of us dared say anything. We were all running away, Sam, all of us...not from that bungalow, but from our conscience... our guilt of covering up the girl's death. We are all guilty...all of us. We expect them to do the right thing, but we are so scared of doing it ourselves. We look at their guilt to hide our own. All of us are running away, Sam...all of us are running away!'

Adi fell silent, suddenly aware of what had been haunting him all this while. Yet surprisingly, the awareness didn't hurt; instead, he felt tears of relief well up in his eyes.

His defense of their actions shocked Rajeev and Harsha into silence. It was as though the credibility their account received from Adi's endorsement made them start believing in their own innocence. In relief and shame, they came over and hugged Adi. With tears streaming down his cheeks, Rajeev kept saying, 'I'm sorry, I'm so sorry, Adi.'

Adi patted them on the back in a feeble attempt at consolation. Then, in a spontaneous catharsis of their pent-up feelings, they huddled together and wept.

Adi's heart went out to the girl. He remembered her youth, her beauty and her smile as she had walked away with the cook. One life, so beautiful and yet so delicate – the injustice of her death gnawed at his soul.

He had one more thing to do.

❧

A few hours later, they headed for their train. Before boarding, Adi bought some envelopes with pre-printed stamps from the post office. Inside one, he put the sheet from the guesthouse ledger that prominently displayed the license plate number of the Law Minister's car. Carefully sealing the envelope, he wrote in block letters.

TO
MR ARUN GOGOI,
'THE NORTH-EAST DAINIK'

133, BHADRAKALI BUILDING
MAIN ROAD, GUWAHATI, ASSAM

He held it for a minute and then dropped it into the
bright red mailbox at the station.

Then he started writing another letter.

THIRTY

*M*y *dear Isha,*
I'm writing this letter well aware we'll get home before this letter does. In fact, if anything, this letter should be addressed to me. But who writes a letter to himself? Someone confused? Or maybe someone stepping out of confusion? I'm not sure which category fits the state of my mind…but that is the point of this exercise: I'm writing to myself through you, because sometimes it is easier to put thoughts down on paper than think about them randomly.

Our return journey to Bombay has been remarkably free of incident and yet the end of innocence mauls us emotionally. Although you don't know about her, the disturbing thought of a dead girl weigh heavily on our minds. This trip to meet Toshi's family has become a journey into our souls.

The night is the hardest; there is nothing to see outside and nobody to talk to as we ride the train in silence. Ten years have flown by in these ten days.

Rajeev has changed the most. He is a shadow of his confident, narcissistic, cocky self. He sits at the window, silently staring out into the darkness on the other side of the glass. Occasionally I see a tear course down his cheek, betraying the emotions behind the barren face.

The conscience is such a terrible taskmaster

Now I know why he disliked me: he felt threatened by my popularity. Ten days ago, I despised him intensely for what he had done to me – a sentiment I'm sure he reciprocated. But today, I feel no joy at seeing him suffer. Forgiveness may be the greatest act of vengeance, because I have nothing other than pity in my heart for him.

Harsha lies on his bunk, weeping with his face buried in his air-inflated pillow. He reminds me of the quintessential nice guy who finishes last. I admire the simple honesty of his character; only such a person would think of verifying Princess Diana's HIV status before making love to her, even in his imagination. But simplicity, unless rooted in certitude, is a handicap in the real world. It is heartbreaking to see him so ravaged with guilt. I let him weep – I hope the tears wash away his pain and turn him into a sensitive, caring and idealistic man, who will break the shackles of conformity to find his own bearings. I wish I could show him the silver lining in the cloud of guilt that weighs him down.

I look at Sam and wonder who it is I see as he stares impassively at the train's ceiling with blank, glassy eyes.

There is such dissociation between what the eyes see and what the mind envisions. The final thought is just a matter of interpretation, coloured by our experiences. We all saw Toshi, but perceived him differently: some saw a Naga, some an Indian, some a privileged student, a friend, or a combination thereof. And is Sam the class clown, a friend, a Maharashtrian, an Indian or a Christian?

There are so many shades of grey in the world. Sam and Toshi looked nothing alike, shared few common experiences, spoke different languages at home and, even though they shared the same faith, they felt a kinship because they saw the similarity in their dissimilarities. It was that shade of grey that matched. I suppose there is comfort in belonging to an order, a disposition, even if it means sharing an imperfection. Sam's self-deprecating buffoonery – his attempts to overcome this imperfection – have failed to gain him acceptance in the 'other' crowd. I saw Sam cry for the first time. I've never been so shocked, Isha – the tears of a clown look like drops of blood.

It is 2.30 in the morning and Pheru should be getting ready for his exam in a few hours.

Life is so strange, Isha. The only thing certain about it is its uncertainty. When we started on this trip, Pheru had jokingly dedicated his failure in Pharmac and the subsequent end of his career in medicine to the memory of Toshi. Ironically, it is Toshi's death that will give Pheru his first real chance at passing the exams. Toshi's untimely death was as unexpected as Pheru's having a fair shot at passing the exam. And the two events are so closely related! I think the randomness of events in the world is so lacking in logic that we give it names like destiny, fate, karma and kismat to deal with the irrationality of its sequence.

John Lennon said it best: 'Life is what happens to you while you're busy making other plans'.

Toshi loved listening to Lennon.

I'm starting to miss Toshi. I wonder what it will be like without him in the hostel. I wonder who I'll turn to for the 2 a.m. discussion about life, politics, friendship, pathology or sex. I wonder what I'll do with the silence of his guitar and the emptiness of his room. I wonder if I'll miss his laughter and long for his companionship in the days to come. I wonder because I was filled with doubt while standing next to his grave, Isha. Doubts that arose when I tried to say goodbye to my friend, but couldn't grieve at all.

Even now, as I sit here alone and think about Toshi, I can only remember him laughing, or singing, or strumming his guitar, or regaling us with the stories of his amorous adventures. I recall Toshi lying on his bed, weak with malaria, with a sign above his head 'Toshi Lying in Bed for World Peace'. I remember him scratching out the title of a biochemistry book and imprinting on it in big letters, 'GREEK'. I remember him trying to patch up the differences between Pheru, Rajeev and me on our way to the airport. I remember the night we stayed awake, studying biochemistry in the wards. I remember his happiness after the exams.

Like poring over a scrapbook full of happy thoughts, I can only remember him from all the happy moments he spent alive. And just like we accept the unpredictability of life by giving it names, I'm learning to accept Toshi's death by living with his memories. Even if they just remain as images in my head, I can still feel the warmth of his friendship. His death has taught me about forgiveness, about second chances, and, most importantly, how short and beautiful life really is. So how can I say goodbye to someone who gave *me so much? I can't, because he is alive in my memory and will live with me till I die. I will never, never say goodbye to my friend Toshi.*

So much has changed in the two years since Baba and I travelled on this train to Bombay. What a simple, wide-eyed eighteen-year-old I was, stepping away from home for the first time. I can still remember the exuberance and excitement I felt at the promise of the new discoveries that lay ahead. And it has taken two years to discover what was closest to me all this while: myself. My entity, my identity, my being: all shaped by the choices I made.

I remember the first night in Bombay, when Baba worried about the experiences that would shape my future. And just like Baba said, my unfeigned belief in all things good, and fair and just has been shaken by so many of my experiences. For, in these two years, I have seen jealousy, anger, fear and betrayal, while discovering friendship, integrity, courage and love. I have seen injustice and bigotry as much as I have seen fairness and tolerance. I have experienced emptiness in the power of public adulation, as well as peace in the isolation of excommunication.

It is mind-boggling to think that our lives, our entire future of who and what we are, is simply a matter of choice. Shaping our choices, as Baba had said, are our experiences, the choice to believe in one or the other, choosing to hope or despair, love or hate, believe or doubt, trust or betray.

So many outcomes...just as many choices. And so it all comes down to this...what does one choose to believe in?

For me, the choice has become so simple, Isha. Just like I can only remember the happy moments of Toshi's life rather than his painful death, my implicit belief in all these virtues of humanity stand reinforced by my experiences.

I choose to hope, to trust, to forgive, to believe and...to love.

I've thought about you every day, Isha. I've missed you every minute of every day.

But what I have often wondered is why it was so difficult for me to say 'I love you' that night. There was the time, there was the occasion, and the mood...but I just couldn't say it. This statement is probably as stupid as it is honest. But the truth is, I just couldn't say it! I still remember the light on the sign of the ladies' hostel flickering, and I kept thinking, okay, the next time it flickers, I'll say it... I'll tell you that I love you...

But I couldn't! I just couldn't!

Of course, soon after that Sam broke the news of Toshi's death.

My uncertainty has frustrated me since then.

Why couldn't I just say those three simple words? So this entire trip, I have thought about it, reviewed it, considered it and reconsidered it, and I think I finally know why. It is bizarrely twisted, so bear with me.

The thing is, you didn't ask me if I loved you...you asked me if I had ever told Renuka I loved her.

I had.

But why was that as important as knowing whether I loved you?

Because to you, it meant defining love. It meant knowing what I meant when I said it. Both of us have felt betrayed in what we believed was love. And both of us have searched for the answer to the simple question: what does it mean to be in love?

I suppose love is everything we want it to be and nothing we don't. I've seen love make the harshness of life disappear for a young woman as she mollycoddled her mentally retarded child. I've seen it motivate someone to fight for life and I've seen it instigate someone to try taking his own. I've seen it bring out the best and the worst in the same person. And so, it surprises me to think that we cry and laugh with the same feeling, find courage and fear in the same emotion, nurture and kill for the same word...and still profess to understand what love means.

Everybody knows what is love— everybody except me. I don't know it although I feel it inside me like the beating of my heart. I cannot tell you what love is or how I feel in love. I suppose it is trust. I guess it is also friendship; it may also be passion, and fondness, adulation and affection, respect and devotion, infatuation, attachment and appreciation…those are all the words I can think of! But they are words, and none describes exactly what I feel. And so, the honest answer is that either I don't know what I feel, or I don't know the words in the language to describe what I feel.

But Isha, I do know that I love you so much, that I couldn't tell you that I loved you without knowing what I meant.

So, I love you and I know I love you, because I couldn't tell you 'I love you'.

Doesn't that sound strange? Yet, it is the simplest reason, the most elegant explanation, and the most definitive proof in my head that I love you.

Of course, there are other things too: I feel complete when you are with me. I feel happy when you smile; I feel alive when you laugh. You inspire me and make me want to be the best person I can be. I love your honesty and your spirit. I love your clarity of judgment. I've missed you every moment of this trip and have thought about you all the time.

But, I know I love you, because I couldn't tell you 'I love you'.

And I find comfort in this seemingly absurd interpretation, remembering what my English teacher told us once about enjoying poetry. 'Sometimes,' he said, 'to judge good poetry, it is best to just let the words soak into your thoughts and not analyse them at all. Like feelings, over-analysis corrupts them, and robs them of charm, such that a simple poem like 'Twinkle Twinkle Little Star' becomes

Twinkle twinkle little star
I do NOT wonder what you are
For through the spectroscopic cane
I know that you are hydrogen'

So, today, when we are still some hours away from reaching Bombay, I'll simply savour the feeling of being in love with you, and open the envelope you gave me as soon as I finish this letter.

I love you.

Adi.

❧

Adi's heart was bursting with anticipation as he opened the envelope.

A bunch of bus tickets poured out. For an instant he was surprised, but then, as he sifted through them, he remembered Isha collecting the tickets every time they went out together. The tickets were neatly stapled into pairs and their empty backs catalogued, in her handwriting, a brief memoir of that outing.

A flood of happy memories surged through Adi.

Only one ticket was not paired. It was for the bus ride she had taken to meet him at Victoria Terminus, before they had set out for Nagaland. On the back of that was written 'I miss you terribly. I'm so glad you are reading this. I love you too.'

THIRTY-ONE

Adi's Epilogue

It was late evening when we reached Bombay. The sun had just disappeared beyond the horizon and the lights of the city lit up the cloudy night sky. There were even more people everywhere I turned to look. The same loud-speakers played trendier music, as the noise from animated street vendors and honking cars brought the silence we had experienced in the tranquillity of interior India to an abrupt end. The wet pavements and glistening roads reflected the colourful neon displays of the evening. Small puddles provided instant fun to shirtless street urchins. Huge, gaudy posters of movies cried for attention, while people walked past them with the single-mindedness of worker ants, unmoved by the promise of entertainment they made.

Big, beautiful, bawdy Bombay. It looked, smelled and sounded the same: crowded, cacophonic, colourful and chaotic. The excitement I had experienced when Baba and I rolled into VT two years ago, returned with a gush of nostalgia. But this time it felt safe; it felt comfortable; it felt like home. The same anonymity that had felt cold and impersonal two years ago, now promised forgiveness as the crowds camouflaged our guilt. Nobody questioned our intentions, our origins, our past, or our motives, as the big city shifted to make space for yet another person stepping off the train. For those few moments, I loved being just another face in the crowd. And yet, I knew there was someone who would recognize *my* face in the crowd.

❧

As our taxi rolled into the hospital campus, my heart was bursting with anticipation. I got off at the ladies' hostel. Khadoos Baba smiled knowingly, then turned around and shouted in his trademark accent, 'Isha Banerji…visitor!'

I saw Isha look down from her window and, on seeing me, gasp with surprise. Then she turned around and disappeared from view.

The evening was pleasant, and what had begun as a slow drizzle now turned into a heavy downpour. The few people standing near the main entrance ran for cover.

I stood in the rain, feeling the drops caress my face. The cool water drenched me and washed away my weariness. There was so much beauty, so much happiness in my world. I felt intoxicated…intoxicated with life.

Isha came running towards me in the rain, barefoot in her excitement. Her face shone with delight as she ran into my arms. I hugged her tightly as we kissed passionately in the rain.

'I love you,' she cried.

'I love you, Isha!'

***

On learning that I was going to study medicine in Bombay, someone had said to me, 'You've got to see two things in Bombay: the Bombay rains and the Bombay girls.'

ACKNOWLEDGMENTS

There are many people I have to thank for this new adventure in my life and so I'll start at the very beginning.

My parents, for giving me life and so much with it. My immediate and extended family: without your colourful stories I'd be missing my imagination. My in-laws, for their encouragement and affection.

Saugata Mukherjee, for giving me the all important break when so many wouldn't. Karthika, my wonderful editor for her superb suggestions and comments. HarperCollins India for agreeing to make this dream a reality.

My children, Nina and Nikhil, for making me believe that I could tell stories that people would want to hear. My wife Swati, my beautiful Bombay girl, for filling my life with so much love.

And Imbi, my friend, I still miss you.